TRAVELER

Part II of the *Anthanian Imperative* Trilogy

Roger Floyd

TRAVELER – Part II of *The Anthanian Imperative*, by Roger Floyd

A science fiction novel of 139,000 words, set in *Book Antigua*.

Cover illustration and interior art work prepared by Kathy Schuit

Trade paperback ISBN: 979-8-9867419-2-5

To strive, to seek, to find, and not to yield.

— Alfred, Lord Tennyson (1809-1892)

CONTENTS

Illustrations:

SUMMARY OF ANTHANIAN MEASURING SYSTEMS

The summary below gives the major Anthanian systems of measurement and the closest *approximate* value in Earth-based systems.

Anthanian	**Earth-based**

Time

On a planet tidally locked to its sun and which rotates only once on its axis in its yearly trip around the sun, no convenient shorter period is available to use as a basis for marking the passage of time. The Anthanians divided their planet's year into 1000 *Time Sectors* (usually shortened to *T-sector*), and each T-sector was further divided by elements of 10.

Anthanian	Earth-based
Year	400 days
T-sector	9.6 hours (10 subsectors/T-sector)
Subsector (10 per T-sector)	1 hour
Millisector (10 per subsector)	5 min 45 sec
Microsector (10 per millisector)	35 seconds
Nanosector (10 per microsector)	3.5 seconds

Instantaneous time values were grouped as a *Time Element*, containing in order, year.T-sector.subsector.millisector, for example, 483.886.3.5. If the year is known or otherwise understood, it may be omitted.

Distance

Anthanian	Earth-based
Link	10 inches
Decilink	1 inch
Anthan	1.57 miles

(*Note*: One anthan is 10,000 links.)

Astronomical Distances

Light-year (distance light travels in one year): 4.15 trillion anthans

Light-sector (distance light travels in one T-sector): 415 million anthans

Weight

Krill	3 lbs, 3 oz
Dekakrill	30 lbs
Kilokrill	3000 lbs
Millikrill	5 oz

Temperature

1 Tal	1° Centigrade

(*Note*: Water freezes at 0 Tal and boils at 100 Tal.)

Angles

100 degrees	90°

Volume

Trilink	985 cubic inches, or 16,000 cubic centimeters
Eighth-trilink	2 quarts or 2 liters

A MESSAGE FROM THE PEOPLE OF ANTHANOS

To all those concerned in this sector of the galaxy

Make no mistake about it, it has always been the sun. An immense orange-red star, Arteamos by name, it began its slow but inexorable swelling toward becoming a red giant several million years ago. Even now, expanding like some huge incandescent balloon, the surface of that star creeps closer and closer to our planet Anthanos, increasing its pull on this tiny golden-brown orb, gradually raising the air temperature and threatening to engulf it the same way it devoured the innermost planet, Altamnos, in eons past. The powerful gravitational pull of the star has already slowed the axial rotation of our planet, and one side, scorched and sterile, now perpetually faces the sun. Under the sun's increasing heat, all the planet's water evaporated and condensed on the cold, dark side in huge packs of ice, often more than an anthan thick. Our fore-inhabitants were forced to migrate to the Lifezone, the ring of cities that encircles the planet at the terminator, the dividing line between light and dark, where the living conditions were at least tolerable. From the Lifezone, the sun appears as a reddish ball directly on the horizon.

Arteamos insinuates itself into almost every aspect of the life of our people in a way nothing else can. It remains the motive force behind the constant breeze that sweeps out of the dark side of the planet, bathing the Lifezone in cool, delicately moistened air. It is responsible for the sterile golden-brown sand beneath our feet—the sand that gives our planet its nickname, the Golden Planet—and, indirectly, for the cloudless deep blue sky overhead. But the most menacing thing about the sun now is that it is responsible for the gradually increasing air temperature.

Eventually, in the distant future of several hundred thousand years, the sun will undergo a nova blast as it depletes its hydrogen fuel and begins to burn helium. That blast will certainly render all planets in our solar system incapable of harboring life, if not incinerate them altogether. Well before that time, however, the air temperature will have risen above a level acceptable for Anthanian habitation, and we will have completely evacuated the planet.

Therefore, and faced with the urgent need to maintain our civilization, we feel we have every right to examine and colonize another world.

This we assert is our Anthanian Imperative.

In the year 459 we found a good candidate planet, thirty-five light-years away. A small Blue Planet, covered mostly with water, but with desert areas similar to Anthanos, it possessed all the elements necessary to sustain life on its surface. We sent a team of ten explorers to make a detailed examination.

But for us, sincere but somewhat naïve explorers accustomed only to the simple, modest, almost monochromatic existence that characterizes our planet, we were unaware of many of the biological, geological and meteorological phenomena on the blue planet—vicious animals, quaking of the ground, fierce storms accompanied by brilliant flashes of light and thunderous reverberations, sudden floods that can destroy areas of habitation, and fires that sweep large areas of vegetation. The planet became a death trap, striking down one explorer after another until only two were left: Lilea Kalatarian, the team's anthropologist, and Jad Til-Lentos, the astrophysicist. All eight others perished.

After they returned, Lilea became the face of the disaster.

Such a lilting name, "Li-*lay*-a," somewhat unusual in the naming of an Anthanian woman with its three syllables and repeated consonant. But in its time it became an expressive name, poignant with the frustration of the Anthanian people toward their planet, their government, their scientists, their situation.

A person who has visited another world does not return unchanged. After Lilea arrived home, she expressed her concern for the Blue Planet and for the Anthanian people. Almost alone, she believed the planet could be a viable option for her civilization and she pressed our Legislative Assembly repeatedly to fund a return expedition. "Wild and beautiful," she called it. "We could learn to live there," she said. Lovely it certainly was—we could see that from the images she brought back. She knew it and she wanted her planet to know it. But deadly, too, and that scared us more than anything.

Lilea never returned to outer space. She settled in her family's ancestral home city of Kalarias with Leos, her only child by her husband Bent, born onboard the huge interstellar spaceship *Star Voyager* during the return trip. Starting life as a single mother, she never faltered in her efforts to persuade the government to send another expedition. But no new expeditions were ever sent, and about eighteen years after she returned, with the air temperature still gradually rising in the Lifezone, she succumbed to the necessity for an air cooling unit in her home.

That was about the same time the Black Sands[1] Tavern did too . . .

---

[1] No black sands actually exist on Anthanos. The name most likely was a 'paradoxical' or 'frustrating' reaction to the ubiquitous golden-tinged sands on our planet. This reaction became especially prominent among the population after images returned by the Blue Planet Exploratory Team showed large areas of inviting cool blue waters and spectacular green vegetation covering much of that world.

CHAPTER 1

A COUPLE OF VISITORS

The Black Sands Tavern resided comfortably in one of the more affluent areas of the city of Kalarias on the planet Anthanos, not far from the home Leos Kalatarian shared with his mom, Lilea. Whenever Leos walked through the front door of this decidedly upscale establishment, the sudden blast of cool air spanked the skin of his face with such a satisfying nip that it almost took his breath away. It gave him a welcome relief from the gradually warming outside air. He liked it like that.

But more than the cool air, Leos's main reason for frequenting this watering hole was the private rear-corner booth it provided to extra-special guests. The presence of that quiet, isolated nook suited his insistence on privacy as he and his companion enjoyed a quiet time together.

His most frequent companion in these T-sectors of his twenty-second year was his current flame and next-door neighbor Tama. Her slender stature and light green eyes, fair skin, and strawberry-blonde hair which cascaded in layered ringlets well past her shoulders, provided a striking contrast to the tall—about six-and-three-quarter links—blue-eyed Leos. His short, dark hair and light umber skin he inherited in roughly equal measure from the fair skin of his mom, Lilea, and the deeper, darker brown skin of his dad, Bent. He and Tama had been dating for more than two years now, and at nineteen, with her graduation from tertiary school group on 483.884 only two T-sectors behind her, and after she and Leos had filed the required Notice of Intent for Betrothal with the Office of Interpersonal Affairs—the first step on the road to marriage—they reserved the special booth for a private, but quiet, celebration.

They settled into the booth around 886.5.6, and ordered their first round of drinks. Leos ordered his favorite, a pinkish-orangish concoction called a *Qootaie*, made of imitation fruity flavors in crushed ice, served in a tall tumbler with an even taller straw. It contained about three percent ethanol. At twenty-one, Leos was allowed to consume low-alcohol drinks—three percent or below—but on orders from his mom, the tavern was supposed to serve him no more than two drinks, and those had to be at least two subsectors apart. But he found that by slipping a few extra monetary units into the personal account of his favorite drink steward he could get additional drinks, especially with his mom out of town. Tama ordered a non-alcoholic version.

A small monitor screen had been built into the table, and by glancing at it from time to time Leos could keep a close eye on the entire room, especially the entrance around the corner. So it came as a big surprise to both Leos and Tama when, around 886.8, and after five rounds of drinks, two visitors appeared almost out of nowhere, unannounced and uninvited.

"You are Mr. Leos are you not?" the first one said.

Startled at the intrusion, Leos looked up directly into the face of the inquirer. "Uhh . . . yeah. Who are you?"

"Please to introduce myself. I am Krok." He pointed to the man standing beside him. "This is my associate, Grok."

Leos grinned at the unusual and almost humorous names, and snickered to himself. "Yeah, what ish it you want?"

"May we sit down?" Krok said.

"Leos—" Tama muttered as she squirmed closer to her boyfriend.

Leos stiffened. "Ah, I guess so."

The one who called himself Krok slid first onto the bright red plastic seating of the booth across the circular table from Leos and Tama. Grok followed, sitting on the outside edge of the curved seat, and Tama scrunched even closer to Leos. Leos studied both visitors closely, watching for any sudden movement that might indicate an ulterior motive. Under more sober circumstances, he might have resented the intrusion of these visitors, but in his inebriated condition he'd become so fascinated with their benign, comical appearance that he decided to take his chances. Still, he moved his left hand slowly and furtively toward the button under the table that would alert the tavern security squad. Just in case.

What the heck, he thought, *these guys can't be too dangerous.*

The two visitors were short, only about six links tall, pudgy, and each had a perfectly spherical and almost completely bald head. Two dark eyes peered at Leos and Tama through puffy eye slits, situated in a chubby face of cherub-like proportions. They could have been twins. What was most interesting to Leos, though, was their skin, a medium-to-dark umber, considerably darker than his. With their thick pouty lips, he immediately assumed they were in the same racial group as his dad, that they were Morokuu, or maybe a racial variant.

They were dressed in a fairly typical Anthanian garb, a dark gray jumpsuit, open at the collar, but fastened tightly all the way down. That type of dress wasn't unusual on Anthanos, though it wasn't common either, but outside of their odd faces and queer cranial construction, what next drew Leos's attention was that their suits were scruffy and unkempt, as though they'd worn them for many T-sectors, even slept in them. When Krok smiled, and he seemed to be constantly smiling, a large gap appeared between his two front teeth. As the smile grew broader, a gap appeared between every tooth.

Grok, though, never smiled. He seemed oblivious to emotion. He remained completely silent, sitting quietly, right on the edge of the seat, staring uncomfortably at Leos, shifting his gaze occasionally to Tama or to Krok.

"What ish it you want?" Leos asked again.

"Your mother is Lilea, is that not correct?" Krok talked slowly, enunciating each word carefully and thoughtfully, as though reading it from a dictionary. In that manner, his speech stood in strong contrast to the rat-a-tat-tat delivery of most Kalarians. "She is one of two survivors to return from the blue planet?"

"Yes, tha's right. Wha's this all about?"

"You are very famous. Your mother is very famous. She is in Sabean now. She attends a meeting of the Spaceflight Command Oversight Subcommittee. Is that not correct?"

"Tha's right. How did you find out about that?"

"It is on the news. The Information Services. It is easy to find out."

"Oh, yeah, I guess so. So, what ish it you want?" Leos took a nip from his drink.

"We have come to visit you. We have noticed you have obtained your pilot's license. Is this not correct?"

Leos smiled. "Yeah, tha's right."

"And you are passed with 100 percent. We are much depressed."

"Yeah . . . huh? Depressed?" Leos screwed up his face. "Whadda ya mean?"

"Yes, yes, we think it very highly that you passed by such a high margin."

Tama whispered to Leos. "I think he means 'impressed'."

"Oh. You mean '*im*pressed'."

"Yes, yes. 'Impressed.' You are right. Sorry. I am of the mistaken type."

"How did you find out about that, anyway?"

"You are very famous. It was on the I.S. You are a very famous pilot. No one passes by 100 percent. Not on the first test. That is our understanding."

Leos smiled even more broadly. "Well, you know, I doan like to brag, but, well . . . " It's true, Leos was a good pilot and he wasn't above letting people know about it. With a 100 percent passing grade on his pilot's exam—unheard of, as Krok said, for a first-time student—he had good reason to be proud. And a little self-satisfied.

". . . ish that what you want to talk about?" Leos looked askance at the visitors. "Are you guys from the Information Services? Do you want me to make a statement?" Leos took another sip from his drink and moved his hand closer to the button under the table. He wasn't about to make a statement to the I.S., which might get spread all over the planet and quoted and misquoted in and out of context for several years, leading inevitably to more quotations and misquotations from his mom trying to repair what was really the minor damage of the original statement.

"No, no." Krok smiled even more broadly and chuckled a few times in a deep, guttural snort. "We are visitors only. We are not from I.S."

Grok still sat impassively, occasionally glancing at Krok as if to wonder what he was saying, but turning his attention back to Leos and Tama within a nanosector.

"Then what are you guys getting at?"

"We would like to make an offer. To you. We have an invention, a contrivance if you will, a discovery. We ask little only that you examine it."

"What kind of invention?"

"A spaceship. To take you to the most farthest reaches of the galaxy."

"A spaceship that can travel the galaxy? Wow. I thought only Spaceflight Command had those kinds of spaceships. To do tha' you haffa travel fasser than light. We already have a spaceship that can travel fasser than light. It's called *Star Voyager*. I was born on tha' ship."

"Yes, yes, we have heard of your curious beginning. But your spaceship does not travel faster than light."

"Huh? It doesn't? Then how did it get to the blue planet?"

"The antigrav drive of your spaceship. It opens a wormhole and your ship travels down the wormhole. It is simple."

"Tha's ridiculous. You can't just open a wormhole anytime you want."

"Of course you can. Your engineers are of the mistaken type. They do not know that. Their math is flawed. Your engineers think they are traveling on the surface of a gravitational wave. Propelled from one wave to another. Flinging you along faster than light. But really opening they are a wormhole and traveling from star to star through a tube between them. A tube through the texture of time. Like the flexible tube that connects one spaceship to—"

"I don' believe it." Leos took another sip from his drink. "Where you guys from, anyway?"

"It is true. Nothing can travel faster than light. Our ship does not travel faster than light. But drive causes wormhole to open and can travel through wormhole. I can show you the calculations. Once you understand mechanism, you can travel from one part of galaxy to another. It is easy."

"Are you saying that our engineers mishtook a gravity wave for a wormhole? Tha's abshurd. How would they do that?"

"Your mathematics is flawed. Your math is a product of your species. Your math developed from your point of view on this planet. And that mathematics will serve you well for designing spaceships. You went very far with that mathematics. But it is limited. You must use mathematics of the cosmos. Mathematics of the cosmos says all universe is curved. Everything in universe is only short distance from everything else. Space-time continuum takes very complicated shape. Thirty-seven dimensions. Not possible to calculate that many dimensions in your mathematics. It is possible to travel very far if conditions right. It is essential to exploring universe. We can show you. Our engineers were of the mistaken type, too, but we corrected. It is minor discrepancy, really, when you look at it closely. Now we travel by wormhole. We have learned how to regulate."

Leos became more and more fascinated with the two visitors, especially with Krok and these new and unusual details of curved space-time which he seemed to throw around so casually. Leos had studied the basics of spacetime and relativity and quantum theory in tertiary school group and later in more detail in college, and many of the terms Krok used weren't unfamiliar to him, but he'd never heard of this "mathematics of the cosmos," and it sounded to him like so much hot air and gibberish. But he was at least willing to give Krok the benefit of the doubt and let him ramble on. He was beginning to think of Krok not so much as a guest as an entertainer. He relaxed at the table as he watched and listened to Krok with his weird smile and the way he used his large, coarse hands with the short, stubby fingers in wide, easy gestures. Leos drew both hands up from below the table and set them on top, resting his chin on his left palm. His eyes glazed over and his eyelids drooped as Krok rambled on. "So," Leos said during a short pause in Krok's monologue, "how doesh your ship travel, I mean, what makesh it go?"

"We have seen drive system on your space ships, and they are adequate. But we have more advanced drive system, more advanced than yours. That is why we are here. To show it to you. Would you like to see it?"

"Sure, why not?" Leos jerked his head up. "I'd like to shee it."

Tama placed a hand on Leos's arm. "Leos—what are you doing? Aren't we going to spend the T-sector together? You promised your mom and me . . ."

"I'sh okay, baby. I'll only be gone a few shubshectors. You gowann home. Take my runabout. Can you guysh give me a lift?"

"Certainly we can, Mr. Leos, sir."

Leos rose from his seat and stood unsteadily at the side of the table— "Lez go," he said—but he had to hold on to the table to stand upright, and Tama slipped out and stood beside him. He slung his arm around her neck as she reached into his pocket and filched his runabout drive card. Then she helped him sit back down at the table.

"Are you okay, Mr. Leos, sir?" Krok asked. "Perhaps we can . . ."

"I'm okay. Any time you're re'ay."

The two visitors stood and stepped away from the table into the dim light of the rear quarter of the tavern, talking quietly between themselves. The one who called himself Krok seemed to do most of the talking, and used his hands in a cursory, almost perfunctory manner, but Grok stood still, listening, his arms crossed over his chest, his feet about a link apart. This was no argument, merely a discussion. Occasionally, Grok would nod his head and appear to make a small comment, though their voices weren't audible at the table. That didn't make any difference to Leos now. His interest in the visitor's "contrivance" was waning and all he wanted to do was sleep. Alcohol always made him sleepy. He leaned back and rested his head against the wall cushion above the back of the seat. He closed his eyes. But he jerked awake as Krok and Grok approached the table and Krok spoke.

"Come, Mr. Leos, sir. We will go now and see our ship."

"Great," Leos said as he jumped up. "Lez go."

"Leos," Tama whispered. "Are you sure you want to do this? I thought—"

"I'sh okay, baby, I'll be back in a couple shubshectors. This ship isn't very far, ish it?"

"No, Mr. Leos, sir. Not far at all."

"I'sh it, like, in your backyard, or sumpin'?"

With his arm around Tama's neck, Leos shuffled to the front door of the tavern and into the dull red sunlight of the eternal Anthanian sun. Krok and Grok led the way. They turned left as they exited, directly away from the sun, leading Leos and Tama around the corner of the building into the constant shadow. They made their way across the parking lot and approached an odd-looking silver-colored runabout hidden in a back corner of the lot. Even in his inebriated state, Leos understood that this runabout was something unusual—something special. "Wow. Tha's quite a spaceship. Tha' goes fasser'n light?"

"No, no, Mr. Leos, sir," Krok said, grinning broadly and chuckling again. "This is our ground vehicle. We will take you to our space ship. It is not far from here."

"Oh, okay. Lez go."

"Leos—" Tama protested.

"Please to enter."

This wasn't a typical Anthanian runabout. The front end of this 'ground vehicle' was cone-shaped, but a short, stubby cone, and one large headlamp occupied the apex of the cone. Only one seat, apparently for the driver, sat behind a windshield at the base of the cone where it joined the cylindrical main section. Even as juiced as he was, Leos realized this runabout couldn't contain the usual small, heavily shielded nuclear power source that powered most Anthanian runabouts. But he didn't stop to try and figure out exactly how it was propelled—he had neither the time nor the inclination. Tama helped him stagger around to the right side of the vehicle where he stood beside the only door on that side. One of the two visitors entered the driver's seat from the left—that was probably Krok, but as sloshed as he was, Leos couldn't tell them apart. The other visitor entered the left rear seat. The right side door swung open and Leos clumsily crawled into the back seat.

"Leos," Tama said, "are you sure you want to do this? I mean, let's go back home and you can lie down. It's almost . . ."

"I'm okay, baby, I'll shee you later. I love ya, baby." Leos leaned back in the seat and closed his eyes. The door closed automatically, pulling itself out of a surprised Tama's hands. "Say," he mumbled to his visitors, "did I ever tell you guys 'bout the time I fought the big-toothed mons'er on the blue planet? Well, it was like this, y' see, I got hol' of his tentacles . . . no, his teticles . . . his tensicles—oh, crap, I grabbed hol' his fuckin' balls an' see, he was like 'bout eight links tall an' he jumped me from this big rock, see, an' I grabbed him by his—oh, yeah, I said that—or was it his tail—I ferget—anyway, I swung him around so fas' his eyes were jus' bulgin' out of their sockets, an', then, well, see, it's like this, I grabbed hol' his . . . and I threw him so far it was . . . like . . . a huner' T-sectors 'fore he got back."

That was the last Leos remembered of the tavern. Or the runabout. How could he? He was practically inert.

CHAPTER 2

THE DRIVE SYSTEM

"What time is it?" Leos asked, but no one answered. Before he opened his eyes he thought he was in his own bed at home, and the pounding in his head and the nausea in his belly told him he was hung over once again. *Oh, God, too many Qootaies.* The bed clothes felt familiar—the soft foam pillow beneath his head and the sharp, crisp, cool feel of the artificial fabric from which Anthanian bed linen was made. But when he opened his eyes . . .

"Hey! What the hell?" He sat up and banged his head against the upper bunk. "Ow!" He plopped back down and opened one eye. "Where the hell am I?" He cautiously rose up on one elbow and looked around the room. The pounding in his head grew worse. "Ooohh . . ."

He lay on the bottom of a set of bunk beds in a long narrow compartment, probably of a space vehicle. The room was about six by twelve or fourteen links, and it seemed everything was metal—walls, ceiling, floor—a shiny silvery metal, but with a delicate gold, or maybe coppery, hue. A faint metallic smell permeated the room, and cool, fresh air flowed into the room through a vent high on the wall above the bed. The head of the bed butted against a wall that curved slightly outward from top to bottom which he took to be the outside wall of the ship. A small wash basin with a metallic mirror above it and a small shelf to its right jutted from the long wall across from where he lay. His wrist chronometer had been placed on the shelf, and the display read '888. *something*', but his eyes were too unfocused to read the rest of the numbers. From a fixture above the sink, a single white light provided all the light in the room. Oddly, the basin wasn't made of the same gold-luster metal of everything else, it possessed more of a dull, stainless steel appearance. A closed door punctuated the wall at the far end of the room, and about three links to the left of the basin was another slim door. But something else seemed to be missing. He checked his pockets and realized—

"My PersComm," he muttered. "Where's my PersComm?" It wasn't in any of his pockets, or on the shelf, or on the lower bunk — nothing.

Oh, God, what have I gotten myself into now? Leos lay back down, his head pounding through his temples. He longed for a yanto, his favorite fruit that had the almost miraculous power to abort a hangover so easily and deliciously. After about a millisector, the far door opened and Krok entered. He had a big wide grin on his face

"You are awake. You are feeling wonderful are you not?"

"Not exactly." Leos raised himself up to a sitting position on the edge of the bed and placed his stocking feet on the floor. From where he sat he could just barely see his face in the mirror above the basin. His hair was unkempt and he needed a shave, but what most occupied his mind was the penetrating fullness in his bladder. He stood shakily beside the bed. The pounding in his temples increased. "Ooohh . . . where the fuck are we?" He closed his eyes and grabbed hold of the upper bunk.

"In our space ship. We will see drive system. You would like to see drive system now, yes?"

"Ooohh . . . maybe . . . okay. But first, I need to, you know . . . uh, where's the restroom?"

"Oh, yes. I am of the forgetting type. Rest room is here." Krok opened the narrow door in the side wall and Leos entered. It was a bathroom as much as any on Anthanos, though the fixtures were a slightly different style than Leos was used to and composed of the same dull metal as the wash basin. He relieved himself and returned to the main room.

"Yes," Krok said. "Now we will see drive system."

Leos didn't really understand what Krok was talking about. The vague memory of agreeing to look at the drive system of this "contrivance," as Krok put it, was only now beginning to wiggle its way back into his brain, and a few tiny details of the conversation he had with Krok and that other guy — what was his name? Crock? Spock? Knock? Grok? Wait — that's right, Grok — were beginning to return. He wasn't sure what Krok had in mind or where the "drive system" was, or even what it was in the first place, but he decided to follow him. Better than staying in this insipid room with nothing to do.

Leos jammed his feet into his boots he found at the end of the bed and followed Krok through the far door of the compartment. They turned right into a corridor only slightly more brilliantly lit than the room they departed. The low level of light helped keep the throbbing in his head to a barely acceptable maximum as he and Krok trod down the hallway.

The walls, ceiling and floor of the corridor were made of the same shiny, gold-luster metal as the room he just left, and the same faint metallic odor permeated the atmosphere. Several other narrow doors led into unknown rooms off both sides of the hallway, but Krok passed them all, headed toward a larger red door in the bulkhead at the far end. A black nameplate had been fixed to the center of the door, though the white lettering on the nameplate was in an alphabet Leos didn't understand. But his head hurt too much to ask and he followed Krok through the door.

On the other side of the door was a ladder, a bright, shiny red metal ladder with handrails on both sides, and fifty or more steps. Krok started up. For such a short, chunky man, he was amazingly spry. He zipped up the ladder taking two steps at a time, not stopping until he reached the top where he turned around and waited for Leos, who was now clumping up the steps, one at a time, holding his head against the throbbing.

At the top was a small landing leading to another door, much narrower than the one below. It, too, had a black sign with funny white lettering. Inside the door, another guy who looked exactly like Krok waited for them. It might have been Grok, but what the hell, they both looked alike anyway.

They were in a room about ten-by-ten links, and everything in the room was composed of the same shiny gold-tinged metal. To their right, a long narrow control panel sat on top of a cabinet that jutted out about two links from the wall. Several dials and gauges interrupted the smooth steel surface of the control panel, and a small computer screen, set into the left side of the panel, glowed off-white. Four doors had been built into the base of the cabinet, and a gentle hum came from within.

"We must put on these insulated suits." Krok grabbed some pale blue fluffy items from the top of the cabinet and handed one to Leos. Soft and fleecy like a comforter, it had a slick, nylon-like surface. Krok pulled off his boots and slipped one over his jumpsuit, and Leos did the same. As he finished, Krok held up a pair of bootie-style slippers and handed them to Leos. "Please to put these on." They were also heavily insulated, particularly on the soles which had about two decilinks of a dense, closed-cell-foam type insulation. Leos slipped them on, and his feet—in fact his whole body—felt toasty warm in this fleecy suit and booties. Had he not been standing up, he might've fallen asleep.

"Now gloves." Krok and Leos put on mitten-style gloves that overlapped the far ends of the sleeves. "Now to put warmsuit on."

"What? I thought we had warm suits on."

While they were donning the insulated suits, the other guy opened two of the four doors at the base of the side wall cabinet. From each door he removed a funny-looking contraption and handed one to Krok and one to Leos. Each was like a spacesuit, but a form-fitting spacesuit, and without a backpack for life support. A fine chain-mail-like sheath covered the entire suit, and when Leos took the suit from the other guy, he almost fell over. It seemed to weigh a ton.

A large number of thin insulated wires, perhaps as many as forty or fifty, emanated from different points all over the surface of the suit—front, back, sides, arms, legs, torso—all flowing out toward the back where they were collected together in one large cable. Some of the wires were black, some red, some green or blue, but one was bright yellow. Much thicker than the others, it was attached to the suit through a silver fitting just below the front neck opening.

The cable of wires itself lay coiled on the floor, and from the underside of the coil the cable ran a few links farther, ending in a complex-looking plug which the other guy inserted into a corresponding latch-point at the apparatus on the wall. Then he gave each plug a sharp left-hand turn, apparently to lock it in place. Two more similar latch points remained unused, as though four of these funny suits could be operated at one time.

Wait . . . what are these suits for?

When the latching of both plugs was complete, two lists of words in the same funny lettering as on the hallway door appeared on the screen. The other guy touched a few of the words on the screen, and each word turned bright red. The hum from the cabinet intensified.

"Wow, what's all this?"

"Warmsuit," Krok answered. "We will enter fuel tank." Krok set his warmsuit on the floor collapsed down like a pair of pants, and stepped into the feet through the neck opening which could be expanded like the iris diaphragm of a camera to accommodate the entire frame of a person. Then he pulled the suit upward, slipping his arms into the sleeves as he brought the suit up to his neck. "Fuel is liquid hydrogen," Krok said as he wiggled into his suit. "Very cold. Suit will keep us warm."

"What? Wait! *Liquid hydrogen?*" Now Leos's eyes were wide open and the pounding in his head paused momentarily. "Holy dinfrizzle! Did I hear you right? We're going to swim around in *liquid hydrogen?*"

"Yes. Drive system is in liquid hydrogen. It must be supercooled. Same as yours."

"You're kidding! We're going to enter a tank of *liquid hydrogen?* Is this safe?"

"Yes. Very safe. We will be protected by warmsuits. You will see." Krok had his suit on by now. The final step was to narrow the neck ring around the collar of his fleece-suit.

Leos wasn't sure what Krok had in mind, though he was familiar with Anthanian anti-grav drives with their three drive coils that had to be kept supercooled. They, too, were in the fuel tanks of the ship, cooled by the liquid hydrogen that fueled the fusion rocket engine that gave the ship its forward momentum on which the anti-grav drive fed to initiate the gravity wave. At least that's what they taught him in the course in astro-physical mechanics he took in college. So Leos thought he knew what Krok was trying to tell him, but he definitely knew he didn't want to walk a-round in liquid hydrogen. Yet Krok seemed willing to jump into the tank— he was now completely inside his "warmsuit," and that other guy was about to jam a clear plastic helmet on top of it.

That turned the decision for Leos—he decided he'd see for himself. He dropped his suit on the floor like Krok and stepped inside, wiggling through the expanded neck opening, pulling the suit up to his neck. The other guy collapsed the neck opening tightly around the collar of the fleece-suit and jammed a bulbous plastic helmet onto the neck ring and gave it a sharp 50 degree turn that locked it solidly in place. A crackling sound came from the earphones inside the helmet as Krok spoke.

"Are you hearing me, Mr. Leos?"

"Yes. I can hear you fine. Can you hear me?"

"Yes. Communication is excellently good."

A cool refreshing snort of oxygen passed below Leos's nostrils, and his head pounded a little less. He could feel a gentle warmth coming through the suit, a warming that would shield him against the extreme cold waiting for him in the fuel tank. Krok shuffled over to a small door in the floor of the room next to the far wall, and at his signal, the door, hinged at one side, swung up and open. The door had about a link thick of insula-tion, and as it opened, a wisp of moisture, condensed out of the air by the ultracold liquid below, drifted up from the opening. Leos's suit got warm-er and warmer.

"Here." Krok's voice crackled through Leos's earphones. "We will enter fuel tank." Krok stood beside the open door for a nanosector, moni-toring a few items on a check-list on the left sleeve of his suit, then with his left hand he gave a thumbs-up sign. The other guy picked up the near end of Krok's cable and slung it over a hook hanging from the ceiling. The hook lifted him off the floor about a link, shuttled him over the opening and lowered him into the frigid liquid. A tremendous flash of liquid hydrogen boiled up around him as his feet hit the cold fluid, and a huge cloud of condensed water vapor surged upward from the open door, concealing him almost entirely for several nanosectors. The boiling didn't stop until he was completely immersed. When he reached the bottom, the hook released the cable and rose back to the ceiling. As he moved through the fluid in the tank, headed toward the rear of the ship, his cable snaked its way through the door following him.

Holy friggin' dinfrizzle — he actually went in! Leos could hear Krok's voice crackling and spitting through the earphones. A few syllables of his words were garbled, but he was able to make out most of what he said.

"You must enter also," came Krok's command through the earphones. Leos took a few halting steps toward the door. Though the suit was a bit stiff, walking wasn't as difficult as he first thought. When he reached the door's edge, he leaned forward slightly and peered into the tank. A wisp of vapor still drifted up from the surface of the shimmering liquid a few decilinks below the open door, yet he could see all the way to the bottom of the tank. Krok was still walking forward in the tank, just disappearing from view. The surface splashed and swirled around like water as Krok's cable continued to slither into the liquid.

Leos was fond of water. He enjoyed swimming and he loved to swim under the surface, puttering around near the bottom of a swimming pool, holding his breath for as long as two millisectors at a time. But this liquid he was about to enter wasn't water, it was liquid hydrogen, and it would freeze him into a solid crystalline mass in less than a nanosector if he wasn't well protected — at least he presumed — so he hesitated.

Krok's cable continued to slither across the floor, working its way into the void as he walked toward the rear of the tank.

Krok must be still be alive somewhere down there. Well, hell, if he can do it, I guess I can too.

He gave the other guy the thumbs-up sign and crossed his fingers. The other guy slung Leos's cables over the clasp which raised him slightly off the floor, shuttled him over the door, and lowered him into the tank. Leos peered down toward the liquid, gritted his teeth, said a little prayer, muttered "holy dinfrizzle," and held his breath.

Another huge cloud of boiling hydrogen enveloped Leos as his feet hit the supercold liquid, and he instinctively closed his eyes when the liquid bubbled up around his helmet, but he wasn't conscious of any cold at all — he was still warm inside his suit. He could breathe easily inside the helmet even though he wasn't sure where the oxygen was coming from.

Through that yellow tube, I guess.

As he reached the bottom, he saw Krok at the far end, motioning in slow, easy gestures for him to come to the other end. Leos began walking, dragging the cables behind him as he moved. He first estimated Krok was a hundred links away, but distances were deceiving in the cold liquid, and after only a few steps he stood at Krok's side.

"See. Here is drive system."

Arranged around the periphery of the tank were several large rings of a highly polished metal. They bore a striking similarity to the coils of the drive system of *Star Voyager*, the ship that made the epic journey to the blue planet. All Leos could see of these coils in the tank was the metal covering which sparkled and gleamed in the glare of the lamps inside the liquid hydrogen tank. The coils themselves, within the shiny coverings, were undoubtedly made of some superconducting alloy, probably wound in a tight coil around a ceramic-nickel-iron-cobalt-aluminum-whatever magnetic core. Attached to each of the first three rings, at four points equidistant around each ring, was a larger globular mass of shiny metal, itself attached rigidly to the inside of the tank. Projecting from each mass was a small pinion gear on an axle, and this little gear meshed with a ring gear laminated to the inside of the coil.

Those must be the motors that make the coils spin.

Leos didn't pay much attention to these coils. He'd seen pictures of the antigrav propulsion system of *Star Voyager*, and they looked just like the rings he saw here. They were exactly what he was familiar with.

Yet, even as he stared at the rings, something about them didn't feel right. He traced his confusion to the fourth ring, the ring farthest from where he stood next to Krok in the sea of liquid hydrogen. Laminated like the others to the sidewall of the fuel tank, it possessed the same external diameter, but it was much thicker than the other three, and it didn't have a rotational system attached. It looked like an inflated version of the other rings, and it dominated his view once he stepped toward it to get a good look. He walked back toward Krok.

"Mostly it looks like the drive system in our space ships," Leos said. "I see the superconducting rings. And the mechanism that makes them spin. But you have one large ring at the back, and three smaller rings. Is that what makes it so much better?"

"Count the rings." But the sound in Leos's ears was even more muffled and crackly than it had been.

"What? I can't hear you. You're breaking up."

"Count the rings." Krok's voice came through a little louder. He pointed upward at the rings.

"Count the rings? Okay. One, two, three, four. All I see is four."

Leos stared at the rings, still confused. The number didn't register on him for a nanosector or two until he counted them again. The front of his helmet was fogging up where the moisture in his breath hit the cold plastic, and he was having a hard time seeing all the coils in one view. He craned his head right and left to get a good look at the coils and confirm in his mind that there really *were* four rings. Then the significance of the number hit him.

"Wait a microsector! Four?! You use four? How do you control it? I heard our engineers tried four rings a long time ago, but it was uncontrollable. They couldn't figure out how to regulate it. Have you figured out how to regulate it?"

"We have learned to control. Large fourth ring is control ring. Must use new mathematics. Mathematics of cosmos. This type of drive system opens larger wormhole and can go longer distance in shorter time. But doesn't go faster than light. Nothing goes faster than light."

"Have you tested it? How do you know that this ship will travel long distances? And what is this mathematics of the cosmos you keep talking about?"

"Our engineers have developed new mathematics, it—" Krok abruptly stopped speaking.

Leos jumped into the silence. "Hold on a nanosector. *Your* engineers? What engineers? Where are you guys from, anyway?"

Krok held up a hand toward Leos as if to ask for silence, and he remained quiet for several nanosectors. Through his foggy helmet, Leos couldn't see Krok's face clearly, but he seemed to be listening to something through his earphones. Finally, he spoke.

"I have heard your temperature is going down. We must leave fuel tank. Please to return."

"What? I don't feel cold." Leos was lying. His feet were chilled, though not uncomfortably so, and the middle two fingers on his left hand were frigid too, as though the warming system in that area wasn't functioning well. He tried to pull his hand backward into the interior of the mitten, but there wasn't enough room for his hand to move, and his fingers were chilled close to numbness.

"Please to return. You will be cold soon if don't leave."

"Okay."

Leos turned around and walked as briskly as he could toward the front of the tank. He followed the cables as they led forward to where they swung upward toward the entrance.

"Stand under access hatch." Krok pointed upward toward the opening.

"How do you get up?" Leos asked, but as soon as the words were out of his mouth, he felt a tug on his suit. He popped out of the fluid and landed on his feet beside the hatch. Krok followed immediately, sloshing out of the fuel with a loud *sploush* as the ultracold liquid, dripping in sheets and plies from their suits, hit the floor and popped and sizzled like water boiling on a hot griddle. A thick mist of condensed moisture filled the room.

The other guy gave Leos's helmet a sharp right turn and pulled it off. He could breathe the ship's air for the first time in almost two millisectors, and that faint metallic scent was back. But above him came a sound he hadn't heard before, a heavy whirring sound. Large fans in the ceiling were evacuating the hydrogen that evaporated from his and Krok's warm-suits, sending it outside into the planet's atmosphere. As he watched the mist radiate toward the fans, a soft 'thunk' behind him came from the fuel tank door as it dropped closed.

"Please to remove suit," Krok said after his helmet was off. "Then we will talk."

Leos wriggled out of the heavy warm suit and the blue fleece suit as fast as he could, but he was still suspicious of his two hosts, and he decided to confront Krok.

"Who are these engineers you keep talking about? Where are you guys from?" Leos massaged his hands and feet to warm them, and put his boots on. "Are you guys from Bes? I've heard there are a lot of kooky people down there. I've never been there, but I've heard—"

"Mr. Leos, please to come out of drive system." Krok moved toward the entry door, motioning for Leos to follow him out onto the landing.

"What's going on here? What ship is this? Where are you guys from? Are you guys even from Anthanos?"

"Not," Krok replied. "You are very intelligent. You have surmised our secret."

"*Not*? You're *not* from Anthanos? You're offworlders? Holy dinfrizzle! I've never heard—"

That certainly wasn't the information Leos was expecting to hear from these guys, and at first he was astounded at what they said, figuring he might be the first person on Anthanos to have the opportunity to speak to someone from another planet. Even his mom never got to speak with the natives she saw on the Blue Planet. But that feeling passed as quickly as it came on and he was alternately frightened for what they might do to him, yet excited to be able to get to know these new offworlders and speak with them. If he could get this information to someone back in Kalarias, like Public Safety or Spaceflight Command or even his mom, they might pin a medal on his chest. He pulled himself up to his full six-and-a-half-link height and stared down at Krok.

"I thought so. So, where *are* you guys from?"

"We are from far away. As I told you that when we first met. Are you not remembering?"

"Yeah, yeah, I remember, but *where*, exactly?"

"Our home planet is ninety-six of your light-years away. A long way."

"Ninety-six light-years! Yeah, that's a long way, but *where*?"

"You are knowledgeable about the constellation Diinn? It is as your mythology has designated, 'He Who Melts the Ice' is that not correct?"

"Yeah, you can only see it from the northern hemisphere. But I've seen it."

"We are from a planet around a star in that constellation."

"Oh, wow. That's a long way. But how did you get here, anyway? How did you land without being detected? Our planet is covered with extra-planetary intruder detection beams."

"We were knowledgeable of the detection devices. We landed on the cold side where the detection beams are the weakest. By appropriate shielding and active and passive feedback mechanisms, we appeared to your detection equipment as no more than a small meteor which your Security Service thought became landed on the ice on the dark side. Then we flew over the surface of the ice underneath the detection beams to here, which was near your hometown. Is that not elegant?"

"Ah, yeah, elegant, sure. So this ship is parked outside the city, right?"

"No, to be honest with you, Mr. Leos, we are parked long way from city. Near ice."

"Near the ice?" Leos jerked his head up and opened his eyes. "How far are we from Kalarias?"

"Two hundred of your anthans."

"Two hundred anthans! Holy dinfrizzle! How did you get me here anyway?"

"You became unconscious in our ground maneuvering vehicle."

"'Ground maneuvering vehicle'? Oh, you mean runabout."

"We prefer 'ground maneuvering vehicle.' It is a point of difference with us."

"Whatever. What time is it? Where's my chronometer?" Leos checked his left wrist, but his personal chronometer was missing.

"Not to worry, Mr. Leos, sir. Your chronometer is in your cabin. Perfectly good. Cannot wear chronometer in warm suit."

"Well, you'll have to take me back to Kalarias. I can't walk two hundred anthans."

"Of course, Mr. Leos, we could take you back, but . . ." Krok's voice trailed off and he seemed distressed, almost embarrassed. He cupped his hands behind his back and looked down at the floor and shifted position uncomfortably.

"But what?"

". . . that will not be possible." Krok's voice was low and faint, almost inaudible. He shook his head briefly.

"Not possible? Why not? What are you talking about?" A sense of suspicion and dread shuddered through Leos. He bent over slightly into the stance he used to talk to these shorter guys and stared directly at Krok. "What do you mean 'not possible'?"

Krok lifted his head and looked back at Leos. "Now that you know our secrets, you will be necessary to come with us."

"Come with you? Now hold on a microsector. I'm not going with you. I've got things to do. I've got a girlfriend who just graduated from tertiary school group and she's getting ready for her introduction to adulthood. We just got engaged and we're planning for a wedding next year, and — wait a microsector, is that why you confiscated my PersComm?"

"You have guessed our reason. We cannot have you communicating with friends. It would —"

"Look, PersComm or not, I'm getting ready for my third year in college. I gotta get back. They're expecting me and —"

Leos didn't get a chance to finish his sentence. For the briefest of moments he heard a low rustling noise, like the door behind him opening, and he felt a slight prickling sensation on the right side of his neck which turned into a burning —

Then his lights went out.

CHAPTER 3

THE CONTROL ROOM

Leos woke on the same bed. The room was cool and the lights had been extinguished. A tiny LED above the basin next to the bed illuminated with a pale yellow light a narrow area over the basin and the shelf. But this time his head didn't hurt and he felt relaxed and comfortable. His mind was clear and he knew he was visiting a spaceship, but nothing unusual or inappropriate floated through his mind. He was even hungry. He briefly considered staying on the bed for a while longer, but he didn't know what time it was and he figured he should get going. He looked around for his wrist chronometer. It sat on the shelf to the right of the basin: 889.3.

Eight eighty-nine? When did I come on board? He searched his mind. *Eight eighty-six, I think. Yeah, that's right. I came on board this ship on 886. I remember. Tama and I were at the tavern. I gotta be getting back. I told her I'd be back later that T-sector. She's probably worried.*

Leos swung his legs over the side of the bunk and sat up, taking care not to bump his head again on the top bunk. His head swirled as though he was light-headed, and it concerned him for a couple of nanosectors, but he attributed it to spending too much time in bed, so he dismissed it, figuring he'd feel better if he got moving. He found his boots at the end of the bed and jammed his feet into them. He grabbed his chronometer and walked over to the hallway door and tried the handle. The door was locked. As he jiggled the door handle a few more times, a familiar voice startled him.

"You are awake, Mr. Leos." Krok's voice seemed to come at Leos from all around the compartment. He looked around for a speaker but couldn't tell where the voice was coming from.

"Yes, I'm awake. Can you hear me? The door—"

"Certainly, I can hear you." A light click came from inside the door, near the handle. "The door is now unlocked."

Leos opened the door and stepped into the hallway. To his right, at the far end of the hallway, was the door that led to the fuel tank, and he assumed that direction would be toward the rear of the ship. It seemed logical for the fuel tank to be near the engine or engines it served. He looked left, but all that met his eyes was the same metallic hallway. A bit shorter in this direction, and another door—this one a bright blue color— with strange writing on the nameplate dominated the far end. As he looked toward the door it suddenly opened, and Krok—at least Leos assumed it was Krok—came into the hallway. Krok's smiling face seemed even more cherub-like than usual.

"Mr. Leos, sir. Please to come this way."

"Say, listen, I gotta get going." Leos turned toward Krok and started down the hallway. "Can you guys give me a lift into town?"

"Yes, Mr. Leos, sir, we will talk about this."

Leos met Krok at the blue door. On the other side of the door was another ladder, similar to the ladder that led to the fuel tank, but a bright sky blue, the same color as the door. Krok led Leos up the ladder.

As they ascended, Leos became aware of an unusual sensation. The lightness enveloping his head became more intense, and he almost became disoriented. Krok, above him on the ladder, moved easily, just like he did on the ladder to the fuel tank, but now he skipped several steps at a time as he went up. By the time he reached the landing at the top, he was pulling himself up by his arms only. And as Leos took step after step, he too became lighter.

What inna namea— I'm becoming weightless! How is that possible? Where are we going anyway?

As Krok hovered weightless over the landing at the top, he swung around to watch Leos ascend, still several steps below him.

"You are realizing weightlessness, are you not? You are familiar with this phenomenon?"

"Yes. I've been up in a shuttle a couple of times and got to visit a space station. But how did you do it here? Are we in orbit around Anthanos?"

"Please to come into control room. We will explain."

Krok crossed the narrow landing and pressed a small button on the wall next to another door. The door swung outward, and Krok drifted through the opening. Leos worked his way to the top too, now completely weightless. He grabbed tightly onto the railing that enclosed the landing and peered through the door.

Inside the door was almost complete darkness. Leos's eyes took a few nanosectors to adjust, and when he and Krok drifted through the doorway he began to appreciate the layout of the control room. At first, all he saw were the bright colorful computer screens piercing the darkness from many points within the room. But as his eyes became better adjusted to the dark, he could tell that the screens were laid out in four horizontal rows, counting from the back of the room to the front. Other small lights twinkled in the darkness near the screens and on the walls of the control room. Some flashed rapidly, some slowly, some glowed steadily, but most of the light in the room was from the screens.

The door closed quietly behind them, enclosing them completely in the murkiness of the control room. Across the front of the control room Leos could make out dimly a horizontal row of windows, but outside the windows was nothing but more darkness — total darkness. He strained to see stars in the blackness of outer space, but nothing appeared.

Seated in front of each computer screen was what Leos took to be a person. Illuminated by the diffuse glow from the computer screens, they all looked exactly like Krok and Grok, each with a bald spherical head, short chunky body, all wearing the same drab outfit, each staring at the screen that dominated his station. A few were engaged in soft whispers with one or more of the other 'Krokians' seated nearby. (That was the only name Leos could think to give them.) He counted four or five in each row, and that would make at least sixteen, maybe even eighteen or twenty people in this room.

"Please to come this way." Krok turned right and drifted parallel to the back wall. A long metal bar had been secured to the wall to make maneuvering easier in the microgravity, and small yellow LED's illuminated the bar at about two link intervals. As they reached the side of the room, Krok turned left and drifted toward the front. They went forward to the first row of screens and stopped. There was something familiar about the Krokian seated there.

"Please to meet Grok."

"Yes, I met him before." Grok unlatched the seat harness that held him in his seat and rose. He smiled faintly and nodded his head in Leos's direction, but he said nothing.

"Grok is our leader. He is in charge."

"Leader? I thought you were leader, er, I thought you were the leader."

"No." Krok smiled broadly at Leos's miscue. "Grok is leader. He is Captain of whole ship."

Grok said nothing and didn't smile. He just kept switching his gaze back and forth from Krok to Leos.

Leos's eyes had became adjusted to the darkness by now, and he could make out more detail of the features of the Krokians. Their eye slits had disappeared and the puffiness was gone. Their eyes seemed to be a dark color, either black or dark brown, though in the darkness Leos couldn't tell exactly. He did notice that very little white encircled the large iris and the wide-open pupil of the eye.

Very good for picking up low levels of light. As Leos stared into Grok's eyes, Grok whispered something to Krok, and Krok translated.

"Leader says to show you around ship. To make ship your home. You will be here for many T-sectors during our journey."

"Many T-sectors? Journey? Oh, God, I remember now." Now all that happened in and around the liquid hydrogen tank came flooding back into Leos's mind. He reached up and scratched the right side of his neck. "Look, you don't understand, I gotta get back." He stared both Krok and Grok in the eyes. "People are expecting me. I got things to do. I gotta get going. Are we in orbit around Anthanos? Can you get me a shuttle home?"

"It is so sorry. We are on our way to our home planet. We left in the last of your T-sectors. We are in wormhole now. Cannot turn around. You will like our planet. You will see."

"Like your planet!? I can't go to your planet! I gotta get back. Why do you want me to go to your planet anyway? Why do you have to take me with you?"

"It was necessary to bring you. Our planet has very fine use for you. You will see."

"Use! What are you talking about? What kind of use?"

Krok and Grok took turns whispering to each other, then Krok turned to Leos. "You will find out later. Now we must take tour of this ship to show you around. Please to come this way."

Krok motioned for Leos to follow him toward the back of the control room, and Krok led the way, pulling himself along the bar at the side of the room. Leos hesitated, at first not sure what they wanted him to do, but he eventually decided to follow Krok. He didn't want to stay in this dark place with a bunch of otherworlders he didn't know, and who, from all he had seen and with one exception, couldn't communicate so much as one word with him. But as he started to move, his legs felt heavy and non-responsive. Had he been standing in a gravity field, he certainly would have collapsed. His head spun and he held tightly to the bar that ran around the room. He didn't want to move. He wanted only to lie down in his own bed at home, to see his home and his mom and Tama and his familiar house in Kalarias and all his friends and acquaintances. The image of the tavern where he spent his last waking moments on Anthanos passed fleetingly through his mind, and he could see and taste the Qootaie he sipped from as Krok and Grok sat down across from him and Tama in his favorite booth.

"Take a tour of the ship?" Leos moaned. "I don't wanna take a tour of the ship. I just wanna go home. After I get to your planet, can I get a ship to return home?"

"That will not be possible. It is necessary you must stay on our planet. Please to follow me."

"I can't stay on your planet. I got things to do. Oh, God, this is a nightmare. How long is this trip going to take?"

"Five hundred of your T-sectors."

"Five hundred?! That's half a year! Oh, God this *is* a nightmare."

Slowly and hesitantly Leos made his way along the side of the room to the back wall where he turned and crawled along the bar toward the door. As he arrived at the door, Krok pressed a button on the wall again, and the door swung outward. But the orientation of the landing outside the door had changed. Instead of being situated at the bottom where it was when they entered the room—and where Leos expected it to be—the landing was now near the top of the door, and the ladder's position had shifted, about 180 degrees away from where it was when they climbed earlier. That didn't matter to Krok, he neatly swung himself around so that his feet pointed "down" the ladder, and he began to climb "down." But to Leos, still in the darkness of the control room, it looked as though Krok was climbing "up," and not only was he going "up," he was going "up" upside down and feet first, and that was just too much for Leos to accept right now.

He grabbed hold of the bar along the wall as tightly as the muscles in his hand and arm would allow. His head spun and a slight regurgitation burned in his belly. Under normal circumstances he might have enjoyed the adventure of puttering around in microgravity. But his captors had abolished normality several T-sectors ago, and still reeling from the realization he wasn't going back to Anthanos at all, the sight of the ladder at such an acute angle and of Krok climbing "down" in such a obtuse direction came crashing together with so much force it brought a paralyzing terror to his mind. He couldn't look at it. He couldn't watch Krok on the ladder anymore. It violated every rule of gravity and common decency and good Anthanian behavior he'd ever heard of, and he closed his eyes. He took several deep breaths, swallowed hard, and summoned up the courage to mutter something to Krok.

"Wha-wha-what's going on?" He slowly opened his eyes, then shut them again. "What are you doing? Where are you going?"

"Ship is rotating. Control room standing still. This provides artificial gravity. Is that not elegant?"

Leos made no reply. He was fixated rigidly, perhaps a little irrationally, on the weird position of the ladder outside the door, and he couldn't bring his mind to justify either the ladder or his abduction, no matter how hard he tried. Both violated natural laws—natural laws that were put in place to bring a defining order to his world, and the sight of that ladder, skewed into a wildly preposterous and unreasonable position, just magnified the enormity of the crime beyond what his Anthanian upbringing allowed him to accept. It just wasn't 'right.' It wasn't 'right' at all. He held tightly to that bar and managed to utter in a pale, feeble voice, "I . . . I guess so."

"You will come down, too?"

Leos paused. He wanted to follow Krok and get out of this horribly dark and depressing control room, but he couldn't move. His heart pounded, his forehead broke out in sweat, and his head spun. Nausea erupted in his belly.

"I'll try."

Leos remained in front of the open door, holding rigidly to the bar, his eyes hard shut. He was aware of a slight movement behind him, and again he felt a tingling and burning on the side of his neck, and again he woke up on the bunk in that same room.

CHAPTER 4

VOYAGE

"Ah, Mr. Leos, you are awake."

Krok stood near the door. As Leos lay on the bunk, he could see most of Krok except his head, hidden by the upper bunk. Leos's boots had been removed again, and his chronometer again sat on the shelf next to the basin. He could make out the first three digits on the display: 890. But what most caught Leos's attention was the presence of another 'Krokian' in the room, standing next to the basin, near the foot of his bunk.

"Please to meet Doctor," Krok said. "He is Gadomer."

"Hello," Dr. Gadomer said. And in Anthanian. He placed some shiny instruments into a silvery metal case that looked vaguely like a toolbox. "You are of the good-feeling type?"

Leos didn't reply, he merely groaned. He took a long look at the Doctor—a link or so taller than Krok, his face drawn into a more oval shape with a slightly pointed chin, rather than the perfectly spherical face of the Krokians. His skin was a marginally paler tan than the others—though it didn't approach Leos's sienna-brown skin at all—but he still had the thick pouty lips of Krok, and his eyes still gazed at Leos through thin slits surrounded by puffy eyelids. He wore a bright white jumpsuit, but he didn't smile all the time as Krok did. A small white badge embroidered on the right arm of the Doctor's suit below the shoulder sparkled and twinkled in the room light.

"What happened?" Leos asked.

"You had a panic attack." Dr. Gadomer's voice, pitched substantially lower than Krok's, carried a much more definite air of concern than the shallow and superficial pronouncements of Krok. His command of the Anthanian language was marginally better than Krok's, too, and he enunciated his words more precisely, without the faint slurring of consonants that characterized Krok's speech. "We brought you back here for rest. You will be good. Krok will show you around the ship."

"Okay." Leos said it but he didn't mean it. He didn't want to take a tour of the ship, he just wanted to stay here in his bunk and rest. A gnawing, hungry feeling grumbled in his stomach, though.

"You have not had food or nourishment for three of your T-sectors," Dr. Gadomer continued. "It is necessary that you eat. Your blood sugar is low. We have food on this ship for you. Krok will show you where your food is."

"Yeah, okay." Leos sat up on the side of the bunk and jammed his feet into his boots. He was weak from the lack of nourishment and still somewhat lightheaded. When he stood, he had to grab the top bunk to steady himself before he could walk, and he swayed and tottered slightly as he walked, but he made his way unassisted to the door. His head throbbed in his temples—though not nearly so severely as the hangover from his first T-sector on this ship—and his stomach grumbled and growled, but he wasn't sure whether he was hungry or not.

Krok opened the door and led Leos into the hallway. The doctor followed, and they turned left and walked up the hallway toward the door to the control room at the far end. Leos started to say he didn't want to go back to the control room, but before he summoned up enough courage to speak, Krok stopped short of the control room door and opened a door on the right side of the hallway, and led Leos into a spacious, well-lighted room. Doctor Gadomer continued down the hallway and exited through the end door.

Like everything else on this ship, most of the fixtures in this room were metal, the same shiny steel with the faint gold or coppery tint Leos saw in the room he kept waking up in. But this room wasn't a sleeping room, it was much larger. It seemed more like the dining area of a small cafeteria, with eight tables and four chairs per table placed evenly around the room. But what drew Leos's attention immediately upon entering were the two sofas to his left—large, dark brown, and very comfortable-looking. Each sofa faced a giant computer screen, and he imagined himself stretching out and relaxing on one of them. The sofas weren't metal like everything else on the ship, the dark brown covering—cool and slick to the touch—was a material Leos wasn't familiar with.

Leos turned his attention to the far wall, covered with small doors, like microwave oven doors, each perhaps 8 decilinks high and 12 decilinks wide. He started to count the doors up the wall, but he was interrupted by Krok. "This is day room."

"'Day room'? What does that mean? What do you do here?"

"Ah, it is my mistake. I am of the forgetting type. You are not familiar with day and night."

"Is that anything like the lightime and darktime my mom told me about on the blue planet?"

"Yes, you are very receptive."

"Huh? Receptive? Oh, you mean 'perceptive'."

"Ah, yes, that is correct. 'Perceptive.' You are very perceptive. I am of the mistaken type." Krok's wide, toothy smile appeared again. "Our planet is like blue planet. It rotates on axis, too. Very similar. We have day and night, too. You will see when we arrive."

"Yeah, okay, but why are we in this room?"

"Here is where we eat. Food dispensers are on wall there." Krok pointed to the wall with the small doors. "Each chamber behind door contains one type of food. Your food chambers are on left. All twenty on far left. Come I will show you."

Krok led Leos over to the far wall and opened one of the doors on the left, tenth from the top. He pulled out a bright yellow fruit.

"H-huh?" Leos stammered. "That's a yanto! Where'd you get that?"

"Here." Krok handed it to Leos. "Favorite fruit of yours, is it not?"

"Uhh . . . yeah." Leos stared at the fruit for a nanosector, not really believing what he was seeing. He took the fruit and held it in his hand. It was solid and heavy like a yanto should be, and it was cold as though it had been refrigerated, as it should have been. But Leos was hesitant to bite into it. He wasn't sure whether he should trust food from these people. Still, hunger, now real and insistent, rumbled in his stomach.

"Where did you get this?"

"We purchased it on your planet. For you to eat on our journey."

There it was again, that word. "Journey" had become a catchword for Leos, and it wasn't the word he wanted to hear. All it did was bring up memories of his abduction, and of the tank of liquid hydrogen, and of the ladder from the control room that appeared so out of kilter. That just made his appetite disappear. "I'll eat it later."

"Doctor says you must eat now."

Leos stared at the fruit. "Okay. Has it been washed?"

"Yes, yes. Very well washed. It will be good for you."

Leos took a cautious bite. Yanto had always had the most delicious flavor sensation he'd ever experienced, and this particular specimen didn't disappoint. The sweet and sugary, yet tart and tangy flavor of the fruit swirled around in his mouth just the way yanto always had. He held the chunk in his mouth for several nanosectors, savoring the effervescent chemical reaction that fizzed and sizzled when the fruit touched a mucous membrane and released those delightful endorphin-like compounds that had the power to settle his nerves and calm his stomach. He closed his eyes and let himself feel the wave of luscious tranquility that washed over his body as the compounds reached his bloodstream. The pounding in his head abated, the growling in his stomach ceased, and a sense of calm returned to his mind. He was still hungry, but it didn't bother him now. He opened his eyes and let out a deep sigh. "How did you know this was my favorite fruit?"

"It was in the Information Services. You are very famous on Anthanos."

"Oh, yeah, I guess so."

"And you will be very famous on our planet, too." Krok smiled as broadly as he ever had. Practically every tooth, and every gap between, was exposed.

"What are they going to do to me when we get there?"

"You will see. You will like it. It will be very much fun."

"Yeah, but *what*, exactly."

"I cannot tell you now. You must wait and see. But you will like. You will be very famous."

'Famous.' That was another catchword. First 'journey,' then 'famous.' Nobody would give him any idea of what those words meant beyond their simplest and most obvious definition. That seemed to be all the information he was likely to get out of Krok, at least for now, and he took another bite of yanto. *Maybe I can ask Grok, or Dr. Gad . . . or whatever his name is.*

"Now I will show you," Krok said. "All your food." He opened several of the doors on Leos's column. Kielkus, totsos, laiwai, luts, and more appeared as Krok opened each door, one at a time in turn, top to bottom, and Leos tried to make a mental note of what was behind each door.

"How often are these boxes refilled? I mean, how often can I get something from one box?"

"Boxes are filled immediately. Look, here."

Krok opened the door that held the yanto fruit, and another one sat in the middle of the box.

"Wow, that's fast." Leos started to reach for the fruit, but he hadn't finished the one in his hand, so he decided to leave it for another time. Krok closed the door and showed Leos the ladder that slid along a track in the floor to get to the doors higher up on the wall, but Krok abruptly left the wall of doors and strode over to the two sofas near the front of the room. He picked up a remote control and activated one of the computer screens.

"Here, you see. Your favorite computer games." Krok pointed out the listing, in the Anthanian language, of the "Assignment Annihilation" series of games, all of which Leos recognized, and many of which were among his favorites. His all-time favorite was "Assignment Annihilation: The Blue Planet," which he played regularly, several subsectors every waking T-sector, much to the dismay of his mom, who disliked the fact that the game had been modeled after her experiences on the blue planet.

"Terrible waste of a video game," Lilea used to say. "Subverted. The blue planet wasn't like that at all."

Then Krok de-energized the screen. "You may play as you like. But we must journey down hallway. Two more rooms await your inspection."

Still munching on his yanto, Leos followed Krok back into the hallway. They walked about a third of the way down the hall, past the door to Leos's room, to another door on the left side.

Larger than the Day Room, this room was filled with exercise equipment. Free weights, exercise bicycles, power lifting equipment, bench machines, treadmills, even a whirlpool bath, all the equipment Leos used at the gym where he worked out on Anthanos.

"Here you will exercise. You must stay in good physical condition. Doctor will monitor you."

"Is there a running track?"

"No. This was not possible to do. Come. We will go to next room."

Krok led Leos farther down the hall, stopping just short of the door to the fuel tank, entering through a door on the right side of the hall. This was the library.

"Here you will learn our language. The teaching machines will teach you to speak and read our language." He touched a marker at the bottom of a com screen on a desk situated near the far wall of the room, and the speaker within the computer began to utter a few simple words in Anthanian, followed by the equivalent in Krok's language. "You see, it is simple once you get used to it. You will spend much time here. You must know our language. Is this not okay?"

Leos thought about Krok's words for a nanosector, then grudgingly agreed. "Okay." He wasn't looking forward to spending a lot of time in this room learning a new language, but he figured he'd give it a shot. Krok was right—if he had to spend time on Krok's planet, he might as well learn the language. It would be so much easier to find a way back to Anthanos if he knew how to communicate with the others.

"What is your planet? I mean, what is its name? You told me it was in the constellation Diinn, but you didn't tell me its name."

"Ah, yes. Please to look here." Krok shut off the translator and activated a history program. He ran through several pages of history until he arrived at a representation of the solar system of his planet, and he pointed out its position in the solar system. The names of each of the planets were written in Anthainan, with the corresponding name in Krok's language directly below. Krok touched a small marker at the bottom of the screen and the computer began enunciating the names of the planets.

"Here. Our planet is this one. It is called *Nytandra*. You see, it is closest to our sun. It is desert planet like yours. You will like it. Very much fun."

"So, you're 'Nytandran,' I guess. Right?"

"Yes, this is correct," Krok said. "Now you have seen all rooms. Please return to Day Room and you may finish a meal."

Krok led Leos back up the hallway toward his room. He used the facilities, then walked down the hallway to the Day Room and finished his meal. But he didn't turn the computer games on because Krok had forgotten to show him how to use the remote control.

CHAPTER 5

INVESTIGATION – I

"I don't care what he says. I want to know where my son is."

"Lilea, we all want to know where Leos is, but we just haven't produced many solid leads yet."

The time was 483.897.2 when Lilea and Tama sat in the office of the Chief Inspector of the Division of Public Safety of Kalarias, on the third floor of the sprawling Metropolitan Administration complex that overlooked the downtown district of the city.

Lilea included Tama in most everything she did, and that especially included the investigation into Leos's disappearance. After all, Leos and Tama were a couple. They'd filled out the Notice of Intent for Betrothal with the Office of Interpersonal Affairs, and that meant Tama had taken the first step to becoming Lilea's daughter-in-law. But more than that, Tama was with Leos the T-sector he disappeared, and she'd already told Public Safety everything she remembered about what happened at the tavern when Leos left with the two strangers.

But Tama was so much quieter and reserved than the voluble Lilea. "Let's let them do their work," Tama said when Lilea told her on 483.895 that the Chief Inspector wanted to talk to her in two T-sectors. "I've already told them all I know."

"Honey, we have to get to the bottom of this," Lilea replied. "Leos wouldn't just disappear like that. I can't believe he's just inspecting some stupid spaceship. Well . . . I can believe it, but he wouldn't stay away this long. Maybe they can tell us something, maybe they have some new information."

News stories on the I.S. were graded in importance by shades of blue in the listings in which each item appeared—the more important the story, the deeper the color—and Leos's disappearance was indigo-blue news all over the planet. They'd even begun comparing it to the disappearance of Jad Til-Lentos, the other survivor of the ill-fated expedition to the Blue Planet, nineteen years earlier. Conspiracy theories swirled through many of the news reports: first, one of the two returnees disappears, and now

Leos, conceived on the Blue Planet, though born on the return trip, also disappears. That fact alone made him the "third returnee," and in the eyes of many conspiracy-minded people there had to be a direct relationship between the two disappearances.

The Chief Inspector's office was neat and simply appointed. A row of six large windows behind the Chief's desk overlooked the city. Bright with the reddish-orange light from the sun, the windows provided all the illumination in the room, though louvered blinds cut the brightness to tolerable levels. The Chief sat behind a dark gray metal desk in the center of the outside wall of the room.

But to Tama, the office seemed a dungeon. She sat nervously in the chair beside Lilea, her teeth faintly chattering, her hands folded tightly in her lap in an almost futile attempt to prevent them from shaking. She would've preferred to let Public Safety carry on its investigations without being dragged down here to the city-center into the glare of publicity from the Information Services that—especially after Leos's disappearance— shadowed Lilea wherever she went. She'd never been inside even one of the Security Service Substations around the city, let alone Public Safety Headquarters, and she was afraid they might have come across an inconsistency in her statement, or find out she omitted one tiny detail, perhaps the one detail that would crack the case wide open. And then they'd come down on her hard, and she'd be taken away, and . . . She tried to focus on the conversation.

Several datasheets, some with printed images, some with numbers and other writings lay in a neat pile on one side of the Chief's desk, and a com display and keyboard occupied the other side. Several framed images of the Chief with various city officials hung in neat rows on the wall to the left, just above a large gray metal cabinet that held thousands—if not tens of thousands—of com datadiscs. The grime of constant usage had soiled the area around the handles of the two cabinet doors. Everything in the office, except the desk and the cabinet, was a pasty grayish-green that Tama labeled icky-vomit green.

Lilea sat in the chair provided for her, to Tama's left. But Lilea could not remain still. Occasionally, she would rise and walk around the office, or amble over to one of the windows to stare at the city, or gaze blindly at one or more of the pictures on the wall, pictures of friends of the Chief, only to return a few nanosectors later to her chair.

She wore her hair longer now. The short blonde curls that were so unique to her public image and which she wore proudly during her time in spaceflight, now fell almost to her shoulders, and a few streaks of barely visible gray shot through the curls at her temples. A yellow ribbon kept the curls away from her face.

"We know he didn't come home on 887, Tama told us that." The Chief's voice, a low baritone, sounded soothing to Tama. She surmised the Chief must have been in his sixties with his neatly combed dark gray hair, and slight paunch to the jowls. Yet his face retained the smooth look of a man several decades younger, and he seemed genuinely concerned about Leos's disappearance. Tama was at least willing to cooperate with him and wished Lilea would do the same. "And we know he went with some strange-looking men late on 886. Several people at the tavern, including Tama, have told us that. But we haven't been able to find out where he went. And we don't know much about the two men. The Picomolecular Scent Detector faded out several hundred anthans from the tavern, where Tama said he entered a funny looking runabout with the two men, and our operatives haven't been able to generate any more information."

"Several hundred anthans? I don't understand . . . where . . .?"

"It ended near the ice line, darkside."

"The ice line? Oh, my gosh." Lilea lifted her head and put a hand to her mouth. "But how could it just run out? Where did he go from there?"

"He may have entered an aerodyne or some sort of aerodynamic vehicle."

"Did any of the intruder sensors track anything?"

"No. Neither did deep scanning nor tertiary effectors. He's not anywhere in the vicinity of the ice. We would have detected it."

"I don't understand it." Lilea rose from her seat and stepped away from her chair. "He's got to be somewhere. People don't just disappear off the face of the planet."

The Chief leaned back in his chair and returned Lilea's intense gaze. He nodded almost imperceptibly, then picked up another datasheet. "There are two other things I haven't mentioned. I don't know if they mean anything or not."

"What are you talking about?" Lilea returned to her chair but sat on the edge, leaning into the conversation.

"We detected a small release of hydrogen gas that emanated from the area where the Scent Detectors lost signal. And very shortly after Leos disappeared."

"Hydrogen gas? What does that mean?" Tama asked.

"Hydrogen gas emissions are illegal," the Chief said. "Hydrogen is an ozone reactant, and hydrogen release into the atmosphere was outlawed by the Assembly years ago. A large emission like that is extremely unusual." He turned to Lilea. "You're familiar with the extreme precautions SpaceComm has to take when fueling shuttles on the surface. Even SpaceComm isn't exempt from the regulations."

"Yes, yes, I know that, but what does that have to do with Leos?"

"I don't know now, but the emission came from the same area where we lost the scent, and it happened only two T-sectors after Leos disappeared. That's coincidental, if nothing else."

"How did you detect a hydrogen emission?" Tama asked.

"The nanomolecular spectrograph here at Kalarias monitors the air over the city all the time because most hydrogen emissions occur near large metropolitan areas. The emission was several hundred anthans west of here, and it entered the breeze. When it reached the city, it was a hundred anthans above. It'd almost dissipated, but it was still compact enough to be detected. By knowing how high it was, we could track it back to its origin. Roughly speaking, at least."

"What's the second thing?" Lilea asked.

"Yes, the second point." From the bottom of the pile of datasheets on his desk, the Chief pulled out a folder. "When we found the origin of the hydrogen gas emission, we re-examined some recent satellite images of the area. Unfortunately, the most recent image of that area is more than five hundred T-sectors old, but we found this." He pulled a high-def image from the folder. "You can see here on this broad image, a tiny point of light reflecting from a metal object. We enlarged the area and we found this." He pulled out a second image and held it up to Lilea and Tama.

"This area is where the hydrogen emission occurred. You can see the metal object here."

This image was a much smaller scale, an enlargement of the tiny point of light. A long, slender, conical object projected from beneath an overhanging precipice of ice. A windshield wrapped 200 degrees around the cone where it emerged from the ice, and a short, linear device, possibly an antenna, projected from the tip of the cone. The rest of the "ship" lay hidden beneath the ice.

"I checked with SpaceComm," the Chief continued, "and they have no knowledge of any spaceship or any type of aerodyne like that. We can't see all of it, but we can see enough to make an identification. SpaceComm doesn't know what it is or who built it."

Lilea took the image from the Chief and stared at it. Tama glanced briefly at it, but she couldn't understand why a spaceship was hidden under the ice so far from a populated area. "Do you think Leos was involved in building a spaceship?" she asked.

"That's one possibility," the Chief said. "Or maybe he got involved with the people who were building the spaceship."

"People don't just *build* spaceships," Lilea snorted without raising her head. "It's too expensive. There aren't enough resources for someone to just *build* a spaceship. All the precious metals and electronic components are too well controlled. How would they get enough gold to make electrical contacts? And titanium for the outer surface? And platinum? And rhodium and iridium? How would they get those? You have to have iridium and tantalum to harden the skin. And that means you have to have lots of it. All of those are imported from the moons of Tekaa. And neodymium and holmium for the coils? And yttrium for the lasers? Bent found all those. There's no way. Besides, why build it way out there next to the ice where the light is so dim you can't see anything? That certainly doesn't make sense. SpaceComm must know something." Lilea looked up briefly from the image. "Who did you talk to at SpaceComm?"

"We talked to Linc in the Office of Design and Construction."

"Linc? He doesn't know anything. You have to talk to Tam. Did you talk to Tam?"

"No."

"I'll talk to Tam." Lilea flipped the image back onto the Chief's desk. She stood and turned to leave, but the Chief called after her.

"Lilea, there's a few more questions I need to ask. Could you stay for another millisector?"

"What?" Lilea turned around, scowling, but made no move to return to her chair.

"I need to ask you a few questions. About Leos. Some personal questions. I have to do this. If I intrude on anything personal, I apologize. But I have to ask."

"What are you talking about?" She walked back to the Chief's desk, but remained standing.

"Has Leos ever been missing before? You know, like run off or run away?"

"No. Never. It's not like him. He's always been—"

"Does he frequent that tavern a lot? Ever come home drunk?"

Lilea paused. She seemed hesitant to answer, but nodded, frustration and exasperation now settling on her face. "A few times. But not much. I talked to them at the tavern. They're not supposed to—"

"Did you approve of his drinking?"

"No, really. Well, as long as he was responsible with it, I suppose so."

"What is it, yes or no?"

"No."

The Chief paused, and leaned back in his chair. "You were in Sabean when Leos disappeared. Is that correct?"

"Yes."

"Tama tells us he was drunk when the two men took him. He almost passed out at one point. Is that your understanding?"

"Yes. That's what she told me."

"And that's okay with you?"

"No, I told him not to . . . well, I told him not to do anything stupid while I was gone, but, you know how kids are."

"But he's not a kid. He's twenty-one years old, isn't he?"

"No, he's twenty-two, but—"

"All right, Lilea, thanks for coming in. That's all I need. If we have any more information, we'll get in touch with you."

Lilea turned and left the room. Tama scrambled to follow, and they descended the main staircase in the front of the building. They walked through the front door directly into a small group of waiting I.S. reporters who peppered them with questions.

"What did you talk about?"

"Did the Chief tell you anything?"

"Is there any more information about Leos? Where is he?"

"What's going to happen next, Lilea?"

"Would you care to make a statement? Give us a statement— anything."

Lilea didn't stop. She walked through the little band of reporters and waved them off with a curt, "I'm sorry, I can't tell you anything." There was real anger in her voice—at least it seemed to Tama—and she marched to her runabout in the parking lot next to the building.

"Tam can tell us something." Lilea set the autodrive to take them home. "I'm sure of it. He'll know what's going on." She said nothing else during the rest of the trip.

Lilea's street was quiet when she and Tama arrived. Information Services reporters did not usually approach a celebrity's house, but Tama was still surprised that no one met them as Lilea parked the runabout in the driveway. The I.S. usually preferred to get their information directly from Public Safety, or failing that, perhaps to scrounge a few personal tidbits from Lilea, though, so far—even in all the furor generated by Leos's disappearance—they had left Tama alone. Still, she wouldn't have been surprised to find a few reporters with a camera crew outside her house.

"Lilea," Tam said over the Vis-Comm interlink between his office and her house. "How are you? I think I know why you're calling."

Lilea and Tama sat on the large, dark green overstuffed sofa that faced the com screen in the living room. The screen covered most of the wall, and the visage of Tam dominated the screen. His deep baritone voice boomed from the speakers to each side of the screen, ruffling Tama's hair with each syllable.

"Tam, what is that spaceship?"

"I don't know," Tam replied, shaking his head. "Nobody at Space-Comm knows. I've talked to Security. I can't tell you anything you don't already know."

"Tam, this is Lilea. You know I respect you and all you've done, for me and for Spaceflight Command, and for Anthanos, but you're not leveling with me. What is that spaceship?"

"I am leveling with you. I don't know. It's not one of our designs, I can tell you that."

Lilea stayed quiet for a nanosector. She ran her hand through her hair and pulled off the yellow ribbon. Her face had turned drawn and harried, even a little agitated. She put both hands over her face and held them there for a nanosector, then spoke again.

"Tam, look, please," she said. She balled her hands into fists. "All I want to do is find out where he is. What does that ship have to do with him?"

"Lilea, I don't know, but you know as well as I do that Security is looking into it. We'll let you know as soon as we find anything."

"Okay, thank you." Exasperation seemed to drip from her voice.

She touched the marker **END COMM** at the bottom of the screen and the screen went dark. Only the time element remained in gold numbers in the bottom left-hand corner: 483.897.6.3. Lilea rose from the couch and walked into the food preparation area. Tama heard her pour a glass of some liquid—water or juice perhaps—and drop a few ice cubes into the glass.

Tama stuck her head into the food prep area. Lilea stood at the window over the sink, staring at the other houses across the golden brown sand that comprised her back yard. Before Tama could say anything, Lilea plucked a white pill from a blue plastic box sitting on the counter and popped the pill in her mouth. She washed it down with the liquid.

"I gotta be getting home," Tama said.

"Okay, sweetheart. Thanks for coming." Lilea paused and set the glass on the counter, but didn't turn around. "If we lived on the blue planet, I bet our yard would be green with vegetation instead of this brown sand." Another pause. "I hate this goddamn sand."

CHAPTER 6

RUMINATIONS

Leos sat in the library of his abductor's ship staring at a com screen displaying a list of examples of the conjugation of irregular Nytandran verbs.

"God, there are so many," he mumbled to himself. "How am I supposed to learn all these?" His eyelids drooped, he'd started to drool, and his attention toward the words on the screen had evaporated faster than liquid hydrogen on a hot plate. Behind him, the door to the room opened and someone quietly entered.

"Well, Mr. Leos. How are you doing today?" Grok addressed Leos in the Nytandran language. "Krok tells me you are progressing successfully in your education."

Leos jerked up and tried to look as though he was resolutely studying the screen. Now well enough along in his study of the language, he could understand most of the words and simple phrases that the Nytandrans used, at least around the ship.

"It is coming along well," Leos said in halting Nytandran. "I can speak well enough to be understood by most on the ship."

"That is good." Grok stood in the center of the room, his arms across his chest, his feet planted firmly on the floor about a link apart. He frequently struck a pose like that, sort of an 'I'm in charge here,' posture. He didn't have the constant smiling face of Krok, but he always spoke plainly and calmly, his voice never exhibiting any of the harshness that might be expected in a ship's commander. Leos was never sure if that was just his way of standing and talking, or whether it was common for all Nytandran leaders to take a strong, self-assertive pose that projected a hard-nosed, uncompromising approach to running things. Would there be more of this on their planet?

"It has been eighty days since we started out," Grok said. "We have reached the midpoint in our journey to our planet. I believe that is approximately two hundred and fifty of your T-sectors. Is that not correct?"

"I believe it is, yes."

By this time, Leos had studied the planet of Nytandra sufficiently that he knew that a "day" on their planet was 3.11 T-sectors long, and he multiplied the midpoint time by the appropriate factor and came up with an answer that agreed closely with Grok.

But getting to this midpoint had been problematic for Leos. Immediately, from the time he'd been told to study the Nytandran language and the history and geography of their planet, he decided he didn't want to have anything to do with these people—after all, they kidnapped him and were taking him into some unknown territory they refused to tell him anything about.

I might as well have some fun before we get there.

So he settled himself on one of the comfy couches in the Day Room and pulled up his favorite videogame, "Assignment Annihilation: The Blue Planet." He blasted animals that had huge saber-like front teeth, and he shot great two-legged, bearded, animal-skin wearing, knuckle-dragging hairy beasts that devoured innocent women and children. In his on-screen runabout with its huge electromagnetic positron cannon, he attacked big shaggy monsters with huge tusks and a long proboscis that shot rocket-propelled death charges at him, threatening to blow him out of his comfy position on the couch. He destroyed immense slithering creatures that attacked him, ready to gobble him alive in one horrendous gulp. And he saved the beautiful buxom blonde from a horrible death at the hands of the dark, hairy natives.

"Oh, thank you, Leos," the blonde murmured as the top—and eventually the bottom—of her bikini disintegrated.

Leos would have stayed on that couch blasting monsters over and over for the entire voyage had Dr. Gadomer not entered the room two sub-sectors later and told him in no uncertain terms to get his ass down to the Library and study. The doctor threatened to shut down the games until Leos began his studies, but he said he could have a few subsectors of game time if he spent eight subsectors in the Library and at least two subsectors in the Exercise Room every Nytandran day.

Leos didn't have much choice, and his studies began.

He learned that the Nytandran year was divided into thirteen groups of thirteen days each, for a total of 169 days in a year. But with the day being slightly more than three T-sectors long (31.1 subsectors!) including the long dark time, the Nytandrans had four meals a day, a concept he was slowly getting used to. He learned that each day was divided into thirteen hours, the hour into thirteen minutes and each minute into thirteen seconds, and so on by repeated subdivisions into infinitesimally small periods of time, all by intervals of thirteen.

Why thirteen? It seemed to have come from some obscure element of the rotation of Nytandra around its sun, but really, *who the hell cares?*

He learned that the planet was tilted on its axis only three degrees off perpendicular to the plane of its orbit, and this meant almost no seasonal variation during the year. Being so close to its sun, the days were hot, the average midday temperature was above 40 Tal, but the nights were chilly, cold even. To the Nytandrans, the night was a welcome relief from the oppressive heat of the day.

But Leos was still uncertain how he would take to the phenomenon of regular intervals of light and darkness. He remembered his mom telling him about the rotation of the blue planet, and how she quickly got used to the cycle of alternating light and dark, so he didn't expect to have a problem with it. But he couldn't be sure. Still, he looked forward to arriving at the Nytandran planet. Anything to get off this ship.

The ship stifled Leos. He'd been assigned only a minimally furnished cabin as a place to sleep, and the door was locked after he entered his room for every sleep period. He spent all his time shuttling between his room, the Library, the Day Room, and the Exercise Room, and while all this activity kept him busy for most of his non-sleeping time, for a healthy, active, red-blooded young man, it was suffocatingly boring. He enjoyed the computer games, of course, they took from his mind the tedium of the voyage and allowed him, in at least one small way, to return to his home on Anthanos. He was beginning to enjoy talking to several of the other members of the crew. That gave him a chance to try out and expand his knowledge of their language. But he longed for something else, something far more meaningful—Tama.

Oh, yes, Tama—Tama—Tama. Why are you so far? Why did they take me from you? Where are you now? Do you miss me? I miss you so much.

A few women did comprise part of the Nytandran crew, but with their almost bald spherical heads, puffy eye slits, and thick pouty lips they looked exactly like Krok, and they were about as sexless as the monsters on the screen. Only Dr. Gadomer's appearance was different from the rest and that puzzled Leos. Why should this one person be any different? A different race, perhaps?

"You will enjoy our planet," Grok said as he stood in the Library. "It is very much like yours. You will be very famous."

"Famous. Yeah. That's what everybody says."

But of all the ideas that flowed in and out of Leos's mind during this first half of the voyage — all 240 T-sectors so far — the one that most consistently puzzled him was his fate upon landing. None of the crew would, or could, tell him anything. Certainly not Krok who told him only that he would like his fate and he will be famous all over the planet. Then Krok would smile that great big smile that exposed not only his teeth but all the dark, insidious spaces between them. Neither would Grok or the Doctor say anything. Not even when Leos cajoled them with his best arguments. They merely repeated what Krok said.

"Don't you think I deserve to know?" he would frequently plead. Or, "Everybody else knows, why shouldn't I?" Or, "It's going to happen to me, I should be allowed to know." Everyone agreed with all these arguments wholeheartedly, but they remained enigmatically quiet, or, as usually happened when he queried others on the crew, they merely stated that they couldn't tell him, and Leos finally, in a fit of peevishness, eventually quit asking.

Perhaps the Nytandrans figured it was best for their purposes to not tell Leos what plans they had for him, but the melodramatic way they went about it only served to produce vile and perverted images in Leos's mind. He derived some small hope from Krok's persistent comment that, "you will be famous," and took that to mean that he would, at the very least, be around for a while. But how long? One day? Two days? Ten days? A year? How long is "a while"? Would they feed him to monsters? What kind of monsters? Many of the monsters he blasted on the video games came spitting back into his mind. Will there be some sort of planet-wide event where he will be cast into the den of some fiendish, demonic creatures and be devoured slowly and painfully to the delight of millions of onlookers?

Or would they sacrifice him to their gods? A living sacrifice? Holy dinfrizzle.

"What *can* you tell me about why I'm being taken to your planet?" Leos asked Grok as he stood in the Library.

"You have heard all that we can tell you. It is sufficient that you know you will enjoy your fate and you will be famous. Say I anymore and I am divulging too much."

"So, I'm likely to be alive for a while."

"Certainly. But I have said too much. I can say no more."

Okay — that partly allayed Leos's curiosity about his fate, but still, *What does it all mean*? That one tiny revelation still left lacking a huge amount of information. *Perhaps they want to cross-breed me with some of their women.* A loathsome thought in itself, it begged the next question: *Why?* Is their race facing some sort of genetic disaster? Perhaps they wanted to bring in some outside genetic material to enhance their race. But would he be able to cross-breed with another totally alien race? Leos knew enough of genetics to understand it probably wasn't possible, and from what he could see on this spaceship it certainly didn't look it, but he couldn't be sure. He didn't have enough information to decide if that was true, and like most other theories he conjured up, that theory died for lack of evidence.

Medical experimentation? Surgery? Disfigurement? Germs? Could it be they were going to inject him with some dreadful elixir and turn him into a grotesque, aberrant troll, destined to prowl the sands of Nytandra as a hideous monstrosity? How many others are out there? Have they done this to other Anthanians before? *The possibilities are endless.* His mind contrived all sorts of revolting outcomes, as though his destiny was written on a granite disk sitting on this desk, staring him in the face T-sector after T-sector. He couldn't get away from it. It followed him wherever he went. Sometimes the torment was too much and he had to force himself to think of better times, of Anthanos, of Kalarias, of his mom, but especially of Tama — *Tama, yes Tama, why are you so tantalizing? Why couldn't you be here right now.* But he always returned to the morbid anticipation of his fate on Nytandra. Many times during the voyage he would wake up on his bunk, saturated in sweat, the LED above the basin the only light in the room, and monsters of many descriptions careening through his mind, and he unable to stop it. He would usually decide right there he wasn't going to play their silly game anymore, and he would refuse to leave his room when the lights were automatically up-modulated the next morning. But the growling in his stomach would become so incessant and relentless he would amble down to the Day Room and grab a bite to eat. Then, because the video games were turned off at this time of the Nytandran day, he would meander down the hall to the Exercise Room and his day would begin all over again.

Maybe they have other Anthanians and they want to set up a breeding colony, he thought at one point while he sat in the library staring at the computer screen. *Some good looking girls, perhaps? After all, with me around, their breeding stock would be well endowed — they wouldn't need anyone else.* He looked down at the growing bulge in his pants. Then he looked back at the monitor and the Spartan surroundings of the library.

Well, that would be nice, but let's face it, it's not going to happen.

Occasionally, he would dream of more pleasant fare. Maybe they want him as an ambassador from Nytandra to Anthanos. Maybe they want to establish a trade relationship between the two planets. Maybe we have something they need—precious metals, perhaps? But his dream would collapse when he remembered he'd been kidnapped.

Aside from that, an ambassadorship would be too political for him. He'd grown up in the public spotlight and he grew to dislike it. He hated the pushy reporters from the I.S. when they questioned his mom about aspects of her time on the blue planet, especially shortly after her return when he was so young and impressionable, and he resented her taking time away from him to go to a press conference to answer their inane and exasperating questions. When he got older—around ten years old—they turned their questions on him and bombarded him with queries about what life was like living with a famous mom, and how did he like it, and so on, over and over, and that was way too much for him.

He just wanted to be a pilot and fly around in outer space and explore new worlds and suns and moons. Those video games had gotten under his skin.

He got the exploring bug from his mom. She talked often to him about her adventures in outer space, about her time in training for the expedition to the blue planet, and about the long voyage there and back, and all she had accomplished on its exquisite—that was the word she used—surface. She explained to him about his father, Bent, whom he idolized from afar because he never knew him. There were so many stories she had to tell him about his Dad, about his visits to most of the moons of Tekaa and of Shaltous, of his discovery of all sorts of metallic elements that were so essential in the building of intra- and interplanetary spaceships. He devoured everything he heard, and read most of the scientific reports Bent had written about his work, and perused the SpaceComm accounts of all he had done. He talked to others who knew him, and so formed an image of Bent in his mind that might have been somewhat exaggerated in its relationship to the real Bent, but which nevertheless was totally real in Leos's mind. His father was genuine, a hero to many at SpaceComm, and a superstar and adventurer (and somewhat of a martyr) to Leos.

But his mom did something else, too. She pushed him to take introductory courses in astronomy and astrophysics and geology in tertiary school group, just enough to whet his appetite for the darkness beyond Anthanos. He enjoyed those courses, and enjoyed even more the advanced courses he took his first two years in college majoring in spaceflight engineering. That was what he wanted, to be a command pilot or navigator or propulsion engineer — hot damn.

"Where will we be landing when we get to your planet?" Leos asked Grok.

"At our capital city," Grok answered. "You have heard of it in your studies, Lox Atendra, have you not?"

"Yeah, I've heard of it."

"It is a very lovely place. You will like it, I am sure."

"Yeah, whatever."

Leos had seen the images of Lox Atendra in the computer history of Nytandra. He called it "Lox," dropping the second name — in Nytandran it was somewhat difficult to pronounce with its guttural consonants and strange vowels. He wasn't impressed by the appearance of the city, either. It looked dirty, though perhaps dusty would be a more accurate word. It was certainly out in the desert — the tan buildings, the dirt roads, the deep blue sky, the simple, unadorned style of construction, the mountains in the distance. Their buildings were much taller than those of Anthanos, some reaching twenty or thirty stories, buildings that would never be stable on the sandy terrain of his home planet. And all those green towers, scattered throughout the city, the water towers, those tall slender erections with a big, rounded head on top, each as tall as many buildings — how unusual. He took that to mean that the soil of Nytandra was 'stronger' in some indefinable way than the sands of Anthanos, though he didn't know how to express it in geological terms. It was an oddity he resolved to investigate after he arrived, assuming he would get the time and opportunity.

"What happens after we arrive?" Leos asked of Grok. "Where do we go first?"

"We will go to see our leader. You will like him. He is very fair."

"Fair. Yeah, okay. But what — "

A beep came from Grok's communications unit in his left chest pocket and he glanced at it. "So sorry. I am due in our control room. I must leave. You will like our leader. You will see." He strode over to the door and left the room, almost slamming the door behind him in his haste.

"'You will like our leader. You will see.' Yeah, right. Isn't it time for your nap?"

CHAPTER 7

LANDING

Leos lay on his bunk, trying to keep his stomach calm. The Nytandran ship was pushing through the atmosphere of its planet, and the vibration was far stronger than any he'd experienced in an Anthanian ship. Grok and Krok had warned him before the de-orbit burn to expect some vibration as well as other unusual movements of the ship. But he certainly didn't expect to feel the ship swinging from left to right like a drunken pendulum, and he could never have anticipated the ship pitching up and down as though it were on the surface of some stormy body of water, or rotating around its longitudinal axis as though it was screwing its way into the atmosphere. It frequently pitched upward, throwing Leos into the air, only to suddenly drop and let Leos crash back onto the bunk like a sack of yanto. Several times the ship rolled over almost 200 degrees, pitching him toward the head of the bed or down toward the foot. Dr. Gadomer had wisely cautioned Leos not to eat anything before landing, and he was glad he didn't. But he did wonder how the pilot was able to control the ship with all this extraneous movement.

Must be computer controlled. How come I don't have any memory of these same wild maneuvers on takeoff? Oh, that's right, I wasn't awake during takeoff. They drugged me and I slept through it.

The wild episodes came in waves. Sometimes the ship would settle down and the ride would be smooth and turbulent-free, like moving through deep space. Then, without any warning whatsoever, the ride would turn rough again, threatening to send Leos hurtling to the floor or flying off the foot of the bed. They *had* offered him a seat in the control room during the landing, but he declined.

"The control room? No, thanks. I'll take my chances on the bed."

I'm going to have to talk to Grok about this landing, he thought as he grabbed hold of the sides of the bed to avoid being pitched onto the floor for about the tenth time. Finally, Krok's cool, rather banal voice came over the intercom.

"You are feeling good are you not, Mr. Leos?"

"I'm okay," Leos yelled back. "When do we land?"

"Very soon. We are through with difficult part."

True to his word, the vibrations smoothed out and the wild maneuvers ended, leaving Leos with the recognizable sensation of flying through a planetary atmosphere.

The ship must be flying below the speed of sound by now, and that means we can't be very far above the surface. Landing should come soon. But did this ship land horizontally like a surface-orbit shuttle, or vertically like most Anthanian spaceships?

"Standby, Mr. Leos," Krok's voice came again. "We will land at our spaceport. Then you will see our planet."

"Yeah, okay, whatever."

The ship turned quiet, the only sound a mild hiss as the environmental system supplied fresh air to the cabin. The gravity of the planet was stronger than the artificial gravity provided by the centrifugal force of the rotating spacecraft, and he weighed more now than during flight through the wormhole. As he lay on his bunk, a whirring sound came from somewhere deep below.

"Our landing gear is down, Mr. Leos," Krok said over the intercom. A few microsectors later Leos felt the gentle bump as the landing gear hit the ground. The ship drifted along the ground for a short distance, stopped, and then, after a couple of Nytandran minutes, started rolling again. When it stopped again, Krok's voice came over the intercom.

"We have landed, Mr. Leos. Please come with us."

A familiar click came from the door to Leos's room as the locking mechanism was released, and Leos took a few steps out into the hallway. His legs were weak against the full 1 G of the Nytandran planet, and he stood by his door for a couple of nanosectors flexing his legs and doing a couple of deep knee bends, when the door to the control room at the end of the hallway opened and Grok and Krok came out.

"This way please, Mr. Leos," Krok said, and Leos walked down the hallway toward the end door. To the left of the end door, Krok pressed a button on the wall and a door slid upward. Behind it was another small anteroom—actually a pressurizable airlock. A few links away was another door, this one with steps built into it. This door, hinged at the bottom, was a part of the curved outer surface of the ship, the main entry door. When Krok pressed another button on the wall beside the door it swung downward. As the door opening grew, the brilliant light and heat from the Nytandran sun swelled into the little entryway, and Leos shielded his eyes with his hand. Now he knew why the Nytandrans had such heavy puffiness around their eyes, and he wished he had the same kind of built-in shielding.

"I should've brought my sunglasses," he muttered.

"So sorry," Krok said. "I am of the forgetting type." He pulled two pair of sunglasses from his pocket and handed them to Leos. They were the wrap-around kind that shielded the eyes in all directions, and printed on them was a recognizable Anthanian trademark. "For you, Mr. Leos. We purchased these on your planet. Our sun is magnificently bright."

"Thanks."

Now that the door was fully open Leos had become aware of a roaring sound, like applause, but mixed with shouts and hoots and hollers and catcalls. *There must be a thousand people out there.*

Grok stepped first down the steps onto the tarmac, and the shouting and hooting grew. Krok went next, and it became even louder. But Leos hesitated. As the only person remaining in the little anteroom, he was to go next, but he wasn't sure he was ready. Krok, standing at the bottom of the steps, turned and peered back into the darkness of the entryway.

"Mr. Leos, please to come out. Minister has desire to meet you."

Minister? Oh, that's just dandy.

Leos's heart pounded and a tightness developed in his chest and in the pit of his stomach. Beads of sweat formed on his forehead and they weren't there because of the heat. He wiped his mouth on his sleeve, grabbed hold of the bar that served as a handrail down the steps, and with his right foot, cautiously stepped toward the door.

But that's as far as he got. He paused again, then turned and looked behind him. No one else was around. The door from the hallway was closed, and the ladder room beyond was almost certainly empty too. Even the door to the control room at the top of the ladder was undoubtedly shut tight. The next step was his. No one was around to sneak up behind him and plant that little prickling device on his neck and put him to sleep.

But Leos would never allow himself to be knocked out and arrive comatose for his first visit to this planet. He would make it on his own. He wanted no one to hold his hand and escort him down that short ladder into the Nytandran sunlight. He was beginning to feel that he'd arrived, that this was his situation to make as much of as he could. This was his move now. The fear that cascaded through his chest and into his gut he would have to overcome by whatever willpower he could summon through his own determination and resolve, and pour into the musculature that would bring his right leg forward and carry him into Anthanian history. *Hell, even Mom never got to speak to the intelligent beings on the blue planet.* If this was to be among his last few days of existence on this planet, well, why not take advantage of the opportunity? Hold his head high and go out in style. He smiled at his good fortune and took the cautious first step down the steps in the door.

As Leos reached the bottom of the ladder and stepped onto the landing platform—made of concrete or a concrete-like substance—he ducked his head to clear the top of the entry door and stood up in the brilliant sunlight. As he did, the noise stopped altogether.

The air he stepped into was hot, above 40 Tal, and the scorching Nytandran sun screamed off the concrete back into his face. About fifty links away approximately a hundred Nytandrans stood in a loose semi-circle. But his attention was drawn immediately to a tall imposing figure standing directly in front of them. At least seven links tall, he wore around his shoulders a multi-hued brocaded cloak with gold and silver thread in gay and gaudy designs and intricate weavings, speckled throughout with a mosaic of red, yellow, green, blue, silver, and purple. The cloak reached to the man's ankles, covering most of the grayish-green boots he wore. On his head he wore a scarlet turban, wrapped round and round in many layers, held together with a gold multi-pointed star-like emblem in the center. A brilliant silver jumpsuit-like outfit sparkled in the sun from under the cloak, and the buckle of the belt around his waist contained the same star-motif as the turban. His dark tan face was more oval, similar to Dr. Gadomer's, and his thick eyes were almost entirely shut.

This must be the Minister.

In his left hand, the Minister wielded a tall rod in the manner of a baton or scepter. At least seven links long, it seemed to be made of solid gold, and Leos's eyes almost bulged out of his head when he saw all that brilliant metal.

Wow—on Anthanos that rod would be worth millions. Billions, maybe. Yeah, billions.

Four round-headed Nytandrans stood beside the Minister, two on each side. Dressed in the same silver outfit, they lacked the cloak or turban, and their bald heads gleamed in the sunlight.

The Minister took several steps toward Leos, and Leos instinctively took a small step back. The tarmac was quiet now, only a faint hissing came from Leos's left as several holding tanks in the ship were depressurized.

"Minister," Grok said. "Please to meet Leos Kalatarian."

The Minister took a few more steps toward Leos who watched carefully every move he made as though he were about to be gobbled alive. Abruptly the Minister raised his scepter and tapped it three times on the ground.

"Mr. Leos," he said in a booming bass voice. "You have come. We have waited a long time. You are welcome on Nytandra. Our Ruler is waiting to meet you. Please follow me."

There it is again — the Ruler. "Ah . . . okay."

The Minister turned around and strode toward the buildings beyond. His entourage fell in place behind him, two on each side. Grok and Krok followed them, and Leos tagged along in last place. The semicircle of Nytandran onlookers opened quietly to let them through.

As Leos walked, he scanned the crowd and they stared back at him. He could take only a brief glance at the accumulated sightseers as he passed through the semicircle, but he was struck with the pervasive similarity of the Nytandrans. They all had the same round, bald head, the same slits for eyes and the same pouty lips that appeared dry and cracked in the intense sunlight. They all wore the same drab clothing, a light shirt and dark pants. Leos found himself wondering if they were male or female or both. The only distinguishing features of the females he'd seen on the spaceship were a slightly higher pitched voice and longer eyelashes peeking through the slits from which their eyes gazed at him.

Many of the onlookers held what appeared to be cameras, apparently recording the arrival of this new visitor to their planet. *Are they press? Or just personal?*

Leos followed the entourage into the building, feeling very much like an animal in a zoo for all Nytandra to gawk at. The building was darker and much cooler, and he took off his dark glasses and wiped his forehead on his sleeve. But the Minister didn't stop. He pounded his way through the building, down several corridors, turning left, then right, then left again, and finally emerged on the other side of the building, delving back into the intense sunlight. More Nytandrans lined the sidewalk outside the door — as though they'd had advance warning he was coming — held back by about ten security guards with bright, shiny but strange-looking weapons. Many of the onlookers also held cameras. Parked in the street outside the building was a long, yet familiarly shaped vehicle.

Leos didn't remember much about the "ground-maneuvering vehicle" in which Krok and Grok took him to their ship — in his mind he called it the "abduction vehicle" — but the sight of the Nytandran vehicle here on the street brought back enough recognition that the image of the vehicle came dribbling back in bits and pieces to his mind. The drunken stupor he was in at the time prevented too detailed an image, but he could generally picture it, especially the unusual conically-shaped front end. What was most significant about the limousine he was about to enter — and it was obviously a limousine with four doors along the side — was that the driver sat in the center, not on the right or left side. There didn't seem to be much room for an engine in the front, either. He briefly wondered what kind of power plant this vehicle could have.

The Minister entered the last door of the limousine, and three of his minions entered the next door forward. Grok and Krok entered the front door just behind the driver, while the fourth of the Minister's associates opened the second door from the front. He smiled at Leos with the same gap-toothed smile that Krok had, motioned for Leos to enter, and Leos climbed in.

Ah, cool.

"It is much cooler in here, is it not?" The Minister's voice boomed through the vehicle as though he spoke from inside a bass drum. "Our sun is quite brilliant, and our weather can be magnificently warm."

"Yes, it is much cooler," Leos replied. "Very nice." He took off his dark glasses.

Leos's seat was on the left side of the limousine, but it faced toward the right side, back the way he'd just come. Many of the crowd that had welcomed him on the tarmac followed them through the building, joining the others lined up outside. All those onlookers, several hundred at least, gathered around the limousine, rubber-necking at Leos through the darkened windows. They didn't wave at him or make gestures of any sort, and they probably couldn't see much through the smoky-gray windows, but they seemed content to try and stare anyway. A few poked cameras at him. At the Minister's command, the limousine moved silently away from the building into the heavy traffic.

The Minister sat in a slightly raised chair in the back of the limousine, his associates in a single row in the next row forward. Leos had difficulty seeing much outside the car through the dark windows, but he could make out a few details of other vehicles that ventured nearby as the limousine sped along the highway. They all had that funny front end with the driver sitting right in the center. And they were all a highly polished metallic silver with a faint gold tint.

"Where are we going?" Leos asked.

"We are going to the Ruler's Palace. You will like the Ruler. You will be famous." For the first time the Minister smiled. That same gap-toothed smile.

Oh, brother. Famous — here we go again. Whoop-de-do.

Yet for all his mental sarcasm, Leos was growing more and more to like the Minister. He seemed honest and genuine, and in that respect he was like the doctor. Leos took his smile as an attempt to be friendly, rather than the haughty and supercilious smiles of the round-headed Nytandrans for whom he felt little more than disdain anymore.

The limousine moved faster now, fifty to sixty anthans per sub. They'd left traffic behind and entered a single-lane up-ramp. With a grade of only about 5 degrees this was a relatively shallow ramp, but it swung in several broad S-curves toward a stand of imposing buildings in the distance. Leos craned his neck in several different directions, trying to see out the front window which was not darkened, or to see out the side windows, but he was constantly frustrated by the lack of detail.

"We have entered the Ruler's Highway," the Minister said. "You can see from here. I will open the window."

One of the Minister's associates leaned forward and pressed a small button on the side of the limo, behind Leos. The window descended about a link, and Leos turned around.

The sunburned warmth of the outside air blended with the coolness that develops in air as it moves, and the breeze felt warm on his face. The limousine still sped along the up-ramp, now several hundred links above the ground and still rising. Leos peered into the distance, letting the rushing wind ruffle his hair.

"You are able to see the Ruler's palace from here."

With the late afternoon sun behind the vehicle, Leos's eyes were in shade. To the north and east of the city, and through a remarkably clear atmosphere, a row of craggy, spike-peaked mountains jutted from the flat city floor, forming half of a natural bowl, with the city nestled comfortably within the protective shadow of the hills. From the northeast region of those hills, at the point where the east-west hills swung neatly south, sat a vast, sprawling palatial edifice. Minarets and towers, domes and arches, mosques and arcades thrust themselves into the sky creating a mélange of architectural structures that dominated the skyline. A magnificent construction, designed to be as much a part of the mountains as to simply sit on top of them. Yet one aspect of the structure seemed oddly out of place.

There was little definitive color in the palace. Every part of it was a tan to light brown, not much different from the hills on which it sat, or the surrounding terrain below.

As the limousine scurried up the ramp, continuing its broad curve to the left, Leos turned his eyes from the palace and scanned the cityscape through the open window of the limousine. Just like the palace, the unvarying tan of most of the buildings seemed all the more remarkable for the almost total lack of any other color. From the images of the city he'd seen on the com screen in the library during the voyage, Leos expected to see the water towers. Placed on strategic sites around the city, they held what little precious water the Nytandrans could extract from the ground. When new, those towers were a rich, warm green, but after years of abuse by the intense Nytandran sun they'd faded into a sort of ghastly chartreuse. But those towers were the exception to the drab, generally characterless colors of the rest of the city. A few buildings were a faded red or blue or even dark brown, and looked as though they'd been peppered out sparingly from a giant shaker. Leos had hoped for more vegetation, more cultivated fields, more of any color indicative of growth. Perhaps he expected too much. Maybe he'd been brainwashed by the alluring images his mom brought home from the blue planet, or maybe it was simply a matter of having his expectations raised too high by the travel brochure-like images on the com screen. He certainly never anticipated such a stark terrain. It was too much like his own planet, vast and bare. Nytandra had more hills and mountains than Anthanos, yet all was a light to medium tan, all hot and barren.

As Leos turned back to look toward the palace, he estimated those buildings were at least an anthan away. He could still visualize the ramp ahead of the limousine as a thin ribbon of pale white growing thinner and thinner as it tapered off into the distance.

After about three millisectors of upward travel, the ramp leveled off and the limousine began to slow. They were now several thousand links above the valley in which the city lay, zipping along at forty to fifty anthans per sub. Leos turned around in his seat and the window moved back up, closing off the breeze.

"Great view," he said.

"It is a magnificent view, is it not?" the Minister replied.

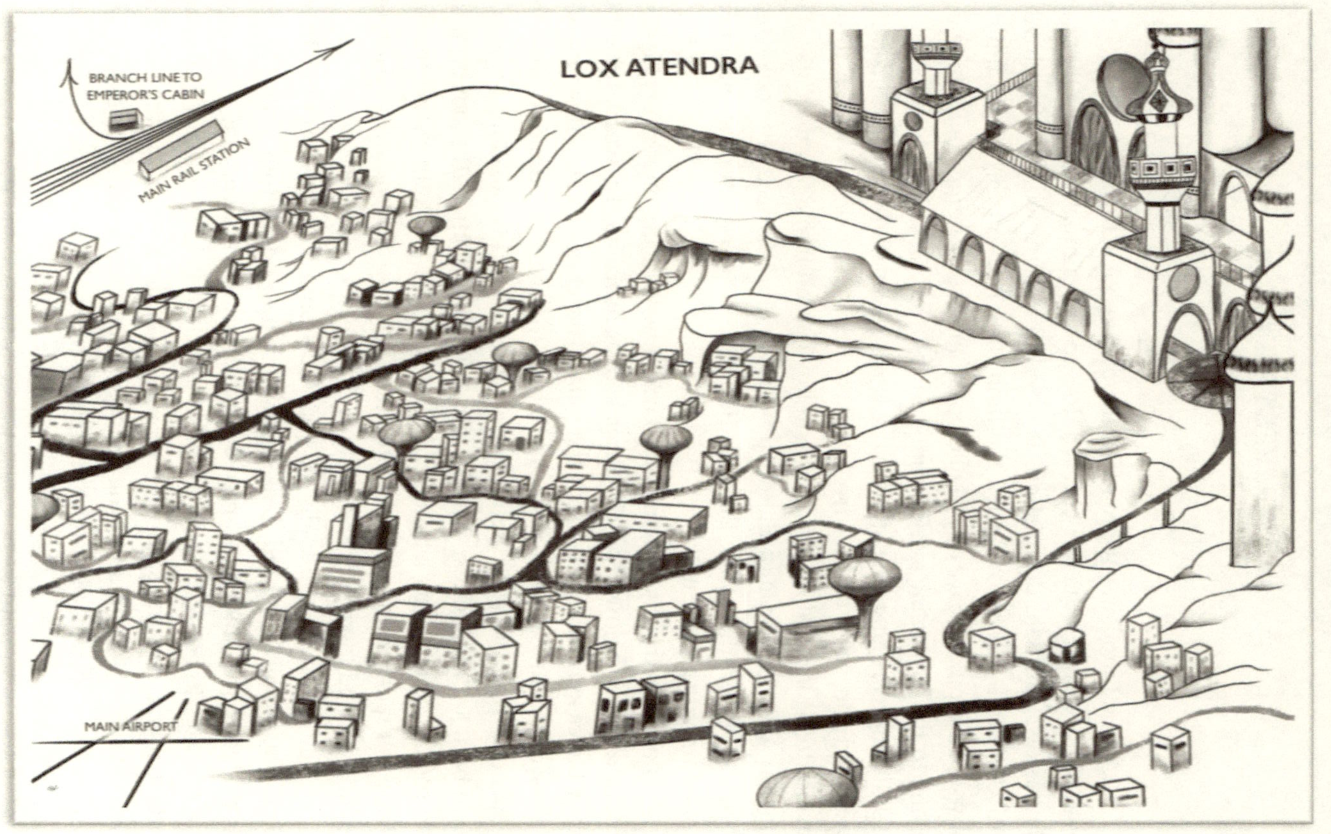

LOX ATENDRA
BRANCH LINE TO
EMPEROR'S CABIN
MAIN RAIL STATION
MAIN AIRPORT

CHAPTER 8

REVELATION

As the limousine approached the palace, Leos turned to his left, trying to look through the forward window to see as much as he could of the limousine's ultimate destination. He couldn't see much past the driver's bulbous head, but he could tell the limousine had left the long ramp and now sped along a driveway sheltered by an overhanging roof. Stone columns to the limousine's left supported the roof, but they whizzed by so rapidly they became a beige blur. A stone parapet about four links high protected the edge of the driveway between the columns. Leos turned farther to his left and lowered the window behind him a few decilinks. The air that whistled through the open window onto his face felt cooler than lower down on the valley floor. It didn't have the penetrating bite of the hotter air of the lowlands.

Between the flying columns Leos now had an unobstructed view into the valley below. The city stretched outward to the west and south from the eastern hills on which the palace stood on a flat, almost monotonous desert of pale tan sand, and north to where it butted against the peaks and precipices of the northern hills. From this position, he would have been looking almost directly into the brilliant sun had it not been for the roof. Farther to his left he could see the long up-ramp they'd just ascended. It faded into the haze of the distance near the southern spaceport as it descended toward the city below.

The limousine gradually slowed and stopped deep within the driveway. The window behind Leos went back up and all four doors on the right side of the limousine opened, almost in unison. Everyone waited for the Minister to get out, and they piled out right behind. Leos was the last out, stepping onto the stone portico where the limousine was parked. The air was cooler here than at the spaceport, but still warm, maybe 25 Tal. Refreshing, though, with not the higher carbon dioxide content of the air on Anthanos.

Directly in front of Leos was the main entrance to the palace, a huge set of double doors more than 20 links high and made of a dark brown material Leos couldn't fathom. Intrigued, he scanned the doors carefully. Six intricate carvings on each door dominated their texture, each set into a panel within the doors, one above the other. Two Nytandran guards, resplendent in black and gold uniforms and wearing a red turban similar to that of the Minister, stood beside the doors. As the Minister tapped four times on the stone flooring of the outer portico, the guards pulled the doors open. In the same way as he led the group through the airport buildings, the Minister strode in first. But Leos was again last in the line of marchers, and again he was acutely conscious of his position. He looked to his rear, afraid someone would sneak up on him. But the doors closed behind him and no one followed.

They entered a large, brilliantly lit, circular entry hall, much cooler than outside, and Leos removed his dark glasses. A magnificent dome-shaped ceiling towered above them, and a large chandelier of a hundred lamps or more hung from the exact center of the dome. Great pieces of colored tile covered the ceiling, placed apparently randomly, but which shone brilliantly in the light from the chandelier. Lower down, the light beige of the circular chamber emulated the tone of the palace exterior, but frescoes of Nytandran figures, probably from deep within the planet's history, adorned the walls. Directly in front of the group was a large set of double doors which dominated the far end of the entry hall, and were attended by a dozen Nytandran guards in two rows. The doors, like the doors to the outside, were made of the same dark brown material and heavily carved with intricate designs and symbolic motifs. They were wider too—opened together, they could admit a Nytandran ground maneuvering vehicle. But they were so heavily guarded that no one could get in without the appropriate permission. The Minister led the little group swiftly across the hall and stopped about ten steps before the doors, and his associates and Grok and Krok stepped aside and fell in line behind Leos.

"This is the Grand Hall where you will meet our Ruler," Krok whispered as he passed. "Please to follow Minister. He will lead you."

The Minister tapped with his scepter four times on the stone floor. Each tap resounded sharply through the hall and reverberated off the ceiling and walls. At the fourth tap, two of the twelve guards stepped out of position and pulled the heavy doors open. Slowly and quietly the doors swung outward in a graceful, majestic arc. Leos watched, impressed, his concerns and apprehensions temporarily displaced as though he were watching an opening into a new and different world. He gazed as best he could through the doors into the room beyond. Unlike the deserted entry hall through which the little group marched in such a hurry, these doors led to a room full of people, perhaps two hundred Nytandrans, both the short, round-headed kind and the taller oval-headed type. They were much better dressed than those in the gawking crowd at the airport, too. Many wore a cloak like the Minister, though their cloaks were invariably a single color. The greatest number seemed to be dark blue, but scattered throughout were maroon, green, yellow, and white. They'd been chatting among themselves, discussing God-knows-what, but after the doors had fully opened and a brilliant musical gong sounded from somewhere within the room, the Minister strode in and the crowd grew silent, stepping back, parting their company to allow the Minister and Leos to pass.

Leos followed, his heart pounding in his chest. Even in the cool air of this chamber, perspiration formed on his forehead and upper lip, and in the palms of his hands. It dribbled into his eyes and stained his collar. The Minister walked majestically up the aisle formed by the crowd, and Leos nervously scanned the multitude as he walked, and they ogled back at him. Cameras poked and peered at him. He saw no outward display of emotion, no smiles, no frowns, no way to tell whether they were accepting or rejecting him.

I wonder what they're thinking? "Such a pity — he was a nice looking kid?"

As Leos walked down that aisle, now as intensely as at any time during the trip, the thoughts that went through his mind focused on why he was here. What could they possibly want with him? Is he going to have to do a song and dance for the Ruler? Or is he a trophy to be paraded a-round like a fool — or a puppet — on the end of a string? Or will he end up swinging from the end of a rope? A drop of sweat dribbled into his left eye. He wiped his eye and mouth with his sleeve and swallowed hard. His stomach growled.

He looked around. The room was brilliantly lighted, not so much by internal lights, though a few of those hung from the beams that supported the ceiling more than thirty links above, but by sunlight shimmering through seven tall stained-glass windows on each side of the room. Pieces of colored glass seemed to have been placed randomly within the win-dows, and in design mimicked the ceiling of the entry hall. The sun, shining through the windows on the right side — the south side of the hall — illuminated them with a penetrating brilliance, as though each piece was lighted from behind by its own individual bulb. Even the glass in the windows on the left side gleamed and glistened in the sunlight reflected off the mountain peaks behind the palace. The surpassing effect was to fill the entire room with a brilliant sense of color and hue, splashed about like paint hurled at an easel. The color permeated and saturated the atmosphere in the room, and it sparkled and danced over the bald heads in the sea of people assembled to greet this visitor to their planet.

As the Minister and Leos reached the far end of the room, the Minister stopped abruptly, then stepped deftly and quickly to his left, leaving Leos staring at a large table set on a platform about three links above the floor. An incense burner on the table filled the air with a spicy odor.

"Please to stand beside me," the Minister whispered. "The Emperor will be in shortly."

The Emperor? Holy dinfrizzle.

The table was made of the same dark brown material as the doors, and it too had been carved with a delicate fretwork down all four legs. Behind the table was a chair, gold leafed and heavy, with comfortable red cushions. But no one sat in the chair.

Is this the Emperor's chair? His throne, maybe?

More beads of sweat drizzled down his face.

Leos didn't have long to wonder. Within a microsector of his arrival, a door in the wall about twenty links to the right of the table opened and the gong sounded again. The crowd had returned to a faint murmuring, but with the brilliance of the gong, all discussion stopped and everyone turned their attention to the door. Through the door in one big whoosh came a man, round-headed, but slightly taller than the other round-headed Nytandrans, overweight and pudgy, wearing a gold jumpsuit-like outfit, his shoulders covered with a cloak as colorful as that of the Minister's. Nothing covered his bald head. He stopped in the middle of the platform and looked directly at Leos. He grinned.

"Leos, m' boy!" the Emperor bellowed. He hopped off the platform in one step, jumping over the set of three steps from the platform to the floor, and strode directly over to Leos, putting his right arm around Leos's left shoulder. "We've been waiting years to see you. How ya doin', m' boy?"

"Ahh . . . okay."

"Great! Great! Nice trip, was it?"

"Yeah, it was okay."

"Great! Splendid! Sounds like you learned our language pretty well. We've got quite a surprise for you, m' boy, quite a surprise. You do like surprises, don't you?"

Leos nodded.

"Great! Splendid!"

Good Lord, is this the great exalted Ruler they told me so much about? I'm confused. This guy couldn't be the ruler of an entire planet, could he? Someone who seems to be trashing the formal rules of etiquette and good taste in meeting a visitor from a different planet? No way—this isn't the Emperor. This is somebody's uncle.

The Emperor took his arm off Leos's shoulder and motioned toward the back corner of the room. "Let's have some music!" he shouted, and a group of eight musicians began to play some rather unusual music—atonal and quite a bit out of tune, even by Anthanian standards.

"Well, Leos, m' boy, we've got quite a surprise for you. You do like surprises don't you? Oh, that's right, I already asked you. Just kidding, m'boy! Let's get right to the point. You aren't married are you? Relax! I already know you're not! Just kidding, m' boy. By the way, did they tell you why we wanted you to come here?"

"Uhh . . . no, not really. They didn't tell me anything."

"Okay, m' boy, suppose we tell you now. Would you like that? Of course you would!" The Ruler signaled toward the door from which he'd emerged a few microsectors ago. "Tell her to come in!" The door opened again and he turned back to Leos but didn't look directly at him. He seemed uncomfortable and hesitant, and took a few steps back as he began to speak. He cupped his hands behind his back and paced back and forth in front of Leos.

"Well, Leos, I have a daughter, and she wants to get married. You know how that is, don't you, m' boy? Good. But she's kinda different, y'know. You understand, don't you? Good." Every time he said "don't you?" he stopped and glanced at Leos, as if to gauge his reaction. Leos just nodded. "She doesn't want to marry one of us. Y'see, she's adopted, and she's, well, she's different, and kind of picky, y'know. You know how that is, don't you? Good. And choosey. Nobody on this planet is good enough for her. You understand how that is, don't you, m' boy? Good."

Oh, that's just great. I've been brought here to marry the emperor's daughter. I can't marry someone else, I'm almost engaged to Tama. Crap. Wouldn't you know. Just my luck. His daughter. I'll bet she's uglier than the hind end of a . . .

Leos was barely able to mumble "Ahh, yeah," to the Emperor's last question when the gong sounded again and a young lady walked through the open door. Leos's eyes opened so wide he wouldn't have been able to open them any wider had he stuck toothpicks between his eyelids. His head jerked back, his lower jaw dropped, and a faint smile curled up the corners of his mouth. "Oh, my gosh," he said quietly.

"Leos, m'boy, this is my daughter. Leos, meet Esmerelda. Esmerelda, come over here and say hello to Leos."

Esmerelda stepped off the platform, walking gracefully down the steps. She wasn't like any Nytandran woman Leos had seen. She had the oval face of the Doctor or the Minister, but he could see her eyes clearly, they didn't peer at him through puffy slits. At first glance, her eyes seemed a radiant emerald green, but as she came closer he could see a faint tinge of blue suffused within the green, tending toward turquoise, and they sparkled and twinkled in the kaleidoscopic light from the stained glass windows. Her long chestnut hair had been put up in a ponytail held by a shimmering gold clasp, and the auburn highlights in her hair picked up the warmer colors of the windows. She had the thin lips of an Anthanian, not the thick, pouty lips of the Nytandrans, and her skin was as smooth as glass. She wore a light gold two-piece outfit, shorts and a halter top, and over those a pale pink gossamer gown that covered everything, yet revealed as much. Rose-gold sandals on her feet clipped quietly as she walked across the stone floor. She moved elegantly, like a princess at her wedding, to where Leos stood and extended her right hand.

She's Nytandran? I've never seen a Nytandran woman like this.

"Hello, Leos," she said in a soft feathery voice that seemed far away. "I believe on Anthanos you greet one another by shaking hands, is that not right?" She looked directly into his eyes and smiled when she talked, and her teeth were pure white and perfectly aligned — no gaps. She wore a delicate shade of pale green iridescent lipstick, and a similar shade of polish glistened from her fingernails.

Leos gulped. "Uh, yeah, that's right." He took her hand. She gave him a firm handshake, and he held her hand in his, feeling her warm, smooth skin, not the warty, pebbly, freckley skin of the Nytandrans.

"Well, whadda think, m' boy? Is she great or what?"

"She's very lovely," Leos said. He couldn't take his eyes from her. He looked at her face and scanned her figure. He gazed directly into her eyes and she met his gaze with hers, a delicate but embarrassed smile on her lips. They stood there for more than a nanosector, staring into each other's eyes, and Leos knew he had to get to know this engaging young woman — the sooner the better. He looked down at her feet, so tiny and so petite and so perfectly proportioned to the rest of her body, not the large, clumsy feet of the other Nytandrans.

"So what about it, m' boy? Ready to get married?"

"Uhh, well . . . I don't know about that . . . yet." An image of Tama floated through Leos's mind.

"Just kidding, m' boy, just kidding! That's okay, you two just met. Take your time, m' boy, take your time."

Finally, the reason for his kidnapping had been revealed. Leos was on this planet to become the Ruler's son-in-law. On the face of it, that was bad enough. He'd been brought against his will to this hot, dusty, god-forsaken planet almost a hundred Anthanian light-years from his home for the sole purpose of marrying someone he didn't know, had never met, and a member of a foreign race at that. But that didn't matter to Leos now. He was staring into the most beautiful pair of eyes he'd ever seen, Tama's notwithstanding, and he could have fallen deeply in love with this winsome lass and married her in a trice and settled down to raise a family on this out-of-the-way planet had it not been for one minor, insignificant, miniscule problem. The problem was with Esmerelda's skin. Oh, her skin was soft and warm and smooth all right—that wasn't his dilemma. The question for Leos, the jolt that almost knocked him off his feet when he first saw her, was the color of her skin. It wasn't the light umber of his, or the deeper, darker brown of the Nytandrans.

It was green.

CHAPTER 9

ESMERELDA

Yes, Esmerelda's skin was green, all right. And not just a pasty yellow-green either—a deep rich green. The kind of green Leos had seen in images of the forests his mom brought back from the blue planet, the vivid green that came from the leaves of the tall stately trees, glistening in the bright sunlight. Her skin had a luster to it, too, and Leos was intrigued by the novelty of such an unusual skin tone. Over the first few days that passed on Nytandra, as he grew to better know Esmerelda personally, his attraction to her grew, and his first impression—somewhat negative—of the unusual tint of her skin began to soften. Eventually, he came to see her as an intelligent young woman, mature beyond her age at twenty-four Nytandran years, and he regarded her skin color as little more than a slight disfigurement, a blemish perhaps, like a mole on her chin.

As a guest of the Nytandran Ruler, Leos had been assigned a room in the Guest Quarters of the Imperial Palace, cool during the day and warm and cozy when the temperature plummeted in the dry desert air at night. They gave him a corner room with a comfortable bed, table and several chairs. And a video screen. Leos translated the term they used for the screen as "television," but he usually referred to it as "the video," or sometimes "the vid." The light brown walls of the room weren't too much different from the exterior color of the Palace, but the door was the same dark brown material he found so interesting in the Grand Hall where he first met Esmerelda. Only the bathroom had the familiar metal fixtures he remembered from the spaceship.

From the side window in his room, he could see the north side of the Grand Hall with its magnificent stained glass windows that turned colorful and brilliant when the morning sun rose over the hills behind the Palace. When the sun crested the Hall, it shone deeply into Leos's room, and a more intense sunlight he had never seen, not on his planet, and from the descriptions he'd heard, not on the blue planet either.

From the front window of his room he could look down on the top of the porch through which the limousine sped as it brought him to this

Palace, and by craning his head farther to the left he could make out the up-ramp, a long, gently curved ribbon of grayish-white that swung deeply toward the city below and ended in an infinitesimal point near the space-port.

*   *   *

In the evening on the third day after his arrival, Leos took supper, the fourth meal of the day, with Esmerelda and the Ruler, whose name he learned was Coreaje, though the Minister instructed him to address him as "Your Eminence," or at the least, "Eminence." They dined in the Family Dining Room of the Royal Family Residence, far on the other side of the Grand Hall from Leos's room in the Guest Quarters. Coreaje occupied one end of the long table, dominating the meal in his special high-backed or-nately carved chair. Leos sat in a more modest chair with a bright red cushion, across the long side of the table from Esmerelda, who sat in a similar chair with a sky-blue cushion. Behind Leos, double doors opened onto a stone patio. Individual panels of etched glass about a link square had been mounted in a framework of that same dark brown material as the doors in the Grand Hall. This particular evening, the doors had been opened, and a warm evening breeze, a remnant of the heat of the day, rustled into the room, flickering the flames of the thirteen candles in a gold-plated candelabra that stood on the table between Leos and Esmer-elda. The flames danced and twinkled in her eyes every time she looked up and smiled at him.

"Well, m' boy, have you reached a decision?" Coreaje asked the same question every time before sitting down to a meal since the second day after Leos's arrival.

"Well, sir, I'm not sure yet." Leos sipped the vegetable soup. "I am committed to a girl on my home planet. We filled out the Notice of Be-trothal just before I . . . ah . . . came here, and we wanted to get married, and, well, you know, I'd—"

"I realize that, but you must realize you cannot go back, either."

"If we were to get married, that is Esmerelda and me, er, Esmerelda and I, well, we couldn't raise a family. We can't interbreed. We're not com-patible."

"That's true, but Esmerelda knows that. She wouldn't be able to breed with any Nytandran either." Esmerelda glanced briefly at Coreaje, but continued to sip her soup politely and properly, as befitted a Princess of the Royal Household.

"So why don't you get someone from her home to be her husband?"

That was the second time Leos had made that suggestion. And like the first time when he'd brought up the subject at supper a few days earlier, he received the same response. Coreaje just harrumphed and said, "That will not be possible," and continued on with his meal. Esmerelda averted her eyes and stared at her plate of food. She put her spoon down in her soup bowl and ate no more until the subject changed. Both times Leos knew he'd said something improper, and wisely said little more for the rest of the meal.

This evening, though, they finished supper adequately and without further embarrassing pauses, and after Coreaje left the dining hall to return to his duties, Leos and Esmerelda strolled through the open doors onto the patio. The patio faced slightly south of west, and the sun had almost dropped behind the horizon at the far end of the valley. The brilliant reds and golds of sunset spun tissues of light over the patio and gave Esmerelda's skin a warm greenish-bronze glow that Leos saw at no other time. The breeze, now gaining coolness in the evening as it swirled through the valley in which the city lay, whispered up the mountain to the Palace and washed over the couple as they engaged in quiet conversation.

"You've never told me where you're from," Leos said. "You know a lot about me, but I don't know much about you."

"Come over here." Esmerelda led Leos into the semi-darkness at the far end of the patio, away from the light that spilled onto the patio from the Dining Room. She pointed upward at about a 40-degree angle into the night sky toward a group of five or six faint stars in an irregular circle just above a peak in the center of the mountain range behind the palace.

"Can you see that little ring of stars?" she said. "In the center of that ring is a little planet. That is my world. That is my home."

Leos stared at the ring. A faint glow came from inside the ring, but he couldn't make out much detail.

"How did you know where to look?"

"The Royal Astronomer pointed it out to me many years ago and I have followed it since. I see my home planet every evening. I follow it all the time. I always know where it is. It is a part of this solar system. It is the next planet outside this planet."

"Then you could go home anytime you wanted. They have space ships that could take you there easily."

"No. Father refuses to let me return. He says I must stay here."

"But couldn't he bring someone from your planet here?"

Esmerelda shook her head and walked away, back toward the light from the dining room.

"Esmerelda, why does everyone turn so quiet whenever I mention your planet? What's going on here? What is it?"

"Leos, you do not know what you speak of. It is hard for us to talk about."

"Why? What is it?"

Esmerelda walked forward on the patio and stopped at the low stone wall about two links high that fronted the patio. Leos followed. About twenty links below lay the roof of the portico under which the limousine sped as it brought Leos to this palace, and several armed guards with highly polished silver weapons patrolled the top. They paced back and forth in sentinel-like attention, oblivious to the two above.

Leos and Esmerelda stayed at the wall for a Nytandran minute, staring quietly into the distance. The lights from the city twinkled below in an irregular crisscross pattern that followed the layout of the city streets. Most of the buildings in the center of the city were illuminated from within, and small yellow lights flashed atop the buildings and water towers in the city. A rotating beacon of white light to the left—south of the city— indicated the position of the airport, and farther to the left, another beacon denoted a smaller airport.

"I was taken from that planet many years ago." Esmerelda spoke softly though she didn't look at Leos. She continued to stare out over the city. "I was very young. My father—my real father—was killed, and my mother and I were brought here. The Ruler married my mother and so became my new Father, and I was raised here in this palace. That was many years ago. My mother died five years ago."

"So you're not Nytandran."

Esmerelda shook her head gently. "No. I am from that planet." She pointed back and upward toward the little ring of stars.

"Couldn't you go back and marry someone on your world?"

"Father says no. I cannot go back. My mother told me all about the planet. I feel it. I am from there, but I must stay here. I want very much to go back, but I cannot. I must do otherwise."

"But couldn't your father bring someone from your planet here? Why did they have to kidnap me from a planet a hundred light years away?"

"They took you because your race is similar to mine. They looked at many races on many planets, and all were ugly, terrible creatures. Not fit for a Princess. Then they went to Anthanos, and you were famous and they could get to you easily. It was easy to learn much about you. And your language. You were about to get married so they took you then. That is why you are here."

"Oh, yeah, of course." Leos was beginning to understand Grok and Krok's calculating ways. They could have learned from the Information Services that alcohol made him sleepy—that'd been on the gossip channels several times—and they knew that once he got drunk they could carry him off without any real protest on his part. "Did they look at the blue planet?"

"Yes, but they did not like the blue planet. The people on the blue planet are not fit for a Princess. Also, there is too much water. They wished someone from a desert planet. Like yours."

"Okay, yeah. But I still don't understand why they don't bring a young man from your planet here."

"Leos, it is hard to talk about it."

"Esmerelda, what is it? Why is it hard to talk about?"

Esmerelda was silent for a few nanosectors. She remained at the low stone wall, not moving, still staring into the distance, and spoke in halting, trembling words.

"My father—my father on this planet—invaded my planet, and my mother and I were kidnapped. But the army that invaded became out of control and killed many of my people. My real father was killed. Many of my people were killed and now very few remain. Only old people remain. They do not have many young people. There is no one to bring here."

"Oh. I'm sorry, I didn't know . . ."

"Father was angry that his armies had killed many people, and it has been hard for him ever since. He did not order the destruction. He wanted only to set up a small outpost. It is a burden he must bear. We called our planet *Jon-Set-Tom*. It means 'Place of the Tall Trees.' We were a peaceful people, we knew nothing of other planets. We knew only our place. That is all. We had no weapons, except knives. We did not even have a government. There was nothing there for them to conquer. Only trees."

"Trees?" Leos raised an eyebrow.

"Yes. It is a forested planet. We wanted only to be left alone, but the armies came and destroyed us."

"I'm sorry, I didn't realize . . ."

"It is okay. That was twenty years ago. I am over it now. But I would like to go back and see my planet and meet my people once again." Esmerelda picked up a pair of binoculars sitting on the patio wall. "Here." She handed them to Leos. "You can see my planet with these."

Leos returned to the back of the patio and stared at the little ring of stars. Through the binoculars he could see many more stars inside and outside the ring, but near the center of the ring was a brightly colored dot—a very familiar color. "It's green!"

"Yes, it is a forested planet."

"What's the forest like? I mean, what's in the forest?"

"There are many trees in the forest, and the trees are very big. It is a small planet, much smaller than Nytandra, and the gravity is smaller. The trees grow very big and very tall. Not like the trees on Nytandra which are small and not so big. We lived in the trees, and we did not harm anyone. We wanted only to be left alone, but the armies came and destroyed our world."

"Are the armies still on your planet?"

"No. Father ordered them to come home when he found out what they had done. Father was angry. They left my planet and brought me and my mother and a few others here. The others died over the past twenty years. My mother died five years ago."

"Yes, you told me."

"Oh, yes. I am sorry. I am of the forgetting type."

Leos stayed quiet for a few microsectors. It must have been very difficult for Esmerelda to talk about her experiences during the invasion of her home planet. From the brief description she'd just given, that certainly had been a challenging and painful time for her, her family, and the others forced to migrate to this hot, dusty planet, so different from their own. With their dark green skin, they would have stood out strikingly within the population of Nytandra—he could visualize how humiliating it must have been. To avoid too much more uneasiness for her, he decided to change the subject.

"Say, did I tell you I'm going to start taking flying lessons here on Nytandra starting in a few days?"

"You are?"

"Yep. I talked to the Minister and he arranged it. I'm going down to the airport and learn how to fly Nytandran airplanes. It'll be fun. I got my pilot's license before they brought me here. I passed with a hundred percent. Flying comes naturally to me. I should be able to pick up their airplanes easy."

"Did Father permit this?"

"I don't know, I didn't ask him. The Minister arranged things."

"Leos, you must be careful of the Minister, there are things you do not know . . ."

"Like what—"

"Shhh, someone is coming." Esmerelda stepped close to Leos and slid one arm around his waist. In a gentle shushing motion, she touched his lips with two fingers. She remained quiet for a nanosector or two, her ears perked up, listening carefully. "It's Mlada," she said. "I must go."

Leos looked around the patio but didn't see or hear anything. "Mlada? Mlada who?"

"Mlada Lontor, the Royal Governess."

Esmerelda left Leos standing on the patio and scampered back into the Dining Room, running past the table down the full length of the room. She reached the main entrance door at the far end and opened the double doors. But, oddly, she didn't walk through the opening. She stepped back about three paces and stood directly in front of the door in the area between the door and the large chair Coreaje used during the meal. She remained there for a couple of Nytandran seconds, her head held high and her arms at her side, projecting her regal position as Princess in the Royal Household. A tall woman, perhaps seven-and-a-half links tall and dressed in a full length dark brown robe with the hood pulled loosely over her head, appeared in the doorway. She nodded and genuflected.

"Your Preciousness." The tall woman spoke in an accent foreign to Leos. Oddly, she didn't seemed surprised by the presence of Esmerelda just inside the door. The encounter suggested that the woman *expected* to see Esmerelda standing there. "Your father wishes to see you," she said.

"Yes, thank you, Mlada." With Esmerelda leading the way, both women disappeared into the Royal Family Residence.

Leos stood at the patio door to the Family Dining Room going over in his mind what had just occurred. He hadn't seen this tall woman before, and like Esmerelda, she didn't look Nytandran. But she wasn't from Esmerelda's planet either. Her eyes were large and dark brown, with whites that seemed more brilliant than any he had seen before, especially juxtaposed as they were to the deep umber of the iris. The ivory white of the skin on her hands and face stood in so much contrast to the dark skin of the Nytandrans, or to his tan skin, or to the deep green skin of Esmerelda.

The exchange perplexed Leos so much that, in the absence of a good explanation from someone he trusted, he hoofed his way back to his room.

CHAPTER 10

OVER THE RAILS AND THROUGH THE WOODS

Leos stood in the hallway outside Esmerelda's private suite. The sun had set several hours earlier and the chimes on a small clock in the hallway near Esmerelda's door tinkled the beginning of the eleventh hour. The family suites were located in the Royal Family Residence, a long slender building that paralleled the Grand Hall which lay to the north. The royal suites were on the third floor, Coreaje's on the north side of the building, Esmerelda's on the south across the hall that ran the full length of the building. The second floor of this building comprised the main kitchen and the private dining area where Leos and the Royal Family took their meals, and the fourth floor contained a family recreation complex that Leos had heard little about, and except for the fact that it contained some exercise equipment which only Esmerelda used, he wasn't terribly interested.

Exactly at the eleventh hour, Coreaje left his suite. "Well, m' boy," he said in his usual expansive voice, "ready to take a trip through the desert?"

Leos turned to greet him. "You betcha!"

Other than this little commotion in the family living quarters, the Palace was quiet. This was Leos's first time on the third floor of the Royal Family Residence. But this would be a short-lived visit. He'd been allowed to enter this area only to meet Esmerelda and Coreaje before their departure on the Ruler's private train.

Coreaje walked down the hallway to where Leos waited for Esmerelda. Leos'd never seen him in anything other than the formal robes of office. Gone now was the multicolored cloak with its many pins and pendants, its tassels and trimmings, its numerous ribbons and medals and ornaments. In its place he wore a much more conventional garb—so typical of Nytandran clothing—a simple pair of dark blue pants and a white pullover shirt containing the royal crest on the left pocket.

Coreaje's casual dress signaled that this was to be much less than an official trip. All three would be taking Coreaje's private train north, toward the mountains that circled the planet at the North Pole. This trip was ostensibly to give Leos a close-up view of the forests and mountains, though Esmerelda made it clear to him that her Father took trips like these for rest and relaxation from the stress of political office. Coreaje had a simple mountain retreat, a cabin near the rail line, which he visited every few months.

"I want you to promise me that you will not bother Father with the cares of daily business," Esmerelda admonished Leos the day before they left. "This is a trip of relaxation. It is important to him and to me."

"Okay."

"Thank you," Esmerelda said and gave Leos a delicate kiss on the cheek.

When she emerged from her quarters, Esmerelda was dressed in the typical Nytandran outfit, but added a light pink sweater against the cool evening air. They left the Palace at the front entrance where three limousines waited. They entered the middle limousine and sped away without the usual flashing lights or sirens, zipping down the north ramp toward the train station on the northern outskirts of town.

"First ride on a train?" Coreaje asked.

"Nope," Leos replied. "I've ridden on the Mag Lev at home."

"This isn't the Mag Lev, m' boy. This will be different. Much different. Great way to travel!"

Seated in the third row of seats in the limousine beside Esmerelda and one row ahead of Coreaje who took the dominant seat in back, Leos craned his neck to scan the railroad and the rail facilities as the motorcade approached the station. As they drove, Esmerelda explained the operating concept of a railroad: two parallel steel rails spiked about six links apart on concrete ties, and the train, made up of individual cars coupled together in lengths of up to a hundred thirty cars, rode directly on the rails rather than being suspended above them like the cars of the Mag Lev.

That concept wasn't totally unfamiliar to Leos. Even the Mag Lev rode on steel rails for a short distance, especially after it left the station until magnetic levitation took over, or when slowing into a station when it settled back down. But he'd never seen a public conveyance that ran on rails the whole way.

After a drive of about three millisectors paralleling several railroad tracks on their right, they neared the main Lox Atendra passenger station in the distance a half-anthan away. A two-story building with several tall towers rising from its peaks, it mirrored the Royal Palace. A passenger train stood at the station, bright and silvery, glistening in the glow from several small bulbs on the station platform and adjacent parking area.

"Is that the train we're going to take?" Leos whispered to Esmerelda.

"No," she replied. "We will take the train over there." She pointed to the right, to a group of three lights in the distance. And just as she pointed the motorcade took a sharp right turn and bounced across several railroad tracks, crossing over the throat of the large classification yard that spread out down the line to their left. Here large freight trains were made up for departure, and arriving freights were broken down into their constituent cars.

Coreaje's special train was held at a separate facility, far on the other side of the yard, hidden from the view of the public passenger trains by the freight cars. Like most conveyances on Nytandra, the freight cars were the usual silver with a faint tint of gold, though the vast majority of the cars had taken on a heavy blanket of red, tan or black dust—in most cases a mixture of all three—from repeated trips through the deserts that ringed the city.

But the Ruler's train, four silver passenger cars and two sleek silver electric locomotives, had been scrubbed and polished to a mirror finish and stood quietly pointed west on a siding next to a small passenger station. Only the black pantograph that reached up from the top of each engine, set firmly against the overhead wire from which the engines drew power, softened the impression of a lustrous arrow poised restlessly on the track.

The motorcade drew to a stop beside the train. In the dim light of the three bare bulbs that illuminated tiny areas of the passenger platform, and with several security guards from the first and last limousines standing nearby, the three travelers boarded the last car of the train, without fanfare, without farewell. Many of the security personnel entered the first three cars, and the train pulled away from the station. It glided quietly several hundred links down the track, click-clacked a little as it negotiated the switch that diverted it from the mainline onto a little-used branch line, and accelerated north.

*   *   *

"Great way to travel!" Coreaje settled into an easy chair and stared through the one-way glass that made up the side windows of his private car. His face beamed with the excitement and enthusiasm of a veteran rail traveler.

"Yep," Leos replied, looking out the window.

Breakfast was over and all three had gathered in the main observation lounge at the rear of the car. It was now the beginning of the fourth hour and the train still sped north through the desert at, by Leos's estimate, more than seventy anthans per sub. To the train's right, the morning sun sat suspended between the cusps of a twin-peaked mountain, low on the far horizon, bathing the train in the warm intense light of morning.

"Wonderful scenery!"

"Yep."

Leos agreed with Coreaje because it wouldn't be proper to openly differ with an absolute ruler who was likely to become his father-in-law. But privately, he disagreed. The only thing he saw from the train was the desert—the flat, unending, monotonous desert. Though occasionally broken by a small hillock or a prominence or a fault line that jutted up from the desert floor—irregularities around which the train scampered easily on its trip north—the vast featureless desert couldn't capture Leos's imagination as it did for Coreaje. The desert did remind him somewhat of his home planet, and he watched in a heartsick stupor as the bleak landscape slipped by, wondering if he would ever see his home again. He brought up images of Anthanos, of the vast, broad, unbroken landscape of home, of Kalarias, of his mom and her home, even his room in her home. He visualized the Black Sands Tavern and felt the cool air on his face he enjoyed so much, and he could taste again the Qootaie on which he sipped when he met his two kidnappers. But the most ardent images in his mind were of Tama. Her eyes, her face, her hair, her touch—oh, yes, her warm, soft, wonderful touch—could anything be sweeter? Could Esmerelda ever imitate that touch? How could he ever replace the image of Tama with Esmerelda? Even when Esmerelda sat down beside him in the railroad car, he remained silent, not acknowledging her presence as he stared through the window in reserved meditation.

An hour later as the train approached the northern mountains with its forest cover, Leos discarded the memories of home and began to investigate the terrain of this planet in much more detail. He and Esmerelda sat watching the scenery to the left of the train when it passed a few trees.

"I love the forest," Esmerelda whispered. "But when I think of the forest, I think of my forest. These trees do not remind me of my forest."

"What trees? I didn't see any trees."

"Those purple plants growing along the track. They were the trees."

"Purple? I thought trees were green. Or brown."

"No. Nytandran trees use purple photosynthetic pigments, not like trees on my planet which are green."

"Oh." Confused and a little perplexed, Leos resolved to keep an eye out for more trees as the train continued north.

Shortly, as more trees zipped past the train, Esmerelda pointed them out. These scrawny specimens, not more than four to five links tall, grew in contorted shapes and deformed curves along the railroad right-of-way. In the intense heat of the day and the stress of the barely sufficient water they managed to eke from the ground, they'd turned gnarly and twisted. They were covered, Esmerelda explained, with shiny purple, waxy, needle-like leaves which helped keep evaporation of water to a minimum.

As the train gained elevation it passed larger and more upright trees. Taller and less contorted specimens, like a tall, slender cone covered entirely from ground level to the top in needles, gave the impression of a purple rocket ship about to blast off. Small buildings, nestled here and there among the trees whizzed by the train too, railroad-associated structures: communication shacks, tool shanties, equipment barns, relay stations.

By the seventh hour the train had entered the mountains proper. It slowed to around forty anthans per sub and headed for the tough two percent grade that would take it to Coreaje's private cabin near the summit of a small peak.

As the train arrived at the cabin near the end of the eighth hour, the sun was a bright yellow-orange disk hovering about thirty degrees above the horizon in the west. The cabin, rustic in its own Nytandran way, had been constructed of the same dark brown material as the furniture in the Palace. The main door of the cabin opened into a large room filled with furniture of the same material, and four bedrooms, two on each side, were situated off the main room. Leos had been assigned a bedroom on the right side of the cabin, and Coreaje and Esmerelda took adjoining rooms on the left. Leos's room had one large window that overlooked a stone patio which extended outward about twelve links toward a panorama of desert plains — the plains over which the train had traveled to this cabin.

The fourth meal of the day was served *alfresco* on the patio in the cool breeze that whistled through the mountains and around the planet's North Pole. Leos and Esmerelda donned jackets against the chill. From the patio, the view extended for hundreds of anthans down into the lowlands at the foot of the mountains, and Leos understood why Coreaje had chosen this place for his mountaintop retreat. The isolation was virtually complete. To the left of the patio, Leos could barely make out the railroad tracks as they curved down the mountain, a line of shiny rail and dirty white concrete ties. In the distance, a speck of glistening white on the horizon caught his eye, and he thought it might be a city, but through binoculars he could tell that it was merely a brilliant cliff of white gypsum that dominated the surrounding territory in that direction. Esmerelda pointed toward it.

"We passed that cliff on our trip here. See, the tracks pass in front of it."

After the meal, Leos picked up the binoculars again and studied the desert. As he scanned the panorama below, he developed a chill. The sun had dropped below the mountain peak on the other side of the cabin, and the air had begun to cool. The breeze picked up, rustling over the patio. Deep scarlet and purple shadows crept over the landscape, shooting over the desert while Leos watched, as though a dark blanket was being pulled over it. Coreaje and Esmerelda retired to their rooms.

But Leos's chill was from more than the cool air. As the final rays of sunlight evaporated from the sky, he saw no lights on the plains below, nothing at all that might indicate cities or towns, not even another train on the tracks leading to this site. The terrain was so desolate and uninhabited, so bleak and forlorn it disappointed him.

There's nothing out there. No vegetation, no animals, no people. Nothing at all.

Leos too finally retired, but couldn't sleep. In his mind the events of the day kept bouncing back and forth, from stepping on the train in Lox, to the barrenness and absolute isolation of this mountaintop retreat. The wildness of this planet was so pervasive it saddened him, and he couldn't get it out of his mind.

* * *

The next day, after the third meal, Coreaje decided to take a walk, and Leos and Esmerelda tagged along. They left the cabin at the front door and turned left onto a trail that wound upward through the rugged, rocky hills that made up the summit of the mountain. The trail paralleled a short spur of the railroad and they passed more trees. Within about an anthan walk, the rail line ended. Here the trees were larger and more numerous, jutting absolutely straight upward to more than a hundred links, each covered with a deep purple sheathing from which emanated hundreds to thousands of tiny, waxy, spicule-like leaves, glistening in the sunlight.

After a few hundred links more, they came to a large stand of trees and several dark brown stumps, denuded of all leaves. Leos stared at the stumps. At first, he thought they were another type of tree, but Esmerelda explained that they were what remained when a tree had been cut down and used to build the cabin and its furniture.

"Only father has furniture and a house made of the wood of the trees," Esmerelda said. "The trees are not plenty, and it is forbidden for anyone else to chop them down. See, over there, several people are chopping down a tree now. This tree will be used to make a desk for father's study at home."

The chopping process fascinated Leos, and he even took a turn himself. Two men, one on each side of the tree, worked with sharp, highly polished axes, and they attacked the base of the tree alternately until it fell with a loud thud. With a special curved tool, they stripped the purple covering from the tree, revealing the dark brown woody core beneath. When the tree was reduced to nothing more than a tall pole, they dragged it down the hill and threw it into a gondola car parked on a railroad siding. Then they attacked another tree, and it, too, was deposited on the car.

Coreaje, Esmerelda and Leos walked on. Their trip took them to the summit of the peak, but they took their time, climbing slowly in the chilly, thin air. Coreaje, though overweight and paunchy, seemed not to notice the altitude. He walked easily, leading the way, breathing heavily but not so hard as to be all out of breath. The chubby, rotund appearance of the Nytandrans, especially the round-headed type, might lead one to conclude they were overweight, perhaps unfit for physical activity. Not so. They did well in many different types of physically demanding chores, and Leos concluded they could be a formidable opponent in a sporting contest, even though they didn't seem to play sports on this planet. Early in his stay on Nytandra he decided not to antagonize any of them. He might not win, even in a fair fight.

As the three hikers crested the summit, the sun sat on the horizon in the distance, appearing from this peak to hover above the cabin below and the dreary plains beyond.

In the opposite direction from the sun was the north pole of the planet, several hundred anthans away, a rugged, mountainous region, clothed entirely in vegetation, thousands of square anthans of a shimmering deep purple carpet that covered everything, peaks and hollows, ridges and valleys. Trees all.

They crested the summit and walked down a short trail on the other side which swung around the peak and led them back to the cabin, eventually arriving at the cabin by the patio.

*   *   *

Leos and Esmerelda took to a two-person porch swing on the patio, waiting for the fourth meal to be served. At first, Leos's mind was on the walk they'd just completed, but as he stared at the barren terrain below, he returned to the thoughts of wildness and isolation that had bothered him so much the previous evening.

"It's a wasteland," he mumbled, carefully speaking just loud enough for Esmerelda to hear. "It's a vast wasteland that isn't doing anybody any good. Why shouldn't we use it?"

Leos sat quietly staring at the desert below, at first not comprehending what he'd said. But as the words buzzed around in his mind, it hit him. "Holy dinfrizzle!" He stood up, gesticulating wildly. "That's it! We could move here! This planet could support us! There's plenty of room."

"Leos, what are you talking about?"

"My planet! Anthanos! Our sun is expanding and the planet is getting hotter. We need a new planet to move to. It's getting so hot we have to have air coolers in our homes and there's plenty of room on this planet so why shouldn't we—"

"Leos, please. You are talking so fast I am not following. Why . . . ?"

"It's our Imperative. The *Anthanian Imperative*. We have a right to colonize another planet. We have to. We have to move somewhere else."

"You are talking of moving? Where?"

"Here!"

"To Nytandra? But why?"

"Look out there. There's a huge amount of space available. There's nothing out there. No cities, no people. It's not just what we can see from here, but all over your planet. The people on your planet live in cities, but the cities are scattered and there's a huge amount of empty space between them."

Esmerelda stared at Leos, still puzzled by his rant. "Leos, I do not think Father will agree."

"He can't say no. He can't turn us down." Leos paced back and forth on the patio, throwing an arm out toward the desert below. "Look at all that space out there. There's plenty of room. What's not to like about this?"

"No, Leos. I do not think Father will agree."

"Why would he not agree?"

"I do not know, but I do not think he will agree. That is a very big decision."

"Let's ask him. He can't say no!"

Leos turned, headed for the patio door into the cabin, but Esmerelda bolted from the swing and grabbed his arm. "No! Leos! No!" Her puzzlement had turned to a mixture of surprise and dismay, and she spoke sharply. "Do not disturb Father! He came here to relax. Wait until we get back to Lox. Please. Do this for me." She led Leos back to the swing and sat down, but Leos was too excited to sit beside her again.

"Okay, I'll do it for you." Leos paced the porch, alternately looking at the desert below and at Esmerelda. "But I need to ask him as soon as possible. This is too big. I can't hold back too long." He walked over to the edge of the patio, eyeing the terrain, imagining the presence of Anthanian cities dotted here and there, each with its large hydroponics garden that fed everyone. He could visualize the maglev zipping between each city and perhaps a spaceport where Anthanian surface/orbit shuttles would arrive and depart. Water, of course, would be a problem, but he wasn't unduly concerned about it.

There must be water around here somewhere. After all, with all those trees, water has to be present. How could the trees grow without it?

Leos eventually sat down beside Esmerelda, his heart palpitating in his chest. All he had to do was get Coreaje's permission and *presto*, in one fell swoop, he could present the people of Anthanos with a tantalizing solution to their expanding sun that was both realistic and imaginative. This would be his legacy—the sudden blast of visionary light that would illuminate the deep inner workings of his Anthanian soul and send shock waves around his world. It would solidify his place in Anthanian history. It would define his life and times. He was already thinking about marrying Esmerelda and settling down and raising a family . . . er, well, maybe not a family . . . but he wasn't averse to marrying Esmerelda and settling in a town where other Anthanians lived, with perhaps the entire population of his planet living in cities scattered about the Nytandran desert, some perhaps even in sight of this very peak.

Wouldn't that be terrific? His chest swelled with pride at the thought of the medals they would pin on it.

So, the day after returning to the Imperial Palace, Leos presented his theory to Coreaje at the fourth meal, certain Coreaje would say yes.

Coreaje thought about the proposal all the next day. Leos was still sure he would say yes.

Coreaje's answer?

No.

CHAPTER 11

TWO HARD DRINKS AND A SEX ACT

The tavern was dim and musty. A faint tinge of dust hung in the air and the aroma of sweat spanked the nose with a fetid display. Leos, still smarting from Coreaje's rejection of his elegant transplanetary migration plan, began his personal visits to the underbelly of Lox Atendra incognito, dressed in the standard brown garb of a day worker, insinuating himself into the bastions of the everyday, the mean, the obscure in Nytandran society. His hair had been trimmed, his skin darkened, his eyes made up, heavy with artificial puffiness to distract the stares of ordinary workers, mostly miners in the ubiquitous gold, iron and bauxite mines in the several deserts and mountain ranges that circled the city. Two round-headed security agents accompanied him, but seated themselves at a small table a discrete distance from Leos, himself comfortably ensconced at the bar, ordering the Nytandran drink, the *kaadz*.

He'd been warned. Kaadz was strong, the product of the fermented glok intestine, heavy with pique and rage, boiled and over-boiled, distilled repeatedly until the still collapsed. Filtered and bottled, it was stored in flagons with ground-glass stoppers because metal caps corroded and disintegrated under attack by the vapors of the swill within.

Kaadz was served in a tiny glass large enough in which to barely insert a Nytandran thumb, aliquoted to each customer individually, yet promptly on demand. Leos took a small sip and held it in his mouth. Its clear, colorless appearance belied its potency. It buzzed around in his mouth, flipping by its own accord from tongue to cheek to gums and back again. It burned his palate, it vibrated his teeth. He had to swallow twice to encourage it to enter his gut, but it finally went down, taking several layers of mucous membrane with it.

He opened his mouth to cool his throat and a faint wisp of condensed vapor drifted out.

"First drink of the kaadz?" the miner seated to Leos's right asked. A husky man, oval-headed, at least seven links tall, hands like earth-moving equipment, fingernails dirty and distasteful. He wore the uniform garb of the miner, a thickly padded one-piece outfit, a plain medium brown with a quilted-like texture, heavy in the sleeves and legs, tightly cinched about the waist and neck. But where Leos's outfit was clean, the miner's was coated with the dust of long intervals spent deep in the soil extracting minerals from the planet's crust. A gold multi-pointed star-like emblem—known to Nytandrans as the "sparkle" because it picked up even small amounts of light and sent it flickering into the observer's eyes—was fixed to the miner's left sleeve, a clue that he worked in one of the gold mines in the mountains to the north.

"Yup." A hoarseness had developed in Leos's voice, compounded by a serious lack of lung power.

"Is it a great drink or what?"

Leos's voice was returning. "I think I'll go with 'or what'." The miner dispatched a deep belly laugh that tinkled several bottles of firewater along the far end of the bar.

"Where you from, mate? You ain't from around here, 're ya?"

"Ahh . . . from Anthatandra," Leos replied, trying to attach a Nytandran suffix to the name of his home planet.

"Where's that?"

"It's on the other side of Nytandra." Leos took a wild guess and figured most miners on Nytandra were not well traveled and probably never ventured far from their own city.

"Never heard of it."

"It's a small town, out in the desert."

"And what desert would that be?"

Before Leos could respond with the name of a fictitious Nytandran desert, another miner sat down to Leos's left.

"What have we here? A visitor, I'll wager. Ready to get 'is hands dirty in the trench."

This miner was different. Arrayed in a dark, loose-fitting long-sleeved cloak covering both front and back, he was dark himself, much darker than any Nytandran Leos had seen. Detail wasn't visible in the dim light of the bar, but Leos did appreciate that this man could be a breed apart—a different race perhaps, a different strain or variety. He had the puffy eye-slits and the thick, well-defined lips of the Nytandrans, but he also had a full head of hair, which he kept cut short in a sort of buzz cut, not too much different from the haircut Leos wore for this occasion. His nose was bulbous and bloated, much more prominent than that of anyone else.

"Says he's from the other side of the planet," the first miner said.

"Ay," the second miner said. "I'll believe that. He don't look from around here."

The second miner's cloak also had the same sparkle as the first, impressed on the right sleeve. Leos couldn't see all of it clearly, nestled as it was within the folds of the cloak, but it appeared to have a single gold bar imprinted directly beneath, an indication that this man was a supervisor or foreman at the mine, or perhaps someone even higher up, an engineer or administrator, not merely a worker in the 'trench,' as the working area of a mine was usually called. The same sparkle-and-bar was more clearly fixed to a small pocket on the chest area of the cloak. Poking its head above the top of the pocket was an unfamiliar gold-colored item, and Leos glanced at it briefly before he looked down to examine the rest of the miner's outfit. The cloak was split about a third of the way up the front and back and on both sides, and as the miner sat on the stool, the cloak fell away from his lap. As Leos dropped his gaze down toward the lower part of the cloak, he realized with a start that the man was barefoot and wasn't wearing pants, and in Nytandran society, that usually meant that underneath the cloak he was totally naked.

Leos had seen public nudity in Lox Atendra before and it wasn't unknown or unfamiliar to him. In the more upscale parts of town which Coreaje and his entourage frequented — and he usually included Esmerelda and Leos — nudity was rare, limited to the discreet appearance of three or four nude women at a party. Coreaje, in his boisterous, pompous way, flirted with the women, disappearing with each, one at a time, into a back room at odd intervals during the party. But Esmerelda — and Leos, too, taking his cue from her — turned away. Esmerelda's friends were mostly younger women, women her own age of the oval-headed type, who seemed — to Leos at any rate — marginally more attractive than the round-headed type. They had more hair and a more attractive face, but Esmerelda was far lovelier than any of the Nytandran women.

But much more common than the nudity at a party, and more apparent through the limousine window during Leos's occasional travels through town, was the display of nude bodies on the streets where favors were bought and sold like trinkets at a fair. So far in his visit to Nytandra, he'd managed to avoid direct contact with the working girls, but now as he sat in a working man's tavern, a nude man — well, almost — was seated next to him, and to make matters worse, talking to him.

What is he up to?

"Name's Gass," the man said. "Greenhouse Gass."

At the laughable, almost ludicrous name of the miner, Leos was caught flatfooted without a return name, and in spite of holding back a smile to keep from snickering at the comical name, he came close to blurting out his real name.

Oops, that won't do, have to come up with something else. "Name's Leok," he said, basing a name on his two friends from the spaceship, though he gave it a different pronunciation. In Nytandran it sounded more like "Leouwrk."

"Leok? Eh, did you say Leok? Hey, Frag, this guy says his name's Leok. Name sounds like that frig Leos. Whadda ya think o' that?"

"Great guy that Leos. Wish I had 'is job." Frag took a swig of the kaadz and swallowed it in one gulp. He slammed his hand on the bar and the bartender refilled the glass immediately.

"Yeah, fucking the green princess. Great job if you can get it," Gass said.

"Now w— Uh, yeah, wish I had his job," Leos said.

"Yeah, I could do his job. I gotta load she'll kill to get. If she'll ever let me in."

"Whadda ya talking about?" Leos asked. His head was beginning to feel light from the kaadz, and he had taken a mere two sips. But his mind still seemed clear and his speech still smooth so he resolved to continue the charade as long as possible.

"She jus' don't know it yet."

As the miner talked, a rustling began under his cloak. Something moved around underneath, pushing up the folds of the cloak. "I'm a friend of Coreaje. You know that?"

"No. You're a friend of Coreaje?"

"Yeah."

"How'd you get to be a friend of Coreaje?"

"He and I went to school together, and we joined the mining companies together. But he got into politics and I stayed in the trench. I gotta get in to see her."

As Gass talked, he removed the gold object from his cloak pocket. Intrigued, Leos paid more attention to it than to the rustling under the cloak. The object was long and slender, about the size of a writing pen, but it appeared to be a nothing more than a simple gold bar about six decilinks long and hexagonal in cross-section. Some unknown characters were scratched or imprinted on it—Leos couldn't tell in the dim light—but Gass held it in his hand, gently tossing it up and down, occasionally holding it vertically and allowing it to slip through his fingers onto the stone bar top. Repeatedly, he flipped it, almost absent-mindedly, as though he wasn't even aware he had it in his hand. When the rod hit the stone bar top it made a heavy, solid *thunk*, not the cheap, metallic *plink* that would come from a light object, such as a pen or pencil. The gold bar didn't bounce when it landed either. Leos took careful note of that fact, and it only added to the concept of heaviness he was developing in his mind as he watched Gass play with it. He almost forgot Gass had spoken.

"Uh, he never—I mean, I never heard that. I mean, in the mining company. I never heard that. Can't you talk to him? Won't he get you in to see her?"

"I did. He tried. Several times. But the green bitch said no every time. She refused to see me. Dirty bitch."

Gass turned slightly to his right to face Leos. As he turned, the cloak separated slightly in front and fell off his leg, and Leos could see what had been causing the movement underneath. His major copulatory organ was growing erect, poking its head out from between the split of the cloak, working its way up, longer and longer, until it was fully extended, almost a full link long. It was dark and black, like the miner, and smelled of an odor that made the kaadz seem almost tame in its fury.

That must be where he got his name. Leos turned his head away and took a sip. "Uh, if she says no, uh, she means it, I mean, she probably means it, like, you know, I guess she means no."

"Yeah, but if I could get in, she'll wanna see this."

As Gass talked, he hesitated slightly, and from his organ, still poking its grotesque globular head between the edges of the cloak, came a single eruption of a brilliant fluorescent-yellow-green ejaculate that spurted past Leos and shot several links across the room before it splattered to the floor, sizzling and popping as it lay. Leos closed his eyes and took another sip of kaadz. Gass barely noticed the discharge. He kept talking.

"I'm a good friend of Coreaje. I've known him ever since I brought her here, and—"

"Gass!" a voice roared from the other side of the room, a nebulous male voice that came from the darkness at the rear of the main section of the barroom well off to the left. Everyone turned in that direction. "Ain't I told you not to do that in here anymore? Now I gotta clean the floor again. You did that last time. How many times I gotta tell you, if you wanna do that go in back. That's what they're for."

"Yeah, yeah," Gass bellowed. "Keep your pants zipped."

Gass left his stool and walked through the bar toward a door in the back wall of the room, slamming the door behind him. But he left the gold bar on the bar top. Leos stared at it, but he didn't touch it.

A round-headed Nytandran, probably a female, and dressed in the usual tan, unkempt jumpsuit of the working class, arrived with a bucket and mop to clean the floor.

"Ay, now you'll hear something," Frag said.

"Why? What's going on?" Leos looked around.

"Just hold a second. You'll hear it."

"Who is that guy? Does he really work for the mines?"

"Ay, he works for the mines. His real name's Gasz." Frag spelled out the last name for Leos to distinguish it from 'Gass'. The pronunciations were marginally different, too. "Just uses the 'Greenhouse' fer fun."

"Is he really a foreman, like the sparkle says?"

"Nope. He's much higher up. Top level. I dunno what 'xactly."

"Why's he wear the sparkle of a foreman, then?"

"Ah, jus' so he don't get recognized. He's like, high up, y'know?"

"Is he really a friend of Coreaje?"

"Ay, good friend. Least they was."

"Whazzat mean?"

Frag took a sip of his kaadz. He hesitated before speaking. "They parted. Coreaje fired him. Gave him the heel of his boot. They got back together later, though. Good friends now."

"What happened?"

"Gasz was the general on the expedition to the green planet. You know about that? He was the leader, ay he was. A general. One-star general. But they screwed up and Coreaje got mad. Killed a few people. Kidnapped some people. Esmerelda and her mother. Coreaje sacked 'im and everyone else on the expedition. Took his star away."

"Way I heard it, they killed a lot of people."

Frag nodded. "Ay, true. Bad news."

"I heard about it from—well, you know, from the vid. Her mom died, like, five years ago."

"Yeah."

"So, he brought Esmerelda here? Izzat right?"

"Yeah."

"So, he's known her all her life, almost."

"Yeah."

Leos paused and took a sip. "Does he usually do that?" Cough, cough, hack, hack.

"What?"

"That. The ejaculation. He usually do that here?"

"Naw, not much. Jus' when he gets talkin' 'bout the green one, you know, Esmerelda."

"He's got a big thing for her, don't he?"

"Sure do. He got a big thing for her, if ya know what I mean. Been tryin' to get in to see her f' three, four years now." Another swig of kaadz.

"I see."

The bar was quiet for about a Nytandran minute, and Leos took two more sips of the kaadz, close to draining the glass. He got a real buzz from it, and he felt loose in his seat. It didn't pound as much on his forehead when it went down. He hoped that Gasz or Gass or whatever-his-real-name-is was gone for good. He didn't want to have to deal with him again, especially the repulsive sight of his nude body and disgusting display of sexual prowess. But as Leos drained the final dram of kaadz in his glass, from somewhere within the deep recesses of the bar came a scream, a woman's scream, a high-pitched penetrating shriek that rattled and tinkled the bottles at the far end of the bar. Just a single scream, it sounded like someone was being tortured or murdered — or worse. It came from the direction of the room Gass had entered. It scared Leos for a few nanosectors and he jumped when he heard it. He held the empty glass tightly in his hand, almost afraid to move, but as he scanned the room no one else in the bar showed any concern, though several people, Frag included, raised their heads and smiled.

"There it is," Frag said.

Leos turned and glanced at the two security agents. He scrunched his face into a deliberately puzzled look and shrugged his shoulders, mouthing silently, "What's that?" but they reacted only by raising their glasses of kaadz in a sort of 'toast' gesture. They smiled and Leos understood they knew what had taken place. But he was still clueless.

"Told ya," Frag said. "He does it every time."

"What was that?"

"Ay, you'll see. Jus' wait."

A couple of Nytandran seconds later Gass stumbled through the door. The entire room erupted in applause, and the ovation accompanied him as he staggered back to his seat, his organ still dripping yellow-green.

"Which one was it?" someone yelled from deep in the barroom.

"Twenty-one!" Gass yelled back. He slammed his hand on the bar and received a shot of kaadz. He downed it in one gulp and slammed the bar again. Another serving immediately appeared.

"Good one, that number twenty-one!" came the voice from the other side of the room. Gass ignored the shout and started talking, addressing no one in particular.

"I gotta get in t' see her. I gotta load that won't wait. I can make her scream better'n that."

"What? Who?"

"The green bitch."

"Well, you know," Leos said. "Maybe she's not that way."

"Man, that's glokshit. I don' fuckin' care if she's 'that way' or not, it's somethin' I gotta do. You know what I mean? You know, like things you gotta do? This I gotta do." Gass slammed the bar again, and another drink appeared.

"Maybe she's not like that. Maybe she's nice. She's not your type. I mean, y'know, like from what I seen on the vid."

Gass downed the next serving and stared at Leos. "Whadda ya mean she's not my type! She's my type as well as anyone! I did her once."

"What!?" Leos said. He started to get enraged, but he decided he better not blow his cover. Besides, he didn't really believe Esmerelda would submit to anything like that, and Gass's bragging sounded more like bluster than reality. But before he could say anything, Frag picked up on Gass's remark.

"Whadda ya mean you ball-creamed her before?" Frag said. He screwed up his face in disbelief and glared past Leos to Gass. "You never said nuthin' 'bout that."

Gass pushed the gold bar idly around on the bar top. "Yeah, well, maybe I did, maybe I didn't, but I sure showed her what I got." A big broad smile crossed his face. A gap appeared between every tooth.

"You showed her what you got?" Leos said. "Whazzat mean? I mean, wha'd she say?"

"Ahh, she done frigged out. Like she was scared or sumpin'. Dirty bitch."

"So you didn't, really . . ."

"Naw, but I sure showed her. You shoulda heard her scream." The smile returned.

Good for her.

Gass was quiet for a few nanosectors. He took another swig of the kaadz that appeared in the meantime. He slapped his hand on the bar and downed the next swig in one gulp. Several more doses appeared and just as rapidly disappeared. Then he turned to Leos. His eyes drooped and he'd begun to drool at the mouth.

"Mee'in' time," Gass said, and he turned to leave. But he was so plastered he couldn't stand on his own two bare feet and he slipped off the stool, falling over onto Leos—"Hey! Watch out!"—who fell into Frag, knocking his drink from his hand. Gass went sprawling on his back beside Leos's stool.

"Glokshit!" Frag yelled. "Whatter ya' doin'? Gass, you bastard! Get up and get outta here."

Gass wobbled to his feet and staggered through the front door.

"Never could hold his kaadz." Frag slammed his hand on the bar again.

Leos finished his second drink. His head was spinning and he wondered if he'd be able to make it out to the Palace Security vehicle the two agents had brought him in. As he debated whether to leave or not, two Nytandrans started a shouting match somewhere within the darkest part of the barroom, and Leos glanced briefly in their direction, to his left, only mildly curious about what was going on. He was more interested in getting his ass outta this place.

But his curiosity jumped several orders of magnitude when he saw the gold bar. Gass had left it on the bar top. "Holy dinfrizzle." So far as he could tell no one else saw it. Frag couldn't see it because Leos sat between him and the bar, the barkeep couldn't see it, he was filling glasses at the other end, and everyone else seemed riveted to the commotion on the other side. Leos turned fully to his left, pretending to watch the shouters, slowly nudging his right hand toward the bar. As he and the others watched the little altercation, one of the shouters pushed the other one, knocking him backward onto another table, and a fight started between the shouters and the other table. The two security agents bounded from their seats, and by the time they got to Leos, he'd palmed the gold bar and dropped it in his pocket. They seized him by the arms and hustled him outside just as patrons at several other tables joined the fight.

As they drove back toward the Imperial Palace, up the southern access ramp at a leisurely forty anthans per sub, Leos examined the bar in more detail. In the dim light in the vehicle he couldn't see well, but he could tell it was heavy, so heavy it almost certainly had to be solid gold. Hexagonal in cross-section and flat on each end, two sets of five narrow lines had been scored completely around the bar, one set at each end. Three unusual marks he couldn't identify were impressed into the surface of alternate faces at the center of the bar.

What is this thing for? Why would Gass carry around something like this? It's solid gold. It must be worth millions of monetary units. Maybe billions. Yeah, billions.

Leos yawned, stuffed the bar back in his pants pocket, and fell a-sleep.

CHAPTER 12

THE THIRD MEAL

"I met a friend of yours last night," Leos said.

He and Esmerelda were at dinner, the third meal of the Nytandran day. Coreaje was not present. He routinely took the second and third meals at his desk, and Leos and Esmerelda sat at a solitary four-person table in an intimate little dining room just off the Palace kitchen, down the hall from the Family Dining Room. The walls of this room were lined with panels formed from the same dark brown wood that was so much in evidence in the rest of the Palace, but a reddish stain had been applied to the wood, and the resulting deep mahogany color imparted a warm, relaxed atmosphere that Esmerelda especially savored. A ceiling-height glass-door china cabinet finished in exotic lacquer sat against the wall across from the table, the wood carved and filigreed down the three visible sides. A table-height storage cabinet, inlaid with etched brass, stood beside it, and bright ivory-white table linen lay neatly folded on top. A large comfortable-looking leather couch sat under the windows that overlooked the stark plains east of the Palace.

This was one of Esmerelda's favorite rooms in the entire Palace, and she took to this room often. Here she could relax and take a respite from the duties of her royal day.

"Who was that?" Esmerelda dipped her spoon into her vegetable soup and took a dainty princess-like sip.

"Calls himself Greenhouse Gass. I couldn't believe the name—"

Esmerelda stopped sipping, her spoon suspended in midair. She looked straight at Leos, a mixture of fear and apprehension on her face. "Oh no, Leos. You did not become involved with him, did you?"

"Not really, all I did was talk to him. Why?"

"He is horrible. I have met him several times. He is a disgusting and horrible person." She began to sip her soup again.

"I can agree with that. Says he's a friend of your father. Leader of the expedition to your planet."

"Yes, you are right." She took another sip. "I have met him several times, but he is dreadful and repulsive. He brought me to this planet when I was young. When I was eighteen, he exposed himself to me and produced his . . . his . . . manly fluid. It was terrible. It was horrible. I despise him much. I do not wish to see him again."

"He wanted to spend the night with you."

Esmerelda's spoon splashed into her soup. "Leos! You did not agree to this arrangement, did you?"

"No, no, I didn't. I told him in no uncertain terms that you wouldn't want to see him. He didn't like it and he wanted to fight about it, but I took care of him. I flattened him. I can still see him lying on the floor begging for mercy." A self-congratulatory smile crossed his lips. "He won't bother you again."

"Thank you, Leos. You have done well." Esmerelda retrieved her spoon, wiped it on her napkin, and began to sip again. She reached over with her left hand and gently touched his arm.

"Speaking of fighting . . ." Leos turned to Esmerelda and spoke quietly. ". . . did I ever tell you about the time I fought the Big-toothed Monster when I was on the blue planet?" He set his spoon down and began gesturing. "Well, see, it's like this, he was on this gigantic rock, see, and he was a hundred links above me, see, like he was way up there, and he was about to jump and then he jumped and I ducked and I grabbed him by his ba —, uh, I grabbed him by his tail and started spinning him aroun' an' aroun' an' aroun' real fast like, and he was like ten links tall and his eyes were just absolutely *bulg*ing out of his head, and I spun him so fast his teeth flew out of his mouth and then I let him go and he flew so far it was six T-sectors later before he got back, an' well, you know, I don' wanna brag, but . . ."

"Oh, Leos! How wonderful!"

CHAPTER 13

INTO THE VALLEY OF DEATH

Leos's Nytandran flying permit allowed him to pilot several jet aircraft, mostly two-seaters, but it included one four-seater, so long as he was checked out by an instructor in each one. He'd had to learn the Nytandran method: the control wheel moved the rudder while the pedals drove the ailerons, opposite from Anthanian craft. He struggled with that for several days, but finally mastered it to the satisfaction of his instructor and he was granted a permit. So, after supper about twenty days after his encounter with Gasz, as he and Esmerelda stood in the cool evening air on the patio outside the main dining room, he asked Esmerelda to come on a flight with him. She hesitated.

"I think we should obtain the Minister's permission."

"I don't think we need to, but if you insist, okay."

The Minister considered Esmerelda's request for several days, finally contacting Leos's flight instructor. The instructor was quite persuasive that Esmerelda would be perfectly safe as long as all they did was fly around in the vicinity of the capital city. They must not stray too far out over the desert. The high magnetic iron content of much of the rock and soil near the city could disrupt a magnetic compass, the instructor said, and even communications could be affected were the airplane's comm system not shielded against stray magnetic fields. Lost aircraft invariably did not return, the instructor pointed out. The Minister made all this clear to Leos and Esmerelda, but he went one step further, insisting that Leos take an escort before he would give his approval.

That didn't sit too well with Leos, but he had no real choice when the Minister emphasized, "All three, or none at all," so the flight was put on the schedule.

But on the day of the flight, neither the Minister nor the flight instructor took into account — nor did they have any real knowledge of — the sandstorm developing in the far reaches of the Abadanádo Desert several hundred anthans southwest of the city.

* * *

The escort's name was Grotuk, a short, pudgy man who was the Minister's personal secretary. He'd been one of the four associates who accompanied the Minister when he picked Leos up at the spaceport. He was also distantly related to Grok, both having the guttural "Gr" sound at the beginning of their names.

The limousine dropped the three at a small airport southeast of the city, rather than the city's main airport because security would be easier with the Ruler's daughter. Leos signed the aircraft rental agreement and found he'd been assigned a small, low performance delta-winged craft with a four-seat cockpit, and a glass canopy like a big bubble that sat on top of the fuselage and seemed much too big for the airplane. He climbed into the pilot's seat on the left side and Esmerelda took the right hand seat. Grotuk climbed into the right rear seat and Leos lowered the canopy.

"Okay, fasten your seat belts!" Leos yelled as he started the engine. "Here we go!" The airplane rolled westward across the hard-packed dirt runway and lifted into the air. He banked left, taking the plane in a big looping curve around to the south, then farther and farther left, finally leveling off at a heading almost 200 degrees from his take-off heading. To their left, about five anthans away and shielded by a faint haze sat the Imperial Palace, tucked away securely within the folds of the eastern mountains.

"How about taking a look at the Palace?" Leos asked his companions.

"No!" Grotuk leaned forward, edging his way into the space between Leos and Esmerelda. "Stay away from the Palace. I forbid it." He waggled a finger in Leos's direction. "We will all be shot down."

"Shot down?"

"Yes," Esmerelda said. "The Palace is protected by anti-aircraft missiles. If you come within four of your anthans of the Palace, one of the missiles will be activated. And do not think you can evade it. They are very accurate."

"This is true. Not in this airplane to be sure." Grotuk sat back in his seat.

"Oh," Leos said. "Okay, let's go east."

Leos held the plane on an eastward heading, still well south of the Palace. He took a broad curve around the Palace, but stayed at least five to six anthans away, and eventually swung around onto a westward heading, well north of the mountains that dominated the city in that direction. They passed over the railroad tracks they'd traveled earlier toward Coreaje's cabin, and flew on for about two millisectors, but Leos spent most of his time scanning the desert below, paying little attention to the front or side horizon. This was his first chance to see the planet from above, and he wanted to make the best use of the limited time he had in this little craft. He was about to turn left to swing back toward the city when he noticed the sandstorm.

The storm approached the city from the southwest. A broad curtain of boiling sepia and ochre, it rose to more than 50,000 links, much higher than the operating ceiling of the aircraft. The winds within the storm picked up vast quantities of sand from the desert below, sucking it upward into itself like a gigantic vacuum cleaner, growing larger and larger as it moved, swelling toward immensity from the merely humongous. It covered the horizon from deep into the south toward the west, directly in front of Leos's aircraft, even stretching many degrees to the north, threatening to block any escape route for Leos and his guests to the right or left. It approached the city from the south and west, and soon the main airport would be blanketed and invisible. Their little airplane was headed directly for the greatest part of the storm.

"You cannot fly into the sand," Grotuk said, leaning forward again. "It will ruin the engine. You must fly around. Or turn around."

"Okay." Leos was only vaguely aware of the destructive power of sand in a jet engine. Sandstorms never occurred on Anthanos, and nothing in his flight training—neither on Anthanos or here on Nytandra—had given him the confidence to deal with one. But that wasn't the most important thing on his mind.

Which way should I turn? He continued to fly west, directly toward the storm. To his left was nothing but churning clouds, to his right lay a small patch of blue, but it was closing rapidly. Behind him lay the best route of escape. Still, the dark brown curtain swirling all around him confused and disoriented him. He'd never seen anything like it. The needle on the magnetic compass swung widely from side to side and he couldn't rely on it. As he kept flying west, the storm grew bigger and bigger, filling the sky, pushing fingers of sand at him, making good on its promise to engulf him at any moment. The boiling sand had almost blocked all light from the sun in the southern sky, and an ominous darkness settled over the plane. He looked back and to his left, but the storm had curved around him.

"Return east," Grotuk said. "You cannot go around. You must return to the airport."

"Leos, please turn around."

At the Minister's insistence, the airport had given Leos only a half tank of fuel, to keep him from straying too far from the city, and though the fuel gauge showed he still had most of that left, he wondered if he had enough to return. Again and again, Grotuk pushed at him, warning, "You must return. You cannot go around." Leos wanted to turn south, but he couldn't find a clear route. Big lobes of blowing, billowing sand kept swirling at him from every direction, and finally, under almost constant prodding from Grotuk, and even Esmerelda, he turned north to get away from the storm. Yet even as Leos looked toward escape in the east, a large finger of the storm had swung around from the north and cut off his escape route. He was flying in circles within a small pocket of clear air in the midst of the storm, but the pocket was closing fast, threatening to envelope him and his little aircraft, and he was entirely bewildered.

"You must land," Grotuk said. "Put down somewhere. Anywhere."

"Leos—" Concern invaded Esmerelda's voice. "It is very thick out there. You cannot fly around forever. Put down. Please."

Particles of sand had begun pelting the canopy, audible inside, and that meant sand was entering the engine, too. Leos looked down at the terrain below him and a clear area appeared. Just a sliver of clear desert, protected on both sides by tall, jagged promontories of rock and stone, and he circled down toward it. It looked like a canyon, a slender cleft in the rock of the desert running east-west, but it was clear and long enough for a landing.

I can enter at the eastern end and roll to an easy stop near the western end.

At first Grotuk agreed. "This is good. This will be accept—" but he stopped and looked intently at the ground below. He shifted seats, hustling back and forth from right to left and back again, staring through the plastic of the canopy at something below. Then he began to yell. "No! No! Do not land here! Do not land here! I forbid it! Stay away from here!"

"Well, do you have a better landing place?" Leos studied the clear area below, relieved finally to be able to see a clear section of ground within the boiling sand that completely surrounded the plane. He discounted Grotuk's warnings. After all, Grotuk first insisted that he land, and he even approved this place, yet now he was bellowing about staying away. That annoyed Leos, and he decided to head directly for the canyon. *In a sandstorm like this*, he reasoned, *we're not going to find a better place.* He banked left, then right, lowered the flaps and the landing gear. "Hold on tight!" he yelled. "Here we go."

"No! No!" Grotuk continued to yell. "I forbid it! I forbid it! Stay a-way! Stay away! Do not land here!"

The sand from the storm swirled around the little plane, closing in and spilling over the peaks that guarded the canyon, but Leos maintained a firm eyeball grip on his chosen landing point.

"It is dangerous," Grotuk said. "Very dangerous. I know this canyon. We should not land here. It has been called—Ay!"

Grotuk's words were cut short by the thump of the landing gear as the plane hit the surface. The ship rolled along the narrow cleft in the rock, but as it moved, the walls of the canyon grew closer and closer, threatening to pin the plane between the side walls before it got to the end. At the far end of the canyon the walls narrowed rapidly to a gap that appeared only a few links wide.

If the ship hits that gap, it'll rip the wings off. Leos applied the brakes and flipped the switch that shut down the engine, and the plane rolled to a stop about twenty links short of the far end. That was narrowest part of the canyon. He breathed a heavy sigh of relief. "What did you say?" he asked Grotuk. "What's it called?"

"It is called Death Canyon," Esmerelda said. "I have heard of it."

"'Death Canyon?' Well, why didn't you say so." He looked again at the narrow gap directly ahead of the airplane, and at the walls to right and left. "It doesn't look very 'death' to me."

"I have heard of it," Esmerelda said. "I have heard stories of this canyon. Many airplanes have been forced down here. It seems a refuge from a storm, but none have ever come out of it alive. There is no way to take off, and the winds in the canyon are very fast."

"The winds? Oh."

"She is right," Grotuk said. "It may be impossible for us to take off. The canyon walls are too narrow. There is no way to turn the airplane a-round."

"Well, we're here anyway," Leos said. "Let's get out and have a look-see." He flipped the switch that raised the canopy, but as the canopy began to rise, a brisk wind slammed through the circular cockpit, pinning the canopy it at its most upward position. The blast almost blew Leos out of his seat.

"Whoaaa!" he yelled as he tumbled out of the cockpit. Esmerelda and Grotuk followed, dropping onto the sand of the canyon floor. Leos held his arm over his face and dashed to the side wall of the canyon, squeezing into a narrow cleft in the rock where he could get out of the gale.

Esmerelda and Grotuk ran around from the other side of the plane and joined him.

From the cleft, Leos could look up and see the sandstorm still raging above the canyon, but little of the dusty grit dropped down to the canyon floor. The wind whipping through the narrow cleft at the head of the canyon was completely free of sand.

"We're in the middle of a sandstorm, but the wind coming through the crack is clean," he yelled above the roar of the wind. "How is that possible?"

"I have heard of this," Grotuk yelled back. "There is a large funnel-like formation of rock many hundreds of kilos to the west. The sandstorm does not cover it and it is clear. The air travels through the funnel to this place, and the funnel becomes narrow here. In the evening the wind will reach many kilos per hour. Maybe up to one hundred."

"One hundred kilos per hour? That's several hundred anthans per sub. That's fast."

"It will blow the plane over."

"Uh-oh. Can we turn the plane around and fly out?"

"No. The canyon walls are too narrow. See the wings." Grotuk pointed to the wingtips. The left wingtip sat only about four links from the canyon wall, and the right wingtip wasn't much farther away, about five links. The plane seemed immovably trapped with no way to turn around.

Leos stepped into the wind to examine the canyon more closely. He held his right arm to his head to shield it from the wind, and gaped upward. The walls were a deep brick red, approaching purple, with streaks of black and umber shooting vertically through the rock. Several small patchy areas of tan were spotted through the red, but the most conspicuous color was the intense burgundy and rust on both sides. At this end of the canyon, the walls were close to vertical, a smooth cliff that to a visitor from Anthanos and unfamiliar with deep canyons, looked absolutely intimidating. On the south side where the three stood huddled in the tiny recess, the wall rose vertically, but near the top it bulged inward, narrowing the side-to-side distance by almost ten links.

"What if we walk back the way we came in?" Leos asked.

"The canyon walls are steep all the way around," Grotuk said. "We cannot climb without rock climbing equipment."

"But the far end of the canyon is flat," Leos said. "I saw it when we landed. It merges with the ground up there." He pointed upward.

"That is a mistake," Grotuk said. "I have seen this canyon from the air. It is sheer cliff and cannot be climbed as we are."

"But how did we get down into it?"

"We went down farther than it looked in the sand. The wind that comes through the canyon prevents the sandstorm from coming down in. It blows much fast and it appears as a clear place in the storm. Many have been fooled by this canyon. This has happened before. See, over there."

Grotuk pointed back down the canyon to a site about 200 links from where they stood in the recess. A skeleton, partially covered by sand, lay next to the canyon wall. The skull, staring upward as if hoping someone would come along and rescue it from the canyon, lay about six links away from its grotesquely twisted spinal column. Esmerelda gasped and turned away.

"Oh, I see," Leos said, also turning away. He scanned the bottom of the canyon in more detail. He noticed the debris—metal debris—scattered about the canyon floor, apparently the remains of airplanes forced down into the canyon, either because they crashed, or landed safely but were destroyed by the wind. And he noticed something else.

"The wind is picking up."

"I am afraid we may suffer the same fate as those," Grotuk said.

"But they must have seen us go down on the long-wavelength band."

"No, that may not be. It will not penetrate sand. They lost us in the storm. They do not know where we are."

"Hold on, what about the radio? I can call out." Leos ran back to the pilot's seat and grabbed the mic. He activated the comm signal but the only return sound was the thin screech of static. Occasionally, he thought he heard a voice, but it faded in and out so rapidly he couldn't latch on to it. It may have been his imagination.

"That is what makes this canyon so deadly," Grotuk said when Leos returned. "There is much magnetized iron ore in the walls of the canyon. It interferes with the signal. You cannot call out."

"Don't tell me, they can't call us either."

Grotuk nodded. "The truth is in your words."

"But they do know we are down, don't they?" Esmerelda asked.

"That may not be," Grotuk replied. "The sand has interfered with much radio imaging. They may be waiting for the storm to end."

"So, what do we do now?" Leos's question wasn't addressed to anyone in particular, he just threw the question into the air.

"We must get away from the plane," Grotuk said. "The wind coming through the canyon will increase as the night approaches, and it will blow the plane around. Perhaps fast enough to blow the plane off its wheels. We must wait and see."

"If the plane is destroyed, we may be here for a long time," Esmerelda said.

"We will have to wait and see if they can find us," Leos said. "But that may take days."

"If I am out overnight, Father will be furious. He will take it out on you."

Leos didn't reply. His mind was alive with visions of the punishment that Coreaje might dole out if Esmerelda were not back by nightfall. But he put it out of his mind and turned his attention to something more immediate: the wind. He looked up at the top of the canyon. The storm seemed to be slowing down. The sienna color of the heaviest part of the sandstorm had largely dissipated, and all that remained of the sand was a weak khaki. Tiny patches of blue flickered in and out as the swirling abated. But the wind through the narrow cleft had not decreased. It had become a deep bellowing roar, pounding at everyone's eardrums and drowning out all other sound. The open cockpit canopy acted like a drag chute, capturing the wind and exaggerating its effect, and the plane bounced up and down on the shock absorbers in its landing gear like a child on a pogo stick. The plane's wingtips were flexing, flipping up and down, as they did during flight.

Daylight was fading, too, and the shadow of the southern canyon wall edged its way slowly over the airplane.

There's plenty of fuel. If we could turn the plane around, we could fly out of here. But the canyon is too narrow. Besides, we can't push the ship. It's too heavy.

As Leos stood in the narrow cleft in the side wall, watching the plane jounce up and down in the roaring breeze, a new plan formed in his mind. He visualized himself sitting in the pilot's seat. *The wind will eventually blow the plane over. But if we lower the canopy, the plane will be as aerodynamic as in flight. Except for the landing gear. If I push the control column forward, that should produce enough negative lift to keep the plane on the ground. Then maybe we can wait out the wind.* He mulled that idea for a few nanosectors, but he didn't know how fast the wind would ultimately become, and it still might flip the plane over.

We can't turn the plane around in the narrow canyon anyway.

The plane bobbed around more now. It flipped up and down on its spindly landing gear, and the front wheel occasionally rose off the ground a few decilinks.

"Eventually that wind will be fast enough to fly in . . ." Leos paused and stared at the plane while a solid image materialized in his mind—an image of the plane lifting off the surface, flying by standing still in the high wind through the canyon. "That's it!" Leos yelled in his native tongue, then switched back to Nytandran. "We can fly it out of here!"

"What did you say?" Esmerelda yelled.

"Everybody in the plane! Get in the plane! Hurry! Now!" He stepped out of the cleft in the rock holding his left arm over his face for protection, making urgent 'Come on' gestures with his right arm.

"What?" Esmerelda yelled. "Leos! You are crazy! The wind will blow the plane down the canyon soon."

"No! We can fly it out. We can do this. We can fly it!"

"How do you know?" Grotuk asked. He hadn't budged from his place in the rock cleft, and he looked at Leos, scowling.

"The wind will eventually reach a speed high enough to fly in. It'll pick the plane up, but if we start the engine, it'll be like the plane is flying."

Esmerelda shook her head. "Leos, you are crazy."

"It will never work. I forbid it."

"Sure, it'll work. What've we got to lose? We've got plenty of fuel. Look!" He pointed upward toward the storm. "The sandstorm is decreasing." The plane behind Leos rasped and groaned in the wind, bouncing up and down even more now. The canopy cracked and creaked, straining against the hinge that held it to the rear of the cockpit, almost ready to snap off and go flying down the canyon by itself. "Quick! Get in! Hurry! We don't have much time before dark."

Esmerelda hesitated. "I do not know . . . it seems unlikely."

"It will never work. We will all be killed. I forbid it."

"Of course it'll work, but we don't have much time."

Leos bolted for the plane and jumped into the pilot's seat. Esmerelda shook her head, but ran around the back of the plane and climbed into the right hand seat. Grotuk entered the left rear seat, just behind Leos who was by this time running through the engine start checklist. When he reached 'Close Canopy', he flipped the switch on the control panel, but the canopy refused to budge. The hydraulic mechanism that retracted the canopy screeched and whined and groaned and carried on like tomorrow would never come, trying with all its might to pull the big bowl-shaped canopy down against the wind, and Leos and Esmerelda had to reach up and pull it down.

As the engine roared to life, a fierce but short blast of wind—much faster than what had been coming through the cleft—knocked the nose of the ship upward two or three links. The ship held that position for several seconds, then slowly settled back. That was significant. The wind speed was now high enough to fling the plane down the canyon, and that meant it was high enough to fly in. Leos advanced the throttle, increasing the engine power to the point where the ship crawled forward—slowly and imperceptibly, but forward—against the wind. The wind continued to buffet the plane, and sudden gusts kept jerking the nose up. Leos kept the control stick pushed slightly forward, hoping to keep the nose down and prevent the plane from being flipped over.

With one hand on the control column and the other on the throttle, Leos fixed his eyes on the front canyon wall, and as he watched, the little airplane rose slowly from the surface. Esmerelda gasped, then screamed.

CHAPTER 14

INVESTIGATION – II

"Tama, sweetheart, thank you for coming over," Lilea said.

Tama stood beside Lilea at the front door to Lilea's house as the dark cobalt blue runabout came down the street. Lilea had invited Tama over because, she said, Tam Kos, Director General of Spaceflight Command would be coming over.

"He said he has some news about Leos and some of the events surrounding his disappearance. I really hope he has something positive."

The time was 483.995.3 when the runabout slowed and pulled into the driveway. The bright gold seven-pointed stars on each front door identified it as an official SpaceComm vehicle. Tam stepped out.

Tama wished she'd dressed more appropriately. She'd never met Tam, but she'd seen him on the I.S. many times, and she recognized him as soon as he left the runabout. With his sandy hair and freckled face and big expansive smile, he looked too young to be Director of Spaceflight Command—couldn't be out of his fifties, she imagined. He wore the official white uniform of SpaceComm, looking as though he'd just come from the fitting room. The shirt with its gold trim on the pockets and around the short sleeves, the pants with the wide gold stripe down the outside of each leg, both clean and sharply pressed. The epaulets on his shoulders bore a trio of gold seven-pointed stars, the insignia of the Director. That outfit contrasted with the relaxed attire of Tama and Lilea, both dressed in shorts and light-weight blouses to counter the heat from the Anthanian sun.

"Tam, this is Tama," Lilea said. "I've included her in all my inquiries. You can speak freely with her."

"Hello, Tama," Tam said. "I've read all your accounts and descripttions of what happened when Leos was last seen, but we've never had a chance to meet." Tam and Tama shook hands, then Tam turned to back Lilea. "I have some good news," he said. "Let's go in and sit down."

Lilea ushered both into the living room of her house, and all three sat on the comfortable sofa in the center of the room, Lilea in the middle. Tam opened a small electronic notebook and set it on the coffee table in front of the sofa. He removed an electronic scanner from his pocket and set it beside the notebook. A short cable about two links long originated from the bottom of the scanner, and he plugged the other end of the cable into a port on the side of the notebook. He held the scanner—an undistinguished metallic cylinder about six decilinks long and one decilink in diameter with a hemispherical top—above his head. A gentle hum came from the unit as it scanned the entire room. Tama watched, intrigued. He held it for about a microsector, then shut it off.

"I'm looking for electronic listening devices," he said. "But the room is clean. What I have to tell you can't go out of this room." He looked directly at Lilea and Tama, his deep blue-gray eyes meeting theirs. "That's absolutely essential for both of you."

"Okay," Lilea said.

Tama nodded.

Tam pocketed the scanner and switched to another datafile on his notebook. The gold seven-pointed star appeared.

"Do you have some more information about the spaceship?" Tama asked. For Tama, this little meeting had become exquisitely fascinating. Twenty-year-old girls rarely attended meetings with the Director of Space-flight Command, and with Tam's insistence on electronic scans and total secrecy, she felt as though she was in a top-secret briefing. Like all those secret agents she'd seen in movies on the Entertainment Services. The goose bumps she got weren't just from Lilea's air cooler.

"No, not about the spaceship," Tam said. "We sent a team out to ex-amine that area where it was spotted, but there was nothing there. But we do have some other information that will interest both of you. We've been looking into several accounts of unusual persons in and around Kalarias over the past several years."

"What do you mean 'unusual'?" Lilea asked.

"Well, let's call them people who have demonstrated strange be-havior and characteristics."

Lilea screwed up her face. "Explain yourself."

"All right—and this goes back to what Tama told us about the two men Leos went with the T-sector he disappeared—we've been able to find out more about these men and their motives. It seems they may not be from around here."

"Around here? You mean . . . wait, what *do* you mean?"

"First of all, they had unusual facial features, not characteristic of Anthanians. Like dark skin, dark like most Morokuu, like Bent, even darker than Leos's skin."

"I remember," Tama said. "I didn't think much of it at the time, but their skin was dark, but not so dark that I thought anything about it."

"That's right, but skin color wasn't the only thing that was unusual. In our investigations, we've found that these people, and there were at least two of them, have been around on this planet for at least several years—"

"'On this planet?'" Lilea said sitting up straight. "Are you saying they're from some other planet?"

"There's a very good possibility they may be."

Lilea didn't say anything, she seemed to be processing the information. She ran a hand through her hair.

"Wow," she said quietly. "Aliens. That's hard to fathom. We've never had aliens on our planet. At least not knowingly. Where are they from? The blue planet?"

"No, not the blue planet—I'm sure we dispensed with that possibility a long time ago—but we have identified a candidate star system they might be from."

"Oh, my gosh. What are you—"

Tam held up his right hand in a sort of 'stop' sign. "Let me explain. As I mentioned, they seem to have been on Anthanos for several years because we've developed leads from people who've seen them. They all describe the same people. We know there are at least two of them because they've been seen together. They look alike, like twins. They've got almost spherical round heads, they're totally bald, and their eyes seem to be protected by big puffy eye ridges above and below both eyes. They've got big gap-toothed grins. This confirms what Tama said."

"I remember," Tama said, nodding her head. "Funny looking eyes. And stupid smiles."

"Right. We've got lots of sightings over several years. There's no one on this planet with facial characters like that."

"Big gap-toothed grins?" Lilea asked. "Puffy eye ridges? Round heads?" She screwed up her face in disbelief. "Tam. Are you leading . . ."

"Wait, there's more. They spoke our language, but with a strong accent. But no one we've talked to recognized that accent. Their accent wasn't like any of the dialects that've developed over the years on Anthanos. Not like the Sabean drawl, or the Kalarias consonant merge, or the Bes vowel flip. They've been seen in stores and on the street, and in a tavern, especially the tavern where Leos and Tama were when he disappeared."

"When Leos gets back I'm going to kill him for going to that bar," Lilea said. She glanced briefly at Tama, but she had a sly smile on her face. She made fists with both hands.

"You do that. But that's not the most interesting thing. We've developed two significant leads recently. The first occurred several hundred T-sectors before Leos left the bar. One of these visitors was drinking at the bar. Nobody seems to remember whether Leos was there, but the visitor was alone and drinking. Heavily. He sat at the bar, and he was drunk—really stoned, and he started talking about a planetary system in the constellation Diinn—"

"Diinn—Tam, now listen, you're getting—what are you talking about?"

"—let me finish. He kept telling people he was from that system. Nobody knew what he was talking about. With his slurred speech and heavy accent, they had a hard time understanding him. He never answered questions directly, just kept rambling on."

"Right," Tama said. "Just like that guy . . ."

"He said it was 100 light-years away and he could travel there in a spaceship no one knew anything about, and he kept talking about something called the mathematics of the cosmos."

"'Mathematics of the cosmos'? Tam, honestly, what the hell are you talking about?"

"Yeah, I remember . . ." Tama said, nodding. "They did mention something weird like that."

"No one paid much attention. They thought it was just the drink talking, just science fiction crap. One person we talked to said he thought the guy was a science fiction writer off in his own little world. You know how weird some of those science fiction people can be. But we decided to check out this guy's story anyway. I talked to Planetary Visualization and had them visualize the area, and they came up with some surprising results."

"Don't tell me—sorry, let's hear it."

Tam paused in his story and pulled up another datafile on his notebook screen. He pointed to a schematic of a small solar system. Tama didn't recognize it.

"There are nine stars in the constellation Diinn," Tam went on, "most of them thousands of light-years away, except for one star which is around ninety-seven light-years. But that's not surprising, we knew that already. That one star is still too far to visualize its planets in detail, but by examining orbital mechanics and planetary gravitationally-induced stellar oscillations, we were able to deduce that this star has at least four planets orbiting it, and three of them, the inner three, are within the Viability Zone necessary to sustain life. At least Anthanian life. They're small compact planets, and all three meet the Primary Standards of the Commonality Report. But most importantly, the star is a G-type star, the same as our sun, Arteamos. That's the same type as the star the blue planet orbited.

"Wow," Lilea said. "That's all good. Very good. How much else do you know about these planets?"

"Not much else. We can't see them so we can't do a visual exam, but we've discussed it among ourselves at SpaceComm, and we've tentatively decided that we want to send an expedition."

Lilea jerked her head back. "What! You're going to send *Star Voyager*? What does the Assembly have to say?"

"We haven't talked to the Assembly, or to the Spaceflight Command Oversight Subcommittee. Yet. Since you're a member of that Subcommittee, I'm officially informing you of the evidence now. You're the first committee member I've talked to. But look at it this way: three planets within the Viability Zone of a G-type star — that's too good to pass up. We've got to check this out. With nothing else available, it's essential. Even without the connection to Leos, I think the Assembly will go along."

Lilea let out a low whistle. "I'd like to read the entire report first, but what you're telling me sounds fabulous." Lilea turned and looked at Tama. "What do you think?"

Tama looked at Lilea and beyond her to Tam. The discussion had been almost too fast for her to comprehend. As a young lady barely out of tertiary school group and not well versed in the worlds of astrophysics and planetary visualization, though moderately knowledgeable, like most Anthanians, of the necessity for finding and colonizing another planet outside their solar system, yet fascinated by the intrigue and secrecy of this little meeting, she wanted to say something, to be accounted for in the discussion. She paused as several thoughts went through her mind. Finally she put enough information together to ask a question, though she hoped it wouldn't sound too simpleminded. "Do you think Leos is on one of these planets?"

"Hard to say," Tam said. "But sightings of these characters ended after Leos disappeared. Oh, that reminds me of the other significant lead we developed recently."

"What?"

"Shortly before Leos disappeared, these guys bought some food. A large amount of food. Enough food for one person for, roughly, 500 T-sectors."

"Five hundred T-sectors? What are you suggesting?"

"I'm not sure, but it's like someone was going on a long trip."

Lilea didn't speak, she seemed lost in thought. "Maybe they were just getting food for a return trip. Back to their planet."

"Possibly, but included in the food they bought were four cases of yanto fruit."

"Yanto?" Tama said. She leaned forward to look at Tam. "Yanto is Leos's favorite. He'd almost kill for a good yanto."

"That's right, it is," Lilea said. "I wonder what it means."

The room turned silent for a few nanosectors. Tam shut off his notebook and closed the cover. Tama sat quietly, not knowing what to say. She was captivated by the information Tam had presented because it could lead to Leos, but the part about the food scared her. Why would these weird characters buy so much food? Especially yanto? That portended a strong connection to Leos, but it sounded suspicious, even a little foreboding, and a morbid feeling developed in the pit of her stomach. He could be in serious trouble—deep trouble—on some weird planet or somewhere, and they needed to get there as soon as possible. But Lilea's voice brought her back to the real world.

"Wanna go?" Lilea asked Tama. "It'll be a long trip."

"Go?"

"On the trip to the star Tam was talking about."

Tama hesitated. "I'll go if you'll go."

Lilea laughed out loud and leaned over and gave Tama a brief hug. "Oh, no, sweetheart, I'm not going. I'm through with spaceflight. You go in my place." She turned to Tam. "Can you arrange for her to go?"

Tam paused a nanosector and then nodded. "I think so."

CHAPTER 15

BACK IN THE VALLEY

"It is working," Grotuk said.

Leos's eyes stayed fixed on the forward canyon wall. He worked the control stick forward and back and the aileron pedals right to left in tiny movements, keeping the plane at just the right position to prevent it from being flipped backward by the wind roaring through the cleft. He stayed calm as he worked, and very little passed through his mind as he stared at the canyon wall. He concentrated only on the relation of the plane to the front wall, not even glancing at the artificial horizon in the center of the control panel—he didn't dare take his eyes off the wall. Slowly, link by link, the plane crept higher and higher, the screaming engine counteracting the wind that kept the plane aloft, the gusts pummeling the plane, knocking it around like a kite in a windstorm.

Every now and then a sudden jolt of wind would jostle the plane and rattle Leos's nerves, and he would manipulate the throttle and control stick and aileron pedals in larger movements than before—forward or backward, up or down, right or left—to keep the plane level for a nano-sector or two to get it calmed down before he allowed it to rise again.

When the plane was about fifty links off the ground, another fierce gust of wind roared through the cleft, but this was much stronger than any before, and it raised the nose of the plane almost twenty degrees and sent it skidding backward away from the wall. The strength of the gust startled Leos and rattled his concentration. He overcompensated and pushed the control stick too far forward, and the nose dropped too far, threatening to send the plane plummeting to the bottom of the canyon. At the same time, the left wing dropped, and he jerked the stick back and pressed the right aileron pedal, but in that brief instant of terror that made him feel that everything was slipping away, he overreacted again and pressed the pedal too far, throwing the left wing up too high. He knew immediately what he'd done and regained enough presence of mind to slowly press the left pedal, returning the wings to horizontal. That was good—that was fine—and he got the plane stabilized, but the unfortunate effect of all these wild gyrations was to throw the nose of the plane into a terrifyingly erratic circular pattern for several nanosectors until he could get it calmed down. It gave Leos the scare of his life, but he never took his eyes off the front canyon wall.

Esmerelda, for her part, grabbed an airsickness bag from under her seat.

As the plane reached an altitude of about a hundred links above the canyon floor, another problem arose—the narrowing of the canyon walls. The southern wall tapered inward, and the left wingtip began to scrape the reddish-brown rock.

Grotuk shuttled back and forth from one rear seat to another, looking out one side of the plane, then the other. "There is no room on the other side either," he yelled.

Leos kept staring at the front canyon wall. He reduced the throttle, dropping engine power to allow the wind to push the plane back and down, past the narrows to a wider section of the canyon. Then he advanced the throttle and let the ship rise. Slowly, surely, and carefully, the ship rose up the canyon like a vertical take-off jet. But as it climbed, the speed of the wind whistling through the narrow opening dropped. Leos reduced the throttle and lowered the flaps a few degrees to keep the plane from migrating forward too fast. He shook his head.

The wind speed is lower the higher we go. Will the wind be fast enough at the top of the canyon to keep the plane airborne? Will we be able to make it all the way to the top?

He'd committed himself to getting out, and he didn't want to go back down, but if the wind speed wasn't high enough at the top, he might have to descend. But if he did descend, he'd have to take the plane all the way down, and that would mean not getting out of this canyon at all. This was their only chance, and he didn't want to screw it up.

He let the plane continue creeping upward, but the wind speed kept dropping. They were high enough now that sunlight glinted off the right wing. He extended more flaps and reduced the throttle, small increments at a time. The slower the wind speed, the slower the plane moved vertically. *Add flaps,* he told himself. *More and more flaps—keep the nose down—maximize air flow over the wings—don't stall the wings. Will we make it? Will we make it?*

"Just a few links more! Just a few links more—here we go—almost, almost . . ." The canyon rim appeared above, about twenty links away. "We've almost made it!"

The sun was still high enough in the sky to illuminate most of the little plane hovering below the rim. Only about half of the left wing was still in shade.

"We've almost made it!" Leos yelled again. The plane rose a few links more.

BONG! BONG! BONG!

"Oh, shit!" Leos yelled.

"What is that?!" Esmerelda yelled, holding her hands over her ears.

"It is stall alarm!" Grotuk bellowed. "The wings are stalling. Go down! Go down!"

"I can't go down! If I go down, we'll never get out!"

"Go down!" Grotuk yelled, more impatiently this time. "Land again! We will never make it."

"I can't! We just need to go a few more links. Just a few more."

"Go down a small amount."

Leos pushed the control stick forward, and the plane settled a few links. The bonging stopped.

"We're okay now, but we can't make it the rest of the way."

"Lower flaps," Grotuk yelled.

"Flaps are fully extended. No more left."

"Let the wind blow the plane backward, then make a run for it," Esmerelda yelled at him.

"What? You're kidding!" Leos shook his head. "That'll never work."

"Of course it will. Let the plane go back. Then fly it out."

Leos didn't answer. He mulled over Esmerelda's suggestion. *How in the name of the Great God Arteamos could the suggestion by a woman who doesn't know the first thing about flying actually work?*

"Certainly, it will work," Grotuk said. "Allow the plane to go back, then increase power and fly the plane out. You can do it."

Leos hesitated, but he didn't have any choice. He had to take Esmerelda's suggestion and make a run for it. "Okay, I'll try. But I gotta say I don't think it'll work."

*   *   *

After two millisectors of flying vertically, Leos had brought the plane nearly to the top of the canyon. As he sat in the pilot's seat holding the aircraft in position, still staring at the west canyon wall, for the first time since he conceived the idea of trying to fly the plane vertically out of the canyon, he began to wonder if his plan would get them out at all. He'd been so sure they could do it, and he maintained that optimistic attitude all the way to this point, just short of the canyon rim. But now he wasn't as sure. He knew that if he didn't believe in his plan—and believe in it one hundred and ten percent—Esmerelda and Grotuk would never believe in it either. But his rosy evaluation of the chances of getting out of the canyon seemed to be dissipating, about to blow away in the wind that whistled through the cleft in the canyon wall. The speed of that wind was barely sufficient to keep the plane aloft, even with full flaps, and he couldn't go any higher without activating the stall alarm and risk crashing on the canyon floor. Should he take it down?

For the first time since the little plane left the canyon floor, Leos allowed his gaze to drift upward. He could see the top edge of the canyon about forty links above, taunting and tantalizing him, just out of reach. The sandstorm raging above them had disappeared and the sky was a deep ultramarine.

Leos swallowed hard. He reduced the throttle slightly and trimmed the wings to keep the nose level. The plane drifted backward, slowly—twenty—thirty—fifty links, and even a little more. But then—**BONG! BONG! BONG!**

"Oh, crap! The wings are stalling again!"

"Go down! Go down!" Grotuk yelled.

Leos gritted his teeth and shook his head. He didn't want to descend if he didn't have to, but the stall alarm was reverberating through the cockpit and banging in his ears, its meaning impossible to ignore. He pressed the control column again about two degrees forward and the plane descended and the bonging stopped. He leveled off.

With the plane stabilized again, Leos reduced the throttle and allowed the plane to drift backward until the stall alarm sounded again, then descended. By this series of alternating back-and-down maneuvers, he worked the plane backward until it was several thousand links from the west canyon wall, but only about thirty links above the floor.

"This should be enough," Leos muttered, talking to himself more than to Esmerelda and Grotuk. He held the plane at this position for several seconds. "I'll have to raise flaps, gun the engine, and try to get up enough speed to clear the rock at the end. It ain't gonna be easy."

"What did you say?" Esmerelda yelled. "I can't hear you over the engine noise."

"Never mind. Hold on tight. Here we go!"

Leos jammed the throttle open, pulled back on the control stick, raised the flaps, and the plane shot forward, climbing toward the western canyon wall. The engine screamed in their ears as the little plane, so unused to such rugged maneuvers, shook and vibrated as though it was ready to disintegrate in mid-air. Leos dipped the right wing almost 100 degrees so the plane would fit between two spike-like pinnacles that projected upward several hundred links on each side of the slot, and with little more than a few links between the plane and the peaks, and with Esmerelda shrieking and Grotuk cowering on the floor in the back seats, he banked right into a crystalline blue sky and headed for home.

CHAPTER 16

AUDIENCE

A few thin streaks of speckled orange light from the setting sun were all that penetrated the stained-glass windows to Leos's right as he entered the Grand Hall through the main doorway. Except for a few dim lamps hanging from the ceiling beams and one small high-intensity lamp on Coreaje's table on the front platform, the Hall was dark.

No gong announced his entrance this time.

Leos had been ordered to attend an audience with the Ruler, but he had no inkling why. In the typical Nytandran fashion he found so distasteful, no one told him anything. All he knew was that Grotuk had relayed a message from Palace Security that he was to be there at the beginning of the ninth hour, the time when most evening audiences with Coreaje were entering their final phase, if not already over. This time he was to enter the Hall through the main doors, those tall, heavily guarded portals which opened into the Grand Hall, the main meeting place so important to the administration of the government of the planet. Now, in the waning hours of the evening, that hall took on the function of a Supreme Court for all who entered.

Most audiences were held during the early evening hours when the Ruler, acting as a court of last resort, gave his opinion on appeals of civil and criminal cases from all over the planet. Late evening sessions were unusual, reserved for those infrequent occasions when Coreaje was required to pass judgment on the worst crimes, those that were considered the most heinous, the most abominable. Those that required the death penalty.

Grotuk met Leos at the doors outside the Grand Hall, and at his command, one of the guards opened the right-hand door.

"Do not speak until Ruler speaks to you," Grotuk said. He remained outside as the door closed behind Leos.

As Leos entered the hall, a delicate coolness drifted up from the floor. The stones in the floor always seemed to possess a welcome chilliness in spite of the heat of the day. Though he wasn't certain of the reason he'd been told to be here, he understood the seriousness of this visit, and wanted to make a good impression on Coreaje. That was nothing new; it'd been true since he first arrived on this planet and found that Coreaje was to be his father-in-law, but his boots made a mortifying clomp on the stone floor with each step that reverberated through the empty hall, and he figured Coreaje must be thinking of him as a complete clod right now.

Earlier this day, Coreaje hadn't appeared for the fourth meal, and that was odd for the gregarious ruler who invariably relished the last meal of the day with his daughter and potential son-in-law. Today Leos and Esmerelda dined alone. Esmerelda had worn an unusual outfit to this dinner: a pair of baggy dark brown pants and an ill-fitting long-sleeved white shirt. She'd never worn this outfit in Leos's presence before, and it looked so improper and un-Princess-like that Leos was astounded she would dare to appear outside her own private quarters dressed so shabbily. When she sat down at the table she tried to explain her father's absence by giving Leos an excuse about affairs of business, but that was all she said during the meal, and Leos didn't really believe her. She ate very little, not raising her head, not looking at Leos, leaving without explanation as soon as her plate was removed. The door behind Leos to the patio, so frequently open during the meal, had been closed and locked.

As he entered the Grand Hall he saw only Coreaje on the platform, seated at the table, illuminated by the harsh glare of the lamp, watching him closely. The incense burner was cold. As Leos neared the platform, he became aware of a tall figure in the shadow to Coreaje's left. At first he took it to be the Minister, but as he grew closer to the table he could just make out Mlada's pale face and the whites of her eyes. Her tall form and dark brown cloak were almost invisible in the shadow outside the dimmest part of the light. She, too, watched Leos as he approached the table. Esmerelda, still wearing that same shabby outfit, her head bowed, her hands folded in her lap, sat in a narrow straight-backed chair immediately in front of Mlada.

"Leos, m' boy," Coreaje said in a quiet voice as Leos stopped about ten paces from the platform, near the spot where he met Esmerelda that first day. "What am I going to do with you?" Coreaje's voice seemed sympathetic, neither demeaning nor judgmental.

"I don't understand."

"Leos, m' boy, you were brought here one hundred thirty days ago as a companion and escort to my daughter Esmerelda, but you have steadfastly refused my offer of my daughter's hand. Yet you and she are conspicuously attracted to each other. That has become obvious throughout these many days. You have spent time together in the city. You have been seen together, in person and on many video channels. Our society is waiting for your proposal, but you remain silent. It is a frustration with us. We are grieving for your answer, yet you flail at our expectations. Do we wait forever?

"I'm sorry, but—"

"But what?"

"I'm sorry, but I can't. You got me in a hard spot here. You know I had a girlfriend on my home planet, and she and I had already made plans, and . . . well, it's a big decision and . . . I'm not ready to make a move now."

"Is my daughter unacceptable to you?"

"No, no, that's not it at all, she's a wonderful girl, I mean, she's a wonderful lady, but it's just, ya see, I've got a girl, I mean a lady, I mean my girlfriend, at home and we're ready to become engaged, see, we filled out the form, the Notice of Betrothal, and well, see, she's not my type, that's all."

Coreaje's face turned puzzled. "Your girlfriend is not your type . . .? I don't understand."

"Ahh, no, see, Esmerelda's not my type."

"I see. Not your type. What—"

"I just don't feel that spark, that's all."

"Spark. I see."

"Not like I did with my girl back home."

"Is that your reason? That you don't feel a spark?"

"Uh, yeah, that is, well, see, Esmerelda's a wonderful girl, er, lady, but she's a Princess and I'm not, er, I'm not a Prince, that is, y' see, well, besides, I just don't feel a spark, like I said, and, well, sorry, that's the best I can do."

"I see. Most men on this planet would instantly take my daughter's hand without question. She has many suitors." Coreaje leaned back in his chair, throwing up one arm in a gesture of content.

"Yeah, I know. I've met some of them." An image of Gass floated into Leos's mind. "But I'm not from this planet. This place isn't home to me. I'm more like a visitor here."

"But this planet is not home to Esmerelda. Yet she has adapted to this planet, and she has become queen to my people, and they have accepted her. They have accepted you, but you have not accepted her. How can this be?"

"I dunno, I guess I've still got a place in my heart for my girl back home."

"Do you not like Esmerelda?" Coreaje leaned forward again, folding his hands on the desk.

"Oh, no, it's not that—er, I mean, well, yes, sure I do, I like her very much. She and I are great friends and we've had a great time together. She's taught me a lot about Nytandra. But it's just that—"

"Friends? Is that all? After all we have done for you and Esmerelda you are only friends?"

"Ahh, yeah, I guess so. Sorry. Besides, you haven't given your permission for my people to move to this planet."

A wave of annoyance crossed Coreaje's face. "Leos, we have discussed that. I have made that clear to you. What you are asking is impossible. It cannot be done."

"You know how important it is to me."

"I am of the understanding of this. But it cannot be done."

"You never gave me a good reason, though. I thought—"

Coreaje shook his head. "We cannot permit you to return to your planet, or communicate with them. This would be impossible."

"I don't understand."

"If you communicated with your planet, they might come here. They would be too many."

"Oh, but—"

"We cannot have that many people coming to our planet. Our planet could not support them." Coreaje looked away from Leos, turning to some papers on his desk.

"Yeah, well—"

"It is the water. There is little water enough for our people. All our water is in underground reservoirs. We cannot provide sufficient water for your people, too. I have made my decision. There can be no other."

"There's enough water around the north pole. Enough to support all those trees."

"There is sufficient water only for the trees. Our scientists have said this to me. We cannot take from them. They would die."

"Oh, I see." Leos stayed silent for a few seconds, Coreaje's reasoning still muddled in his brain. He understood the water problem the Nytandrans had to contend with, and in the short time he'd been standing before Coreaje he couldn't come up with a good counter-argument.

Maybe we could bring our own water. But that would require huge water-

carrying spaceships. They'd have to transport water almost a hundred light-years for all the Anthanians who wanted to come to this planet. That's out of the question.

But as he mulled over the dilemma, a modified possibility occurred to him: would everyone on Anthanos want to come? Would all two million Anthanians want to travel to this planet? Probably not. Some may prefer to stay home—only a few people need make the trip. Those people could start a new colony in the desert and maybe they could bring enough water for themselves. Just a few hundred people. That might work, and maybe it would be acceptable to the Nytandrans.

Leos turned his attention back to Coreaje, ready to make his suggestion, but Coreaje had already moved to a different subject. He continued to shuffle papers around on the table, placing them in folders which he set aside one by one, then picked up a familiar-looking object. Leos lost his train of thought.

"Leos, I grow weary of this conversation. Perhaps you can tell me why this was in your possession?"

Coreaje held up a small gold bar. It was the same gold bar Leos . . . er, borrowed from Gass, and its surfacing here startled him. Confused at first, he searched his mind and remembered seeing it last on the table in his room. He wanted to deny ever owning the rod, but he'd been caught red-handed. Better to own up to it now, and not prolong the deception. Coreaje wasn't in a good mood and Leos didn't want to antagonize him further.

"We found this in your room," Coreaje continued. "It is called the oroban. How did you come to the possession of it?"

Leos cleared his throat. "Um . . . how did you get that?" Esmerelda raised her head and glanced at Coreaje, leaning forward to see the oroban he held. Then she stared straight at Leos, a look of surprise, perhaps even astonishment on her face.

"Our Personnel of Housekeeping found it when they cleaned your room this past day. I am surprised at its appearance. It belongs to the mine companies. It is an insignia of office of a very high-ranking person. I ask you again, how did you come to the possession of it?"

"I got it from a guy in a bar."

"What is the name of this 'guy'?"

"Said his name was Gass. Greenhouse Gass."

Coreaje laughed. "Hah! Gasz! I am of the correct type. I might have expected him to be involved in this. That *is* his mark upon the bar."

"He left it on the bar top. I just grabbed it . . ." Esmerelda closed her eyes and lowered her head.

Coreaje was silent for a nanosector. The smile disappeared from his face and he glared at Leos. Leos shrank to about one decilink tall.

"I know Gasz," Coreaje said. "But even I do not believe he would just leave it on the top of a bar. It is his insignia. He is a high-ranking person in the mining company. He must keep it with him at all times."

"But he wore the sparkle of a foreman."

Coreaje snorted. "A common misconception. Gasz is not a foreman. He is much higher. He is the leader of the mining company."

"But he was plastered. From the kaadz. He—"

"Yes, this I am of the understanding."

"He said he was a friend of yours. An old friend or something."

"Yes, he is an old friend. He was the general in charge of the expedition to the green planet. But he killed many people. He encouraged the men under him to do so. He performed obscenities on many of the women. I had to discharge him. I disbanded his army. It was not pleasant. But he would not just leave the oroban lying around. It does not belong to him. It is worth much."

"It's worth lots more on my planet."

"This I am of the understanding, but it is solid gold. It—"

Leos nodded. "I thought it might be."

"Do not interrupt. It is not yours for the keeping."

Leos remained silent. He shrugged his shoulders absentmindedly, then looked at the floor. Coreaje continued.

"We cannot permit this type of behavior to continue. This is a serious offense. The theft of gold deserves a punishment of the harshest type. I have no choice but to sentence you to the Kazo Dela Tan."

Esmerelda's head jerked upward. "No, Father! No!" she yelled, and stood to face Coreaje. She took a step or two toward him, stepping into the cone of light from the lamp. Her eyes glistened and her hands were balled into fists. "You promised!" she yelled, her voice cracking. "You said he could go! You promised!"

"Esmerelda! Remember your place! You will become of the silent type!" Coreaje paused and turned back to Leos. "That was before the oroban appeared in his room. I must do this. I can do no other."

"Father! He saved my life. Remember? He got us out of the canyon. We told you about it. No one has ever done that before." Tears poured down her cheeks and fell silently to the floor.

"But he flew farther over the desert than he was allowed. And he landed in the canyon when he was told not to. Grotuk forbade him to land there, but he disobeyed."

"But he was forced to. He had to land there. By the storm. There was no other place."

"Nevertheless, he should not have flown so far from the city."

"We got trapped by the storm."

"Nevertheless—"

"Grotuk told him not to try and get us out of the canyon, too, but he did it."

"I am aware."

"And he got us back before nightfall, as you wished." Esmerelda sniffed loudly and wiped her face on her sleeve.

"I remember," Coreaje said. "I have accepted all of this. Now you will be silent."

Mlada stepped forward and placed a hand on Esmerelda's shoulder. Without saying a word, Esmerelda whirled around and scurried toward the side door. Mlada followed. A gong sounded.

Coreaje watched the two leave, then turned back to Leos.

"You will stay in your room tonight, but tomorrow, at one hour before the rising of the sun, you will be taken to the Kazo Dela Tan. Have you anything to say?"

"What's the Kazo, uh, Kazo what? I never heard of it."

"You will find out tomorrow. That is all. You are dismissed."

Coreaje stood from his desk and gathered his papers. He extinguished the lamp and left the Hall by the side door.

Leos winced . . . *There's that damn gong again . . .*

The sun had disappeared from the sky and the stained-glass windows were inky dark, as though a cloak had been pulled over them. Only the dim light of the ceiling lamps provided any illumination as Leos turned around and clomped back toward the main doors to the Hall. One opened as he approached. Grotuk waited on the other side amid the usual contingent of guards, but now two extra guards carrying shiny weapons stood nearby. He wasn't smiling.

"We will return to your room," Grotuk growled. "Please to follow me."

CHAPTER 17

KAZO DELA TAN

No, the gong didn't sound when Leos left the hall. He was aware only of the slam of the door as it closed behind him.

As he followed Grotuk back to his room through a side door in the entry hall, and with the two guards marching behind, he mulled over in his mind what'd just happened. All he knew for sure was that he'd been sentenced to this crazy 'Kazo' thing, and from the sound of Coreaje's voice he figured it must be serious, like a contraption, or a device of some sort. He also figured his relationship with Esmerelda was probably finished. But his mind kept jerking back to one particularly confusing item. Something odd, something a little inconsistent, kept popping up and he didn't know what to make of it. Esmerelda said that before the oroban was discovered in his room, Coreaje had decided he could "go." But go where? Back to Anthanos? That couldn't be. Coreaje didn't want him to communicate with his home planet. Where else could he go? Nothing suggested itself. But now, because of the oroban, he had to visit this 'Kazo' thing. What did the oroban have to do with it? And what the hell *is* that damn thing? The whole meeting left him confused.

Leos stayed in his room all night. He didn't venture down the hall to the ice machine to get a cold drink. He watched a movie on one of the entertainment channels, but mostly he stared out the window, wondering what the stupid contraption was. "Kazo" was Nytandran for "head," but head of what? After several hours of ruminating uselessly about the meaning of the term, and of the object itself, and of watching what he thought was an inordinate amount of traffic on the Palace up-ramp, he went to bed and slept soundly, awakened only when Grotuk pounded on the door and bellowed through it.

"Please to get ready, Mr. Leos. In thirteen minutes we must leave."

"Do I get any breakfast?"

"No."

Leos glanced outside into the black sky through the front window of his room. The clear desert air sparkled with the lights of a million stars, and a few lights of the city twinkled in the valley below, though most of the buildings were dark. As he stared out the window, a twinkle of light well to his left caught his eye and he looked down toward the up-ramp. Headlights of hundreds of Nytandran vehicles stretched in single file up the ramp from the city. Each vehicle had one headlight set right in the apex of that stubby cone that constituted the front end. The line ran so far the lights merged into one continuous line of white that petered out well past the airport. Yet the northern descending ramp was empty.

I wonder where they're going?

Leos donned a clean set of dark blue pants and a white shirt, and combed his hair and brushed his teeth. He stepped to the door and opened it. Grotuk and the two armed guards stood outside.

"Please to follow me," Grotuk said.

Grotuk led Leos down the hallway in the Guest Quarters. The guards, walking in lock step a few strides behind, held their weapons tightly against their chests which produced a spooky *click-click-click* as the weapons tapped against the heavy buckles and clasps on their uniforms. At the far end of the building Grotuk turned, not right as was Leos's usual route to the Royal Family Residence, but left into an unfamiliar side hallway. This hallway led into other hallways, and the little group kept walking, turning right, then left, then right again, over and over, headed into what seemed like a maze that led deeper and deeper into the hills behind the palace. They descended dusty stairs and trudged through dark, grimy tunnels past wretched, shabby doors leading to side rooms containing God-knows-what. They wound around balconies that overlooked deep chasms, and they marched along flimsy, swaying catwalks suspended over sheer cliffs from which tentacles of darkness and dread reached up and snapped at them. They plunged back into a long hallway smelling of moisture and mold and mildew and must, lit by tiny ceiling lights that gave barely sufficient illumination to walk by. They strode on and on, gradually circling downward like a helix. At the end of the hallway — it must have been a quarter-anthan long — was a large door, perfectly circular, perhaps six links in diameter, and made of the same dark brown wood as most of the other doors in the Palace.

Grotuk knocked. The hinges of the door, rusty and weary after what may have been many years of supporting the grotesque mass of the door, creaked and groaned and spit as the door slowly swung inward. The room beyond was dark.

Grotuk stepped through the door and Leos and the guards followed.

The guards took positions on each side of the door as it creaked shut, not with a loud bang which might be expected from such a massive door, but with a soft, almost imperceptible thump. A loud metallic clunk from inside the door signified the door had been locked.

As Leos and Grotuk stood in the room for a few nanosectors, lights began to slowly illuminate the immediate area where the two stood. A sound that Leos didn't recognize filled the air — like a group of people far away, milling around and whispering or murmuring, similar to what might be heard from a crowd waiting for a show or cinema. Grotuk led Leos away from the door and directed him to a chair standing oddly by itself in the middle of the dirt floor.

"Please to sit here."

"What's going on?"

"Remain quiet." Grotuk latched a seat belt around Leos's waist. "Keep your hands down at your side."

As soon as the belt was tight, Grotuk took a few steps back. The chair began to rise, pushed from below by a hydraulic ram that shot Leos upward into the chilly darkness.

"Hey! What the . . . ?" The chair swayed a little as it ascended, and Leos grabbed the arms to stay in the seat, though the belt would have held him anyway. About fifty links in the air the chair stopped. It swayed somewhat, forward and back, side to side, but the swaying stopped after a few nanosectors. Then it inched upward a few more links. Leos looked around, trying to gain some perspective of where he might be, but he couldn't see anything in the intense blackness. He glanced down, but the light at the bottom had been extinguished. He lifted his head, again to try and figure out what was going on, when, with a loud *wham* that startled him so much his heart skittered into high gear, from his right and left sides two metal plates, each with a C-shaped cutout along matching edges slammed shut around his neck, holding him tightly in a rigid neck-lock.

"Hey! What the hell? What is this? Let me outta here!" Leos banged with his fists on the bottoms of the plates, but the plates were cold, hard steel and they held him tight. He was trapped.

As soon as he started yelling and struggling to escape, from below and from all sides came a huge chorus of the same hoots and hollers and catcalls he'd heard the first day he was on this planet, and he jumped when the noise hit him. He stopped struggling. This time, the jeering was from hundreds, maybe thousands of Nytandrans, and as the lights illuminated larger and larger areas of the room, he could see the people in grandstands on all sides in a circular formation, thousands of people, round-headed and oval-headed, taunting and heckling him.

"What the hell. What is this?"

He took a look at his predicament. He could turn his head from side to side and even tilt it a little upward, but there was much more to his imprisonment than the two steel plates that held him. He was trapped in a huge apparatus, a smaller version of the railroad tracks that crossed the deserts all over the planet. Two steel rails, about two links apart, were held together by ties of a rusty-looking metal, and his head was clamped between the rails at one side of this contraption. Something red stained the rails and ties. The track took the form of a huge circle several hundred links in diameter, and the entire monstrosity was suspended fifty links in the air, over the jeering crowd below. Something must run on this circle of track. But what? And why was his head clamped between the rails?

He faced inward, toward the center of the circle, and he couldn't tilt his head very far backward to look up, but as the illumination in the room increased he saw that immediately above the track in which he was held was another circular track, exactly the same size and shape, about five links higher up. The upper track paralleled the lower track precisely, the two tracks the same distance apart all the way around. But nothing rode on either track—and that just added to his confusion.

"What's going on? Where the hell am I?" Leos said, loudly for all to hear, but that just made the shouts and laughs and heckling from below grow louder. He decided to keep his ponderings to himself. *Is some train supposed to come along and run me down and slice my head off?* The thought scared him as soon as he conceived it and he tried to put it out of his mind, but he couldn't tell if he was right.

Confused and disoriented, he sat there for a full Nytandran minute, staring at the upper and lower tracks. The jeers and shouts and whistles continued from below, heckling and flustering him, driving him to distraction, and he struggled even more to free himself, but he soon came to the discomforting realization that those two plates weren't going to budge, and he decided to examine the apparatus in more detail.

That's when he saw the blade.

Shaped like an axe blade without a handle, the blade slid on its side on the rails of the upper track, the sharp edge forward. Only a few deci-links thick at the back end, the blade tapered to a broad, slightly curved front end that appeared to be about three links wide, wide enough to overlap the rails on which it slid. Made of a shiny, highly polished metal, it reminded Leos of the metal that covered the anti-grav coils in the fuel tank of Grok's spaceship, and it flashed and glistened in the lights that now illuminated the entire room.

That's one helluva big axe blade.

The blade started from Leos's left. It came around above his head and passed off to his right, sliding easily on the upper track, as though it slid on a thin film of oil between it and the track. He wondered what made it move. It wasn't attached to anything, and nothing pushed it. It was just the blade, moving slowly along the upper track, singing and zinging against the rails as it went.

The blade swung slowly around the circle, picking up speed as it moved. Occasionally it passed over what sounded like a sharpening stone set between the rails, a stone that zinged the blade and sharpened it, readying it for slicing . . . but for slicing what? It was on the upper track and that didn't make sense.

Is this thing just supposed to scare me? Make me think it's going to chop my head off with that blade? It would have to be on the lower track to do that. Is there a way for it to get down to the lower track? Or is there another blade on the lower track?

He scanned both tracks, up and down, over and under, above and below, but he couldn't find a second blade, and he couldn't see any way for the upper blade to descend to the lower track.

The blade continued to pick up speed. The first few revolutions took several Nytandran minutes, but the blade gained speed with each revolution, and after about the tenth revolution it zipped around in under a minute. And by that time it wasn't passing over the sharpening stones anymore.

It must be going a hundred anthans per sub.

But Leos still couldn't figure out what made the blade move. Or how it could get down to the lower track — if that's what it did.

As the blade's speed increased, the calls from the audience grew louder and more insistent. Each time the blade passed above Leos's head, it made a loud *zwing*, rising in pitch as it approached, and dropping as it passed over his head and moved away. The hooting and hollering from the audience rose and fell exactly in sync as the blade passed over his head.

By about the twentieth revolution, the blade seemed to have settled down to a constant speed, and Leos became less concerned with his own welfare. At first, when the blade passed over his head, he instinctively ducked — as well as he could trapped between the rails — but by now this whole contraption had become almost a novelty as he watched the blade slide over the upper track, round and round, going nowhere in one helluva big hurry. *Maybe they're just trying to scare me.* His heart pounded a little less and he wasn't bothered as much when the blade swooshed by above his head, nor when the shouts and hollers rose and fell, still in sync with the blade. He didn't duck anymore, but he still didn't understand why he was trapped in this stupid device.

Then he found out.

As soon as the blade passed the point on the upper track diametrically opposite from where he was held, Leos saw the one thing about this apparatus that made his heart freeze in his chest. The blade had made about its twenty-fifth revolution—he lost count a long time ago—and the rails of the upper track split crosswise into two parts. The tip ends of the rails on the right side settled into a notch in the lower track, forming a long, gently-sloping curved ramp that descended from the upper to the lower. The blade swung around one more time, back over Leos's head, headed for the ramp. It still moved rapidly, over a hundred anthans per sub. It slid down the ramp as easily as a train changes tracks through a switch—it even gained a little momentum in the transition. But now it was on the lower track.

The noise from the audience grew. They yelled and screamed. They applauded and hooted.

Leos's eyes turned as large as soup bowls. He swallowed hard. "Oh, shit."

Well, I guess this is it, folks – it's been nice. I had a good life to now, until I got kidnapped and brought to this miserable planet. What a glorious end. What a magnificent departure! Am I on the video? Where's Tama? Why isn't she here? Am I in her heart? Doesn't she realize the sacrifice I made for her? All I did for her? Tell the Information Services to remember me in the news reports. I'm here, folks, I exist! I think, therefore I die!

Leos watched the blade approach and his eyes grew even larger. He let out a sickening scream and struggled to free himself, but he was securely trapped, and those metal plates wouldn't budge. The blade came closer and closer. The noise from the crowd grew into a chanting—swelling and expanding, rising and spreading, gaining in fervor and intensity as the blade approached. He clamped his eyes shut, gritted his teeth and grimaced hard, jamming into spastic rigidity every muscle in his face. He whispered a tiny prayer for his mom and Tama, and waited for the blade to slice into his neck.

The blade approached. His heart pounded faster and faster, the chanting of the crowd grew louder and louder, the blade drew closer and closer. Then from a point about two links beside his left ear came an absolutely sickening metallic sound . . .

CHAPTER 18

THE ROCKET SHIP

. . . **CLANK!**

A huge cry of applause and cheers, of excitement and elation, of bravos and hurrahs rose from the audience as the blade slammed into the heavy metal sheath that flipped up from between the rails of the lower track mere decilinks from Leos's naked neck. The two metal plates snapped apart and the chair dropped like a stone down to ground level. The belt unlatched automatically as the chair neared the bottom, and when it slammed to a stop he skidded out feet first, landing on his butt on the dusty floor. The applause and shouts turned to laughter, a high-pitched laughter that, coming from those hundreds of onlookers, throbbed painfully in his ears and threatened to burst his eardrums.

But Leos didn't consciously recognize the laughter. His mind was still confined between the metal plates, still waiting for the blade to arrive, still screaming silently for an end to the horror that'd been courted on him by this hideous device. He rolled over and lay face down on the dirt floor, slowly coming to grasp the reality of his situation. His head spun, he was weak and he couldn't stand, and he felt sick to his stomach. His side hurt too, but he didn't understand how the apparatus injured his side. Above the laughter and the catcalls was another voice behind him, yelling.

"Run! Run!" the voice said. One of the guards stood over him, poking him in the side with the front end of his weapon. "See the light over there? Run!"

Leos looked at the guard and vaguely understood that the guard wanted him to do something, but he didn't know what. His head still spun and he wasn't sure what his real situation was. Was he dead? Did the blade slice his head off, or was he still alive, still able to function? He felt at his neck—it was still there, his head was still attached. What the hell was going on? He became angry. Could he do as he was told—run? Most of the lights in the room had been dimmed, and when he looked around for the light the guard pointed to, he found it as a tiny point of light on the other side of the room. Sunlight streamed through the opening—it looked like a door to the outside. He got up and ran.

Yes! Yes! Get out of here. Get outside. Get away from this horror. Get away. Forever.

He ran as fast as he could, but he stumbled and fell repeatedly, and eruptions of laughter jabbed him at every misstep. But he kept getting back on his feet and kept scrambling toward that door as fast as feet and legs would carry him. His only thought, *get out of here.* His clothes were dusty and dirty, and the dust stung his eyes and felt gritty in his mouth, but he made it to the door and ran into the bright morning sunlight, into the precipitating heat of the coming day.

Outside the door lay a broad, flat plain, stark and naked for many anthans to the north and east. To Leos's left, a line of Nytandrans led toward—*what is that?—an airplane—or, no, it's a spaceship*—like a smaller version of the one he came to Nytandra in. Its long slender wings had been folded back into a delta wing configuration, and it ended in a T-tail with the horizontal stabilizers at the top of the vertical. A narrow beam of sunlight glinted off the shiny rocket engine bell at the rear of the craft. As he ran, the onlookers laughed and jeered at him, and pointed toward the ship.

"Run! Run! Run toward the ship! Run!" Some picked up dirt and pebbles and threw at him as he ran.

Now Leos ran more easily, he didn't fall as much. He ran and ran, toward the ship, closer and closer, leaving the noise behind—finally to get away from all the noise! The door to the ship stood wide open, and he ran up a short ramp into the ship. The door led into a small entry room, like an airlock, and in the bulkhead to Leos's left was another open door to the front cockpit with seats for a pilot and co-pilot. Standing just inside the cockpit door was Grotuk. His arms were crossed over his chest and he snarled as he met Leos.

"This is your spaceship. Eminence has given it to you. In about five minutes it will take you to green planet. It cannot be deprogrammed. There you may live out your days. You must land by yourself. Landing is not programmed. All instructions for operation are on the ship's navigational computer. In the back of the ship are food and water and bunks to sleep, and we have packed a valise of your clothing. Good luck."

Grotuk turned and left the cockpit, but as he reached the entry door, he shouted back over his shoulder, "If you are to return to our planet, we will not sheathe our blade."

The outer door swung closed behind Grotuk as he left the ship. The ramp rolled away, and the ship was ready to leave. Leos sat down in the left-hand seat, the pilot's seat, in the cooled air of the spaceship.

Still dazed, he couldn't comprehend what'd just happened, and he had to take a minute to examine his situation. He was alive—at least he thought so. Or was he? Was this merely the result of the random and chaotic firing of his cerebral neurons as they began to die from the anoxia of exsanguination? He looked around at the ship. It seemed real enough. He touched the control panel. Cold hard metal it was to be sure, the same silvery metal with the faint gold luster he'd seen in so many other Nytandran vehicles. It was all real and he seemed to be alive, but the events of the past few minutes were swirling around in his head like a monstrous whirlwind, and it made him dizzy and weak. His whole body trembled.

He thought by now everything would have been over, that he would never live to see anyone or anything ever again. He couldn't believe what had happened. He was relieved to be alive, no question, but nothing about the past hour or so made sense, and it made him angry that they would treat him this way, that they would play with his life and his emotions like this. He felt like a child's toy, a rattle to be shaken whenever the child wanted, carelessly tossed aside when unwanted. He covered his face with his hands, trying to control the shivering.

"Why didn't they just tell me to leave, and get it over with?" he mumbled. "Why go through all this?"

Now he hated everyone and everything about this planet. He hated Coreaje and Grotuk and Grok and Krok and the Minister and even Esmerelda.

Oh, God, Esmerelda! Why is she so tantalizing? Why did I permit her so easily to enter my soul? Why was she so captivating and lovely? And that skin! That dark green skin that's so elegant and so royal—so Princess-like. Still, it's so unusual and odd and bizarre. How dare she live on this planet—a planet that puts up with the likes of Greenhouse Gass and public nudity and public fornication and all that crap—she should be ashamed of herself. She should go back to her planet, wherever that is.

As Leos sat in the coolness of the ship for a few more minutes, trying to make sense of his situation, he became aware of the sound of laughter and jeering again, but faintly, as though far away. He looked up. Thirty or forty Nytandrans had congregated around the front of the ship, laughing and pointing at him through the front window and making threatening, obscene gestures. Some threw dirt and small stones at the ship.

I better get my ass off this planet as soon as possible. Time for commiser-

ation will come later. How long 'til the engine starts? He quickly scanned the control panel to find the main computer screen, hoping that the time was near for the ship to leave.

The screen was black except for a countdown of white numbers in the Nytandran system, approaching zero. As it neared zero, the ship came to life. Another screen came up, white now, with a list of several options. Lights came on all around the control panel as instruments were activated, and secondary com screens flickered to life. Servo control mechanisms began clicking, sending power and electronic instructions to all areas of the ship. A turbine started whirring and fuel flowed into the engine. The crowd around the front of the ship scattered as the whine grew louder, and when the countdown reached zero, the engine ignited in a huge thud of noise from the rear, and the ship began to roll forward. Slowly it picked up speed, and with Leos scrambling to fasten his safety belt and shoulder harness, it roared across the dusty plain, lifted into the air, and shot upward at a 50-degree angle.

The acceleration built up to almost 3 G's—it appeared as a digital display on a small com screen in the center of the control panel in front of him—pressing him solidly into the cushioned seat. The ship took him higher and higher, up into the stratosphere, past the ionosphere, through the mesosphere and thermosphere, and eventually into outer space where it settled into a holding orbit around the planet. When the engine stopped, about five breathless Nytandran minutes after leaving the surface, Leos relaxed in the microgravity to consider his position more calmly.

Where am I now? He looked at one of the smaller com screens in the control panel. All of the information about the orbit, including orbital period, orbital velocity, altitude, apogee and perigee, and a few other odd notations, was arranged in a short list.

But nothing in that list told him where he was above the surface of the planet. One of the entries in that list, the elapsed time indicator, let him know that he had about ten Nytandran minutes before the engine would start and blast him out of orbit toward the green planet, and with nothing to do until then, he grew curious about where the ship was above the plains of Nytandra below.

Mixed with that curiosity, though, was a dread, a real trepidation about his fate. Esmerelda had told him tales in considerable detail about her planet, she described the trees that gave it its dominant color, she portrayed her people and their life. They were the original people of the planet, with no sophisticated infrastructure like Nytandra, living quietly among the trees in a primitive, classless society. They knew nothing of rockets and spaceships and interplanetary travel. So, he gathered, once he arrived he likely would never leave. No one will come to get him, either.

She'd also mentioned a vague danger to living there, but she never went into detail, leaving him to puzzle over the details in his mind.

With nothing to do until the engine burn that would send him on the long trip to the green planet, he unfastened the shoulder harness and leaned forward to get a better look through the front and side windows, straining to see if he could identify any visible landmarks. This was a spectacle he'd seen only on images on a com screen, and he quickly became fascinated with the desert planet below. The ship's orbit was tilted about thirty degrees to the planet's equator, and he was treated to a view of large areas of the planet's deserts. But he didn't recognize any geological features.

Patches of brilliant white or umber or magenta or ebony dotted the tan sands of the Nytandran desert, but from orbit, the predominant color was the drab of the desert. Vast areas of sand and rock drifted by, broken occasionally by fault lines that poked above ground as long slender cliffs, towering over the lowlands as rocky precipices or craggy rock walls.

Leos gazed longingly at the terrain below. "There's so much room on the planet, but so little water," he mumbled. He saw no lakes or rivers or oceans, not like those his mom had shown him on the blue planet. Nor did he expect any. Coreaje's elegant descriptions and illuminating portrayals with which he regaled Leos and Esmerelda every evening at the fourth meal, as well as the images Leos had seen on the com screen in the ship's library during the long voyage to Nytandra, had vividly impressed on him the immensity and total lifelessness of the open desert that lay just outside the cities. Yet, as he continued to scan the desert below, the vast areas of emptiness reminded him, at least in one small way, of the empty areas outside the Lifezone on his own planet. He noted one important difference, though — the sands of Nytandra didn't possess the rich golden brown tint of those of Anthanos. Nytandran sands were more of a pale tan, a washed out khaki, a blanched beige, and they looked much less inviting.

Every now and then, a few patches of green appeared randomly on the sands below. These were the cities with their surrounding cultivated fields, sitting like oases in the desert, able to survive only because of the presence of water below the surface.

Green? I thought photosynthetic pigments on Nytandra were purple. Oh, that's right, I remember Esmerelda telling me that domesticated plants used a green pigment. That's wild. Green and purple. What a weird combination.

From this point of view, Leos now understood in substantially more detail why Coreaje had vetoed his idea of having Anthanians move to Nytandra. So much room, yet so little water. Coreaje loved his planet, that was clear, but he could be intensely realistic about its limitations and drawbacks. His absolute rejection of Leos's request was a sound, if irritating, example of his pragmatism. Leos shook his head sadly at the thought.

As he continued to scan the planet below, his eyes drifted to the railroad lines that connected the cities, barely visible from orbit as grayish-brown threads. He could also make out the photovoltaic arrays, three long narrow black filaments circling the planet at the equator, their collecting panels pointed directly toward the sun, the primary source of power for the cities and railroads.

As he stared out the front window, entranced by the planet beneath, a sharp metallic click came from somewhere in the room.

"What was that?" It wasn't a loud click and he wasn't alarmed. But he hadn't heard anything like it since he arrived in orbit, and he became curious about its source. He glanced at the control panel, but nothing seemed amiss. The computer screen showed no incorrect readings, still several minutes before engine start. He thought it might be a relay doing its job, but the click had come from behind, and the right side of his neck began to tingle and he instinctively reached up and massaged the spot.

"That couldn't have come from behind. There's no one else on board. Or is there . . .?" He raised his head intending to turn around, but he glimpsed a reflection of a dark object in the front windshield and a faint shadow that moved across the control panel. From behind came a familiar voice.

"Hello, Leos."

CHAPTER 19

VOYAGE TO THE GREEN PLANET

"Aaahhh!"

Had it not been for the waist belt holding him down, Leos would have come straight out of his seat. He whirled around to face the stowaway.

"Esmerelda—holy crap! What the dinfrizzle are you doing here?" He unfastened his seat belt and stood up in the microgravity. His eyes were like saucers and you could have run a train into his mouth.

"I must come with you," Esmerelda said. She wasn't wearing that ridiculous white-and-brown outfit now. She had on a much more logical dress for someone moving around in microgravity, a neatly pressed pale blue jumpsuit with her royal crest embroidered on the chest pocket. In the center of the crest was the Nytandran equivalent of the letter 'E,' the first letter of her royal name. The suit fit her graceful figure in a much more dignified manner. She drifted toward the two pilot's seats from the door, pulling herself along using the handholds built into the ceiling.

"What!? Good God, no! You can't come with me." He pointed directly at her. "You gotta leave."

"I cannot leave. I must come with you. I have spoken to you about this before." Esmerelda spoke softly and quietly, and under any other circumstances her words would have been warm and soothing. Leos wasn't about to be soothed.

"What are you talking about? Your father will kill me. He'll hunt both of us down."

"I do not think he will find us on my planet." She gave him a soft but passionate kiss on the lips.

Leos just stared at Esmerelda. He took a few seconds to try to collect his thoughts and think of something to say. Grotuk's final words, "We will not sheathe our blade," and the image of the Kazo Dela Tan erupted in his mind. He could see the blade coming at him on the lower track, but this time the sheath didn't pop up miraculously at the last nanosector to keep the blade from shearing his head off.

"Oh, God, I'm a dead man," was all he could think to say.

"I must return to my planet. It is important to me."

Leos pulled himself back down into his seat and stared into empty space. "Oh, God, I am so screwed. I'm a friggin' dead man."

Esmerelda drifted to the co-pilot's seat and settled in. She latched the seat belt and shoulder harness. "Oh, no, I do not think you are dead. I must travel to my planet. I know of it. We will travel there, and I will meet my people. I have wanted this for many years, and I must do this. I can do no other. My father will understand."

"Understand?" Leos jerked his head up, now for the first time in his relationship with Esmerelda, angry with her. "Do you realize what you've done? He'll hunt us down. He'll bring us back to Nytandra and he'll chop my head off. God knows what he'll do to you." Leos paused and glared at Esmerelda. She shook her head and started to say something, but he lit into her again. "Did Grotuk know about this? Did he let you on board?"

Esmerelda remained cool against Leos's anger. She seemed to be trying to diffuse it by maintaining her princess-like demeanor. "No, Grotuk did not know about this. He almost discovered me as I hid in the back storage room when he made his final inspection before they gave the ship to you. But I hid well from him, and he is innocent. Leos, listen—"

"How did you get on this ship, anyway?" Leos rotated his seat toward the front and latched his belt.

"I sneaked upon the ship last night. I brought some food and water. There is plenty of oxygen for two people, and there are two bunks. This is a spaceship for two people, and we will be comfortable."

"How did you know what was going to happen? When your father sentenced me last night, you left the room."

"Father told me later what he desired to do. Then only I decided what I must do. Mlada and I gathered some food and clothing, and she and I came and I remained through the night. Please do not be angry with me. I must do this."

Esmerelda's voice sounded so comforting, but Leos didn't want to be comforted. "Mlada? Mlada helped you? Your father will kill her."

"She will be quiet. She will deny. She has been through much before."

"Did anyone see you and Mlada coming to the ship last night?"

"I do not think so. It was dark and the ship was dark. No one saw us."

"Weren't there guards around?"

"Yes. Several. But we were of the sneaking type. We waited until they left. They did not see us."

"That's good. I hope." Leos put his elbows on the control panel and buried his head in his hands. "I can't believe this is happening. I'm a dead—" But then he jerked his head up. "Hold on a microsector!" he yelled in his native language, then went back to Nytandran. The excitement sent his heart racing. "We're still in orbit! We can land and let you off." He scrutinized the center com screen, scanning all the different options, looking for the one that would order the ship to land again.

"You cannot land. The ship is programmed to take us to my planet."

"Oh, crap. That's right. Of course." Landing back on Nytandra was not one of the options. He settled back in his seat, staring straight ahead, dejected and spent. "You're right. We have to go all the way."

"Leos, do not be concerned for yourself or for me. We will be safe. I am certain of this."

"God, I hope so."

As Esmerelda had done so often at a meal or during gentle conversation in the evening as they sat together on the patio outside the Family Dining Room, she reached over and placed her hand on Leos's arm. "Leos, look at me."

That was her signal that what she was about to say was very serious. He turned toward her. A glimmer of light reflected from the planet's surface flickered in her green-blue eyes. "There is another reason I must come with you."

"What is that?"

"They will kill you."

"What? Who? What are you talking about?"

"The people who live on my planet. You remember, it is called *Jon-Set-Tom.*"

"Yes—yes! I remember. But . . ."

"They are my people. I am afraid for you that they will kill you after you land. You do not speak their language. I will help you. I know of the planet. I will talk to them for you."

"That's good of you."

"Then we will live there. Together."

"Okay. If you say so. By the way, I have to ask. How did you survive the take-off? The G-load meter went up to 3 G's."

"I sat on one of the bunks. My back was to the wall. I used two pillows. It was okay. I do not wish to do it again."

As Esmerelda spoke, a broad warning tone came from the computer, and the numbers signaling a short countdown flashed on the screen. The engine was about to start and blast the ship out of orbit onto the long, looping elliptical path to the green planet.

"Holy dinfrizzle! We don't have much time! Hold on tight! Here we go!"

CHAPTER 20

DECEPTION

"Mlada! Mlada! Where is that old bitch?"

Coreaje stormed up and down the hallways of the Royal Family Residence. He banged on doors, yelled out windows, and generally raised an uproar in the corridors. Mlada sat in her room at the far end of the hallway in the Family Quarters of the Palace, adjacent to the suite of rooms occupied by Her Royal Preciousness, the Princess Esmerelda. She could hear Coreaje's rantings and she dreaded having to meet him. He'd done this before. His tirades always brought back memories, terrible unpleasant memories of her own planet, memories she would rather forget, but which dominated her every waking hour now that Esmerelda was gone.

Mlada held her breath as Coreaje pounded on her door. But she knew what to say. Her instincts for deceit and deception had been honed through years of life on her native planet. She stepped to the door and opened it.

"Yes, your Eminence?" She genuflected in the presence of an absolute ruler.

"Oh, there you are. Mlada, have you seen Esmerelda? She did not appear for breakfast."

"I have not seen her, your Eminence. She revealed to me her wish to be left alone."

"Nonsense. She didn't come out of her room all day yesterday. She knows we have a meeting with the Minister of Culture and Displays at the beginning of the fifth hour. She is to attend the meeting. This she knows well. Go into her room. Tell her to attend the meeting. I expect to see her at the appointed time."

"Yes, your Eminence."

Coreaje turned on his heel and stomped down the hall. Mlada walked the few steps down the hall to the main door to Esmerelda's suite. She knocked on the door, but as she expected, no answer came. She knocked again, pretending to be concerned that no one was inside. She tried to open the door, but the door was locked. Upon leaving to hide in the spaceship that was to take Leos to the green planet, Esmerelda had locked the door to her chamber from the inside, then exited through Mlada's room.

"If anyone asks," Esmerelda warned her as they walked down the hall toward the rear stairs to begin their trip to the spaceship through the hills behind the Palace, "I told you I wanted to be left alone."

"I understand, Your Preciousness. I will carry out your wishes."

Mlada retreated to her apartment and entered the Princess's Suite. She walked through the empty Suite to the main door, unlocked it, and stepped into the hallway.

"Now it has become time to inform the Ruler."

*   *   *

The knock at the thin wooden door of the house of the Lontor family on the eternally shrouded planet *Non-Dre-Ahdenu* was unexpected—yet in many ways it was not. It was a hard knock, not the gentle tap that might be expected from a good friend coming over for an evening visit. The light had almost faded from the sky, and the darkness—as pervasive a darkness as could be found on any planet—had settled over the little house on the outskirts of the town where the young Mlada and her family lived. The cool air of the evening edged between some of the boards of the house, forcing the residents to start a fire in the cast iron stove that sat to one side of the living room. At five years old, Mlada played on the floor at her parents' feet with her favorite dolls. When the knock came, she stopped play immediately and gripped tightly one of the dolls with both hands. Her mother and father stiffened visibly, and her mother raised a hand to her mouth to stifle a gasp.

"Mlada!" her mother whispered hoarsely. "You know what to do. Go to your special place. Now!"

"But mother—"

"Do as your mother says," her father warned, his voice strict but not harsh.

"It's the Talatan Guards, isn't it?" Mlada's older brother Tlan said.

"Hush," their mother said. "Mlada, run!"

Mlada knew what to do. She gathered her dolls and dropped them into the small satchel her parents provided. She removed her shoes so her feet would not make a sound on the bare floor and scampered toward the rear of the house. She ran past the kitchen and bathroom and through her parents' room. She headed into the small bedroom she shared with her brother—it was really nothing more than a small storage room off the main bedroom—and tiptoed across the floor, reaching her bed just as her father opened the front door to the Guards.

Mlada fell to the floor and froze, not wanting to make a sound while the Guards were in the house.

"You were late in opening the door," the Captain of the Guards said. Mlada could hear his dark booming voice from her place on the floor in the bedroom. "You are required to open the door in twenty seconds or less."

Mlada crawled under the bed from the foot, past the boxes of her brother's clothes that her parents stored there, and with her fingertips carefully pried open the narrow trap door lying beneath the bed. The old metal hinges that held the door creaked with a tiny mouse-like squeak and she stopped, holding the door in one place for a second, then she slowly pressed the door open slightly more, hesitating briefly at each creak. She held it open with her left hand while she dropped the satchel in, then she herself slipped into the recess between the door and the floor joists onto the small rug that gave her the slightest cushion against the wood panel on which she lay. She kept the door cracked open only the tiniest amount so she could hear, ready to drop the door completely closed should the Guards enter the room.

"I am terribly sorry," her father said. "We were in the back room. It will not happen again."

"I am giving your house twenty marks," the Captain said. "It happened once two weeks ago. I am very concerned about this house. We have heard that you are keeping a young girl here. Is that true?"

"No," Mlada heard her mother reply. "We have only the boy, Tlan. Here he is. He is our only child. That is the regulation. We have complied."

"But we have reports from several people that they have seen a small girl in the vicinity of your house. Do you deny it?"

"Yes, we deny it."

"Then how do you explain this?"

A sudden quietness developed in the front room, and the lack of conversation seemed only to magnify the clomp of heavy boots as several of the Guards began to search the house. It wasn't an exhaustive search; they poked their noses into the various rooms, pausing at the door to the bedroom where Mlada lay hidden, but only to turn on the light. They did not enter or search the room. Mlada silently dropped the trapdoor completely shut and listened for the footsteps as the Guards withdrew.

Mlada learned later the Captain had shown her parents a photograph of a small girl in the backyard of her house, and the girl was her, but her parents denied it, saying it was the daughter of a friend, not Mlada at all. Only a friend who had come to visit.

At first it'd all been a game. Her parents showed her the trapdoor hidden under the bed and taught her how to use it, quietly and surreptitiously, repeating the drill over and over until she could enter with her playmate dolls within a minute or so, and stay until her mother or father called her to come out. Each time she stayed quiet and hidden, repetition after repetition, through drills and the real thing, waiting patiently to come out, staying quiet, breathing slowly and calmly to avoid detection by the Talatan Guards.

But by her fifth year, she knew it was no longer a game, that she was expected to hide and stay hidden for an hour if necessary, and that it would happen over and over, almost every other week, or even every week, or several times a week, until other arrangements could be made. And she lived like this with her family year after year, hiding from the guards when they came to the house to search for her because she was the second child, and two children in one family were forbidden on her planet.

It scared her, too. She was too young to understand the real reason for hiding like this, but she knew it was serious, and she began to be scared more and more often. She hated the little recess, the terrifying closeness of the opening, the musty smell of the floorboards that lay over her, only inches from her face, the darkness that left her unable to see. She could run her hands over the little valise that contained her beloved dolls, but she couldn't play with them, only touch, and she wanted so very much to pull them out and hold them close, but her parents said no, and she complied. Her heart would pound, tears would stream down her face, and she would emerge when her parents called, crying and scared even more than when she went in because she knew she would have to go back again, soon.

Eventually, she grew too big to fit comfortably in the little recess hollowed out among the floor joists, and other arrangements were made.

*   *   *

"What the hell are you telling me, old woman!? Are you saying Esmerelda is nowhere to be found?"

Coreaje, fists on hips, stood in front of Mlada in the Minister's office, which also served as the outer receiving chamber to The Ruler's private domain. The Minister cowered majestically behind his desk in a far corner of the room while Coreaje questioned Mlada.

"It appears that this is true, your Eminence."

"Where is she, then?"

"I am not knowledgeable of her whereabouts, your Eminence."

"She has to be around somewhere. She couldn't have left the city. She can't just get on a train and travel. She would be noticed and I would have heard about it. Security may not always be on top of everything, but even they couldn't miss *her*."

"I am in complete agreement, your Eminence."

"The only place she could go without attracting attention is to remain on the Palace grounds. Unless she took a limousine into town." Coreaje turned to the Minister. "There are some places in town where her presence would not be unusual. She has many friends in the city. Did she requisition transportation?"

"No, your Eminence, she did not. All our ground-maneuvering vehicles are accounted for. None have been removed from the storage depot. None of our drivers report having taken her into the city."

"Therefore, she must still be in the Palace. Or on the grounds. Search the place! Search everywhere! Bring her to me."

Coreaje stormed back into his private suite and slammed the door. The receiving room was quiet as the Minister stalked out from behind his desk. Mlada was about to leave when the Minister spoke.

"Hssst—old woman."

Mlada turned back to face the Minister. He stared directly into her big brown eyes and his angry scowl set off an alarm in her brain. "If you are of the knowing type, tell me now and save from yourself the fate of the Anthanian—and without the clemency." He practically spat his words at her. "You and Esmerelda were close—very close. I know this for a fact. She confided in you much. It is hard to believe you do not know something of where she is, even if you are not knowledgeable of her exact presence at all times."

Mlada stiffened. She stared back into the Minister's eye slits, barely able to see his eyes in the bright light of the room, and barely able to conceal her contempt for the man. "I don't know what you're talking about," she said, and left the room.

*   *   *

The rest of the day came and went uneventfully, and the passing of the evening and the rising of the sun brought a new day.

Mlada spent this day in her room. She admitted no one. She would not leave. Coreaje and the Minister were becoming increasingly agitated about the disappearance of the Princess, and the pain of deceit that Esmerelda had asked of Mlada was taking its toll. Mlada slept little during the night. She skipped breakfast and her morning toiletries were disrupted. She desperately wanted to tell Coreaje or the Minister what she knew. She wanted to spill everything and relieve the torment in her mind, but she didn't want to sacrifice her bond with Esmerelda, a bond she cherished in her heart above any other friendship or obligation she'd ever had. But this deception and subterfuge was too much like her life on her own planet and she wished it to stop.

She turned her mind to the day she arrived on Nytandra six years earlier. The necessity for the lies and fabrications, the isolation that was forced on her by the stealth in all her dealings, the deceit that had dominated her life on her planet had ceased the moment she stepped off the spaceship at the Lox Atendra spaceport. She felt free for the first time in her life, free at last to be herself, to use her own name, to have friends.

She immediately met with a small group of other émigrés from her planet, *Non-Dre-Ahdenu* (which she abbreviated as *'Non'* for the Nytandrans who had difficulty pronouncing the third, fourth, and fifth syllables) and began to learn the Nytandran language. As one of the few from *Non* on Nytandra, Mlada had become something of a celebrity. With her experience as governess to the children of a high-ranking official on *Non*, she soon attracted the eye of Coreaje, and about a year after her arrival the job offer was made.

Esmerelda didn't immediately accept Mlada. Her mother had only recently passed away and Esmerelda was still in mourning, still in denial that she needed anyone at all to provide guidance to her life. The first few months Mlada spent with Esmerelda were turbulent, even chaotic at times, and frequently brought tears to Mlada's eyes. At nineteen, Esmerelda was fully convinced she'd become a mature woman, even though she knew the legal age for maturity was twenty-four, and that level had been set several years earlier by Coreaje's planet-wide decree.

But Mlada recognized immediately the potential of the young princess. She appreciated in her a degree of intelligence and poise rarely seen — or at least rarely allowed to surface — on Nytandra, and Mlada understood, perhaps better than Coreaje himself, that the young woman could bring a valuable counterbalance to the male-oriented society that dominated life on the planet. Mlada pushed Esmerelda to take an interest in arts and culture, so long languishing in the brown-collar, labor-intensive society of the planet, and to speak out against the despicable treatment of women: the prostitution, the public nudity and fornication, the sexual slave trade, and the pornography that were all too prominent in Nytandran society.

Coreaje assigned Mlada this room in the family living quarters because it was adjacent to the Princess's suite. She was to remain close to the Princess, to not let her out of her sight, to keep control and instruction over the Princess and to bring her into adulthood.

"Discipline!" Coreaje demanded of her when she started the job.

And discipline she delivered. But the Princess was still missing.

Now the morning light streamed wildly into her room, and the air cooling unit had been activated to counter the heat the intense Nytandran sun would soon deliver. Mlada stood at one of the rear windows in her apartment. Her apartment lay in the southeast corner of the Family Living Quarters, and from either of the two corner windows she could see the mountains that spiked up behind the Palace, still dull in the shade of the morning sun behind them. From the east-facing corner window that overlooked the rear of the Palace she could see the hill that contained the Kazo Dela Tan. On the other side of that hill lay the dusty plain from which the rocket ship had departed. She wished she'd been on that ship.

As she stood at the window, a knock came at her door. It was a quiet knock, two light taps, not more, not hurried or panicky. She opened the door and Grotuk stood outside. But two armed guards stood beside him, and none of the three were smiling. Grotuk growled that characteristic snarl of his.

"You will come with me."

"What is the meaning of this?" Mlada asked. She stood fast at her place in the doorway.

"Come with me." Grotuk said again. "Minister wishes to see you." He turned and walked down the hall toward the Minister's office. Mlada reluctantly stepped into the hall and closed and locked her door. The two guards accompanied her toward the Minister's office.

"So, old woman," the Minister said. He stood just inside the door and accosted her as soon as she appeared in the doorway. "You don't know anything about the disappearance of the Princess, is that true? Well, I have information that will change your mind. I have found out that you and the Princess were seen in the vicinity of the spaceship that Eminence gave to the degenerate Leos. I talked to a guard who informs me that he saw you and the Princess approach the ship. Do you deny this?"

Mlada knew exactly what she had to say. "I do not deny it. The Princess wished to see the ship. I accompanied her."

"Wished to see the ship? Is that all? She carried a satchel, did she not? Do you deny this?"

"No."

"You were outside the room of the Kazo Dela Tan. The darkness was upon you, but you hid in the shadow and waited until the programmers had left the ship. Do you deny this?"

"No."

"Why carried the Princess a satchel? A bag. A large bag. A full bag. That is unusual, is it not, if she merely wished to 'see' the ship?"

Mlada hesitated. Now the deception had come back onto her. Core-aje and the Minister were beginning to figure things out. She didn't know a guard had seen the two of them as they approached the ship. Her instincts, her sentience, honed after many years on her own planet, had told her that no one was watching, that the way to the ship was clear. But she'd been mistaken, and she went back to review in her mind the details of their surreptitious trip. She and Esmerelda hid in a tiny alcove outside the door to the Kazo Dela Tan, waiting for the programmers to finish and leave. Two guards stood near the boarding ramp to the ship, but they left when the programmers did.

And leave the ship unguarded—why? Well, for one thing, no one would tamper with the ship. Who would want to? It was suitable for one purpose, to take Leos, and Leos alone, to the green planet and strand him there. Only the programmers knew how to override the instructions, and when they were gone she and Esmerelda could board. But one guard must have lingered after the others left. He'd seen them, and now the time had come to end the deception.

"Well, old woman? What have you to say for yourself? Are you in the clear or are you not? Know you where the Princess is? Board the ship did she and leave with the devil Leos?"

"Leos is not a 'devil.' He is a decent young man."

"He is a thief! He is a traitor!"

The Minister's voice pounded in Mlada's ears and she winced at his yelling. "He is not a traitor. He was a good friend to Esmerelda. He listened to her. She spoke of him well at all times. I do not think that—"

"I do not care what you think! He was a traitor! He could not see his hand before his face! Now, old woman, will you tell me where the Princess is or not? Am I to take measures with you?"

Mlada paused. "I will talk only to his Eminence. There is something I must tell him."

"You will tell me!"

"I will tell only the Ruler."

"He is busy."

"Interrupt him."

"I cannot."

"You have the authority. He is in his office at this time. Morning session has not yet begun."

"I will not interrupt."

"You will, or you will not hear what I have to say."

"I am suspicious, old woman. You know something."

"Nevertheless, Coreaje or not at all."

Even behind the darkness of the Minister's face, the flush of anger was visible. "Do not use his personal name in that way in my presence or I will have your head! Come with me."

The Minister and Grotuk led the way. They traveled through the Family Living Quarters to the main building of the Palace, toward the rear of the Grand Hall where Leos had first met Esmerelda. They arrived at a small outer office behind the hall, adjacent to the elaborately appointed anteroom where family members waited before entering the main hall through the side door. The small office led into Coreaje's primary study chamber where he scrutinized the many reports and documents that crossed his desk daily, preparing for the morning session of meetings, appeals, hearings, and conferences that constituted the life of an absolute Ruler. The Minister approached Coreaje's personal assistant and asked for an audience. Coreaje granted it immediately and they entered his office.

Mlada had been in Coreaje's office only once before, when she was formally appointed to the position of Governess to Her Preciousness, The Royal Princess. At that time she was not as much in awe of the Ruler as she probably should have been, and entering his private office had been an adventure. She treated it as a story to be told and retold to friends and acquaintances. But now she trembled when she entered, unsure of her fate in such a precarious position.

The office was as she remembered. Dark paneling lined the walls, and pictures of previous rulers of Nytandra reaching back into distant memory hung from the rafters. Coreaje's desk stood at the far left end of the room. Situated prominently on the wall behind the desk was a large portrait of Esmerelda, painted when she was fourteen Nytandran years of age. She sat in one of the chairs from the little dining room she liked so much, turned slightly to her right, her hands folded in her lap. She smiled for her portrait, and the warm disarming smile she had as an adult was very much in evidence in the painting. But the artist had taken liberties with her image. Perhaps unsure how to depict skin tones of such a deep, rich green, he lightened her skin color slightly and placed her image against a dense maroon curtain as a backdrop in a feeble attempt to diminish the powerful color of her skin.

The Minister and Mlada approached the desk. Coreaje sat reading from a folder of papers, but he looked up as the two entered, glaring directly at Mlada. She stood directly in front of his desk.

"I have read the report from the guard." Coreaje put the papers down and leaned back in his chair. "What have you to say for yourself?"

Mlada bent her knees and nodded her head in obeisance. "Forgive me, your Eminence, I admit I have not been honest with you in this matter, and I offer my apologies. Esmerelda swore me to be of the secretive type, but it is as I feared, the truth will come out. Esmerelda left on the ship you gave to Leos. It was her decision. She has wanted to return to her planet all these many years. This is the truth, so as I swear."

"Yes, I see." Coreaje slumped forward in his chair. "When I first heard the report from the guard, I thought she might board the ship and leave. It would be like her. She was headstrong enough to do this. She wanted to return to her planet."

"She has spoken much of this before, your Eminence."

"Of this I am aware. Perhaps I should not be surprised at her actions."

"She is an adult, now, your Eminence. She has passed her twenty-fourth birthday."

"But she disobeyed my instructions to *not* return to the green planet. This I cannot permit."

"I do not think she disobeyed, your Eminence."

"What?" Coreaje stood and put his fists on the desk and glared at Mlada. "What are you talking about, old woman? Of course, she disobeyed."

Mlada paused, intent on diffusing the anger of Coreaje. His decree to Esmerelda that she never return to her planet had always been so rigid and unyielding that his bullheaded approach had only made her want to go back even more. "Perhaps directly, your Eminence, but in her heart she did not. She spent many hours thinking about her planet and she chose to do as her heart told her. She went to be with her people. She obeyed the beating of her heart. It was to her the only option."

"Curse you, old woman!" Coreaje ran his hands over his bald head and sat back down at his desk. He angrily pushed the papers on his desk aside.

"Eminence," the Minister said. "May I suggest the Kazo Dela Tan? After all, there has been much deceit and deception here on the part of —"

"No, no." Coreaje shook his head slightly without looking up. A drifting tone of sadness filled his voice, a sort of resignation. He swiveled his chair all the way around, away from the tall woman. Mlada couldn't tell what he was looking at, but she did notice that he tilted his bald head backward, as though he was looking up at the painting.

"That is all, Mlada." The gloominess in Coreaje's voice was so heavy it seemed to drip from the walls. "You may leave."

CHAPTER 21

LANDING

"Hold on tight! Here we go!"

For the first time in the ninety Nytandran days since Leos and Esmerelda left orbit around the desert planet, they sat strapped in the two pilot seats of their little ship, waiting for the engine to come to life. The ship was quiet now, their journey nearing its end. They were excited at the approaching termination of the flight, but too tired to become passionate about it—tired of sleeping in microgravity, tired of the boring food selection the Nytandrans imposed on them, and just generally tired of each other and of being cooped up in a cramped spacecraft for so long. Personal hygiene was spare and privacy almost non-existent. In spite of the food Esmerelda had brought, their supply of consumables, especially drinking water, had run low, and they had to limit food intake during the last several Nytandran days to make supplies last. But as the voyage progressed, they watched in fascination as the planet grew slowly larger. Now as they waited for the ship to go into orbit, the planet before them had become a huge ball that took on a deep viridian hue in the brilliant light from the sun and cast an emerald tint on everything in the cockpit. It dominated every hurried preparation the two weary space travelers made for orbit and landing. A few white, wispy clouds dotted the surface of the planet, but by and large the planet's atmosphere was clear.

Their tiny rocket ship was eight thousand anthans from the surface as it began its final approach toward orbital insertion. The ship's computer rotated the ship so the engine faced forward, and when the planet disappeared from view, Leos and Esmerelda turned their attention to the countdown displayed on the central computer screen as it wound its way toward zero. Leos was relieved to know that the program still worked. During the long flight, the computer had few chores other than routine tasks, though it did maintain a constant check on the ship's position and attitude in space. When the countdown finally reached zero, the engine spat out another explosive thud that slammed the two travelers back in their seats and shot the G-load level to 2.2 G's where it stayed for several

Nytandran minutes when it abruptly shut down. Leos checked the com screen.

"We're in orbit. Now we have to find a place to land." He instructed the computer to flip the ship over so the planet was again visible through the front window, and he and Esmerelda scanned the planet's surface below. He was surprised—and a little concerned—at what he saw. But one feature alone, one overwhelming impression, stood out so markedly above all others.

"It's so green. Nothing but forest. I don't see any place to land."

"The trees have grown all over the surface. I remember my mother said this. But she also said when the army invaded, they cut down many trees to make room for their spaceships."

"Do you think any of those places are still open? It's been twenty years."

"I do not know. We will look and see."

The two travelers continued to scan the surface through the front window of the spaceship, but the greenness was pervasive. Even through 10-power binoculars, the green continued unabated, like a carpet covering the surface. It was as though the carpet possessed a furry, fuzzy nap—Leos couldn't see individual trees, but he came to realize that the surface was filled with tiny irregularities. But so complete was the green cover that nothing even remotely resembling a potential landing site appeared in his binoculars, and he wondered if they would ever find a landing site at all. After almost one full orbit, Esmerelda poked Leos. She pointed to a pale area in the midst of the green—a tiny streak, barely visible to the naked eye, like a scar on the surface situated exactly at the planet's equator.

"Look, there. It is a light area."

Leos unsnapped his chest and waist belts and grabbed the binoculars. He drifted over to the right-side window and examined the area more closely. "It does seem to be clear, doesn't it? At least a little. Like there's some vegetation, but it's minimal. It's long and slender, like, maybe, a runway. Maybe once for airplanes or spaceships. It looks like it's, I guess, a couple anthans long. Should we try it?"

Esmerelda borrowed the binoculars and stared long and hard at the spot. "I see nothing else. We have no other place for which to land."

"But when we went around to the dark side of the planet we couldn't see what was down there. We should wait until the planet rotates and the dark side comes into the light. We should check that side, too."

"But we have seen this place. We should take it. It would be foolish to wait longer. Our food is almost gone. There will be food on the surface. This is where the invading army landed. They cut down many trees. I recognize it. I wish to land."

"Are you saying this is where Gass and his men landed? Back when they invaded?"

"Yes. It is near my home. I will show you. We must land here."

"Okay. I'll start the landing procedure." He returned to his seat and re-snapped his waist and chest restraints.

During the long trip to the green planet, Leos had examined the ship's computer in complete detail, and he found — to his immense relief — deep within the software the instructions on de-orbiting. Those instructtions weren't part of the flight program of the computer, though they could be used, given the proper coordinates, to take the ship out of orbit and into the atmosphere. But, as Grotuk said, there was no program for landing, so once the ship entered the atmosphere and crossed into subsonic flight, Leos would have to fly it down to the surface manually. He called up the de-orbit parameter query list, and began entering data. In the absence of latitude and longitude on a planet that was a uniform green, he imaged the surface and indicated the landing area on the image. The computer, knowing where the landing point was beneath the orbit of the ship, calculated the trajectory needed to reach the site, computed the length of the de-orbit burn, and flashed the numbers on the screen. Leos touched the red "Start" marker on the screen, and the computer began a short countdown.

"Hold on tight! Here we go!"

The ride was nauseatingly familiar. Like the de-orbit burn on Grok's ship, this ship took the same skip-and-settle approach, diving into the atmosphere, bouncing off and dropping back, losing speed and altitude with each dip. But to Leos, there seemed an inordinate amount of time before the ship reached the first skip, almost twelve Nytandran minutes, and that just added to the confusion he'd felt seeing the planet up close just after reaching orbit. *Something's not right here. Should it take that long?*

Then, when the ship finally began to encounter the atmosphere, every slam and bounce sent the ship rolling and yawing, pitching up and down, throwing the wings high and low, tossing Leos and Esmerelda around in their seats like vegetables in a salad. *This isn't good either.*

"Leos! Make it stop! Make it stop!"

After the final skip, the ship entered the upper atmosphere for good, and the flight became more stable. At least it wasn't rolling and yawing so much. But now came a new problem. As it settled into the thin upper atmosphere, still supersonic, the ship began to vibrate. And not just lightly, either. These were large-scale vibrations—the whole ship was shaking and creaking and groaning like no other re-entry Leos had ever experienced.

What's going on here? He pulled out of long-term memory the de-orbit burn when Grok's ship went through re-entry. That ship also pitched and yawed and rolled, but after it settled into the atmosphere, a thin, almost imperceptible vibration began that swept over the ship in gentle, rolling waves, and didn't disappear until it reached subsonic speeds.

But that was nothing like what this is little ship was experiencing—it was about to be torn apart. Leos' heartbeat shot up more than forty points and he could hear it pounding in his temples. He held his breath against the time when the ship would just simply disintegrate around them. That could be any time now.

"Leos! Make it stop!" Esmerelda yelled again, her voice quivering in sync with the vibrations.

"There's nothing I can do! We have to wait for the ship to slow down!"

Though it seemed the vibrations had gone on for several hours, they actually lasted for less than five Nytandran minutes, and as the ship dove deeper into the atmosphere and the velocity dropped further, the vibrations diminished, settling out into a high-pitched buzz coming from the tail section. The ship was now in a denser part of the atmosphere, though it was still zipping along at several thousand anthans per subsector, and the nose and leading edges of the wings took on a pinkish-red glow as the atmosphere heated the metal skin of the ship. After three more millisectors, the speed had dropped far enough that the rosy glow dimmed and faded out, leaving the wings their usual gold-tinted silvery color. The ship shuddered slightly as it moved through the transonic region, emerging subsonic into still air about three anthans above the ground. The vibrations were gone and the wings swiveled forward and outward into long, glider-like wings, perfect for low-speed flight.

"Holy dinfrizzle!" Leos exhaled and began to relax in his seat. "What a re-entry flight. I'm glad that's over." He wiped his forehead with his sleeve and grabbed the control column.

Esmerelda, for her part, grabbed an airsickness bag from under her seat.

But what a glider the ship was! The green planet was so much smaller than Anthanos or Nytandra, the gravity only about one-quarter of either. The little spaceship glided serenely, almost tranquilly, through the atmosphere, slowly losing altitude, far more slowly than the rate Leos was familiar with when he took glider aircraft training back on Anthanos. The ship seemed to fly itself, whistling through the air as though it were skating on the surface of some glassy-smooth ice pack, and at first, Leos did little to control the craft.

"Where's the landing site we picked?" Leos said. "I don't see it." He looked at the computer screen where the flight path was displayed. The flight path, a thin yellow line, had been superimposed over an image of the surface, and the little line pointed directly toward the landing site. But when Leos scanned the surface of the planet through the front window of the spacecraft, still several anthans above the treetops, everything was still a solid forest green.

"I don't see it," Leos said again. He looked forward, he studied the com screen, he glanced at the navscreen in the center of the control panel directly in front of him. On the navscreen was a computer-generated airplane, seen from the rear, superimposed on a thin set of crosshairs, and if Leos kept the plane in the center of the crosshairs he was on the correct glide path. He dare not let that little airplane image drop below the line or he would crash short of his target. So he thought.

"It should be ahead of us. I am hopeful."

Leos looked again at the com screen. They flew on a west-to-east trajectory, and the flight path should lead directly to the site. He checked the navscreen — still on the glide path, not too low, not too high. Leos shook his head. "We're almost on top of it. But we're still several anthans above the ground. We're way to high."

"Look! There it is!" Esmerelda stared almost straight down from the right side window. "The landing site! See! It is open."

"That couldn't be it!" Leos yelled. But the longer he stared at the site, the more convinced he became — yes, that is the site they'd selected, a sort of crude runway hacked out of the forest. "It's too far below us. We're way too high to land. The computer brought us in too high. We'll have to circle to lose altitude."

Leos put the ship in a shallow glide, circling downward in a left-hand spiral toward the opening in the forest below. He let the ship glide by itself, losing altitude slowly and carefully. He relaxed in the pilot's seat, his confidence boosted by the fact that they'd come through the difficult re-entry without any real problem. Other than a terrific scare.

This shouldn't be too difficult. Just circle and land. What could possibly go wrong?

The air remained smooth and calm. The sun had just risen on this site, and Leos had plenty of time to get the ship down before the site was immersed in evening darkness.

Easy does it.

As the ship swirled lazily downward, Leos tried to visualize the landing itself. He would put the ship down in a smooth three-point landing on the runway—albeit a rather crude runway—a landing that certainly would impress his instructors on Anthanos and Nytandra were they here to watch, and then he and Esmerelda would emerge from this magnificent spaceship to explore the green planet with a swagger and a style that would befit a conquering hero.

Ha! That would teach them to kick him off their planet!

That's nice, you twit. But first you have to get this spaceship on the ground, so wake up and get your mind back to landing.

The runway Leos aimed for had been used by Gass and his invading army twenty years earlier. They chopped down trees and removed underbrush, clearing out a long slender area slightly more than two anthans long, which they used to bring in spaceships carrying all the men and matériel they needed for their invasion. But in the twenty years since the invasion, the runway had become overgrown with bushes, tree seedlings and saplings, and other nondescript underbrush. Landing was looking more and more problematic.

The plant life on this planet was colorful if nothing else. The bushes were various shades of red, some a pale pink, some a deep scarlet, some tending towards maroon or even purple. The broad leaves on the trees and saplings were a deep green, exactly the same color as Esmerelda's skin, and the ground cover, the low sprawling grasses and flowering plants, was so varied in color it reminded Leos of an artist's palette—yellow, gold and ochre, pink and red, blue and lavender.

But as the ship grew closer to the surface, the most significant objects that caught Leos's eye were the trees—the big trees that outlined the old runway. He was able to make out individual trees for the first time, and he was impressed by their size—hundreds of links tall, just as Esmerelda had said. Those giant green trees defined the planet and gave it its identity. The vibrant green of the leaves was the hue seen from space, and from that color was derived the planet's nickname—*The Green Planet*. The trees dominated the terrain on the planet's surface so completely that nothing else shone through, and only under cataclysmic circumstances so rare as to be almost unimaginable, as, for example, an invasion from outer space when an artificial opening is created in the forest, were the smaller colored shrubs visible from above.

But the presence of the big trees left Leos with a deep apprehensive feeling, too.

The trees grew right up to the edge of the runway, forming a palisade all around. They outlined the runway. Only the lack of these immense towers allowed the runway to exist at all, and they'd begun to invade the runway proper.

"There's a lotta crap on the runway," Leos said.

As the ship closed on the runway, Leos scanned the surface in detail through the binoculars, relieved to find that portions of the runway were still useable. Many of the bushes and small trees were up to three to four links tall. They weren't big enough to seriously affect the ship when it landed, and even if they slowed the ship down a bit after it was on the ground, well, so much the better. But what most caught Leos's attention was one big tree near the eastern end of the runway. It was a large tree, maybe a hundred links tall and a brilliant shimmering green in the sunlight that covered the ground in the open area, but it blocked any approach from the east.

"I'll have to bring it in from the west," Leos said.

"I am in agreement," Esmerelda replied.

At an altitude of one anthan above ground, Leos took the ship out of the circling glide and swung around well beyond the western end of the runway. He ordered the computer to calculate a new glide path, and when it popped up on the screen, he swung the ship back to the east and put it on that new glide path. He watched the navscreen and kept the ship in the crosshairs. It should have taken him directly down onto the runway.

But when the ship passed over the end of the runway, they were still eight thousand links in the air. "The computer calculated the wrong glide path," he said, and ordered the computer to make new calculations.

Again, he swung the ship to the west and put it on the glide path, and again, the glide path was too high. They were still five thousand links above the runway.

"There's something wrong. The computer is giving me crappy info. I can't tell what's going on. We aren't descending like the computer says we should. I'm going to calculate a new glide path."

"All right," Esmerelda said, "but I do not understand." She looked at Leos, her eyes drawn up in a perceptible squint, a look of consternation, even faint panic, on her face.

Leos made the new calculations and scanned them as they appeared on the screen.

"Those numbers won't work." Now, having run through two—no, make that three if you count the descent from orbit—incorrect landing attempts based on calculations from the ship's computer, it became clear that this glide path would still leave them too high. He decided not to even try to use it.

"We aren't going down at the rate we should. It's like the computer is using the wrong info—holy crap!"

"What? What is it?"

"The calculations are wrong! The computer thinks we're going down faster than we really are. There's a mistake in the computer. But I can't recalculate. The computer won't let me. They fixed it before we left. They screwed us! I *knew* something was bad. When we first went into orbit. The orbit was too high!"

"What can you do?"

"I'll have to take it in manually. Hold on tight! Here we go!"

Leos swung the ship around to the west again. He made a mental estimate of how far he would need to travel before he could turn back and bring the ship in on this, his third attempt to land. But the lower gravity of this planet confused him, and not a little bit either. He wasn't used to piloting a glider in the light pull the planet produced. So when he swung west, he let the ship glide just a little too far before he made a 200-degree arc back toward the runway. He almost forgot that a glider loses altitude in a turn faster than when flying in a straight line, and now—*holy dinfrizzle*—*we're coming in too low!*

The tall trees that enveloped the runway, especially those that stood tall and proud at the east and west ends, prevented Leos from aiming for the near end of the runway. He would have to land near the midpoint of the runway. But as he made his final approach from the west, the ship got uncomfortably close to the tops of some of the trees.

"How tall are these trees anyway?"

"They are many of your links tall. Maybe one thousand."

"A thousand? Holy crap! They're jutting up into the glide path. I can't keep the ship in the air much longer. We're coming down! We're coming down!"

As the ship approached the landing site it began clipping the trees in the flight path, making a subtle *whisssp* sound as the tops of the trees swooshed by across the underside of the ship. Every time one of the wings nipped the top of a tree, he could feel it in the control column as a slight jerk to that side. The tips of the trees were slim and feathery, not substantial at all, and when they collided with the ship they didn't cause any real damage, but every contact slowed the ship infinitesimally in its glide. The runway was dead ahead—

"We're not going to make it!"

Leos kept the nose as low as he could to maximize what precious little forward velocity he had, but the ship still drifted downward, still stinging the tops of the trees. He maneuvered around some of the taller trees, but each turn threw him off his glide path, and he had to turn back to regain control. And that just slowed the ship even more.

"I'm having trouble keeping the ship in alignment." He swung the ship right and left to avoid more treetops, but the runway was too far a-head. "We're not going to make it! I can't glide that far!"

"Can you use the engine to boost us?"

"What? The engine? No way! There's no fuel! We used all the fuel in the de-orbit. Wait. Maybe there is. Just a little. Look in the computer. I can't take my eyes off—"

"I do not know how to . . ."

"Hit 'Engine.' Then hit 'Fuel Load.'"

Esmerelda punched a few keys on the computer keyboard. "There is no more than a second of fuel remaining."

"That might be enough! Hit the engine."

"I do not know how to do it . . ."

"Go to 'Manual!' Manual engine control! Look on the com screen."

Swish—thunk—jerk on the underside of the ship.

"Oh, yes, here it is."

"Punch in one . . . no, *two* seconds. Hit 'Start'!"

"It says it cannot do it. Not enough fuel remains."

"Hit 'Override', then hit 'Start'!"

Esmerelda punched those two keys and the engine blurted out one final thud that lasted slightly more than one Nytandran second, but it jerked the ship forward and practically knocked her from her seat.

"That did it!" Leos yelled. "That's enough! We're going to make it! I love ya, baby!"

The short engine burn knocked the nose of the ship up a few degrees and added several links per second to the airspeed, just enough to drive it forward to the runway. Within a few nanosectors the opening appeared.

"Here we go!"

Leos found the best line of approach slightly off to the ship's right, and he swung over. The trees were marginally shorter here, but now he was coming at the runway at an angle, and he would have to make a quick left bank to line the ship for landing.

Should I lower the landing gear? Or take it in gear up?

Leos didn't have time to mull the question, all he did was react—he lowered the gear.

That way we can take off again.

He swung left to align the ship with the runway and pulled back on the control column to stall the ship. It settled onto the surface and bounced back into the air. In the weak gravity of the planet, the ship drifted more than twenty links into the air and continued to glide down the runway, and by the time it hit the ground again it was well forward of the runway's center point—almost to the eastern end. It plopped down again, easily, not with a jolt, and sped along the crude runway. Not bad.

"At least we're down," he shouted to Esmerelda, but then he saw that one large tree at the eastern end of the runway, and the ship was headed directly toward it.

That tree is going to be a major problem.

In the light gravity of the planet, the ship sailed down the runway so much more easily than he expected. He thought the ship would come to a stop well before it reached the end. Had he landed on Anthanos or Nytandra it would have.

Now I know why the Nytandran army made the runway so long. Then he yelled, "The brakes! Where are the brakes? During the flight I forgot to find out where the brakes are!"

"I do not know."

He felt with his feet on the aileron pedals, expecting to find smaller pedals that activated the brakes. "Where are the brakes? Never mind—where's the ground control? Maybe I can turn the ship."

"I do not know. Leos—the tree—"

Leos hunted all over the front control panel for a lever or knob that would control the front wheel. He thought briefly about grabbing Esmerelda and flinging her to the floor, but he wanted to keep hunting as long as possible. He expected to find a small lever that controlled the front wheel similar to the one in the little jet he flew out of the canyon, but he couldn't find anything even remotely similar to it.

"Leos, that tree is coming closer! Do something! Turn! Please turn!"

"Here it is! I found it!"

"Leos! The tree! Look out!"

Leos grabbed the master control, a small greenish knob well down on the aft end of the central control console, and jerked it all the way left. The ship turned but he was a fraction of a nanosector too late and the right wingtip smashed into the tree.

The impact sheared off the wing about halfway out. Esmerelda screamed again and threw up her arms to cover her face. Leos closed his eyes and held his breath. The collision flung the ship into a right-hand spin. It whirled around 400 degrees like a toy top, ripping off the landing gear and most of the left wing, and what remained of the ship was sent careening over toward a clump of bright red bushes. A small stub of the left wing remained and dug into the ground as the ship spun. At least it didn't flip over.

When it finally shuddered to a stop, Leos exhaled.

CHAPTER 22

JON-SET-TOM

The ship lay canted to the left about forty degrees. Leos sat still in his seat—very still. He didn't want to move, afraid that any sudden movement might cause the ship to roll farther over. He stayed completely quiet for several microsectors, finally beginning to wiggle his arms, just a little, to test the solidity of the ship. It held. It didn't roll any farther.

Esmerelda still held her arms over her face. At first, she didn't move either, then she slowly lowered her arms. She was shivering and a perceptible tremolo invaded her voice. "Are we of the living type? I am so scared."

"We're okay. The ship's stopped moving."

Leos unbuckled his chest and waist straps and slid out of his seat to his left. In the lower gravity of the planet, he dropped onto the sidewall of the ship, but it seemed more of a drifting sensation than a real drop. He stepped back a few paces along the joint where the curved sidewall met the floor. Esmerelda followed, climbing over the central control panel into Leos's seat, then joining him below. They inched their way to the airlock door at the rear of the cockpit, but when Leos pressed the door-open actuating button, the door didn't move.

"Well, of course, the door won't open. There's no power. We'll have to open the door manually."

He stood at the juncture of the ship's side with the floor, the door above his head. He reached up and released the door-lock mechanism and pushed the door upward and clambered through the opening. He held the door for Esmerelda as she crawled through into the airlock, and they both dropped back onto the sidewall next to the main entrance door. Esmerelda scrambled through the rear door of the airlock into the back room, the personnel compartment of the ship, and came out with a small leather bag.

On Nytandra, the main entrance door would have been too heavy to move by hand, but in the lighter gravity of the green planet, and after Leos released the mechanical interlocks that normally kept the door tightly sealed, they popped the door inward and slid it back onto the side wall in the fully open position.

The first thing they saw was the soil of the planet, a dark, black soil with a few grasses and flowers strewn about. A narrow opening at the top of the doorway was just wide enough to let them squeeze through. But when they stood in the warm, humid air just outside the wreckage of the spaceship, the view was so unlike anything Leos had ever seen, he had to blink several times to convince himself it was real.

"Wow. This is . . . wow."

The wrecked ship lay at the eastern end of the runway. It'd been thrown by the force of the collision to the edge of the cleared area, and came to rest near a stand of several large trees. As they exited the craft, Leos and Esmerelda were facing slightly east of north, directly into the forest that surrounded the runway.

"We must be careful," Esmerelda said. "There is much danger here for people in the open."

They wandered forward a short distance toward a narrow opening between several trees. Walking on the green planet was a series of hops. Each step sent a person flying a few links into the air. The gravity was only about a quarter of that on Anthanos, about a third of Nytandra, but Leos and Esmerelda adjusted to it easily, and they bounded through the opening and stopped in a small open space within the forest.

"It's like we're in a canyon," Esmerelda said.

Leos paid little attention to what Esmerelda said, and only vaguely acknowledged her meaning. He stood entranced by the panorama of trees all around him. His jaw dropped, his eyes opened brilliantly wide, and he gaped upward. "The trees are huge."

They stood within a grove of eight or ten trees, each with a canopy of leaves that must have been fifty or sixty links in diameter, extending all the way to the ground. Leos remained absolutely still and ran his line of sight slowly up the trees as far as he could. They seemed to go upward forever. Each was absolutely straight and vertical, hundreds of links tall, eight or nine hundred, maybe even a thousand, like Esmerelda said. He couldn't see the tops of the trees; they were so far out of sight they merged into a greenish haze well above him, dissolving into the clear blue sky above. He turned where he stood, working his way around a full 400-degree circle. The trees grew everywhere around him.

He looked around again, staring upward, trying desperately to a-dapt his mind to their immensity. But he was so tiny and insignificant in comparison, standing as he was within this grove, confined and surrounded by these immense arboreal specimens. A chill ran through his body—he was back in Death Canyon. But this time there would be no way out. That spaceship certainly wasn't going to fly them out of here.

As he continued to turn, he glanced back through the narrow opening through which they'd entered this grove. Visible behind the wreckage were the skid marks left by the ship as it spun around after the landing gear collapsed. The tail section had been ripped from the fuselage in the spin, left behind about twenty links from the rest of the ship.

"We must leave this place," Esmerelda said. "It is not safe for us to be here."

"The trees must be millions of years old."

"I do not think they are that old, but they are very old. They are magnificent. My mother was right." Esmerelda wiped a tear from her face.

"I see what you mean." Leos took her hand.

"This is where I must be. I recognize this place from the stories my mother told me. I am now home."

"What do you mean?"

"This is my planet. I have come home. These are my people." Several more tears trickled down both cheeks, and she sniffled loudly.

"Yeah, well, I don't see any people."

"They are here. They are hiding from us. We will find them soon. They heard us."

"How can you be so certain?"

"I know my people."

They retreated to the vicinity of the ship, but Leos continued past the torn rear section into the opening of the runway proper. Esmerelda followed, but when they passed the tail section, she repeated her warning. "Be careful, Leos. There is much danger here."

Leos went farther, stepping into the brilliant sunlight that flooded the crude runway. The local time approached midday, and here at the equatorial landing site the sun shone from almost directly overhead. Several thin shafts of sunlight reached between the trees at the edge of the forest, speckling the surface in little chunks of light. Almost every beam of sunlight reached a bush or small tree growing strategically near the base of the larger trees. Some bushes were red, some a dull pinkish hue, some bright yellow, but each, regardless of color, took the opportunity to soak up its daily quantum dose of life-giving photons. One particular bush caught Leos's eye. A sparkling scarlet red, and illuminated by a brilliant shaft of light, it grew on the ground at the base of one tree near where he stood. In the intense light the bush seemed on fire, the small fan-shaped leaves flickering lightly in the faint breeze that moved through the canyon that was the runway.

Leos looked up at the sun. Standing in the direct sunlight he felt warm, but the sunlight lacked the penetrating heat of the Nytandran sun. A few wispy clouds dotted the sky, and several large black birds soared above the trees.

"We're farther from the sun now. It isn't as hot."

"It is much more comfortable. I enjoy it. But we must get under cover. It is dangerous to be out in open places like this."

"Why? What's the danger?"

"I will tell you. But we must enter protection."

Leos followed Esmerelda back toward the cool, humid air of the inner forest. As he walked — or, rather, bounded — Leos inspected the trees in more detail. The big green tree that made up by far the greatest segment of plant life on this planet was cone-shaped, but a tall slender cone, tapering to a thin, tenuous point many links above ground. This was the tree whose apex slapped against the ship during landing and threatened to take the ship down before it could reach the runway. The large, flat, spade-shaped leaves of the tree were almost a link across, and tapered to a slightly rounded point at the tip. But what was most interesting to Leos was that the leaves provided a complete cloak-like covering to the entire tree — from the top of the tree to the soil in which the tree grew.

How are the leaves are held in place? I don't see any branches.

After they'd walked a short distance into the forest — no more than forty to fifty links — they edged their way between two trees and stepped onto a separation among the trees. About thirty links wide, it appeared to stretch infinitely in each direction, paralleling the runway on which their ship landed. The soil of the separation was hard, much harder than the soil among the trees, as though it had been tamped by many feet passing through over many years.

"This is the *suota-hoa*," Esmerelda said. "I do not know how to translate it into Nytandran. It is the trail we travel among our people. It runs all around the planet. It is like the highway between the towns on Nytandra. I traveled on it much when I was young. We can use it to meet my people."

Esmerelda turned right and began to hop down the trail, Leos directly behind. Abruptly she stopped beside one tree, an immense tree, one of the widest at its base in the vicinity. She reached up to spread several of the leaves apart, and for the first time since landing, Leos noticed how closely the color of her face and hands matched that of the leaves.

Almost as if it had been made that way.

"We must get inside," Esmerelda whispered. "Come with me. Come over here."

"Get inside? Where?"

Leos hopped over to the tree. Esmerelda turned her body slightly sideways and with a *whooshing* sound as the leaves brushed against her clothing, she stepped into the tree. The leaves fell back exactly as they had been, and the opening disappeared, leaving a seamless green covering. Leos pushed one leaf aside and looked in as Esmerelda had done. At first he couldn't see anything in the darkness within the tree, but as his eyes adjusted to the dim light, he too entered at the same spot.

"We are safe in here."

The interior was illuminated only by what little greenish light could penetrate the leaves or squeeze between them. Esmerelda stood near the trunk of the tree, looking upward. The trunk was about ten links in diameter, and the branches protruded from the trunk like the spokes of a wheel, each set of spokes about three links apart. The branches emanated perpendicularly from the trunk, splitting into smaller and smaller branches near the tip, ending in many tiny sprigs on which the leaves were attached. In the interior, the branches formed a crude ladder, each directly above one another all the way up.

Esmerelda showed Leos how to climb the tree. She reached up and grabbed one of the branches at the highest level she could reach—the third branch from the ground, about eight links up—and with one big jerk of her arms pulled herself up. In the lower gravity she landed with her feet on the same branch. Leos was impressed.

"Wow. Nice trick. You got a real knack for climbing."

"It is not difficult. I remember my mother showing me how to climb the tree. I was very young. Come. We will climb this tree. You can too." Esmerelda reached up and grabbed a higher branch and jerked herself up again. But this time she used the power in her legs as well as the strength of her arms to propel herself upward, and she passed four levels of branches in one jump. Then she repeated the process, higher and higher, rapidly climbing out of sight in the darkness of the inner tree.

"Okay, here I come." Leos, a few decilinks taller than Esmerelda, grabbed the fourth branch up, and with one big yank he pulled himself up. But he yanked too hard and passed the branch and went one level higher.

Well, almost. He spent too much time watching his feet, and so didn't grab a branch with his hands. He tried to catch himself and scramble up, bringing his feet up to the next higher branch. As he did, he whacked his chin. "Ouch!"

He massaged his chin and looked up, but by now Esmerelda was out of sight. He decided to try Esmerelda's leg/arm technique.

"Wow!" he exclaimed when he passed five branches in one jump. He tried again, then several more times, rapidly getting the hang of the process. He learned how to coordinate his arm jerk with his leg thrust, and just how much power to put into each jump. He learned how to grab the proper branch with his hands as he rose, and how to drop his feet on the correct branch several levels below. But he still scraped his chin and occasionally his nose.

About a quarter of the way up the tree, Leos and Esmerelda entered the lighted part of the tree. The sun had entered the western sky, and the sunlight now illuminated only the upper levels of the trees. The leaves took on a translucent glow in the direct sunlight, giving an eerie greenish cast to the inside of the tree. But they kept climbing, jerk after jerk, branch after branch, until they came to a point about two-thirds of the way up the tree.

The branches were shorter here, and as the leaves edged in closer as they climbed, the illumination got brighter.

Esmerelda, still above Leos, glanced upward, and in the lighted area of the upper tree, she saw something. She stopped climbing and stood on one branch, looking upward.

"What is it?" Leos asked.

"It is a platform."

"A platform? What are you talking about?"

"There are people living in this tree. We will meet them."

"People? You mean . . . some of your people?"

"Yes." After a few more jumps, Esmerelda arrived at the bottom of the platform.

The circular platform wrapped entirely around the trunk—about three links in diameter at this point—and it extended outward ten to twelve links. It was composed of individual boards, arranged radially, held together from below by five sets of concentric joists that circled the trunk of the tree. The joists themselves were set on one level of branches, lashed down by a brown cord. A railing encircled the entire platform at its outer edge, and an access opening in the railing about two links wide led out onto one of the branches. Esmerelda ascended to the level of the access branch and stepped onto the platform. Leos followed. He was out of breath and sweating profusely in the humidity.

"There's no one here," Esmerelda said. She dropped her leather bag on the platform.

The platform was bare. A few shriveled leaves, dried, brown, and crinkly, lay scattered over the grayish-brown wooden planks, and a thick layer of the dust of years of neglect covered everything. The railing was cracked and broken in places. Several of the planks were soft and rotten. Leos stepped on one and pushed his foot all the way through, and the remains of the plank went tumbling downward in a sort of slow-motion plunge, swirling around as they sank through the air as though they were suspended in a viscous liquid that held them back, retarding their fall.

"They have left," Esmerelda said. "I am thinking that this tree was too near the landing place. They did not like being near to the invaders. They left many years ago. But we will use this home until we find my people."

"Your people? What are you talking about?"

"My people live in the trees like this. This day we will find them."

"Okay, if you say so. But this place is a real fixer-upper."

Leos made his way around the platform, scrambling over each limb in turn, checking the integrity of each of the boards and the railing all the way around.

"There's about twenty boards that need replacing," he said, "and the railing needs fixing at four or five places. There's one place out back where the boards are like, twenty links long. Some of them —"

"That is the sleeping area. If people were here, it would be covered with blankets. It would be enclosed. Like a room. To be warm. It is cold at night here. Many blankets would be here."

"Oh, yeah, I see. But otherwise, the place is okay."

"That is good," Esmerelda said, but she was preoccupied looking toward the upper levels of the tree. "I am looking upward," she said. "I wish to see higher." She began to climb again and Leos followed.

CHAPTER 23

THE ZOLOPIL

As they climbed, the branches became more tightly bunched. Still the same distance apart vertically, but because of the narrowing diameter of the trunk, smaller and closer together horizontally. The leaf covering was tighter, too, and as they neared the top, Esmerelda stopped about forty to fifty levels below the absolute pinnacle of the tree where the branches were too light to carry their weight. Here they sat in a sort of conical tent, green and glowing from the bright sunlight that saturated the leaves. Leos started to pull back a leaf and look out, but Esmerelda stopped him.

"Leos!" she exclaimed in a coarse whisper. She didn't shout. Her temperament, her training, her demeanor would never permit her to shout openly. She would insist on a quiet voice, a voice that would command attention yet be unobtrusive and unpretentious. So she asserted herself with an emphatic, vehement whisper, "Do not open the leaves at this level. The zolopil may see you."

Leos whispered back, "The what?"

"The zolopil. My mother told me about them. They are flying animals and they can take you from the top of the trees. They wait and snatch. They will eat you."

"Oh." Leos swallowed hard and closed the little opening. Esmerelda reached forward and separated several leaves, opening only a tiny port less than two decilinks wide, peering carefully out. She looked right and left, and up and down. She scrambled from branch to branch around the tree, doing the same thing at the end of each branch, carefully peering in all directions. After looking out everywhere around the tree, she pronounced it safe.

"We can look out now," she said, still in a whisper. "But only for a short time. And do not stick your hand out. It could draw the zolopil."

"Okay." Leos separated two leaves, peering through the small port. "Wow! We're way up high here. You can see a long way! You can see for anthans—wow—and in all directions. We're above most of the other trees. This is one tall tree. You can see the landing site down below. I can't see the ship, but I can see the old runway."

"The ship is at the bottom of this tree," Esmerelda said. "You cannot see it from here. Now we will go down. It is time for me to join my people."

Leos closed the last opening he'd made from between the leaves, and just as he let the leaves drop together, he heard a funny *whop-whop-whop* from outside the tree. The sound puzzled him at first, but he didn't have much time to think about it when, at exactly the point on the surface of the tree where he'd made his last little opening, came a roaring *whoosh*, followed immediately by a ripping sound, a piercing, tearing, slashing sound, and from that same point on the tree, several twigs and leaves exploded back into his face. Esmerelda screamed, and Leos fell backward into her lap. She cupped one hand over her mouth as though she had said something wrong, and Leos sat upright.

"Yow! What the hell was that!"

"Leos! Be quiet!" Esmerelda slapped a hand over Leos's mouth. "It was the zolopil! It had seen you. You are very lucky."

A permanent opening to the outside about a link across now existed where the leaves had been ripped away. Leos peered through the opening, careful not to get too close. He looked straight ahead and cautiously to his left, keeping his head well back from the opening, but it wasn't until he turned his head to the right that he saw a large flying creature swooping away — coal black all over except for a bright red band at the end of its tail feathers. Its tannish-yellow curved beak seemed way out of proportion to its tiny head and long slender neck, and its wingspan looked to be thirty links or more. The zolopil was looking over its left shoulder directly at the opening it had created. It gave a couple of *whop-whop* flaps of its great wings again — "That was the sound I heard!" — then held its wings straight out in a glide as it circled. It was returning, aiming for the hole from which Leos peered.

"Leos! We must go down. It will attack again. Hurry!"

Descending from the top of a tree was easier than climbing. Esmerelda simply jumped. First, she worked her way out several links from the trunk of the tree on one branch, then, while facing the branch, she jumped backward. In the low gravity she didn't plummet as she would have on Nytandra, she drifted down, slowly gaining speed, but caught herself on one of the branches about ten levels down. Then she repeated the jump, stopping again when she got going too fast, hesitating only long enough to dissipate her momentum. Then she jumped again. Leos was surprised at the method—he had envisioned more of a ladder-like descent from one branch to another—and he hesitated before he made his first jump. He knew the low gravity wouldn't pull him down as fast as he was used to, so he made a tentative decision to try it. Like Krok plunging into a tank of liquid hydrogen, he figured if Esmerelda could do it, he could too. But he was tentative in his first jump, dropping only two levels—he didn't want to allow himself to get going too fast. When he grabbed the branch, he banged his nose again.

"Ouch!"

He stopped to massage his nose, but as he stood on that branch he heard the *whop-whop-whop* sound again and another slash from the zolopil at the top of the tree. Several leaves and pieces of woody debris trickled down around him. As he looked up, the zolopil thrust its head—at the end of a neck that must have been four links long—through the opening, and with a piercing *caw – caw – caw* it started slashing and tearing at everything in sight—leaves, branches, bark. It must have held itself in place with the power of its huge wings, and it spied Leos, several branch levels down. He jumped again just as the crash of the zolopil's beak ripped the air apart right beside his left ear.

This time he dropped so far he almost caught up with Esmerelda.

"It is time for me to join my people," Esmerelda said as she reached the platform.

Leos dropped down beside her, massaging the nose he bruised several more times on the descent. "What do you mean?"

"We will go and eat, but I must prepare to meet my people."

"Eat? There's not much food left in the ship."

"We will eat not from the ship. We will eat my food."

"Where do we get your food?"

"On the ground. I will show you. But I must prepare." She turned away from him.

Unaware of what Esmerelda was about to do, Leos sauntered over to the edge of the platform. He stood at the railing looking out at the canopy of leaves, wondering idly if going down to ground level was going to be as painful as coming down from the top of the tree. He stared downward for a few nanosectors trying to gauge his descent. He imagined trying the same sort of descent as from above, picturing Esmerelda in his mind as she drifted down from the upper branches. He ran over the process in his mind, working out to his own satisfaction how it should go, and when he satisfied himself he could do it without banging his nose again, he turned around to ask Esmerelda when she intended to leave. What he saw stopped him dead in his tracks, and he didn't get his question out. His jaw dropped and his eyes bulged out as much as they did the first time he saw her in the Grand Hall on Nytandra. But this time Esmerelda had done something he'd never seen her do.

She'd taken her clothes off.

CHAPTER 24

A FEW MINOR DETAILS

It was a short, simple meeting. Mlada had been summoned before Coreaje to finalize her dismissal from the Ruler's service. She stood in front of Coreaje's desk, watching as he signed her termination order. Only once did she glance up at the portrait of Esmerelda, but so many vivid memories assaulted her that she forced herself to look away.

"That's all, Mlada. I will write in your favor. You may go."

"Thank you, Your Eminence."

Mlada stepped back from Coreaje and bent in obeisance. With Esmerelda gone, her services as tutor and confidante to Her Royal Preciousness had come to an end, and she had been given three days to pack up her belongings and leave the Palace grounds. But finding another position elsewhere didn't present a problem to Mlada. Over the years of her relationship with Esmerelda, she'd picked up many contacts within the city, and she was able to obtain several, albeit temporary positions as tutor or instructor to youngsters of the upper class intelligentsia with whom Coreaje regularly mingled. But now, ninety days after her dismissal, a permanent position still eluded her, and with a highly regarded recommenddation from His Eminence, a good job should be no more than few days away.

She turned to leave, but she'd taken only two steps toward the door when the door flung open and the Minister hurtled into the room. His face was drawn and tight, his lips clamped shut, his jaw rigid. That was so unlike the Minister whose face was usually more relaxed. He rarely smiled, granted, but he was not generally given to outbursts either. Unless provoked.

He dashed past Mlada, acknowledging her presence only by deftly stepping around her. He approached the Ruler's desk, clicking his heels and bowing. Mlada continued toward the door, interested not the least in any information the Minister might have for His Pudginess, the name she'd recently — and quite privately — given the Ruler.

"Yes, what is it?" Coreaje stared only at some papers in his hand.

"Eminence. My apologies for the interruption, but two, shall we say, circumstances have arisen of which you should be informed."

"Circumstances? What are you talking about?"

"About the vessel," the Minister said, and paused. He took a deep breath.

"The vessel?"

"The spaceship in which the devil Leos traveled to the green planet."

Mlada had just passed through the door and was about to close it, but at the mention of the spaceship which took Leos to the green planet—and on which Esmerelda stowed away—she stopped, compelled, and listened carefully. The urgent manner of the Minister and the grimness in his voice filled her mind with a sense of dread. Her heart skipped a beat. She stayed just outside the door frame, hidden from the view of Coreaje and his tall minion by a large chair and one of the paintings hanging from the rafters. She could spy Coreaje through a narrow space between the chair and the painting, though the Minister remained hidden.

"What about the spaceship?" Coreaje looked up.

"A few, uh, let us say, important factors have been brought to my attention."

"Important factors?" Coreaje put the papers down and looked up at the Minister. His face turned serious, his eyes stern and somber. "Explain what you mean."

"Two factors, Eminence. First, a minor factor. The landing program of the ship. Our programmers could not anticipate the exact nature of the landing on the green planet that the devil Leos would take, and the de-orbit program was not modified."

"Yes, yes, as I was told. What about it?"

"So they left it as it remained. The devil Leos was required to land manually. This was your intention was it not?"

"Yes, it was. What of it?"

"The programmers did not change the gravitational constant in the landing program. They left it alone. It remained with Nytandra's value."

"Are you saying . . . dammit, what are you saying?" Coreaje's eyes narrowed, his brow furrowed.

"When the devil Leos attempts to program a landing, the computer will calculate based on Nytandra's constant. Such a calculation will leave them high in the air."

"Is that dangerous?"

"Our programmers think not. The devil Leos is a sufficient pilot to land without the program. We are of the thinking type that it will not harm the Princess."

"That's good. What's the other factor." Coreaje picked up the papers again.

"Yes, Eminence. Of a more serious nature."

"Oh?" He looked up.

Now the Minister's voice trembled and vibrato set in. "The spaceship was an older model. A prototype. It had not flown before. Only two of the prototypes were made."

"So? That is what I was told. They were throwaway ships. No longer of any use to us. Is that not correct?"

"Yes, Eminence, you are correct. But I have learned these prototypes were discovered to have a design flaw. A defect."

"Defect?" Coreaje put the papers down and rose from his chair. He put both fists on his desk, leaned forward and stared directly at the Minister. "I was not told about any defect. Explain yourself."

"These prototypes were discovered to be unstable on re-entry. I am sorry, Eminence, but the flaw could be serious. There was much vibration in them. Too much vibration during re-entry. They were, uh . . ."

"Yes? They were *what*?"

"Computer simulation discovered the vibration. It was . . ."

"It was *what*?"

"It was in . . ."

"Yes?! It was in *what*?"

"In the tail, Eminence. Too much vibration in the tail. The tail could fall off."

"The tail could fall off?!" The picture near the door rattled against the wall.

"Yes, Eminence. During re-entry."

Coreaje sat down and stared straight ahead. His face turned white, and he seemed to be in shock. He spoke slowly and quietly. "My daughter was on that ship. And the tail could fall off?" He stood again and his voice rose to a bellow. "Why the hell did we give him a defective spaceship?!"

"Eminence, when we selected that ship, we did not know The Princess Esmerelda would board and leave with the devil Leos. It was selected because it was, as you say, of the throw-away type. It was only for the devil Leos. And if by chance the tail would fall off during re-entry . . . so be it. This was by your orders, Most Eminent."

Coreaje sat back down and spoke quietly. "I was told only that those ships were not of use any more. Not needed. But not defective." He put his head in his hands.

"As was I, your Eminence."

Mlada slipped away from her position at the door and retreated hastily to the parking area where her ground maneuvering vehicle waited. She took a back route through a little used hallway in the palace so no one would see the tears streaming down her cheeks.

CHAPTER 25

WELCOME HOME

Esmerelda took everything off—boots, socks, jumpsuit, under-clothes, everything, and hung them neatly over one of the branches. Then she reached into the leather bag she'd set on the platform when they first arrived and pulled out three items. Around her waist she strapped a brown leather-like sheath that held a knife, letting the knife hang down her right thigh. She replaced the gold clasp that held her ponytail with a brown leather-like strap, and around her neck she tied a green ribbon. Several colorful symbols in red and yellow, perhaps characters in some language Leos didn't understand, had been inscribed on the ribbon, and she adjusted it so the symbols were in front, immediately below her chin. The ends of the ribbon hung over her right shoulder.

"Esmerelda! Holy dinfrizzle! What are you doing?"

"I will meet my people." She spoke without even turning around.

This was so completely unlike Esmerelda. She'd changed when she reached her beloved planet. On Nytandra she'd been so quiet and demure, yet still in charge of her life. She was so lady-like, so Princess-like. She lived up to her title, and Leos had grown fond of her. But now she was a climbing acrobatic gymnast, a nude Amazon strapping on . . . *a knife*? She was ready, it seemed, to fight for something. But what? Her dinner? Her home? Was this what she wanted to return to? This was so different from the Esmerelda Leos knew.

Even during the long voyage from Nytandra to her planet, she'd maintained the Princess persona. She shooed Leos out of the cramped personnel compartment of the spaceship when she prepared for bed. Leos hung out in the cockpit and waited for her signal before he could enter and get ready for sleep time himself. She would already be in bed—she took the lower bunk—and Leos would enter quietly and use the cramped bathing facility, and drift to the upper bunk, only to be banished from the room again when they woke several Nytandran hours later. But he adjusted to it, taking it as a requirement of living with a real Princess.

Leos adored Esmerelda. He considered himself lucky to even know her personally, let alone be privileged to live with her and escort her a-round town and be seen with her and be talked about by the population in the same breath with her, not to mention escorting her to another planet.

But now this enchanting Princess had taken her clothes off. Right in front of him. He didn't know whether to be concerned or aroused. He opt-ed for a little of both.

"Do you want me to take my clothes off, too?" He started unbuttoning his shirt.

"No, Leos, you should remain clothed." She turned and faced him. Frontal nudity it certainly was, yes, and Leos took it all in, but she didn't seem embarrassed by it, nor was there any awkwardness in her manner. Her face remained calm and even, her carriage and poise still Princess-like. "It will be best for you."

Flustered, Leos could only stare and stammer. "Oh. Okay." He re-buttoned his shirt.

"Now we must descend to the ground. Come. I will show you."

Esmerelda stuffed her clothes into the now empty bag and walked a few steps through the access opening in the railing onto the branch. Then, exactly as she did when she and Leos were near the top of the tree, she jumped, starting her trip down. Leos watched as she descended — *look at the muscles in her shoulders!* — trying to get some pointers on how it was done. She didn't just jump downward, she also jumped backward a short dis-tance to clear the branches as she fell, and kept her legs together and her toes pointed downward so she wouldn't bang a limb as she passed. But she kept her arms extended in front, and when she came to the branch she wanted to land on, she swung her feet forward and hit the branch and grabbed a branch two levels up with her hands, slightly flexing her knees to absorb the shock of landing. She hesitated briefly on the branch, then jumped again.

Elegant. He crawled out onto a branch and jumped himself.

Esmerelda made it look easy and Leos was beginning to get the hang of it. But this dropping procedure was more complicated than he first thought. He learned to keep his feet together as he dropped — that was easy — and he allowed himself to pass ten or twelve branch levels at a time, then swing his feet forward onto a branch and grab hold of a branch two levels above his feet. That brought him to a sudden stop. But the lower gravity made descent slow at the beginning, and that confused him. He didn't immediately comprehend that the longer he remained in the drop, the faster his speed became. Gravity worked the same way on this planet as it did on Anthanos or Nytandra, it just took longer to get started. Occasionally, he would let himself fall several branch levels too far, usually because he was concentrating on looking downward instead of watching the branches as they passed. But he would be going faster than he thought, and he'd impulsively grab for the nearest branch and swing his feet forward to stop, and his boots would slip off the branch and he'd grab whatever branch he could to stop and he'd whack his shins — *ouch*! It wasn't until he'd made several jumps that he mastered the concept of counting the branches as they passed, and not let himself go more than ten or twelve levels at a time.

His worst miscalculation came as he approached the bottom level. He couldn't see the black soil in the darkness, and he tried to stop to avoid hitting Esmerelda on the ground below him, but he almost missed the branch entirely, and his boots slipped on the branch once again, but this time he whumped over, landing on the branch on his stomach.

"Whoa!" he yelled, and slid onto the ground on his back. "Umph!"

Esmerelda smiled at him as he lay on the ground, a little dazed, the wind knocked out of him.

"Leos, you are being silly," Esmerelda said. Her voice was quiet and soft, not judgmental or demeaning, as though she had nothing better to do in her world than to watch Leos tumble from the upper branches of the tree. She extended her hand and helped him up. "We have not the time for silliness. Now we must get some food. You must stay inside the shelter of the tree and remain quiet. I will check if it is safe."

Esmerelda crept soundlessly through the darkness toward the outer edge of the tree. In her bare feet she brushed dead leaves and twigs away to avoid stepping on them. She stood still at the leaf curtain, listening carefully for a full microsector, then peeked out between several leaves. She looked right and left, listening quietly. As she'd done at the top of the tree, she repeated this procedure at several places, carefully examining the area all around the tree, checking for something. Then she motioned for Leos to join her.

Leos tried to tiptoe quietly over to where Esmerelda was standing, but he cracked a few twigs and crunched a few dead leaves as he walked, though Esmerelda didn't seem too concerned about the noise.

"It is safe. We can go out."

Safe? Leos didn't like the sound of that word. It implied danger. "Can the zo . . . lo . . . whatever-it-is get to us down here on the ground?" he whispered back.

"No, they cannot. But the zil can."

"Another flying monster?"

"No, it is a monster on the ground."

"Oh."

"That is why it is dangerous to be outside a tree—shhh." Esmerelda placed her fingers on Leos's lips in a shushing motion and cautioned him to be quiet. She stood quietly, listening, just as she did that evening on the patio outside the dining room of the Palace.

"Shhh," she whispered again.

Like that evening on the patio, Leos heard nothing. And he didn't understand what Esmerelda was listening for. He stood quietly with her, listening carefully, and soon he became aware of a faint thumping sound in the distance.

"I believe it is the zil," Esmerelda whispered. "Hurry. We must climb up a short way." She scurried over to the deep interior of the tree and pulled herself up about three levels of branches and sat down. Oddly, she didn't seem concerned about making noise as she ran. Leos joined her, but as he sat down he became aware of a foul odor, an extremely foul odor, the odor of rotting, of putrefaction.

"What is that?" Leos asked, holding his nose.

"It is the zil."

Something passed by the tree, rustling the leaves as it passed. It paused at the tree, exactly at the point where Leos and Esmerelda had entered. It started poking around, rustling the leaves up and down, over and over. A heavy sniffing or snorting noise came from the area.

"It is smelling us. It can tell us by our scent. We must be very quiet."

"The zil. Wow. You don't have to listen to tell if it's coming. You can just smell it."

"I remember my mother telling me about these animals. They are very dangerous."

"What else did your mother tell you about them?"

"She told me much. They are the life of my people. They give us everything we need—blankets, meat, sinew, bones, and much other. Very little is discarded. You will see."

"You eat the meat of the zil?"

"Yes, but we eat berries, too. Especially the berries."

Berries? Ah, yes, berries. That sounds much better. "Where are the berries. How do we get them?"

"They are in the pink trees. I will show you."

The beast continued to nose around the tree, trying several places along the outer edge. It would jam its nose between the leaves, trying to force its way in, bending inward the curtain of leaves, but always it met with resistance from the branches and it never succeeded in entering. Each time it tried, Leos's heart pounded a little faster, and he recoiled a little, edging closer and closer to Esmerelda on the branch.

"Don't you think we should get up higher? What happens if it gets in?"

"It will not get in. It is too big. The branches are too close together."

Too big? Now that was something Leos didn't like the sound of, and he tried to imagine some vague large animal struggling to get between the leaves and limbs of the tree, but he wasn't sure what the zil looked like, so he brought out of memory one of the large wooly animals from his favorite video game, and that gave him a rough idea of the size of the animal. After about three microsectors the zil gave up and the rustling stopped.

"I think it has gone. But we will wait and see."

They stayed on the branch for almost a millisector before Esmerelda dropped to the ground and crept toward the edge of the tree. Leos followed. She went through the same routine as before, checking all around the tree, watching and waiting for a sound that would indicate the zil had returned. But she still maintained an attitude of quietness as she returned to where Leos stood. She whispered.

"My mother told me the zil may wait beside a tree for the people to walk out. We must be careful. They have good hearing and smell. But they are not of the good-seeing type."

"We should be able to tell if they're around just by their smell. They stink."

"This is true. But we would be wrong to rely on it. We must check all around the tree. Now it seems safe. Hurry. Follow me." Esmerelda opened a cleft in the leaves and stuck her head out. She looked in all directions. "It is safe. Run!"

She took off running as fast as she could. She ran in the usual bouncing gait they'd used before, and Leos stayed right behind her, his arousal growing more intense as he admired the rippling of Esmerelda's muscular thighs, calves and buttocks as she ran.

Esmerelda ran deeply into the forest, down the main trail, away from the wrecked spaceship and the old runway. No underbrush grew here, the trail had been trampled into an almost concrete hardness after many years of use—by the natives, no doubt—and in this respect it became a super-highway where natives trod—every day?—moving to and from . . . ahh, now that's the question, isn't it? Where *did* the natives go when they trod this trail?

In her bare feet, Esmerelda ran almost silently, but Leos's boots made an embarrassingly uncomfortable scrunching sound on the hard-packed trail as he ran.

After several thousand links, Esmerelda diverted her run, turned abruptly right, and disappeared between the leaves of another tree. The leaves folded back to their original position, obliterating her entrance point. Leos followed, popping into the same tree. But as he entered, his clothing made a high-pitched *sswiiishh* against the leaves, and only then did he realize he hadn't heard that sound when Esmerelda entered the tree. Her smooth green skin was completely soundless against the green leaves.

"We will stay here for a short time," Esmerelda whispered. "I will check for the zil. "We must be careful. One may be near. We could meet it on the trail."

Esmerelda went through her usual procedure, checking all the areas around the tree to see if any of the zil were around. When she was satisfied that everything was clear, she bolted from the tree and ran on, farther into the forest, Leos right behind her. Then she chose another tree and slipped inside. Here she repeated her process, examining carefully all around the tree to be absolutely certain, then sprinting from the tree, running deeper into the forest. This was her course, her routine. This was her technique for moving about the forest.

Sometimes she would pop into a tree so quickly that if Leos wasn't watching, she disappeared with no trace of where she'd been. He would have to check a few trees before he found her, then they would set out again.

"I hope you know where we are," Leos whispered as they entered what he estimated was the twentieth tree. They were by now so deep in the forest, perhaps a full anthan, that he'd become completely lost, and he wondered out loud if they would ever get back to the tree near the landing site, the tree Esmerelda wanted to use as a sort of home base.

"Yes, I know. We have come into the forest to meet my people. My people would never live near the landing site. We will meet them. But now we will eat. Come."

Esmerelda finished her usual inspection of the area around the tree, and then snuck out, but instead of running farther into the forest, she stood at the edge of the tree and surveyed the area. She darted across the trail toward a bright pink tree, illuminated by a shaft of sunlight that managed to squeak its way between the trees. She slipped into the tree. Leos snuck in right behind her.

They were inside a pink conical tent. The sunlight shimmered through the thin translucent leaves, giving a roseate color to everything inside. The architecture of this tree was the same as the larger green trees, a straight central trunk with branches that spread radially from equidistant points up the trunk, though the branches were only about a link apart. The tree was about thirty links tall. Except for the bottom two or three levels, the branches were too small to support the weight of a climber. But this was the tree that held the berries. Pale pink berries, less than one decilink in diameter hung from the branches in clusters near the periphery of the tree. Esmerelda picked one berry and popped it in her mouth.

"Mmm. It is lovely. Here, Leos, taste. This is the food that my people eat."

"What are the berries like?"

"They are sweet and full of flavor. They are delicious."

Leos took a berry from Esmerelda's hand and placed it in his mouth and bit down. The juice that squired out tasted sweet, a fruity sweetness, but it had a tartness, too, like nothing he'd ever tasted, and he had difficulty comparing it to a flavor he already knew. Certainly not like yanto, which he desperately wanted, but the last yanto he had was on the ship that brought him to Nytandra, and long ago he resigned himself to doing without until he got back to Anthanos. These berries would have to do. They were juicy and they quenched his thirst and assuaged his appetite.

Surprisingly, the more of them he ate, the more he wanted. He grabbed another cluster from the tree and crammed several in his mouth at one time. They had a thin skin-like covering that enclosed the soft juicy insides, and when he bit down on a berry it ruptured, spurting the luscious juice all over the inside of his mouth. Some of the pink juice leaked out and dribbled off his chin onto his shirt.

But as he stood in the safety of the pink tent, scarfing down the sweet berries, Esmerelda placed a hand on his shoulder and whispered, "Hush! Someone is coming. I can hear the footsteps."

"I don't hear anything." Leos continued to munch on the berries, though he tried to munch quietly.

Esmerelda stood still, listening. She stayed quiet for a few nano-sectors, when from the other side of the tree, one of the native inhabitants of the green planet slipped into the secluded interior of the bush. He saw Esmerelda immediately, but apparently wasn't able to distinguish Leos, hidden from his point of view on the other side of the tree trunk. Leos, for his part, still munched on berries, and he didn't realize another person had entered, so quiet was his entry. But when the man spoke to Esmerelda, the sudden presence of an unfamiliar language and a strange male voice caught Leos's attention, and, with cheeks full of berries and pink juice drizzling down his chin onto his white shirt, he turned and glanced around the trunk to see who was talking.

"Whazzat?"

At the appearance of this strange and odd otherworlder, the man — an elderly man with deep green skin and graying brown hair, totally na-ked and wearing a knife and neckband like Esmerelda — shrieked, uttered an unfamiliar expletive, and fled from the tree. Esmerelda called after him in her native language.

"Who was that?" Leos stopped chomping on berries, and looked at Esmerelda quizzically. But Esmerelda gasped.

"He was a native of this planet, but he was scared of you. He thought you were a soldier from my father's army."

"You speak his language?" Leos swallowed the rest of the berries in his mouth.

"Yes, my mother spoke it to me much while I was young. She want-ed me to have the culture of my planet. That was in case I return. That is why I came with you. To return to my planet."

"Well, you've certainly arriv —"

Leos didn't get to finish his sentence. From deep in the forest came a ghastly, low-pitched, full-bodied scream. It was followed by a second, but much higher-pitched scream which turned into a muffled, gurgling cry, and the foul odor returned.

CHAPTER 26

THE INHABITANTS

Leos's world had become absolutely quiet. The warm, moist breeze that rustled through the forest and down the trail evaporated, and the screaming of the zolopil from on high ceased. Heavy dark clouds moved in, obscuring the shaft of light that illuminated the tree, leaving Leos and Esmerelda standing in a darkened pink tent. Leos was aware only of his heart palpitating in his chest. His hunger faded and the berries didn't seem delicious anymore.

He stared at Esmerelda and she stared back. A look of bewilderment and confusion covered her face, and she turned to look at the place on the side of the tree through which the native had darted only a few nano-sectors earlier. She stayed quiet, saying nothing. The vein on her left temple throbbed with each pulse.

Funny, I never noticed that before.

"Oh, Leos. I am afraid. He was caught by the zil."

Now Esmerelda's lithe nude body didn't seem so sensuous anymore.

The forest remained quiet for a short time, maybe another nano-sector when the cry started. From one of the trees, somewhat deeper in the forest and from the direction the native had come, came a thin, high-pitched wail, a cry that sailed out over the forest like the spreading of a wave, a fabric of sound that rose to a tremulous shrieking and howling, joined immediately by others, first in a few nearby trees, then spreading, jumping from tree to tree, swelling down the trail, deeper into the forest and back the way they'd come. It spread outward like ripples on a pond, eventually coming from all around. It came from the treetops, it descended the trunks, it came from deep within the forest and nearby. It turned into a caterwauling, a painful screaming of high pitch and low, it became a shrieking that rained down on Leos and Esmerelda standing in their little pink nest, safe and secure against physical assault.

As the cry developed, Leos became aware of footsteps, of creatures running past the tree, a few of them at first, but soon several at a time, and then many, all sprinting past the tree, screaming and shouting, occasionally brushing against the tree as they ran.

He flinched when the crowd passed, recoiling from the sound and the swishing against the tree. He worked his way through the tangle of branches and berry clumps to the other side. But Esmerelda remained still, statue-like, staring at the inside of the little pink tree, not moving, frozen in space and time. A tear stained her left cheek.

Almost as soon as it began, the running stopped, but the weeping and the shouting continued, and the sound worked its way deeper into the forest, away from the pink tree, and as it did so it became subdued. But it did not stop.

"Leos, I must talk to these people. These are my people. I must explain what happened."

"Uh, yeah, okay. Are you sure you want to? I mean, let's be careful."

"Yes, I must. You will stay here."

"Wait! What happens if the zil returns?"

"You will be safe here. The zil cannot enter the tree."

"Okay." *I hope you know what you're talking about.*

Esmerelda stepped from the tree. Leos crawled over to the trail side of the tree and peeked out between two leaves, watching Esmerelda as she walked down the trail. Farther down the trail in the diminished sunlight stood a large group of the inhabitants of this planet, as many as fifty or sixty. The shadows in the deep forest made seeing difficult, but they all had the same green skin, the same knife hanging from a band around their waist, and the same neckband as Esmerelda. Many of the group were still crying, some on their knees, some wailing to the heavens.

Esmerelda was not out of place in this group. As she approached the natives, no one made any movement in her direction. She blended in with the rest of the group, and they did not immediately recognize her as a visitor.

Then Esmerelda began to speak. First she spoke to one person, then several at a time, and the news of who she was spread through the crowd. Many did not hear, still involved in the mourning process, but one by one, they turned to look at Esmerelda. Several came over to greet her, and many of the women gave her a hug. Some even smiled while brushing tears from their eyes.

The group was far enough away from Leos that he couldn't hear the voices, but within a few nanosectors the crying had stopped, except from one woman still crouching on the trail at the exact spot the man was killed.

Everyone in the group watched Esmerelda. She turned to her right and pointed back toward the tree where Leos hid. Several men stepped out of the crowd and stared at the tree. They seemed confused, and they weren't smiling. Esmerelda turned around and motioned to Leos to come out of his hiding place.

"Leos! Come. It is okay."

Are you out of your mind? The sight of the visitor to the pink tree floated through Leos's mind.

Esmerelda yelled again. "Leos! Come!"

Against his better judgment and his most fervent desires, Leos slipped out of the tree. A collective gasp rose from the crowd, and most everyone drew their knives. A shout rang out from several of the natives. Leos didn't know what it meant, but he recognized it as the same epithet the man used just before he left the tree and ran to his death. Esmerelda turned back around and spoke to the crowd, holding her hands in the air, palms toward the crowd in an emphatic "stop" gesture, but four men, two on each side of the group, took several more steps toward Leos, knives drawn. They didn't look happy to see him.

Esmerelda yelled again at the group, especially at the men who approached Leos. They stopped, they didn't take another step, but neither did they sheathe their knives. One of the men spoke to Esmerelda, and she answered quietly. A short conversation ensued and Esmerelda yelled again.

"Leos! Come. It is good."

Leos stood outside the tree, his fear level hovering somewhere between *run like hell* and *get your friggin' ass outta here.*

"It is okay, Leos. They will not hurt you. I have spoken to them and they are only protecting themselves and the others."

Leos took several hesitant steps toward the group. Every knife was held vertically, one flat side of the knife facing him. His name seemed engraved on each blade. He took two more steps, and two of the men who'd stepped out of the crowd took several side steps, closer to the edge of the trail, near the trees. They blended closely with the foliage, their green skin so perfectly matched to the color of the trees.

Leos took a few more halting steps and everyone held their place. He watched the two outside men carefully, even more than he looked at Esmerelda. She stood quietly in the middle of the trail in front of the group. The men held their ground, and Leos approached.

I sure could use one of those weapons the security guards on Nytandra had.

"Come, Leos. Do not be afraid."

Leos stopped about a hundred links from the group. "Tell them to put those knives away."

Esmerelda turned back to the group and spoke to them. Hesitantly, all the women and many of the men returned their knives to their sheaths, but the four men who'd stepped out of the group did not. Now another male, an older man, stepped forward from the group. He had a full head of grayish-white hair and a slight pot belly, and he projected a definite air of authority within the group, possibly an elder or the head of the group. He stared long and hard at Leos, his face rigid and grim. He spoke quietly to Esmerelda, then turned and spoke to the group, and two more men—two who had not yet sheathed their knives—joined the four others at the side of the trail.

Uh-oh. Six men with knives. This doesn't look good. What the hell is going on?

The man spoke to Esmerelda, quietly at first, but soon he raised his voice, though it never rose to a shout. He stood directly in front of her, between her and the rest of the group, his arms crossed over his chest. He leaned back on his heels, staring at her as he talked. She wasn't intimidated, she retained the straight-backed regal look Leos had seen so many times on Nytandra, and she appeared to understand what the man was saying. She nodded several times and once shook her head, but in most respects she agreed with him. As he spoke, he made an abrupt gesture, a cutting motion of his right hand diagonally across his chest, rapidly from left shoulder to right hip. Esmerelda nodded, but Leos swallowed hard. His forehead began to perspire.

Esmerelda turned back and spoke again.

"Leos, please come. It is all right. They will not hurt you. They are only protecting themselves."

"If you say so." Leos took a few hesitant steps toward the group. He kept one eye on the men at both sides of the trail, and one on the older man. The group watched as he approached. At about five steps from Esmerelda, the men on the side of the trail circled around him, blocking any retreat. They held their knives straight up in the air, one flat side toward Leos.

"Leos, this is Jaiete, he is the Chief of this tribe. I have explained to him who you are and that you will not harm them. They make you to be one of my father's army, and they think you are here to kill their men and children and perform horrible acts on their women. I have said you are not. I have explained that you do not have a weapon. I have explained why you are here."

"Ahh . . . that's right. I'm just here to look around."

Esmerelda translated Leos's words, but the group was not amused. Esmerelda continued. "They are very angry that the man was killed here. They blame you for his death since he did not know who you were, and he was afraid of you. But they will accept you to stay here for not a long time if you will respect all others. You must not touch any of the women."

"Okay, that's good by me."

"Or he will personally kill you."

Leos swallowed hard again and his palms grew sweaty. He nodded and glanced at Jaiete who stood quietly listening to Esmerelda, his arms still across his chest.

Esmerelda turned and spoke to Jaiete, relaying Leos's agreement, and the Chief spoke again. Esmerelda turned to Leos but she didn't get a chance to translate. Several female voices in the group screamed —

"Zil! Zil!"

CHAPTER 27

THE ZIL

Everybody in the group froze—solid—rigid. With a smooth, quick, quiet action, developed over a lifetime of practice, every knife in the group was unsheathed. Even Esmerelda drew hers.

"Zil?! What? Where?" Leos looked around. He didn't smell anything.

"Hush! Do not speak!" Esmerelda whispered, and she clapped her left hand over Leos's mouth. Her eyes were wide open and she seemed to be staring back down the trail in the direction she and Leos had come.

Everyone in the group listened carefully. Oddly, and unlike Esmerelda, no one else in the group turned to see from which direction the zil approached. Leos found out later that these inhabitants of *Jon-Set-Tom* used their ears to pinpoint the sound of the Zil as it approached—not their eyes. The entire group stood absolutely still, no one moved or breathed for several nanosectors. Even the woman mourning the death of her husband had become quiet, though she still knelt on the trail in the middle of the group. Slowly, quietly, cautiously, several people in the group turned slightly. Esmerelda released her hold on Leos's face, and as he looked at the group, he found everyone else also looking back down the trail.

From that direction came a faint thumping sound, a series of slow, heavy foot beats, a *clump-clump-clump* sound like an army marching in step. As he looked down the trail, from behind a tree perhaps a thousand links away, a large beast-like creature thundered out onto the trail. As it stood cross-wise on the trail sniffing and snorting at a tree on the other side, four of the men who had been behind Leos fled toward the sides of the trail and vanished into the forest as quickly and quietly as Esmerelda melted into a tree. The other two remained still.

The foul odor also returned, wafted in on the breeze that drifted up the trail.

Okay, this must be a zil.

This was the creature everyone was afraid of, that everyone lived high in the trees because of (though not *too* high in the trees, mind you), and that everyone snuck from tree to tree to avoid because it was so dangerous and it could kill you with one swipe.

Did you get a look at its claws?

This was the monster of the ferocious reputation that made you want to hide in a tree and never come out, except that you had to come out to get food to live, and that meant you had to face the monster every day. And by its appearance, this beast lived up to its reputation, too. It most certainly looked the part of a deadly, vile creature capable of terrorizing an entire planet. At least twenty links tall at the shoulder, its back arched upward toward a muscular center hump that gave it a total height of more than twenty-five links. It must have weighed several krillic tons. Well, it would have on Nytandra or Anthanos.

The beast walked on four feet, but the front and rear feet were not even remotely alike. The rear legs were thick and heavy and ended in flat stump-like feet, but the front legs were narrower and more muscular and carried five long, slender, bright yellow claws, each almost a link long and curved into a vicious dagger.

One swipe with those claws and it's no wonder that guy was killed.

The fur of the animal was mostly a deep, dark brown, but splotches of lighter brown and tan were dappled randomly over the back. The face of the animal was drawn into a long slender muzzle around two links long which ended in a pinkish nose with a single trumpet-bell-shaped orifice through which it breathed. It carried its head down near the ground where it could detect the scent of natives or visitors moving through the forest. Situated prominently smack in the center of the upper muzzle was a bright yellow horn, a larger version of the claws on its front feet, and as the creature carried its head down, the tip of the horn projected straight forward.

You won't get past that horn.

The beast stayed quiet and remained in one place, sniffing around the tree—the same tree Leos and Esmerelda had stayed in just before they bolted over to the berry tree. It stayed there for several nanosectors, then raised its head and sniffed the air. It looked to its right—nothing in that direction—then it swung its head left, and—you could tell what it was thinking: *hold on, what do we have here?*

The big animal turned to face the group—it was surprisingly nimble on its feet—opened its mouth and let out one intense blast, one deep-throated, ear-piercing scream. It certainly didn't seem to be concerned about letting its prey know it was attacking, and when that huge behemoth saw the group of natives, it acted as though it had heard a clarion call to dinner. It galloped toward the group as fast as its bulky legs could carry it.

I could outrun that thing.

Surprisingly, the group did not bolt for the trees. They not only held their ground, they began walking *toward* it. All except Esmerelda, Jaiete, and two women in the center of the group, one still weeping and the other doing her best to comfort her. All spilled past Esmerelda and Leos, moving down the trail a few steps, facing the zil as it approached. They formed three parallel lines, fifteen or sixteen people per line, each line stretching in a shallow concave curve across the trail, blocking the zil's path.

"Now you will see what my people can do," Esmerelda whispered to Leos. "I have not seen this for many years. My mother told me about it much."

The zil slowed in its charge, and when it got within about twenty links of the group, it stopped. It seemed confused by the presence of so many people. It swung its head left and right as though inspecting the green-skinned beings standing before it. It whiffed the air in several husky snorts and took a few hesitant steps toward the group, but it made no real attempt to attack. Leos had been ready to scoot over to a tree and climb a few branches to get out of the animal's way, but no one else was surprised at all at the animal's hesitancy. They seemed to know it would stop.

"The zil has good hearing," Esmerelda said. "And it has good smell. But it does not have good sight. It knows there are many of us, but it is confused. It does not know where to attack. We will attack it."

"You're going to *attack* it?"

"Yes. Stay here. I will join the group. I wish to be a part of the kill."

Leos raised his eyebrows. "The kill?"

"Yes. You will be safe here. It will not get past us."

"God, I hope not." Leos glanced at Jaiete. He stood quietly, his arms still crossed over his chest, watching the group and the zil. He turned around and yelled something at the two women who had stayed behind. The comforting woman left the other and ran forward to join the group, drawing her knife as she ran.

Esmerelda took a place in the third row. Everyone held their knife by the handle, cocked behind their head, ready to throw. Jaiete barked orders at the group, and the three lines took two steps forward. He barked again and again. At each command, the line took two steps forward until the group came within ten links of the zil. The big animal still seemed confused and bewildered. It took two or three steps backward as the lines approached, swinging its head from left to right, its long horn swooshing viciously back and forth. Finally, it refused to retreat further and held its position. It pawed the ground and snorted and bellowed a few more times, and took several short, repetitive lunges at the line of people in front of it.

Farther down the trail, just behind the zil, the four men who had slipped into the forest appeared from the trees. The zil didn't see or hear them—it was focused on the people in front of it. The four men had drawn their knives, also cocked behind their heads. Jaiete raised his left arm, his index finger pointed directly at the sky, and when he jerked his arm down, the four men slung their knives into the zil's rump. All four knives hit home, slicing into the heavy musculature of the animal's backside.

The zil let out a tremendous bellow but it didn't bolt forward—it rose straight up on its rear legs. Standing like this, it must have been forty links tall. It slashed the air with its claws and bellowed a huge cascade of sounds that echoed up and down the trail.

As soon as the animal reared up, the front line of natives unleashed their knives, fifteen or sixteen knives plunging into the zil's belly just below the rib cage. All the knives penetrated fully, up to the bony shaft that served as a hand grip. As soon as those knives were flung, the throwers dropped to the ground to make way for the next row. The second row flung and dropped, and the third row flung, all three in rapid succession, one right after the other without hesitation, all in the space of no more than a half, maybe three-quarters of a nanosector.

Blood spurted from every wound. All of the knives of the second and third waves pierced the animal's rib cage, and when the zil dropped to all fours, even in the lower gravity of this small planet, its chest slammed into the ground with such a grisly, crushing thud that all those knives were driven deeper into the animal's chest. They must have ripped the animal's lungs to shreds. The zil released one more snort, its head fell to the ground, and it rolled onto its left side. A few more weak snorts puffed from its nose, followed by a billowing bolus of bright burgundy blood, and the animal lay still.

A huge cry rose from the group. Except Esmerelda. She allowed nothing more than a bashful smile to cross her face. She would never have participated in a celebration. Her royal demeanor would not permit it.

In the midst of the celebration, the group separated, stepping aside to let Jaiete through. He stood at the head of the zil, then walked all around it, pointing to various parts of the carcass, giving orders, probably on how to divide up the spoils. When he reached the head again, he drew his knife and with one quick slice sheared off the horn of the animal at the base.

With a big smile on his face, he presented the horn to Esmerelda.

"Look, Leos. They have given me the horn. It is a sign of respect. They killed the animal in my honor."

"Yeah, that's quite an honor."

As soon as the horn was removed, the group went to work skinning the animal. Even lying on its side the animal was more than six links high and at least twenty links long.

"They will skin it in a short time," Esmerelda said.

They skinned the animal in about a subsector. Their knives seemed to melt through the flesh. They sliced the skin over the back into four roughly square pieces, eventually to be made into blankets. They spread all four inside up over the trail to allow them to dry, then turned their attention to the rest of the carcass. They cut out the meat, sliced it into strips, and hung the strips from the branches within several of the trees. Several women rubbed salt over the strips.

"Salt? Where did they get salt?"

"From the ground. From the water in the ground. It is very salty."

They spread the bones out on the ground next to the trail, and dumped the entrails in a specially prepared pit north of the trail, almost an anthan away. "The other animals will devour it there," Esmerelda said.

"Other animals? What other animals?"

"You will find out later."

"Er . . . okay."

To reach the pit, they passed through an open grassy area about eight hundred by five hundred links. A stream of clear, cool water ran through the grass. Remnants of small trees that had fallen over into the grassy area dotted the field.

"This is where we get our drinking water," Esmerelda explained as several others dipped large flasks of zil hide into the water and carried them back to the trail.

By the time the zil's remains had been disposed of, the air temperature had begun to drop and the sun hung deep in the evening sky, ready to plunge below the horizon at the far end of the trail.

CHAPTER 28

LEARNING

"We will spend the night here," Esmerelda explained to Leos. "They have told me of a tree which has a dwelling place in it, and we can use it."

"We're not going back to the place near the runway?"

"No, it is too late, and we do not have a blanket for the night. They have many extra zil blankets and we may have one. Jaiete has said so. We will be warm tonight."

"What are they going to do with the four blankets they made from that zil?"

"After the zil skin dries, they will prepare it. It takes many days to make a blanket. It must be dried and soaked in diluted zil brains to soften, and scraped to make it smooth."

"Zil brains?"

"It makes it soft and warm. You will see."

"Oh, okay. But what tree are we going to use?"

Esmerelda showed Leos a tree farther up the trail which she'd been told was not in use, and several others from the group brought over a large zil blanket. The platform that circled this tree was in much better condition than the one near the runway, and this platform had one feature the other lacked. A separate walkway connected it with the tree next door.

"All the living spaces are connected. Except across the trail. It is too far."

Within the security of the upper tree, Leos and Esmerelda were insulated to a modest degree against the plummeting temperature when the sun finally dropped below the horizon, but the chill had begun to seep through the canopy of leaves into the living space. The coolness felt good, a welcome change from the saturating humidity and warmth of the day. They spread the zil blanket on the sleeping area of the platform, fur side up, and as they sat on the blanket with the darkness enveloping them, the glow began.

It started on the trunk of the tree, near where Leos and Esmerelda sat. It spread upward and crept around the trunk. Even some of the branches near the couple glowed. At its maximum, after all light was gone from the sky, the glow spread entirely around the tree and encompassed all the branches. The orange glow contained a hint of yellow, and it illuminated the living space with an eerie, supernatural flavor, but it gave them enough light to see each other. Esmerelda's green skin appeared much darker, nearly black, but Leos's tan skin wasn't affected. He glanced around at the glowing trunk and branches and wondered about its origin. He found that if he exhaled on a small area of the tree, the glow intensified into a brilliant yellow for several nanosectors, then faded to its normal orangish tint.

"Before we become of the sleeping type, there are things I must tell you." Esmerelda and Leos sat cross-legged on the blanket, facing each other. She smiled at him, her eyes softly focused on his.

"What?"

"We must leave tomorrow and find my *san*, that is, we must find my group."

"Your group? I thought this was your group—er, what?"

"My group, my blood group, my family. The people I am descended from. They are my family and my relatives. They live farther from here. But there is another reason we must leave."

"What's that?"

"They will not let you stay here. They blame you for the death of the man."

"But that was an accident. I didn't do anything."

"But if you had not been here, he would still be alive. He was afraid of you."

Leos shrugged his shoulders. "Yeah, I know, I'm sorry about that, but I didn't realize . . . you know . . . these guys with the knives . . . I didn't know."

"This is true, you did not know. But there is more that you do not know and you should know."

"What?"

"This group lives closest to the runway. They lived near where Gass and his men landed. This *san* was the first group they found, and they destroyed them much. Many from this *san* were lost. Many men were killed, and the women—I cannot explain it—you understand. You know how Gass is. His men were . . . that is . . . similar. He is disgusting. I despise him much. After Gass left, they moved here."

Even in the soft, orange glow from the tree, the look of hatred and revulsion at all the terrible atrocities that Gass and his men perpetrated on these people was visible on Esmerelda's face. She turned her head away. Leos touched her face and she took his hand in hers.

"Yes, I know," he said.

"That is why this tree is empty here. This tree belonged to a family of whom many were killed. Many from this *san* were killed."

"I'm beginning to understand."

"And when you came, you looked like a man from the attackers. You understand why still they blame you?"

"I understand, but there's nothing I can do about that now."

"Leos, you should show some pity for the woman. She is pregnant and now her husband is dead."

"She's pregnant? Wow. I didn't know that."

"Yes, she is pregnant. She will give birth. Not many women are pregnant. It is hard for women of this age to bear children. Now her husband is dead and the child has no father."

Leos lowered his head. He had a real sense of compassion for the woman, but he also now knew why Esmerelda had told him that had she not been with him when he landed, he'd be dead by now. But he wasn't sure how to express his sympathy to the woman, so he reverted to a familiar theme. "Oh, I see. But it wasn't . . . I mean, y' know, I didn't really . . . well, you know."

"Yes, I know. And you should apologize to her and to Jaiete. But there will be no time. We must leave early tomorrow." Esmerelda removed her neck band and knife, and took her hair out of its usual ponytail. A light rain had started outside and the drops made a faint metallic plinking sound as they hit the leaves. But as each leaf overlapped the one below it, the rain trickled down the outside of the tree and the two residents inside remained dry.

"I didn't come to this place for my health, ya know. I had to. Remember?"

"Yes, this is right. And I will teach you about this planet. This is my planet."

"You had a choice. I didn't."

"You are right. I chose to come. But you must understand how they feel about you and the invaders. You have the appearance of an invader."

"Yeah, I guess I do." He looked at his clothing, the typical Nytandran garb. The invaders would have been dressed similarly. "Sorry about that. But there's not much—"

"That was the word the man said when he saw you in the berry tree—'*doa-ta*.' That means 'outsider' in my language. A person different from our *san*. We do not have a word for 'invader', or for 'attacker'. It does not happen here."

"I see. I guess I understand now."

"I understand, and Jaiete understands, too, but many do not. You must not touch any of the women."

Leos nodded. "Okay."

"They will kill you if you do." She took off her knife and tossed it onto the platform.

"Yeah, I remember."

"That is good. Now it is time to go to bed. I am chilled. Please to get ready. This night you may enter me. I desire it much. I will be your mate forever." She leaned over and gave him a hot, passionate kiss. She'd never done that before. Not on the lips, anyway.

Oh.

Now the moment of truth had arrived—now the time had come to make a decision. He'd known Esmerelda for about two Nytandran months now, a couple hundred T-sectors in Anthanian time, not counting flight time to *Jon-Set-Tom*, which didn't count in his mind because Esmerelda remained so aloof during the flight, not allowing him anything like intimacy—she wanted to wait, she said—and so many images went through his mind, of Tama, of Esmerelda, of other women he'd met. Where did his devotion lie? Who was he committed to? Tama? Esmerelda?

Esmerelda's right here. Ready to go. I'm not likely to see Tama again. If I reject Esmerelda now . . . I don't even want to think about it. Might as well . . .

"Okay," Leos said, and dropped his clothes into a pile on the platform. They nestled together in the blanket, sealing themselves in a cocoon of warmth against the plunging temperature. As he lay on top of her soft, warm body, he caressed her satiny hair, kissed her luscious lips, stroked her muscular arms, and reveled in every quiet moan she made with each passionate thrust. The images that materialized in his mind were of the naked women he'd seen during the day. One by one they paraded through his head.

No wonder Gass and his men went wild when they came here.

CHAPTER 29

HER SAN

"Leos. Rise. It is time to go. Please to get dressed."

Esmerelda's voice seemed muffled or far away, as though in a dream. Leos turned over within the zil blanket and reached for her but she wasn't there. He opened a sleepy eye to investigate, but she'd left the warmth of the blanket. Within a nanosector he heard her soft voice behind him.

"Leos, I have brought you some berries. Please eat. Then we will leave."

Leos sat up in the blanket. The sun had barely risen above the tree line, and the upper part of the tree was brilliantly illuminated. Leos had only to look upward through the branches to appreciate the deep green of the tree's interior. At the level of the platform where the two lovers had spent their first night on this planet, a single shaft of sunlight lit up the leaves just above where Leos sat, and gave him enough light to see by. The only remnants of the orange glow from the trunk and branches were small pockets of color which remained hidden within dark recesses in the tree bark. Esmerelda squatted next to the blanket and handed Leos a handful of berries. The air was beginning to warm, yet even in the chill, Esmerelda seemed not to notice. She'd already donned her knife and neckband, and put her hair back in its usual ponytail. Leos munched on a few berries, then stood and retrieved his clothing. Esmerelda rolled the blanket into a tight cylinder and secured it with a couple of strips of zil leather. Leos slung the bulky blanket over his shoulder, and they made their way down the tree. They saw no one on the trail, and set out again, continuing in the direction they'd come the day before. Behind them, a single prolonged note of a trumpet-like call, followed by the lyric chant of a mellow baritone floated through the trees.

"That is Jaiete. He is announcing the start of a new day. I am not so familiar with the chants of this group, but I believe he is calling for a sharpening of the knives. Their knives have not been sharpened in a year. The early morning is a good time for this."

They bounded down the trail as fast as they could, popping into a tree now and then. Leos found it astonishing how quickly and silently Esmerelda could change direction and enter a tree, and how seamlessly the leaves fell back together, obscuring where she'd gone.

All the better to hide from a zil.

Finally, after slipping in and out of another twenty trees, Leos began to understand that the number of trees you entered was a crude, but convenient, method of measuring distance on this planet. Then, suddenly, Esmerelda stopped, right in the middle of the trail, in front of one particularly large tree.

"Should we be standing here?" Leos asked, looking around. "Isn't it dangerous?"

Esmerelda touched Leos's lips again and spoke in a whisper. "There are people here."

"How can you tell? It's just trees. Looks the same as every other place."

"I know this place. This is my home. This is my *san*. This is where my people live. I know these trees. I have been here before. My mother told me of this place. See the horns?"

"Horns?" Zil horns, similar to the one Esmerelda carried, but colored in reds and yellows, festooned the trees on both sides of the trail about twenty links above the ground as though they marked the boundaries of something—yes, the boundaries of the living area of a different group, a different *san*. The horns hung with the point downward, and each horn had been inscribed with two or three symbols running vertically. Some symbols were different from the others, but all had one marker near the top that was the same among all the horns. And that was one of the same symbols on the ribbon around Esmerelda's neck. An identifying marker perhaps. It identified the group of which she was a member—her *san*.

Esmerelda held up her hand. "There are people here. I can hear them."

Without any warning, ten men, all with knives drawn, slipped out of trees around Leos and Esmerelda. One of the men shouted something to Esmerelda, motioning for her to move away from Leos. They fixed their eyes on Leos, every knife held vertically, one flat side facing his direction.

"What's going on?" Leos said, and he dropped the zil blanket on the ground.

Esmerelda held up both hands and shouted at the men. Slowly, one by one, they turned toward her, but just as quickly turned back to Leos, all the time keeping their knives pinned on him. The man who'd shouted made his way toward her. Like Jaiete, he was older, perhaps in his sixties and with the same air of superiority, but much taller and without the paunch. All the men appeared to be in their forties or fifties, and, like the men of the other group, muscular and fit, especially in the upper body. All had angry scowls on their faces.

"Esmerelda, what's going on?" Leos said again. His eyes darted from man to man, trying to gauge their intentions, but they stared at him, that angry look and flash of knife so intimidating.

Esmerelda remained quiet. The man approached and she spoke a-gain. A look of puzzlement crossed his face. He briefly seemed to relax, then turned and yelled toward one of the trees. Several women appeared.

Esmerelda spoke again, and one of the women approached her.

"Kao-tsin?" the woman said.

"Kao-tsin," Esmerelda replied, nodding her head. The woman spoke again and a bright smile splashed across her face. She began speaking rapidly in a language Leos didn't understand.

"Leos!" Esmerelda exclaimed, she too beaming broadly. "She remembers me!"

"Yeah, right. Uh, listen, could you tell these guys . . ."

But Leos was interrupted when the woman let out a shriek and clasped her hands to her face and began yelling so all could hear, "Kao-tsin! Kao-tsin!"

Several other women took up the chant, and it shot from one woman to the next.

"What's going on?" Leos wondered. "What's 'Kao-tsin' mean?"

"She remembers me," Esmerelda said, the smile still broad on her lips. "She knew my mother and she remembers me as a little girl before I was taken. Kao-tsin is my name before I was captured and taken to Nytandra. I have not heard that name since my mother died. It is so wonderful to be with my own people again."

"That's great. But, uh, listen, say, about these guys with, you know, the knives . . ."

"Yes, I will talk to the Chief." But Esmerelda didn't have to say anything. The Chief spoke sharply to the men and they re-sheathed their knives. But they didn't look happy about it. They held their ground and stared at Leos who breathed a cautious sigh of relief.

"Come, Leos," Esmerelda said. "I will introduce you to the Chief. His name is Senalar. I knew him from before. He was a young man then."

Like the others, Senalar kept a suspicious eye on Leos and studied him up and down. His face had returned to an angry, tight expression. Esmerelda kept talking to him, probably prodding him to accept Leos. He finally nodded and the angry look on his face mellowed slightly. But he still scowled at Leos, and that told him that—as Esmerelda translated—though he might be welcome in this group, he was definitely on probation and better keep his hands off . . . well, he knew.

"They are suspicious of you," Esmerelda told Leos. "Just as Jaiete was suspicious of you. I have told them that you are a visitor, and that we have mated, and he understands. You are welcome to stay here with me. But you must not touch any of the women."

"Ah, okay. That's what I thought."

Now the party began. Many more men and women appeared, slipping out silently from the trees, all mature, perhaps in their forties or older. Leos saw no youngsters, no young couples. He and Esmerelda were the youngest present. The women brought out leather flasks of a pinkish liquid which Esmerelda explained was made from the berries and fermented.

Ah, fermented. Leos licked his lips in anticipation. They brought out strips of zil meat and started a little party on the trail, forty or fifty people standing around munching on salted meat and several types of berries, and getting tipsy, if not downright drunk. They hugged Esmerelda and showered her with kisses. They played crude flute-like musical instruments which, to Leos, produced a much more lyrical sound than any music he'd heard on Nytandra.

But they left Leos alone. They forced him back toward the edge of the trail, pressed into the trees like a wallflower at a dance. No one spoke to him. The men eyed him suspiciously and formed a loose line between him and the rest of the group. No matter where he looked, at least one pair of dark, intense eyes glowered at him. No one passed the flask to him until Esmerelda did, and after he took a drink, they threw the flask on the ground.

As the sun made its way across the sky and inched down behind the trees in the west, the celebration ended, and the others of Esmerelda's *san* returned to the more mundane tasks of daily life. Some entered the trees and effectively disappeared from Leos's view. Some used their knives to cut and trim pieces of wood, and several walked away up or down the trail or to one side. Senalar showed Esmerelda and Leos her old home, a hundred links or so off the main trail. An absolutely magnificent tree, one of the tallest in the area, shielded well in the shadows of the afternoon light, a home befitting the return of a prodigal soul. Leos and a giggly Esmerelda climbed the tree and settled in on the platform more than four hundred links above the ground.

The next day, they rose with the sun and Senalar's call—his tenor voice seemed to penetrate through the leaves of the trees better than the baritone of Jaiete—and made their way to the bottom of the tree. They took a meal of berries, though Esmerelda didn't eat very many. She seemed greener than usual. They met Senalar again who told them he planned to send a runner to the next family east, to let them know of Esmerelda's arrival. Using characters similar to those on Esmerelda's neckband, he scratched a message on a pale pink pad-like sheet, made from the leaves of the pink tree, but blanched in salt water and woven and dried into a smooth, tight surface. He rolled it up and stuffed it into a leather sheath and gave it to a runner. That message would be transmitted all the way around the planet, runner by runner, so everyone would know of the return of a member of their race kidnapped more than ten years ago. Ten years green planet time, that is.

And after the runner was dispatched—with considerable ceremony and attended by everyone in the group—they got busy with the duties of the day.

Out came the knives again.

CHAPTER 30

THE KNIFE

From his first day on *Jon-Set-Tom*, Leos was intensely aware he was an oddity in the *san*, the only one—they assured him repeatedly—on the entire planet who wore clothes. Leos wasn't ready to shed his garments; the thought of dispensing with the custom of living fully clothed just to join these new people was unacceptable—no, that wouldn't do. So he remained fully dressed, and his dignity and self-respect stayed intact in spite of standing out rather obviously among his green-skinned hosts. Esmerelda never pressured him to join them. In fact, she accepted and approved of his decision. He—and she—learned to live with it, and only when he was alone with her in the sleeping area of their platform each evening, ready to join her in the zil blanket, did he remove his clothes. A pleasure he looked forward to every day.

But that wasn't the only way Leos stood out from the others.

Within the first few days after Leos and Esmerelda arrived, Senalar finally, and at Esmerelda's insistent prodding, allowed the two of them to return to the crashed ship and retrieve the suitcase of Leos's clothing. But—and this was the only way Senalar would never let him go—Esmerelda had to go with him. Leos had no knife, and his hearing wasn't acute enough to detect the zil from far enough away to prevent being impaled by the horn.

And Senalar did something else.

Life on *Jon-Set-Tom* was more than picking berries from a tree. They cooked—always on the ground, never in any of the trees—they made rope, they captured rainwater for drinking, and they extracted salt water from the ground and used it to preserve zil hide. They had gardens, well off the trail in an open space near a narrow freshwater stream that trickled off the larger stream through the greenspace, and they picked fruit and vegetables that grew on trees near the grassy area, fed by the water from the main stream. They could treat the berries in two ways, ferment the whole berries to make a strong drink, or skin the berries and soak the insides in water to release the sugar to make a wonderfully thick, rich sauce they ate as a sweet desert after a meal of the strong, pungent zil meat.

Leos eventually became fascinated with the mechanics of living on this planet and threw himself into learning all about it. He had to. He had little choice.

Even from the beginning of the long flight from Nytandra to *Jon-Set-Tom*, Leos understood he would probably have to live on the green planet for the rest of his life. *There's no damn way anyone is going to come and pick me up. Coreaje isn't going to send anyone. Why would he? He kicked me out of there. I'm dead to them. And Anthanos doesn't know where I am. How could they? I never got to talk to anyone and tell them where I was going. Grok and Krok wouldn't let me. I'm going to be on this damn green planet for a while. A long while. At least I have Esmerelda to keep me company.*

So Leos went to work. But first . . .

At the heart of much of the work was the knife. Everyone had a knife. Esmerelda had the one given to her by her mom, the one she used to help kill the zil. These were special knives, unique to these people and Senalar insisted Leos make his own.

The blade of the knife was not metal. The natives had no access to metal, and couldn't refine it even if they had. They made knives from a special mineral they called *skar* which they found in small deposits off the main trail. A dark grayish-blue material, it resided in thin sheets that jutted from the ground in sharp, angular plates. Struck at just the proper angle by a large rock, a piece would break off, and with several more precise and skillful whacks, it could be worked into a rough shape, and a small piece of hollowed-out zil bone shoved onto a narrow section to act as a handle. That was the easy part. Next came the long, tedious sharpening.

The only material hard enough to sharpen it was more of the same. Leos took a small, flat piece of *skar* and with a circular motion he smoothed the blade until it approached a sharp edge along one side. He kept at it all day, and when the daylight was gone from the sky he set it aside and slept on it—literally. He put it under his zil blanket and retrieved it the next morning. And he worked on it all that day, and the next, and the next, and that was all there was to his life for many days. When it began to look like a real blade, he gave it to Senalar and he told him to work on it some more, and so he did, until his arm was so sore he could swear it was about to fall off. And as he worked on it, within those small circles that sharpened the blade's edge down to molecular thinness, the blade began to glow, much like the orange glow on the trees after the sun went down. But this was a brilliant yellow-white glow which started at the edge and gradually spread to encompass the entire blade, as though the blade was a small sun right there in his hand. It wasn't a hot glow—not at all, he could still hold it in his hand, but a sensation developed through that glow, like a bonding. More than a bonding, though, it became a covenant—an obligation—a pledge. He heeded Senalar's warning: if you take care of the knife, it will take care of you. Each day as he worked on it the bond grew stronger, and the knife become a part of him, like a third hand. And when the knife was complete, so was the bond.

After eighty-seven days of smoothing and sharpening, Leos's knife finally passed Senalar's inspection. Leos showed it to Esmerelda.

"Cast your peek-a-boos on that, kiddo!"

"Oh, Leos, how wonderful!"

And, brother, was that knife sharp. It cut through wood as easily as it cut through warm zil fat. Leos found he could shave with it. Later he made a smaller knife with a flat, straight edge that he used for shaving, as did most of the men in this *san*.

The others showed Leos and Esmerelda how to use the knife to trim a small tree to get the wood and cut it into strips. They showed them how to make furniture for their platform home and repair the joists that had rotted since Esmerelda's parents had been captured or killed.

Senalar showed Leos how to throw the knife. Like all knives on this planet, it was single-edged, thicker along one side. "Grab it lightly by the handle," he told him, "let it rest gently in your hand. Cradle it, don't choke it or squeeze it. Hold the knife flat to the target with the sharp edge to your right, then cock your arm behind your head and sling the knife in one smooth motion. When you do it correctly, it will jump out of your hand as though it had a mind of its own."

It did. They set up a target in the profile of a zil on one side of the trail, and let Leos practice throwing. It took him several days of practice, but Leos eventually understood the spirit that inhabited the knife. It jumped from his hand and landed exactly where he wanted. He still had to fix in his mind where he wanted the knife to go, and he had to throw it hard enough to get it there and throw it in the general direction of the targeted point. But most importantly, he had to learn how to hold it when he released it so that it flew horizontally, and the air streamed across the blade as it did over an airplane wing. That way it slipped easily between the ribs of a zil.

It was a big knife, too. The handle was only about five decilinks long but Leos made the blade much longer, around twelve decilinks, making his knife equal to those of the other men in the tribe. Most of the women's knives had a blade about eight to ten decilinks long, but only the chief had a knife with a larger blade, more than twelve decilinks. That knife, though, was heavily decorated and largely ceremonial, passed from one leader of the tribe to the next. When he had to actually use a knife, he used the one he'd made himself.

That was the daily routine on the green planet. Every now and then they would kill another zil and strip the hide and make jerky of some of the meat, preserving much of the rest in the salt water from the soil. They cooked meat over a small fire on the ground in the midst of the trees, and Leos grew fond of the taste of zil meat. "Tastes sort of like glok meat from Nytandra. Sort of." And they prepared blankets from the hide of the animal. Soon Leos and Esmerelda had enough skins to cover all six sides of the sleeping area in their platform.

One day, about thirty days after the runner was sent out, another runner arrived. But he came from the direction of Jaiete's tribe. He brought the information that the news of Esmerelda's return had traveled all the way around the planet, and everyone—except for his group—was vitally excited that she'd returned. They rejoiced that someone from their planet had successfully left the planet of her captors and managed to make her way home. To them, it was a sign from whatever form of divine providence they considered holy that better days would be forthcoming. But they were also excited about something else, something that was withheld from Leos, even from Esmerelda, and he had no idea what it was. Leos couldn't imagine.

Leos put that aside and learned to relax in his new surroundings. After he finished his knife and learned to throw it, they allowed him to participate in an attack on a zil. They put him in the back row because that row didn't have to drop to the ground like the first two rows, though he never made it to the second row, or to the elite group, the first row.

Soon his thoughts turned to his future on this planet. Always in the back of his mind lay the faint hope that someone would come and rescue him. He clung to the prospect of Coreaje sending a ship to retrieve Esmerelda, but he also knew that with each passing day the chances of that happening dwindled slowly toward nothingness.

So he made do. At least he was safe, he wasn't followed around by guards with intimidating weapons, and he didn't have the shallow and supercilious Nytandrans to put up with. The green folks on this planet were much more honest and open with him. He was eventually accepted as a regular member of the group, as much as any other man, largely because he was Esmerelda's friend, lover, and life partner. He and Esmerelda participated in all the activities of the group. The others were certainly aware he was indirectly responsible for the death of the man in Jaiete's group—news like that spread around the planet as fast as one runner could travel—but most didn't let it interfere with their welcoming.

But Leos still had a problem, and it stemmed from his relationship with Esmerelda.

It wasn't that Esmerelda wasn't a good partner, certainly not. She satisfied him in every way possible. He would lie on that zil blanket and she would attend to his every want, his every need, stimulating every part of his body with a freshness that left him panting for more. Occasionally, he would sit in the crude chair he fashioned with his knife, and in the few minutes before the evening turned too cold to remain outside the blanket, Esmerelda would perform orally on him, expertly, the way he taught her, just the way he liked. The way Tama used to. Then they would retire to the sleeping area and wrap themselves in, cuddling together like the two lovers they were, just the way she liked. Esmerelda had become a master at the art of love.

But in his mind, it wasn't Esmerelda. Leos never fully accepted Esmerelda as his lover. They'd mated, sure, and in the evenings he would stroke Esmerelda's long hair—before bedtime she took it out of the ponytail she wore during the day—pretending it was Tama's rich curls. Esmerelda's warm, muscular body was a ripe substitute for the suppleness of Tama, and with his eyes closed, or in the darkness inside the blanket, Leos could fool himself that he was back on Anthanos with Tama at his side. He assumed he'd never see Tama again and he tried to forget about her. But her tantalizing face and figure appeared in his head almost every day. Only by participating in the tribe's regular day's work could he eject her image from his mind.

No, it wasn't a great life, but all his needs were met and he didn't have to do any hard work, but he longed to be back on his home planet. In some respects even Nytandra was better than this place—a lot more things to do there. Here, life was the same day after day, the same duties, the same chores, the same landscape, the trail and the trees—oh, the trees, so many trees. So he resigned himself to living out the rest of his life as best he could, until one day about one green planet year and a half after he and Esmerelda arrived . . .

CHAPTER 31

VISITORS

Leos stood in the middle of the trail, several of the other natives of Esmerelda's *san* nearby. That was good for Leos. Without the acute hearing of the natives, he wasn't supposed to be away from the safety of the trees by himself. In the past year and a half he'd been on this planet, he'd come to realize two vitally important characteristics about the zil: not all of them had the foul odor he smelled the first day, and they could approach quietly too — well, reasonably quietly, never silently at all — but not always with the heavy clumping and loud trumpeting that indicated they were attacking.

As Leos stood on the trail, he gazed upward into the bright blue sky. This was the dry season, one of only two seasons on this planet, and he longed to see rain clouds to provide some desperately needed moisture. Several zolopil circled above the treetops, at this distance little more than a dark, vaguely arrowhead shape that flapped its wings occasionally. The adult zolopil couldn't easily negotiate the narrow confines of the trail, and only immature ones ever dipped into the tight canyon of trees and attacked ground dwellers, and, with the simple flick of a knife, that usually ended badly for the zolopil. But higher above that small clutch of circling zolopil was another bird, a funny-shaped bird that didn't circle. Like the zolopil it too was dark against the bright sky, and it had long, slender wings, but it flew in a straight line, unusual for a zolopil. Zolopil always circled, waiting for the next opening to appear in the leaves of a tree, usually because a small animal had climbed to the top of the tree and dared peek out. This new bird didn't flap its wings, either. Its wings were straight and rigid, not curved like the zolopil. Silent, too, totally silent, not squawking like the zolopil.

"Funny," Leos mumbled. "That bird looks like a space sh — holy din-frizzle!"

You know how it is when you've seen something terrible, something so horrible that it frightens you deep down inside, so terrible that your heart pounds and your body temperature drops and you visualize with every nerve cell in your brain the most awful consequences, and your mind races ahead to conceptualize in the worst way. Your face grows pale as the blood drains from your head, you feel dizzy and you want to run, but your legs won't move and you're stuck in the ground right there, and besides, you don't know where you would run even if you could, and your entire world comes crashing down around you. Leos knew that feeling. And with the realization that little black dot in the sky brought home to him, his knife slipped from his hand and plunged into the soil of the trail less than a decilink from his foot.

"Leos!" Esmerelda said, joining him on the trail. "You must be careful. You almost cut your foot."

Leos didn't respond. He stared at the sky, watching until the little black dot disappeared, then lowered his head. Esmerelda looked at him, her face quizzical. He was sick to his stomach.

"You are pale," she said. "What are you looking at?" She, too, looked up into the sky but the funny bird had passed.

"Nothing. Just the birds. The zolopil."

"But you do not look at the zolopil. Why now? Why would a zolopil make you . . ." Esmerelda paused, and her face, too, drained of color, as much as a face of dark green can. Her voice dropped to a whisper. "Leos, you have seen something. Tell me."

"Come over here."

They walked over to a tree at the edge of the trail and slipped inside. Leos spoke quietly. "I just saw a bird that wasn't a zolopil. It didn't flap its wings and it flew in a straight line."

"I do not know of any bird like that. Leos, what are you saying?"

"That wasn't a bird. It was a spaceship. It's headed for the landing strip."

Esmerelda remained quiet for a nanosector or two. She looked at the ground, then raised her head and looked at Leos. Her eyes betrayed no emotion, her face remained calm. She spoke softly and quietly. "My father has arrived. He will bring men with weapons. I must go to meet him and try to persuade him—"

"Meet him? Wait, Esmerelda. Do you really want to meet him?" Leos placed one hand on her arm and gave her a little shake, perhaps trying to shake some sense into her. "Maybe we should leave him alone. After all, he probably came to take you back and to get me for taking you with me."

"I wish to talk to him," she said, her voice hesitant and shaky.

"Talking won't do much good. He wants you and he probably wants me. I'm not about to let him —"

"No," Esmerelda said, her voice now firm and steady, just like the Princess he once knew. She straightened and looked Leos directly in the eye. "I must talk to him. We must leave right away. We have a long way to go."

"What? No, you can't." He gave her another shake and tightened his grip on her arm.

"Leos, your hand — you are pinching . . ."

"Esmerelda, think about what you're going to do. This is not a good idea. It could only end badly for us."

"No, I must go. This I must do." Esmerelda wrenched her arm from his grip and stepped out of the tree. She took off down the trail, running west toward the landing site.

"Esmerelda! Wait!" Leos began to run, too.

It took them several Nytandran hours to reach the landing site. They passed Jaiete's area quietly and unobtrusively, and when they reached the opening, Leos slipped into one of the trees bordering the runway, hiding from certain capture. Esmerelda slipped into the same tree, but remained at the periphery, peeking out from between the leaves to watch the accumulating spaceships.

By the time they arrived, several ships had landed at the runway. First to land were three vertical landers. They touched down at the far western end of the runway, more than an anthan away, barely visible in the warm, humid haze that settled over the opening each day. Each ship disgorged seven soldiers, and they scoured the runway, poking with their brilliant silver weapons into the edge of the forest. But as Esmerelda and Leos watched, the horizontal landers drifted in, swooping silently over the canopy of trees at the western end, landing near the center and coming to rest at the eastern end. Eight ships landed, one at a time, deftly missing the one large tree that confounded Leos, each one quietly gliding up behind the previous in a neat single file.

Third in line was the largest ship. Leos and Esmerelda waited silently, watching.

"I believe my father will be in the third ship," Esmerelda whispered. Leos put his arm around her waist and pulled her to him. She shivered in his embrace. They kissed.

After a few minutes, two Nytandrans emerged from the lead ship, and ten more joined them from the second. Armed and heavily armored in the typical shiny metallic body armor of Nytandran security forces, they hurriedly set up a security perimeter around the third ship, joined by a hundred or more troops pouring from other ships down the line.

Several official-looking members of the security team stepped outside the armed perimeter and began poking around the periphery of the runway. Officers, no doubt, with colorful badges and emblems and insignia all over their uniforms. They approached the tree where Leos and Esmerelda hid, so they scooted up several levels of branches to escape detection. When the Nytandrans seemed satisfied the area was secure, they retreated to their ships. Leos and Esmerelda climbed back down and watched as the gangplank was lowered on the large ship.

Down the gangplank strode a large Nytandran man, round-headed, overweight and pudgy, a multi-colored cloak draped around his shoulders. When he reached the end of the gangway, one of the security officers pointed toward the remains of Leos and Esmerelda's spaceship, still lying where they'd left it but now overgrown with weeds and flowers, and home to several furry creatures that scattered as the visitors approached. They glanced inside, taking several minutes to investigate the ship, then walked over to the edge of the runway. Esmerelda stepped from her hiding place in the tree, facing them.

"Father," she said quietly. "How are you?"

Coreaje turned toward her, his smile distorted into a look of utter surprise.

"Esmerelda!" he bellowed as he walked over to meet her. "What are you doing, young woman? Put some clothes on this instant!"

Another soldier marched down the gangplank of the third ship and strode up beside Coreaje. Shorter, pudgy also, swarthy complexion and bulbous nose, he was dressed in a magnificent dark green general's uniform with three bright gold stars gleaming from the epaulets. He had a broad grin on his face, and he unzipped his pants.

CHAPTER 32

RENDEVOUS

In one swift move, Esmerelda whipped her knife from its sheath and held it less than a decilink from Gasz's nose.

"Do not be so foolish, Gasz, or I will cut it off and feed it to the zil." The smile on Gasz's face evaporated, and he zipped up.

The security perimeter around the ships had withdrawn, leaving only one or two men guarding each ship. The rest had lined up in ten squads behind Coreaje and Gasz. At Esmerelda's move, every weapon was now aimed directly at her. Safety locks were released, bolts were opened, and rounds of ammunition were fed into chambers.

"Esmerelda! You get some clothes on right away, young woman. How dare you prance around like that. You will be of the clothed type immediately! And put that knife away! This is not the proper attitude for a Princess."

Coreaje's face was a dark scarlet and turning redder as he bellowed at his daughter.

"That will not be possible, father. I am among my people now and I must do as they do." She gave Gasz a last hard, vicious look, then took a cautious step back and sheathed her knife. "I can no more dress for you than you could undress for me. It is my way, it is the way of my people and I must do as I must—"

As Esmerelda spoke, a commotion began in the group of thirty or so people behind her. Jaiete elbowed his way through the crowd, speaking loudly, gesturing with his hands. He pointed at Gasz and began shouting.

"Esmerelda! What is he saying? Please to translate."

"He's talking about Gasz." She translated in fits and starts as Jaiete bellowed and ranted at Gasz. "He says this planet was peaceful and quiet before *he* came with his men and weapons. They lived here well. They lived in peace. Then this man came with his army and his spaceships and his weapons. They killed many of his people. They killed women and children and all the old ones. They kidnapped many of his people, and they disappeared and were never seen again." Jaiete picked up a handful of dirt and flung it at Gasz's feet, but all Gasz did was scowl back. His hand went to his weapon, but he didn't draw.

Esmerelda continued to translate. "He and his men performed obscenities on their women. Jaiete lost his wife and daughter to this man. He gave them slow death and he will not permit him to be on this planet any longer. Neither will any leader of any other group."

Gasz stood quietly, a bewildered look on his face, but a slight smile creased his lips too.

Jaiete began again, pointing at Gasz and continuing his rant, several times thrusting a pointed finger at Gasz, several times pointing toward the sky.

"Esmerelda! What is he saying?"

"He is comparing Gasz to the lowest of the low. He says he is without honor, and his family has been dishonored by his actions. He is no better than the yellow-bellied zolopil who flies all day and eats bloody pickings from the tops of trees."

Jaiete continued his rant, but Esmerelda hesitated. She stammered, confused. "Uhh, to translate his words, father, he says he is, well . . ."

"Yes! Yes! He is what?"

". . . in his words, he is of 'dubious antecedents and conjectural progeny.' Jiaete's words, father, not mine."

Jaiete spoke again, continuing to point his finger at Gasz, continuing to heap scorn and abuse on him. Esmerelda couldn't translate; Jaiete's speech had become so rapid and vitriolic and intimidating that she couldn't keep up. But you didn't have to understand Jaiete's language to appreciate the derision and contempt he poured over the portly general. And by the look on his face, Coreaje well understood Jaiete's meaning, and he stopped asking Esmerelda for translation. But Gasz, as unfamiliar with the language of Jaiete as Coreaje, stood still, grinning slightly, perhaps a little embarrassed at the attention, though probably not.

"He says if you don't get Gasz and his men off this planet soon, there will be destruction. His men will destroy your men and your spaceships, and you will have to live here and face the zil as we do every day."

Abruptly, Jaiete turned and retreated into the crowd.

"That will not be possible." Coreaje snickered at the suggestion. "Not so fast, young lady. I came here to see you and I meant it. I would like to see more of this planet. We cannot take off. Time is not favorable now. We must wait before takeoff. Where is Leos?"

"Leos is not here. He is hiding from you and your men. You will not find him. What do you want of him?"

"I do not want him. I was merely asking. I came to see you."

"Father. Why have you come here? There was no reason for you to come. We are living well on this planet. This is my home. I will stay here. I will not be of the returning type."

"I guess I came as much to see you as to confirm that you were still alive. That you survived the trip."

"Yes, we survived the trip well."

"There was much concern on Nytandra that you did not survive well. That you were killed during entry into the atmosphere."

"The entry was okay. We survived. I remember there was much vibration."

Coreaje's face went blank. He took a deep breath, and his voice dropped. He glanced around the forest, at the ground, then at Esmerelda. "This, I was told by our engineers. The design of the spaceship was defective. There was much vibration in the tail. The tail could fall off."

Leos's mind exploded as he stepped back from his observation place inside the tree. *What?! Defective? Vibration in the tail? The tail could fall off? What were they trying to do to me? First, they almost chop my head off, then they send me into outer space in a defective spaceship?*

"Father, what are you saying?" Esmerelda put her fists on her hips. "What do you mean, 'the tail could fall off?'"

"It was not my order. I was told only that the spaceship was not needed. I was not told it was defective. I found out about that after he left. It was an early design. We have better designs. I gave it to Leos to let him come to this planet. I meant only that he would live here—"

"Father, he could not live here without me."

"He could live here with all the others."

"No, father, they would have killed him. They would have thought him a member of your army. Come to harm and do . . . things to their women. They would have fed him to the zil—if the zil had not killed him first. He could not speak to them. He would not have known about the zil. To send him here without me would have been a death sentence."

"I see. So that's why you came with him. To save his life. I might have known." A smug smile crossed Coreaje's lips, as though he'd just figured something out.

"No. I came to be with my people. If I saved Leos's life, that was second. I wished to be with my people. I wished to come back to my planet. Now, father, you must leave. Jaiete has said so."

"I have told you, I cannot leave now. Now is not right. I came to see this planet and to make friends with those who live here. It is time to put the past behind us and make friends. We have much to talk about. And to take you back, if you will go."

Esmerelda's voice turned strident. "Father, I have told you. I will not return."

"This I am aware. Now let us see Leos and make friends."

"Leos is hiding. You cannot see him. You tried to remove his head. And now I am understanding that you gave him a defective spaceship. Leos will not think well of you. You must understand that."

"An indiscretion on my part. A mistake I would like to correct. I would like to see Leos and ask how he is doing here."

"Father, I do not think—"

Esmerelda was interrupted by a commotion in the crowd behind her. Jaiete returned and resumed ranting at Gasz. She translated.

"Jaiete says Gasz must go. He must leave or blood will be shed."

Gasz roared at Esmerelda. "This fat bastard does not frighten me! I have men who will take him out and his men in less than a minute. This ain't no fuckin' picnic, sister!" He unzipped his pants. Weapons behind him were raised again.

"Quiet, Gasz!" Coreaje bellowed. "I will give the orders here."

"You should be afraid of him, Gasz." Esmerelda's voice had turned much calmer than that of her father, though intellectually it was just as sharp. "He is the leader around here."

Suddenly Jaiete raised his left arm and uttered an expletive. He pointed his index finger at the heavens, the same signal that started the attack on a zil.

What the hell? What's he up to?

At Jaiete's verbal signal four men appeared from the trees nearest Gasz and Coreaje, their knives drawn and cocked behind their head. Gasz saw the men appear, and from the startled, panicked look on his face, he knew something was about to happen. Whether mere intuition or something he'd learned on his previous visit Leos couldn't tell, but Gasz's right hand lurched toward his holster weapon. He was too late. Jaiete's arm came down as soon as the men appeared and they flung their knives at Gasz in one smooth, well-choreographed motion and disappeared into the trees as swiftly and silently as they'd come. It was over in less than a nanosector.

Coreaje, shifting his focus back and forth between Esmerelda and

Jaiete, seemed confused about Jaiete's intentions, and either didn't notice the men or didn't pay any attention until one of the knives sizzled past him two or three decilinks from his corpulent belly.

"Esmerelda!" Coreaje yelled. "What is this? What have you done? This is treason!"

The knives hit Gasz hard in the chest from four different directions, entering horizontally, slipping between his ribs, slicing his intercostals, and penetrating up to the grip, no doubt shredding his lungs, heart, diaphragm, and the great vessels of his chest. Gasz made no sound that Leos could hear, and nothing more than an intensely painful look spread over his face. The knives had certainly destroyed his ability to force air through his larynx. He dropped to his knees and fell forward, his face buried in the black soil of the trail, his chest propped up on the handles of two of the knives. He lay absolutely still. A faint trickle of blood from the four wounds stained his uniform and dribbled onto the soil.

He was probably dead before he hit the ground.

CHAPTER 33

FAREWELL

"Oh, crap," Leos muttered to himself. "Now they've done it."

Esmerelda screamed, Coreaje continued to bellow, and the crowd behind Esmerelda melted into the trees. Someone barked an order and the infantry behind Coreaje began firing, spraying the trees with unregulated small arms fire. Esmerelda bolted into the tree hiding Leos.

"Oh, Leos, they have done a terrible thing. Many will die. Leos, leave this place. Run, Leos, run." She pushed him toward the other side of the tree. "Take one of their spaceships and leave. Before they kill you."

"You have to come with me." He grabbed her arm.

"No, Leos. I cannot go. I must stay. I must try to stop this. My father will listen to me. Go—leave—before they kill you."

"Then I'm going to stay with you."

Esmerelda jerked from his grasp. "No! Leos! No! You must go. They will kill you if you stay here. They will make you the leader of this. They will say you brought this on. You must save yourself. I will try and stop them."

"Esmerelda—"

"No, Leos, go! Save yourself. Do this for me. Please. I love you Leos. I want to be with you forever, but I do not wish to see you hurt."

Leos started to protest again but Esmerelda grabbed him and kissed him hard, lusciously and passionately, something she never did outside of their amorous adventures in the zil blanket. Almost immediately, several high-powered weapon shots blasted through the tree. Esmerelda broke the embrace and bolted into the forest, cutting back toward the living space of the group.

"Go, Leos!" she shouted over her shoulder as she ran. "Go!"

"Esmerelda—wait!"

Leos watched her bound away, a zil in hot pursuit, but she could outrun the big lumbering animal. She darted into a tree several hundred links away, probably gliding through the branches to come out the other side, leaving the zil sniffing around for her scent while she ran on. Leos wanted desperately to join her, and he took a cautious step in her direction. But before he could get into that typical bounding step everyone took on this planet, several more shots, wild and unfocused, splattered the leaves of the trees around him. He dropped to the ground. "Holy shit," he muttered and turned back around, running and bounding as fast as he could toward the runway. He could still hear Esmerelda in the distance yelling as he had never heard her yell before.

"Father! Tell them to stop! *Please*, Father! Tell them to stop!"

Leos stopped and turned around. A tremendous desire to join Esmerelda ached in his heart. He wanted to try and help her stop the fighting, but he also knew she was right—he certainly would be captured and executed if Coreaje's forces found him with her. She knew Coreaje, and she knew this planet. He shouldn't take the chance.

As he stood in the forest listening to Esmerelda's screams fade in the distance, four of Jaiete's tribal mates stepped out of a tree near the opening. They were the four who'd flung their knives at Gasz and had been waiting for quiet to retrieve their weapons. One glanced in Leos's direction. He hesitated and turned to face Leos, glaring at him. He raised his bloodied knife straight up in the air, one flat side toward Leos in a signal that said, 'I don't like you,' or even, 'I will kill you.'

Leos knew this man. And he knew what he meant by his gesture.

The man disappeared into another tree.

An undercurrent of resentment had simmered not only within Esmerelda's *san*, but also within several of the groups near the runway ever since she and Leos arrived because she'd taken a mate from another planet, not from among her own people. Some members of the groups had been vocal in their distaste for Leos because they knew that if Esmerelda remained with Leos she'd produce no offspring, and they needed children to maintain their culture. They never made any real trouble toward Leos, and Jaiete and Senalar never acted on their complaints. But the man who glared at Leos was one of the most outspoken in Jaiete's group. Now that he had retrieved his knife . . . what would he do in the confusion?

But still, what was it Coreaje said? Something about making friends? Coreaje's words spun around in his head. Maybe he wouldn't be killed if he stayed. Coreaje might even take him back to Nytandra . . .

No, that was before Gasz was killed. Coreaje has undoubtedly changed his mind by now. A good friend of his, killed so brutally like that, and by friends of Leos and Esmerelda. Coreaje would be so angry . . .

But if he could find Esmerelda, she would protect him. He could hide in one of the trees, and no one would find him, and he'd help Esmerelda mediate this mess and everything would be all right, and they'd pin a medal on his chest . . .

Oh, no, that's not right. There's open warfare on this planet now. If he were to stick around . . .

And there was that one guy with his knife . . . he might take advantage of the commotion and turmoil, and take out his frustration on Leos. After all, these invaders were here because of *him*, because of Leos *himself*. Because of Leos, Coreaje and Gasz had come to *Jon-Set-Tom* and Gasz had to be killed. Because of Leos, open interplanetary warfare—*Jon-Set-Tom* against Nytandra—now existed, and people will be injured, people will be killed, *killed*, maybe even fertile women who were *Jon-Set-Tom*'s only chance to repopulate the species. That's right, Leos, you idiot, this war started *because of you.*

You had to steal that gold bar from Gasz in the tavern, didn't you? That was his insignia of office, you asshole. Your insatiable curiosity got you kicked off Nytandra, didn't it? Maybe it would have been better if they had *chopped your head off. Better for Jon-Set-Tom anyway. Now there's open warfare. The only thing you can do . . . yes, Esmerelda's right.* That's *what she meant. Of course. They will make you the leader of this. Not Coreaje's men, no, Jaiete and Senalar's men. That's what she meant. They will kill you. Not her father's troops. No—the others of her group. Or Jaiete's group. That's what Esmerelda meant by "They." The only thing you can do is—*

Several more shots buzzed through the tree near where Leos stood. They might as well have been knives. He turned and sprinted for the runway.

He ran hard, the firing and yelling behind him. When he reached the runway, he paralleled the opening for more than an anthan, staying within the forest, keeping the runway to his left as he ran. He popped into a tree here and there to watch for zil, his sensitivity toward the animal honed after more than a year on this planet. He knew the noise would attract the zil—that was one of the strategies for rounding one up to be killed. They suffered from a terrible curiosity and would undoubtedly congregate at the eastern end of the runway. When he neared the western end, he cut to his left and crept slowly and cautiously back toward the opening. In the distance, the invasion force was still firing. In the reduced gravity of the small planet, the soldiers had trouble trying to walk—er, bound—and shoot at the same time, and many of their shots went wild. Most of their shots hit the trees, but many went aimlessly and haphazardly up into the air. One shot even hit a zolopil which had swooped low over the opening, perhaps to investigate the commotion. It fell to the ground near where Gasz lay, pathetically flapping its wings as it lay dying.

Twelve of Gasz's soldiers had been assigned to guard the spaceships on the runway, but at the start of shooting they grabbed their weapons and took off and joined their comrades at the opposite end, leaving the ships unprotected. That was Leos's opening. He bolted over to one of the vertical landers.

These were the scout ships, landing first to secure the runway. They had one advantage over the horizontal landers: they could leave at a moment's notice. The other ships would have to be turned around before takeoff.

Leos crept cautiously toward the nearest of the scout ships, suspicious that a few guards might still be around. He saw no one. He climbed the entrance ladder and slipped inside.

The interior was empty and quiet. He ascended to the cockpit, carefully checking each level along the way. The ship was divided into three levels, the entrance area with the air lock and what appeared to be a storage area for food and water, a crew area above with bunks for seven, and the cockpit and navigational section at the top. He ordered the entrance ladder retracted and the main door shut and locked, a safety measure in case the soldiers returned.

He grabbed a pair of binoculars from the top of the control panel and stared east toward the far end of the runway. Gasz's inert body still lay there, a lump of malignant green that raised no feelings of sorrow or anguish in Leos's mind. He saw no one else he recognized, neither Coreaje nor Esmerelda nor soldiers. The invasion force had moved down the trail. The ship remained quiet. He sat back in the pilot's reclining chair and queried the ship's computer.

A return flight plan was already laid in, and all he had to do was initiate the program and the ship would take him back to Nytandra safe and sound — oops, no it wouldn't. The two planets were way out of alignment. A flight to Nytandra, were he to try it, would take almost a year, and would take him in a big looping orbit more than three-quarters of the way around the sun before he caught up with it. Food, air, and water wouldn't be sufficient for a trip that long. Nor fuel either. Too many mid-course corrections. Scratch that flight plan.

But would that have been a wise move? Why would he go back there? On Nytandra he would be arrested as soon as he landed, and that bright, shiny, silver-plated blade of the Kazo Dela Tan was waiting for him—he could visualize it glistening in the lights of that room as it sliced the air above his head. Then it would slide down the ramp to the lower track and . . . gulp. Besides, if he arrived without Coreaje and the others, the Minister and his entourage would want to know what happened. What could he tell them? That Gasz was dead and open warfare had broken out on the green planet, started by the inhabitants, and that he ran off without them? That Coreaje could potentially be killed? That he was the only one to escape with his life?

But as Leos scanned the navigational computer, he noticed an odd reading. *Two* flight plans had been laid in. One back to Nytandra, and one to . . . the *white planet*? Three planets showed up on the screen. Nytandra was nearest the sun, and *Jon-Set-Tom* was second. But a third planet lay outside those. That was the white planet—the "mysterious planet" as the Nytandrans called it—veiled in a perpetual cloud cover. It was Mlada's home planet, *Non-Dre-Ahdenu,* and it was the reason Coreaje wanted an outpost on the green planet so many years ago. He wanted to spy on it.

It wasn't in the computer by accident. By Coreaje's orders, all space-ships had flight plans to the white planet, as well as the green planet, pro-grammed within their navigational computers. The plans were constantly updated too, so Coreaje could order his army to the ships any time he wanted and fly there within a few months' time, given, that is, their proper position. But now, that little idiosyncrasy of Coreaje was going to help Leos escape. All he had to do was activate the flight plan to *Non-Dre-Ahdenu,* and this little ship would take him there, quickly and simply, al-most as simply as walking from his room in the Guest Quarters to the Dining Room to have lunch with Esmerelda. The two planets were in good alignment, not optimal, but close enough, and the trip would take about four Nytandran months, a month longer than the trip to the green planet the year before. Since he was the only crew member on board, food, water, and oxygen were plentiful. This trip was shaping up to be easier even than the trip to the green planet in the first place. He punched a few keys on the computer keyboard to activate the flight plan, then ran through the check list:

> **RADIO CHECK**—Now who the hell am I going to talk to?
> **ABORT ADVISORY CHECK**—Right, I'm going to abort.
> **ACCESS LADDER**—Retracted
> **MAIN ACCESS DOOR**—Closed and latched
> **LIFE SUPPORT**—Initiated

CABIN VENTILATION — Good
CABIN PRESSURE — Normal
ORBITAL PARAMETERS — Entered
FLIGHT PARAMETERS — Entered
LANDING PARAMETERS — Bypass
GYROSCOPIC ALIGNMENT — Optimal
VOICE CHECK — What? Again?
ABORT CHECK — Another one? Fuggidaboudit.
TIMER — Started
MAIN ENGINE — Hit the start button!

With that heavy thud of noise from the bottom of the ship — just like before — Leos was on his way.

CHAPTER 34

THE OLD MAN

The old man woke from a fitful night's sleep. His muscles ached, his joints creaked, and the tendons in his knees, already seriously weakened from the constant pounding over many years of jogging and running, sent shards of pain up and down his legs each time he flexed them. But those minor pains didn't bother him anymore. He'd had to put up with a some physical pain ever since he came to this planet, *Non-Dre-Ahdenu*.

How many years ago was that? His mind, still nimble in spite of his advanced age, quickly calculated the number. *Almost fifteen now. Has it been that long? Seems longer.*

He rose from his bed and stretched his arms over his head. That always helped get his blood flowing again. He bent over, trying to touch the floor without bending his knees, but that was a little too far to reach any more, and the pain in his back and hamstrings was too sharp to force it. He straightened and stretched his arms and shoulders. He tried a deep knee bend but the knee pain made him stop half way. When he was through, he doddered off to the bathroom.

He combed what hair he had left. Once he had a full head of rich dark brown hair and he was so proud of it, but it'd turned gray and begun falling out ever since he came to this planet. He brushed his teeth exactly as the Morning Processing section of the Standard of Living Regulations required. He shed the government-issue pajamas and put on his own clothes, a nondescript pair of dark brown pants, a light blue shirt and faded yellowish-brown shoes that needed new soles. As he made his way to the door of his small apartment, he passed the only window that overlooked the street below. He pulled aside the faded curtains and checked the thermometer outside the window. The temperature was up a degree from the previous day.

The warm season is here.

He left the apartment and carefully locked his door—there was just too much crime nowadays—and trod carefully down the dimly-lighted stairs with the worn carpet that always seemed to be waiting to trip him up, to the street one story below.

The morning was just beginning, the permanent cloud cover starting to lighten. All the other planets and moons he'd ever visited always had a brilliant sun that dominated the sky. On one planet, the sun migrated across the sky during the day, rising in the east, setting in the west, giving a strong definition to daytime and night. But here on *Non-Dre-Ahdenu*, the permanent cloud cover diffused and spread the sunlight over the entire sky and a distinct sun wasn't visible. Morning was nothing more than a uniform but gradual increase in cloud brightness, evening the reverse. Most citizens of this planet, he learned soon after arriving, had no idea a sun existed beyond the clouds, or why the brightness appeared and disappeared on a regular schedule, and oddly, they never seemed at all curious why. It was their way of life and they accepted it without question.

As he did most every day, the old man stopped for his morning meal at the little eatery a short walk down the street from his apartment. The food was barely edible even though it met the Food Service and Victuals Standards, and the owner posted his License to Provide Food Service proudly on the wall opposite the door where you couldn't avoid seeing it as you entered. At least the food was cheap.

The old man was on the dole. As a guest of the government and physically unable to work, he was provided with a small apartment free of charge and given a pitiful allowance which scarcely met his needs and left almost nothing for even the daintiest pleasure.

He ordered his usual breakfast, two eggs of the *kuu* bird, a toasted roll—he could swear the cook added ground glass to the flour—and a glass of fruit juice that tasted as though it was pure citric acid with a tinge of pink food coloring. But they said it was good for you, and he downed the vinegary fluid as best he could.

As he glanced around the little dining room, he saw many of the usual customers, the ones who came in every day and, like him, ordered the same breakfast. The man in the business attire who stopped on his way to . . . and that was the question, on his way to what? Corporate enterprise? Government? *Why would he patronize such a cheap establishment? Surely he could afford much better.* Then there was the young lady, a secretary perhaps; the Talatan Guard in his neatly pressed brown and red uniform just starting his day; the older matronly woman who always sat at the same table with the Guard. *His mother? What did they have in common? What were they talking about?* Others were present too, non-regulars, a few who stopped by once, never to return. But on this day it was the customer the old man didn't see that lifted his spirits. The plainclothes Talatan operative wasn't here, and the old man looked around to be sure he hadn't missed him. Nowhere in sight. The old man's scientific training had taught him to be thorough, if nothing else.

He may be running late. Maybe he'll arrive after I leave.

Three Talatan operatives took turns shadowing the old man. He knew them all, their clothes, their habits, their usual food order. Occasionally, the operative who was supposed to be on duty in the morning would fail to arrive at his appointed time to tag along behind the old man, to keep him always in view and note everything he did. And when his shadow operatives missed their turn, the old man took advantage of it.

He finished his meal, paid his bill, and left, carefully counting the change returned by the cashier. He crossed the street, jaywalking against the traffic. Traffic was mostly bicycles and motor scooters anyway, and they swerved easily around him. He turned left on the other side of the street and trudged the short city block to the park entrance, directly across the street from his apartment building. As he walked, the pain in his knees spiked again, but in spite of the pain the old man was still proud of the fact that he didn't have to use a cane. Not yet, anyway. His posture had slipped, his hair thinned, his joints were falling apart, and his eyesight was fading, but the muscles in his legs still retained a faint semblance of their youthful exuberant form. All the running he'd done in his younger years had finally paid off. When he reached the entrance to the park he paused and, shielding his failing eyes against the glare of the cloudy sky overhead, glanced around. It was a feint; he was actually looking to see if the operative had arrived.

Still no sight of him. And no sight of the typical Talatan vehicle the operatives drove.

He entered the park named "City Park of Great Expectations and Wonderful Desires" and passed under the wrought iron arch that marked the entrance. The well-manicured lawn and carefully nurtured shrubs and trees encompassed him as he walked. He shuffled along the sidewalk to the other side of the park and sat on a freshly-painted dark green wooden bench. Behind him, a large broad-leafed plant, one of several in this park, rustled in a gentle breeze.

This park was a good place to meet one's surreptitious contacts because the foliage obscured distant observation. The Talatan Guards didn't like it when he entered the park, and they repeatedly made their objections clear to him, but it was here he met his contact, Tsee. She lived in one of the buildings across the street from the other side of the park. When he arrived he sat on the bench — a bench she could see from her window — and that was his signal to her. She walked through the park entrance a few minutes later.

Unlike most on this planet, Tsee wasn't tall, only about six links, and pudgy. She wore the drab non-descript clothing of a working woman to avoid calling attention to herself. But like all Jhontu, the race of beings on *Non-Dre-Ahdenu*, her deep umber eyes were large, wide open and sensitive to the slightest movement.

She sat on the other end of the bench, but didn't greet the old man. They talked in whispers, she pretending to read a book, he watching the others in the park, putting on a reasonable imitation of an old man whose eyes appeared more photosensitive than they really were.

"You haven't been here in more than three weeks," Tsee said. She mumbled, trying to talk without moving her lips, glossing over her 'm's and 'b's. "Much has occurred."

"I realize that, but the Talatan are effective. I cannot always get away. What information has Tsoder brought?"

"Omani's trial took place last week. He was found guilty."

The old man sighed. "As we expected. Where is he now?"

"He was sentenced to the Callus. We must help him. He will die there."

"It would be difficult to help him now. It was stupid of him to throw that experimental bomb he made. He knew that. We must be patient. At least they didn't trace him back to us."

"Llaann could land on the Callus and pick him up. He finished his pilot's training and he has been admitted into the Flying Corps. He is a co-pilot for the Air Transport. He has been promoted to Pilot Second Class. He is learning to fly multi-engine aircraft. It can be done."

"No, that would be too dangerous. He would be arrested immediately. That could lead them back to us, and everything we have worked for would be destroyed."

"But Omani was our best bomb expert. We will miss him."

"I realize that, but he is gone. We have to accept that. He knew that when he joined. He was warned not to go outside the group. That jeopardizes everything. I was very angry when I heard. He was foolish."

"Tsoder is angry, too. He is impatient. Omani was a good friend. I do not know how much longer I can keep him from doing something, too."

"Tell Tsoder he must be patient. Not to act outside the council's directives. Do you have any other news?"

"No, only about Omani and Llaann."

"This is good news about Llaann." The old man paused, savoring the information, looking ahead to uses for a pilot sympathetic to their cause. "Give him my congratulations. He will be of use to us someday. But tell him to maintain his cover. He is not to make any unauthorized moves without the consent of the council."

"I will tell him. They have put more air marshals on the planes now. He is watched all the time. It will be many months before they promote him to Pilot First Class. Then he will be allowed to fly without a security escort."

A small jet aircraft sheared the morning air overhead. The old man looked up and shielded his eyes against the light. By the direction the plane flew, it was headed for the airport just outside of town. But it was an unusual flight—no flights of small aircraft were scheduled for this time of day.

"This is good," the old man said as he stood, turning away from Tsee. "We must stay together for the good of our group. I have to get back. The operative gets annoyed if I stay away from my apartment too long. I was visited when I stayed in this park for more than an hour. I will see you when I can."

The old man tottered back the way he came, toward his apartment building. When he arrived, he found his usual Talatan operative pacing the landing outside his apartment door.

"Where have you been? We have news for you."

"I went for a walk after breakfast." The old man pulled out his door key. "Come in. You can tell me what you're talking about."

"We have a visitor. From Nytandra. They are bringing him in now."

That was certainly a surprise—the old man hadn't heard anything about Nytandra since shortly after he'd arrived. He turned to face the Guard. "A visitor from Nytandra? When did this happen?"

"He landed a few hours ago, near Tlor. He—"

"Tlor?"

"A small town, several hundred sil west of here. He crashed in his spaceship. It was Nytandran. It had the same markings as the ship you came in. Our operatives recognized it immediately. He was not seriously injured, but they are taking him to the hospital just in case. You will meet him there. We cannot talk to him now. You must translate for us. I will take you."

"Meet him? Translate?"

"Yes, Directorate wishes him to be introduced to you, as you come from Nytandra, too."

"I assume that explains the non-scheduled flight that came over a few minutes ago."

"This is correct. Now, will you come?"

The old man hesitated. His instincts told him not to get involved in anything the government was doing, but since it was someone from Nytandra, curiosity got the better of him. "All right. When do you want to leave?"

"We will leave immediately. Transportation is below."

CHAPTER 35

THE VISITOR

Holy crap . . . where am I? Oh, shit, my leg. What the hell's going on? What is this? A hospital? Looks like a hospital room. Smells like disinfectant. What happened? Oh, right, I remember now, I was trying to land and . . . I picked out a flat area . . . sure looked like a flat area . . . the display from the ship's computer said it was a flat area, but it turned out to be the side of a hill . . . damn, lousy info . . . I remember the ship tilting and . . . I guess it went over . . . damn, that hurts . . . God, my leg, seems to be in some sort of sling . . . hurts like hell. It's all black and blue. My ankle's swollen, almost twice its normal size. I wonder if it's broken. Sure looks like it. But if it was broken, wouldn't it be in a cast? Why is it just in a sling? Where is everybody around here. What's that little bag up there? Oh, that's some sort of IV solution. I see the tube. I wonder what it is. Maybe it's a pain reliever. If it is, it doesn't work very well. Shit, my leg hurts.

Leos lay in a bed in a rather undistinguished room about ten by twelve links, austere dirty white walls, a door to one side across from his bed, and a rickety-looking chair in one corner. A small table to his left held only a glass of water. In a hospital he expected to see instruments, medicines, a com screen with vital signs, a blood pressure cuff, maybe an intravenous line pump. Nothing like that at all. The bed appeared to be an old metal bed, painted white at one time, now reeking of age as did everything else in the room. A window barely two links on each side to the right of his bed looked out over a treeless plain of pale green hills, illuminated by a pall of clouds covering the sky as far as he could see. The clouds scared him, so foreign were they to him. Every time he glanced out the window his mind returned to the landing. But after the ship fell over everything was just a blur. At least he was alive, though he had no idea how much longer he would stay that way.

How long have I been here? Is this the same day I crashed? Or the next day? Or what?

Three people entered the room. *Uh-oh, who are these people and why are they here? Are they doctors? Nurses? Orderlies? Interns?*

Dressed all in white, from white caps and white masks to white gowns and shoe coverings, they certainly appeared to be health care workers and probably held Leos's best interest at heart, but their sudden entry and identical garb and complete body coverings—especially face coverings—gave Leos a momentary start.

Crap, now what?

The only visible part of their body were their eyes—large, wide open, staring, penetrating—just like Mlada's eyes. Leos never liked looking in Mlada's eyes. Those big, dark brown eyes were so unnerving. It was like she was reading his mind.

One of the visitors began speaking—male by the pitch of his voice—but in such a foreign language Leos had no idea what he was trying to say. Mlada never taught him any words in her language; he spoke with her only in the presence of Esmerelda. The man approached Leos and pulled back the cover on Leos's leg in the sling and examined it closely. Several times he indicated to the other two with him particular points on the injured leg and ankle, and pointed once to the bag of IV fluids. After about a millisector, he and one of the others left the room while the third replaced the IV bag with another, and in a few nanosectors the pain in Leos's leg and shoulder seemed to disappear. He felt very tired and slept.

* * *

Leos was able to keep track of the passage of time—crudely, to be sure—as he lay in that bed because whenever he woke he would glance out the little bedside window and keep a mental note of a repeating pattern of light and darkness. One darktime and one lightime made one day. After four days, they reduced the amount of the medicine Leos had been receiving through the intravenous line, and allowed him to wake up more fully. His leg still hurt but not as much, and he could tolerate the pain for short periods without the pain reliever from the little plastic bag.

He didn't like that pain reliever. It did alleviate the pain in his leg and it made him sleepy and gave him a chance to rest, but it made him dizzy and nauseated and he developed a rash on his chest and face. On this fourth day, in a somewhat more lucid state without the pain reliever clouding his mind, he began more and more to remember how he got here. After the ship toppled over and skidded down the hill onto a road, the local people, farmers he figured by the dirt on their clothes, notified the local authorities who turned out to be a militia-like group wearing brown uniforms with accents of red. They wrenched him out of his seat and whisked him away to this . . . hospital.

Oh, yes, those uniforms. Red and brown. I remember now.

*   *   *

On the fourth day, the old man came to visit Leos. He sat on the stiff, rickety chair in Leos's room.

"I've been here each day since they brought you to this hospital." He spoke in halting Nytandran, struggling for words as though he hadn't spoken it in years. "But you weren't awake. They told me to tell you your leg and ankle weren't broken, at least they didn't think so, but it'd been wrenched when your spaceship fell over and trapped you between the seat and the control panel. They said you hit your shoulder on the side of the cockpit when you crashed. But you'd been strapped in the pilot's seat, and that probably saved your life."

Still dizzy and a little confused from the pain reliever, Leos just nodded and mumbled an indistinct, "Thank you." But even through groggy eyes, Leos could tell that this visitor wasn't Nytandran, he was too tall to be from that planet, and he didn't have the puffy eye slits or exaggerated facial features of the Nytandrans, and his skin was much too fair. And he had a full head of grayish-brown hair. His eyes had the general characteristics of Anthanian eyes, and that puzzled Leos, but in the absence of any real information, he decided not to make any assumptions.

"They told me you were Nytandran," the man said. "But you sure don't look like any Nytandran I've ever seen. You're obviously from some other planet. Do you know where you are?"

Leos mumbled something about a 'white' planet, but wasn't sure the man understood him.

"You're on the planet *Non-Dre-Ahdenu*. You're in a hospital in the capital city of *Marktu-Ahdenu*. The race of beings that inhabits this planet are the *Jhontu*. The word 'ahdenu' means a group of people, a coming together, or a gathering. You'll hear that word frequently if you stay here for any length of time. And considering how you got here, you will. Do you have a name?"

"Leos." But in his dazed state he barely understood the question, and blurted out his name only after several nanosectors of thought.

The old man looked mystified and screwed up his face in a puzzled look. He stared askance at Leos, then out the window as though pondering a difficult problem. "Oh," he whispered, "I wonder . . . could it be . . . no, not likely . . . still, I wonder. Did you meet Coreaje when you were on Nytandra?"

Leos nodded. "Yes."

"He still the Leader?"

"Yes."

"I'm still confused. You're obviously not Nytandran. How did you come to be on Nytandra in the first place?"

"I got kidnapped by the Nytandrans. They wanted someone to marry Esmerelda, and they picked me."

"Marry who?"

"Esmerelda."

"She's the woman with the green skin, wasn't she? But she married Coreaje, didn't she?"

"That's her mom. Esmerelda may have been a little girl when you were there."

"Oh, yes." The old man searched his memory. "They did have this little . . ."

"She's grown up now. Twenty-five years old. They were looking for a mate for her."

"Why'd they pick you?"

"They said I was Esmerelda's type. They looked at a lot of planets and chose me."

The old man nodded his head. "What planet *did* you come from, anyway?" He removed his glasses and began to wipe them on a handkerchief.

"It's called Anthanos. Maybe you've heard of it."

The old man stiffened visibly and dropped his glasses. They skittered across the floor. He stared at Leos, and an uncomfortable silence settled over the room. "Ton tatonae," he said in a faint, halting voice. He bent down and picked up his glasses, examined them briefly for damage, and finding none, set them carefully in place.

"What?" Leos blurted out. "You speak Anthanian?"

"Yes," the old man replied, and he began to speak in his—and Leos's—native language. "I am from Anthanos, too."

Stunned, Leos could barely reply. "No kidding. Wow, what a coincidence. Another Anthanian on this planet."

"Yes, even more of a coincidence than you might imagine."

"What do you mean?"

"Now I know why your name was so familiar to me. I knew your mother. I was on the expedition to the Blue Planet."

"What?" The grogginess seemed to abate somewhat. "You were on *Star Voyager*?"

"Yes. I knew her there. I knew you, too. When you were newborn. I held you once."

"Holy dinfrizzle. That's neat. What did you do on the ship."

"I accompanied her to the surface of the planet."

"You went down to the surface with her?" That little bit of contradictory information stymied Leos for a few nanosectors as he searched his mind. Ten people landed on the surface of the blue planet. Eight were killed and only two returned: his mom and—let's see, what was the name of the other one . . . ?

CHAPTER 36

A DISTANT MEMORY

"Jad?" Leos said. "No kidding." Wow, what visions that brings to mind. You gotta dig deep in your memory banks to resurrect that name.

Jad Til-Lentos had been on the original expedition to the Blue Planet and only he and Leos's mom, Lilea, survived. They returned to Anthanos and retired from spaceflight and never left the planet again. At least that's what everyone assumed.

Jad and Lilea spent their first year in Sabean attending the dreary and almost never-ending debriefings, hearings, meetings, public discussions, and assemblies that followed. But when her official duties ended, Lilea left town, settling in Kalarias, her family's home town, buying a house in a modest-income section of the suburbs to live the unassuming life of a single mother.

One year after they returned, the Anthanian Assembly designated Jad and Lilea *Anthanian National Treasures* for their participation in the unmitigated disaster that was the expedition to the blue planet. That was the highest honor that could be bestowed on an Anthanian, and they were the first to be given the honor. They were awarded these fabulous-looking Designations, printed in a delicate scroll-like font of pure gold leaf on a 15 X 24 decilink sheet of plastic, and matted and framed in a brushed-gold metallic frame. Lilea took a great deal of delight in hers and mounted it in a prominent place on the wall in her living room where you couldn't avoid seeing it were you fortunate enough to be invited to her house.

Jad saw retirement differently. He lived well beyond the dignity and nobility the Designation brought. He leased an apartment in an up-scale section of Sabean and savored the lifestyle of the eligible bachelor. But for reasons that never became entirely clear to Lilea or Leos, that lifestyle suited Jad not well at all. Charged several times with public intoxication and once with resisting arrest, he spent forty T-sectors drying out in a private institution. He was never incarcerated—who would dare throw Jad in jail?—but he was ordered by the magistrate of a Misdemeanor Court to seek mental health treatment, though he rarely attended. He stayed away from his apartment for many T-sectors at a time, venturing back only to change clothes and wash up. Eventually he abandoned the apartment altogether. SpaceComm filed a missing-persons report about a year after the Designation was made, and in the ensuing twenty years no trace of Jad was ever found. SpaceComm had the foresight to take possession of Jad's effects, and most of them were stored in a weather-controlled room at SpaceComm headquarters.

Except for Jad's Designation.

Lilea petitioned SpaceComm to be awarded caretaker of it. She stored it, frame and all, in a locked metal box in a secure storage room in her house. When Leos was twelve years old, she brought it out to show him because he was old enough to understand what it meant to her, and to Anthanos.

And so, by the time Leos left Anthanos, to everyone except Lilea and a few others at Spaceflight Command, especially Tam, Jad was little more than a name in a history lesson.

"Jad!?" Leos blurted again. The old man nodded. "Holy dinfrizzle."

"You are very perceptive, as they say on Nytandra."

"How the hell did you end up here?"

"The Nytandrans visited Anthanos years before they came to get you. They'd been on and off our planet for a couple of years. They arrived the first time not long after your mom and I returned."

"What were they doing there?"

"Well, they certainly weren't looking for a mate for . . . whatshername. They'd just discovered the secret to regulating the antigrav drive, and Anthanos was a good place to go for a first trip. Anthanos was so much like their planet, they came here, er, there, naturally."

"But how did you get mixed up with them?"

"They came to me first. They knew who I was, that was all over the IS. They knew I was familiar with astrophysics and anti-grav drives, and all that. They started talking about the mathematics of the cosmos they'd just discovered."

"Yeah, they told me about that too, but it sounded like a bunch of glokshit to me."

"Glocksh . . .? Oh. No—no, don't dismiss it so easily. It really works." Jad shifted position on the chair and glanced briefly at the floor. His face reflected irritation, exasperation. "Trouble was, on Anthanos, no one else would listen. Stupid idiots. I was the only one who would listen to them, and I understood what they were talking about right away."

"So you understand it?"

Jad nodded. "Pretty well. As well as anyone can."

"What's it all about, anyway."

Jad threw his head back and took a deep breath. His face relaxed and the slight smile of a pleasant memory curled up the corners of his mouth. He shifted position on the dilapidated chair and launched into a discussion. "You have to discard regular math. You can't use numbers. Numbers are a way of identifying discrete items, like electrons and protons and so on. But in the infinitesimally small world, there are no discrete particles. There's really no such thing as an electron, there are no protons, no neutrons, no gravitons, no real particles. Electrons and other subatomic particles are just a convenient way of thinking of things. They're really nothing more than agglomerations of wave fronts and wave intersections and wave dynamics. They fit our mathematics. They fit our minds, our perceptions. Our mathematics developed because of who we are and what we are. We developed mathematics to count things, like fingers and toes, or like the number of yanto in a box, or the number of nuts you have to collect when you don't have anything else to eat. Numbers are convenient but misleading. When we wanted to examine the atomic and subatomic, we developed electrons and protons and so on. We were so naïve, so foolish; we were so focused on counting things that we developed discrete items. We totally missed the wave dynamics. And we developed quarks and neutrinos and all the other subatomic particles. But all these particles don't really exist. There's just energy — vibrations — waves. That's why light waves have characteristics of waves and discrete particles, both at the same time. That's why the graviton particle has zero mass. I always knew there had to be a reason."

"Sounds complicated —"

"And the mathematics of the cosmos also eliminates the discrepancy between quantum mechanics and relativity. It merges the two, it shows how the two can work together, though you have to modify each to fit the protocol. The mathematics we used leads in the wrong direction — you have to make assumptions that aren't possible with regular math. Oh, did I mention there are thirty-seven types of matter?" Jad grinned. "I worked out the first equations that pointed that way. Thirty-six forms of other matter as well as the one type that makes up our universe. There are thirty-six other universes out there, but we can't see them. They're there, they're really there, but they're unseen — maybe a better word would be 'dark' — to us. The only common thing between all thirty-seven is gravity.

The speed of light is different in each of those universes, but the gravitational constant is the same." Jad poked the air as he spoke. "They all occupy the same space at the same time, but they don't interact because the wave frequencies are all different."

Oh, wow . . .

Leos lay in his bed fascinated and enraptured, taking in everything Jad said as though he were a child at a puppet show. Here he was, Jad, the big man himself, recipient of a Designation, returnee from the Blue Planet, discoverer of worlds, astrophysicist to the stars, discoverer of the graviton particle—and he was *right here*, right in this room, expounding on all matters physical and cosmological, just for him. A window had opened into the makeup of the universe so that everything could be revealed to him and him alone, everything all at once and he could take it in, take it *all* in.

Leos certainly wasn't as versed in astrophysics and cosmology and corporeal phenomenology as Jad—*not by any means*—though he'd studied the fundamentals of it in college and he could follow along and understand the implications of Jad's revelations. He wanted to know more about it. "How do you do calculations with it?"

Jad stood from the chair and began to pace the room, his head down. "Gravity is really nothing more than the sum total of all the wave fronts and wave interactions and wave dynamics in each universe. But the sum total within each universe is the same, absolutely the same, down to the last electron. That's why gravity is so common and so ubiquitous. You have to use fundamental principles, fundamental values like the primary oscillation frequency—that is, the POF—of all these electromagnetic wave fronts. All the different types in all thirty-seven universes. In each universe the POF is unique, but the sum total is the same. Everything vibrates—everything resonates—even the 'matter'—if you want to use that word—in all the different universes. But the POF is different in different universes. There are thirty-seven possible frequencies the POF can take. No more, no less. I worked them all out."

Occasionally Jad would stop and gesture in subtle ways, illustrating his point. "Each form of matter, that is, in each of the other universes, vibrates at its own resonant frequency, that is, its own POF, and they're all different. I've made all the calculations. Took me four years on that damn supercomputer before they destroyed it. That's why we can't see the other forms of 'matter'. And that's why mathematics of the cosmos explains the presence of other forms of 'matter' and energy much better than regular math. Everything is built on everything else."

"So other universes really exist?"

"Yes, but not in the way we think about them, or *used* to think about them. These values aren't what they are by accident. They're all inter-related. They were closing in on a fundamental theory of everything. Including gravity. Did I mention there are thirty-six other universes out there? A fundamental theory of everything has to take into account all those universes, not just our own. There's a different fundamental theory of everything for each universe. The theory is basically the same, but the numbers are different. The only thing common to all universes is the graviton wave-interaction. It's what holds all those universes together. It's not just in our universe, it's in all other universes too. It's the only thing that can move from one universe to another. If it weren't for the gravity wave-interaction, all those universes would fly apart. It flips back and forth between universes like the maglev from one city to another. Without it, the entire universe—really the multiverse—would collapse and cease to exist. I've thought about trying to communicate with some of these alternate universes. I'd have to use graviton waves since that's the only common link. I couldn't use light waves or radio-frequency or X-rays or anything else, the other universes can't see us any more than we can see them. If I could build a graviton wave generator, it might work. Maybe modulate the wave dynamics. It could be based on the primary graviton wave generator that powers *Star Voyager*. It would have to be much bigger, though, and it would be stationary, feeding off the orbital motion of the planet it sits on. Maybe put it on an asteroid. Or one of the moons of Anthanos. You talk about a God particle, it's the graviton particle. That is to say, the—" Jad stopped. He looked at Leos with a kind of strange and existential expression on his face, and took a deep breath. "But I've said enough. I'm probably boring you."

"Sounds complicated."

"It is and it's not." Jad shook his head, a subtle anger on his face. "You have to be willing to look in different directions, in different ways, to discard so much of what we've already learned." He began gesturing, pointing at Leos and around the room. "Once I talked to the Nytandrans, I saw how things really are. It was so elegant. Nobody else really understands. I'll explain more about it later. But it works."

"Okay." Leos paused. "Why'd you come to this planet?"

"This is where the scientists are. Or were."

"The scientists?"

"Yeah. If you recall, there wasn't much science being done on Nytandra. The society here has degenerated and the Nytandrans left. Most of the scientists came here. And the supercomputers. That is, they were until they destroyed them. This is where they developed the mathematics of the cosmos. This use to be the place to do science. When the Talatan came into power, they . . . well, the bottom fell out. So to speak."

"No kidding. Are you doing, you know, science, now?"

Jad released a mild sigh, then returned to the chair, plucking it from its place in the corner and moving it nearer Leos's bed. It emitted a slight creak as he sat down. "No, I'm retired. I don't do much anymore. After the Talatan came to power, they cut all that astrophysical research. Weren't interested in it. Didn't fit their ideas of population control. Destroyed the computers I needed. Most of the scientists I worked with disappeared. Those were the last people to ever leave this planet. I helped them design some satellites to do some astronomical observations. It's hard to watch the sky through a permanent cloud cover. But I don't work much anymore."

"How'd you get stuck here?"

"I'm a guest of the government. And now you're a guest of the government, too."

"What does that mean?"

"They'll provide all your housing and everything. They've assigned you a small apartment not far from mine. They'll take care of you. You're a visitor here. You can get most anything you want. You'll even get a small stipend to live with. But there's one restriction."

"What's that?"

"You can't leave. You're stuck here. Just like me. You can't go back to Anthanos, or Nytandra. Once you get used to that fact, the better off you'll be."

"That's what they said on Nytandra, but I got out of there."

Jad looked at Leos and frowned. He shook his head. "This isn't Nytandra. The government is very repressive. They don't allow people to leave. By the way, how *did* you get out off Nytandra?"

"They kicked me off. Gave me my own spaceship and everything"

"Gave you a spaceship? What did you do to get kicked off there?"

"I sort of stole something. A gold bar. It fell into my hands. Sort of."

"A gold bar? They're really serious about gold there. I heard about one person on Nytandra, they chopped his head off for stealing something small. It wasn't gold, but if it had been, I bet they'd have gone crazy."

"Yeah, I know," Leos said, and several wild memories flashed through his brain.

CHAPTER 37

THE GATHERING

Leos stayed at Jad's apartment for seven days until his foot and lower leg healed well enough that he could walk around without crutches. He slept on the couch and accompanied Jad to the little eatery for meals. His ankle was still swollen and painful to walk on, but he could climb the stairs in the front of the building without much difficulty.

The night before Leos moved to the small apartment assigned to him, Jad invited several friends over for a *sim-ahdenu*, a small gathering, to introduce Leos. At the height of the party, Leos counted twelve others beside himself and Jad, and in the tiny apartment the walls vibrated with the good chatter of warm conversation.

"That's good," Jad said. "The noise overwhelms the listening devices."

Leos appreciated that the Jhontu seemed congenial and welcoming. They smiled a lot, not in the condescending manner of the Nytandrans, but in a cordial and easygoing way, opening themselves to a visitor. Most of the conversations revolved around what the others did for a living, and Leos found himself talking largely to mathematicians and scientists, including a physician, all professions he could reasonably expect to be friends of Jad. In the din of conversation, they talked openly. The alcoholic drinks Jad served, in bottles or cans, lubricated the discourse, and the noise level in the small apartment soon rose almost to a painful level.

But appearances could be deceiving. Leos came to dislike the wide eyes of the Jhontu, even dating back to his first meetings with Mlada. Their eyes constantly darted around, and being so much larger than he was used to, any movement they made seemed exaggerated beyond what Leos was used to seeing, and he found them difficult to adjust to. But more than their eyes, he had a difficult time gauging the Jhontu, even through mannerisms or expressions. He couldn't read their faces to judge their emotions as he could so easily with the Anthanians on his home planet. The Jhontu kept their feelings to themselves much more than Anthanians, a skill they no doubt developed living within a highly repressive regime where a stray emotion, especially of dislike or contempt which the government might interpret as disloyal or unpatriotic, could get a person imprisoned for many years. Or worse.

Jad seemed to enjoy his role as host. *I wonder if he does this often. Like throwing parties like this. What does the Talatan think about this?*

Jad moved gracefully from group to group, a generous smile on his face, making an apropos comment that brought smiles, if not outright laughter, from the others. Backslapping he didn't do, and Coreaje he certainly was not, but he played the good host well. He also translated for Leos.

"I don't understand," Leos said to Jad late in the party. "If this planet is so tight, how did all the information about the spaceships and the controllable drive, and stuff, get out?"

"Our planet was once much more open," said one person who'd been introduced to Leos as Thembo. An elderly man, tall and distinguished looking, with grayish-white hair and an impeccably tailored suit, he smiled rarely and sipped from his drink even less. "We had a trading agreement with Nytandra. Coreaje's group was friendly, and there was much trade. A few people left the planet over the years. The government sold scientific information to Nytandra in exchange for the metals mined on their planet. It's about the only exportable resource they had. But there was a regime change about ten years ago, and they shut down the exodus. Very little gets out now."

"So that's why Coreaje wanted to spy on this planet."

Jad nodded. "Exactly."

"But now the scientific staff on this planet has been decimated. There's almost no more research going on."

"But you and Jad and several others I've met are still doing science."

"True, there are a few of us still remaining. But it is military science. Only for the regime. We do only what they want us to do."

"There are no more space flights," Jad said. "No one leaves."

Oh, no. I don't like the sound of that.

"There is no trade anymore." Thembo's face turned sour and angry. He snorted slightly. "They imposed strict controls. Everybody has been confined to the surface." He took a sip from the can he held. "They have turned repressive and dictatorial."

Leos turned to Jad. "When did you come here?"

"Almost fifteen years ago when there were still flights in and out. I worked for a while with their scientists." A wistful look passed over his eyes as he talked, and the smile disappeared from his lips. He looked down at the can he held and shrugged his shoulders. "It was interesting. Had a good time. Now most of those scientists are dead. Or sentenced to the Callus. Excuse me." Jad left the group, walking over to the little alcove that served as a kitchen where he opened another can.

"What? What's the . . . Callus? Is that what you called it?"

"Yes, the Callus," said one who called himself Kazeh. Somewhat shorter than the others, with a round expressive face and a full head of deep black hair. He spoke a few words of Anthanian, but slowly and haltingly, barely well enough to converse. He and several others had persuaded Jad to teach them his language, perhaps, Leos surmised, as a way of relieving the boredom and apathy that saturated the society on this planet. There was little public entertainment. A few militaristic concerts and maybe a parade or two, but that was all. The vid was nothing more than government propaganda, and, from what little Leos had seen, it bored the tears out of him.

"The Callus is a big flat-topped mountain," Kazeh continued. "Where they send people to die. People who might cause trouble. Like scientists and intellectuals. Any repressive regime always starts by rounding up the intellectuals."

"How come you never got sent there?" Leos asked Jad when he returned to the group.

"They kept me around to act as an advisor. On anti-grav drives. Shitty work, but it paid the bills. I had to stop when my eyesight began to fail."

"Tell me more about the Callus."

"No one knows much about it because no one who goes there ever returns," Kazeh said. "You go there to die. The only people who have ever seen the Callus and come back are the pilots who fly the prisoners there. But all they see is the landing strip. And they are so well indoctrinated and brainwashed by the Talatan they would never betray the secret of the Callus."

"There is Llaann," Thembo whispered.

"Be careful," Jad whispered back. He glanced around, as though to see if anyone was watching or listening to the conversation.

"Who?" Leos whispered. He gave Jad his best inquisitive look, but Jad put his finger to his lips and shook his head. He said nothing further.

"What's the government like here?" Leos asked. "I haven't heard much about it. I know it's kinda repressive . . . but . . ." He shrugged his shoulders. He thought he was being merely inquisitive, as a visitor to an unknown planet might be expected to be. He wanted only a brief answer about the form of government, the leader, perhaps a bit about the legal system, but the group turned quiet after Jad translated and Leos understood he may have overstepped the bounds of decorum. Or legality. He almost asked Jad to withdraw the question.

"If you want to know something important about our government," Kazeh said in a low, hushed voice, "then let me tell you about the old woman . . ."

"Kazeh, maybe you shouldn't," Thembo said. Kazeh looked at him, but flipped his head back in the typical way that Jhontu marked nonchalance, and went ahead with his story. "He asked, he should know. There was an old woman, Uyanza by name, they arrested her for something . . . well, they never said until her trial came up. She was ninety-five years old and they tried her for jaywalking and treason and sentenced her to the Callus. I was there at the trial. I testified. I watched it myself."

"A ninety-five year old woman? For treason? Holy dinfrizzle. They wouldn't do that would they?" Jad didn't know how to translate "dinfrizzle" into the Jhontu language, so he said it in Anthanian. Kazeh smiled.

"They certainly would. She wasn't guilty of anything. Nobody believed the charges against her. She wasn't guilty of jaywalking. How could she? She couldn't even walk, let alone jaywalk. I know. I examined her. She was a patient of mine."

"You are—"

"A doctor, yes."

Leos paused, digesting the bizarre incident. But it pooled in his brain, and he wondered out loud, "Why would they do that?"

"To make an example of her. To show everyone they will prosecute anyone who steps out of line."

"Oh."

"Do not be fooled, Mr. Leos, by the attention you are getting," Kazeh continued. "The apartment, the clothes they provide, the small subsidy. It may look good now, but realize this—they can be ruthless. They are masters of deceit and subterfuge. You will not see it as do we, we who have lived here all our lives. The Talatan are tricky. They will deceive you as you lie dying."

"Who are the Talatan?"

"The enforcers, the government, the secret police. They will watch you as they watch everyone. They saw us this night as we arrived here, and they will see us as we depart. It is not too bad for us, because we come here often, and we are friends of Jad, and they respect him."

"An operative was downstairs when we came," Thembo said. "He will leave when all of us leave. He has taken down all our names. He knows when we arrived and when we leave."

"Are they the ones with the red and brown uniforms?"

"Yes, but there are plainclothes operatives too. They are subtle. You will never see them unless they want you to."

"My suggestion to you would be to forget you ever heard us say anything about this," Kazeh said. "It would be to your benefit to do so."

As he spoke, Jad introduced a young couple to Leos. "And that is why we must act," the man, Tsoder, said. Tall like all Jhontu, but with a face that burned with the fire of passion, he jumped directly into the conversation. The muscles of his chest and arms bulged through the tan shirt he wore, and wire-rimmed glasses perched precariously on the bridge of his nose. His eyes darted around the room, even more than others, as though wary and discreet in his conversation. His wife, Tsee, stood beside him, but came only to his shoulder. She, too, wore glasses, pink, with tiny flowers on the earpieces. But Tsee was much different than the usual Jhontu woman. Though she had the typical wide, bright eyes, she wasn't tall like the others. Mlada had been so elegantly tall, and carried herself well, never giving in, never stooping to dissemble in the presence of the boot-lickers who mingled around Coreaje (except for Esmerelda, of course). But Tsee was short, at most six and a half links, and somewhat pudgy, given to a roll around her waist.

As Tsoder spoke, a look of anger, even defiance, spread across his face, and his hand formed a fist.

"Patience, Tsoder," Jad said, and he placed a hand on his shoulder. "The time will come. I can guarantee it." He turned to Leos. "You'll have to forgive Tsoder. He is an angry young man. Very impatient. If there's anything I've learned from living on this planet—or on the blue planet—it is that of patience. Ask your mother about that."

I will if I ever get back to Anthanos.

"Does that mean you're involved in something?" Leos asked.

"Shhh," Jad said, and he left to join another group nearby.

CHAPTER 38

TARGET PRACTICE

Leos's apartment wasn't much, just a small room with a bathroom, a sink in one corner, and a hot plate that served as a kitchen. The bed was a fold-out couch, hard and uncomfortable, with a bar that ran through the middle that fell just at the wrong place against his back at night. He'd hoped for a two-room apartment like Jad's, but, the government operative who showed him the room told him, this was the best they could do in such short notice. It wasn't far from Jad's place, only about five city blocks, but it was a rough walk, through angry streets past decaying, crumbling buildings and back alleys littered with the remnants of life and liberty.

A few days after he moved to his apartment, Leos spoke to Jad.

"I'd like to get my stuff from the ship I came on."

"What kind of stuff?"

"A few clothes, my knife—"

"What? Knife?" Jad said, surprised. "Hold on, we're not allowed to have knives, no weapons at all. You could get in a lot of trouble."

"Yeah, but it's a knife I made myself on the green planet. Sentimental value. You know."

Jad hesitated to answer. Clearly he was bothered by Leos's request. "Okay, I'll talk to the Guards. I'll see what I can do. But I won't tell them about the knife. Keep that quiet, will you? Whose clothes were you wearing?"

"It was a seven-person ship. Plenty of extra clothes for all. Extra weapons, too."

"They'll confiscate all those weapons."

"That's okay, I just want my knife. I hid the knife inside the ship's control panel. Underneath. Maybe they won't find it."

"Oh, they'll find it. They'll find it when they take the ship apart piece by piece. It'll take them a while, though. They don't have many scientists left who can understand how a spaceship works. But be *very* careful with that knife. Hide it in your clothes, or something. If they see it . . ."

*　　*　　*

The spaceship Leos came in had been transported to an airport about twenty sil from the main city, about twelve anthans. Jad talked to the Chief at Airport Security and asked him to allow Leos to remove his personal effects from the ship. From what Leos could gather, Jad'd had to fumble around for a convenient lie, telling the Chief something about Leos needing his clothes because the ones they gave him didn't fit too well, and he'd like to have his clothes back, the ones he arrived in. After a somewhat discomforting conversation, the Chief finally said okay, he could get his clothes, and assigned two Talatan Guards to take Leos alone to the ship to retrieve his stuff, but they'd do it at night when no one was around. This was strictly off the record, the Chief said. He could get into trouble if he allowed anyone inside the security area around the spaceship who wasn't on the inspection team.

Later that day, when all light had faded from the sky and the oppressive darkness had settled in, two Talatan Guards picked Leos up at his apartment in an inky-black Talatan vehicle, and took him to the ship. They didn't seem to be happy to be assigned the duty. One, a private or possibly a new recruit, was drunk and reeked of the nauseatingly sweet smell of alcohol. The other one, a sergeant with three silver and red pips on his collar, growled a lot and had been drinking, too. Both wore the usual Talatan uniform, dark brown with red cuffs. The sergeant's uniform had more red on the arms and near the shoulders. The higher the rank, the more red on a Talatan uniform. Both carried side arms.

The sergeant drove. He kept up a blistering conversation with the private who took repeated swigs from a pocket flask. Occasionally, the sergeant would take a swallow, though he never got as tipsy as the private. Every now and then the sergeant would toss a few words in Leos's direction in the back seat, but Leos understood very little of what he said, so he just nodded as though he agreed, and stared out the window at the intense blackness of the night.

The ship lay horizontally on a flatbed trailer inside a fenced-off area in a dark lot behind the airport. From what Leos could see in the patchy light from the vehicle headlamps, the Jhontu scientists hadn't begun to disassemble the ship and he felt better about his knife. *It should still be hidden inside*. The sergeant produced a key to open a padlock through a gate in the fence, and they scrounged up a ladder which they set against the side of the ship. They gave Leos a flashlight, and he crawled in through the opening where the front window had been. His rescuers had removed the window to get him out because the main door was covered in the fall. He worked his way through the ship to the sleeping accommodations on the second level. The bunks looked funny standing upright like that. He grabbed his clothes and went back to the flight deck.

The knife was still where he'd hidden it, in one of the dark recesses within the control panel, tucked up behind the communications equipment. He wiggled underneath, yanked it out, and wrapped his clothes around it.

He climbed back out the window and carefully worked his way down the ladder in the darkness to where the two guards waited for him. Climbing down the ladder with a flashlight in one hand and the roll of clothes in the other was a bit cumbersome, so he tucked the clothes under one arm. But the heavy knife kept shifting within, and he had to keep readjusting it and he was so afraid the knife would fall out, and from below the sergeant kept shouting at him and holding his hands out as though he was saying, "Throw your stuff down to me." But Leos kept his 'stuff' tightly clenched under one arm and inched his way down the ladder.

His clothes were wrapped as firmly as possible around the knife, but as he neared the end of the ladder, he turned around to point the flashlight toward the ground to see how many more steps were left, and the roll of clothing tipped slightly. Before he could grab it, the knife, still in its zil-leather sheath, slipped out and clattered to the ground, right at the feet of the sergeant. At least it didn't break.

"Oops."

The drunk private bellowed an epithet and jerked his weapon from its holster and pointed it at Leos. He didn't seem so drunk anymore.

The sergeant picked up the knife and removed it from its sheath. He stayed cool and inscrutable as his eyes studied the knife. He ran his hands over the blade and tested the edge on a fingernail. But it sliced through the nail into the finger drawing a bright drop of blood, and he let out a squeal and started jabbering in a loud, frantic voice, waving the knife in Leos's face as he took the last step off the ladder. The sergeant's face turned a muted crimson as he yelled to the other guard who grabbed Leos by one arm, sending his roll of clothing skittering across the tarmac. They hustled him over to their vehicle and slammed him against the side. They handcuffed him.

They kept jabbering at each other in that rapid-fire language that made it impossible for Leos to understand even the few words in Jhontu he knew. It became an argument, each yelling at the other, the sergeant sometimes shouting "gdnau" — "no" — repeatedly at the private. Then, in one of those pregnant pauses that so often indicates a change in the direction of a conversation, the two guards turned utterly quiet and began whispering to each other. The sergeant pointed occasionally to another dark section of the airport grounds. A few nanosectors later, the private broke out in a fit of drunken laughter, and the sergeant did too. After a couple of micro-sectors of howling and giggling, they calmed down sufficiently to stuff Leos in the back seat of their vehicle, but they continued to snicker at each other as though they had something in mind they didn't want Leos to know about. They sped away, out of the secure area, not stopping to relock the gate. The trip ended a short distance away in a construction zone, not far from a large, unlighted building, probably an airplane hangar. Piles of wood and metal lay all about, mostly unrecognizable in the dim light from the single small bulb on a temporary pole that illuminated the area with a pale yellow light.

"What's going on?" Leos said as best he could in their language, but neither guard replied.

They staked Leos spread-eagle to a large, flat wooden panel which they stood on one end against a lumber pile, lashed down by rope from their vehicle.

"What're you doing?" Leos protested again, but the guards re-mained silent. He jerked his arms against the ropes, but they held tight. The same horrible feelings of entrapment and frustration he'd felt on the Kazo Dela Tan returned, and it appeared his knife was to play the role of the shiny big blade.

About twenty links from where Leos was bound, near the light pole, the sergeant unsheathed the knife. The other guard pulled the flask from his pocket and took a swallow, then shared it with the sergeant.

Uh-oh. This doesn't look good — two drunk guards with a knife.

The sergeant held the knife in front of his face and muttered some-thing, then, holding it carefully by the straight side of the blade, took aim and tossed it in Leos's general direction.

"Hey! Watch what you're doing with that!" Leos yelled in his own language, but the knife spiraled harmlessly into the dirt about ten links from his feet. The sergeant squealed an epithet and picked it up and tried again, but his aim was high and it sailed over the lumber pile. It took them almost a millisector to find it in the dark.

The sergeant tried again, throwing it as hard as he could right at Leos. He seemed to be aiming at Leos's chest, and this time the knife reached the lumber pile, but it flopped end-over-end as it flew, swinging way out to Leos's right, catching on a stick of wood. The other guard gave it a try too, but his aim wasn't any better. Each time they threw it—either guard, it didn't matter—it swung wide, sometimes right, sometimes left, sometimes overhead, mostly colliding with the wood pile. Occasionally, it stuck, but more often it simply clattered against the wood and fell to the ground.

The guards got more and more frustrated and threw the knife harder and harder each time. But they held the knife by the blade, and that's not how this knife is thrown. Leos had gone through the same frustration when he started throwing, but at least he had Senalar, an experienced knife-maker and thrower, to show him how to hold the knife by the handle and fling it so that it took advantage of the air that moved across the blade as it sailed toward the target. You didn't aim this knife and let it go—that was the worst thing you could do, as the Guards were finding out, though they seemed too stupid—or drunk—to understand. Each knife was like an extension of your hand and arm, in sum, an extension of yourself. In making the knife, a connection developed between you and it, an almost magical connection that linked your eyes and brain through the knife to the target, and when you threw, the knife went where you wanted, where you *willed* it, and it sailed there under its own power. That wasn't aiming. Not at all.

So neither of the two Guards could get the knife anywhere near Leos's body. Throwing the knife harder just made it drift farther from the target. Power wasn't the answer, though after fifteen or twenty throws they were too drunk and frustrated to understand that. Finally, the sergeant, in a fit of rage, grabbed the knife by the handle and threw it in Leos's general direction, as though he was trying to throw the knife away, or maybe he was saying, "This is the last throw we'll make, then we'll do something else."

But he threw the knife so the blade was nearly horizontal.

Leos had begun to relax within the bindings that held him to the board. These two clowns couldn't hit the broad side of that airplane hangar over there, though there was always the possibility they might, by some wild stroke of luck, hit something important. But when the Guard picked up the knife by the handle and raised it back behind his head, Leos's heartbeat shot up and he stiffened against the bindings. He gasped silently. Instead of the tumbling, erratic trajectory of the previous throws, the knife took a smooth, aerodynamic course—just like it should—and struck the knot in the rope above Leos's right wrist. It severed the rope into three pieces and his hand was loose. He grabbed the knife and with three more easy whacks he was free.

Now Leos had the knife. His heartbeat pushed higher and his chest tightened. His jaw clenched, his eyes narrowed. He took a few steps forward.

Okay, you guys . . . look out. Here I come.

The Guards' faces had a comical look. Had they been short and fat, they would have been Grok and Krok. They pulled out their weapons, each unloading one drunken, wild shot at Leos. He held the knife in his right hand as is proper, the blade flat to his prey. The first shot, from the private, zinged past Leos's left ear, but the sergeant's aim was better. The knife flickered left slightly to cover his face—did Leos do that or did the knife move by itself? He couldn't tell, the move was automatic and instantaneous. The projectile struck the knife.

The sound of a ricochet reverberated off nearby buildings. Leos looked at the blade. Only a smudge remained, a splatter of tarnish on the grayish-silver metal near the handle where the copper-clad projectile had struck. Then he heard a scream from one of the Guards. He looked up.

The weapon's projectile had ricocheted directly back into the face of the sergeant. He lay on his back, arms outstretched. Blood covered his face and spewed from one eye. The other Guard dropped his weapon on the ground and knelt beside the sergeant, trying to stanch the flow of blood. He had nothing to use, no bandages or dressings, and he tried to cover the wound with his hand, but the blood kept gushing all over his hand and the sleeve of his uniform, the crimson a perfect match for the red of his right cuff. As he held his hand over the sergeant's eye, screeching and shrieking, perhaps for the flow to stop, it did stop. He gasped, then screamed, realizing what that meant. He turned and glared at Leos, and spat out a stream of vile and venomous rumblings. He wiped his hand on his pant leg and reached for his weapon. He stood, raising it to fire, but he never got off one shot. Leos reacted instinctively and flung. The knife hit the private in the middle of the chest.

He was probably dead before he hit the ground.

CHAPTER 39

ESCAPE

Leos pulled his knife from the Guard's chest. In the dim light around the construction area he found the sheath on the ground near the two bodies. He wiped the knife on the uniform of one of the men, and slipped the knife into the sheath. Then he ran. He ran around the dark building toward the lights in the distance, the lights on the buildings of the airport. The airport was largely closed; on *Non-Dre-Ahdenu* airplanes didn't fly at night. He ran and ran and ran, past the buildings toward the lights of the city, white and twinkling in the distance. A siren, that penetrating wail of sound, alternating between high pitch and low in what must be a perfect sine wave, screeched in the distance and he ducked into a dark corner of one of the airport buildings. The drive through the city to the airport had taken several millisectors in the dark, and he had absolutely no idea how to get back. But he did have his knife, and he knew how to use it, and within that envelope of self-protection, honed by so many days on *Jon-Set-Tom* with his friendship with Esmerelda and Senalar, standing in the third row in the attack on a zil, slinging his blade into the upper chest of the beast, he felt tolerably safe.

But this wasn't an attack on a zil. He had killed a much more sentient organism. All those times he'd been allowed to participate in the killing of a zil had honed his knife-throwing skills to a keen edge, and now one man lay dead because of him. *No, two. No, one — dammit, I'm not responsible for the first, that was an accident. The knife — But the second . . . When they find the bodies they aren't going to look at it that way. But the second one — my God, I killed him. I threw my knife at him and killed him, just like those guys on the green planet killed Gasz. Right between the ribs, like killing a zil. Right into his heart, I'm sure. It must have sliced his heart in two. If I'm lucky, the bodies won't be found until light, but the shooting may have attracted some attention. I'll have to stay hidden.*

He cursed his skill. Was he that good? Yes, he was good. He was so good he could kill two men with a knife. He passed his pilot's exam with 100 percent. Yes, that was good, of course, but is there such a thing as too *much* skill? Could he be *too* good?

248

He walked down the main road leading to the airport, and in the absolute darkness that engulfed this planet at night, he was well hidden. Whenever a vehicle came by, he'd drop into the ditch beside the road and wait until it passed. Then he'd get up and continue on. Most often the ditches were dry, though some of them contained stagnant water. He took his chances.

When he reached the north end of the road where it intersected a main thoroughfare, his memory failed. During the drive here, he didn't pay enough attention to where the guards were taking him—why would he?—his mission was simply to retrieve his clothes and return to his apartment. He had no reason to believe he'd be walking back in the dark. He was fairly sure they'd turned left onto the airport road, so he turned right, but as he started down the road, a Talatan Guard vehicle approached and he dived for cover behind some bushes. Its siren wasn't on and the vehicle didn't stop, so the driver probably didn't know about the dead guards. Leos walked on.

He walked toward light, mostly lighted signs with the city's name on it. He recognized the city's name in the Jhontu language. By following the signs and walking toward the city lights, he came to the inner city as the faint glow of sunrise warmed the clouds in the east. Wet, filthy, exhausted, and hungry he limped badly, his foot swollen and sore. In the short time he lived with Jad he'd become familiar with the area of Jad's apartment house, taking his cue from the city park across the street, and when he found the right building, he hobbled up to the second floor and knocked. Quietly.

He had to knock several times, growing more and more apprehensive with each tap, until music started inside and Jad opened the door.

"Leos," he said in a whisper. "What are you doing here?"

Leos just stared at him. "Can I come in?"

Jad silently motioned him in and signaled him to be quiet. He turned up the volume on the radio, then spoke in a coarse whisper.

"What happened to you? You're filthy. Did you get your stuff?"

"Yes, but—no, I didn't—well, I got my knife, but something happened." He limped over to the couch and sat. He held his head in his hands. His heart pounded, his body trembled, and he had difficulty drawing a breath. "I—I dropped the knife, and they saw it. The guards were drunk, at least one was, well, they both were, and they took it from me and tied me up and threw it at me. Tried to kill me. Shit. Scared the fuck outta me." His voice trailed off and he paused to take a deep breath before talking again. "But they didn't know how to throw it, and, shit, I can still see that knife coming toward me, but it cut the ropes, that is, cut the rope on my right hand, the rope they tied me up with, you know, they got a rope and I got loose. When they started shooting at me, I flung the knife and killed them."

Jad seemed confused trying to follow Leos's rambling story. "You killed both of them with one throw?"

"Yeah. No, no—one bullet ricocheted off the knife and killed one, then I killed the other."

"Ricocheted off the knife?" Leos held up the knife and showed Jad the smudge. "You killed the other one? How the hell did you do that?"

"The knife. I threw it at him. Hit him in the chest. Horizontally. Between the ribs. Ripped his heart—"

Jad sat down on the couch, his face draining of blood. "Leos, are you telling me that two Guards are—holy crap, two men dead. How did you get here?"

"I walked. I walked the whole damn way."

"Once they find out—they're . . ."

"They took me to a construction area at the airport. Away from the lights. There wasn't much light there. They may not find the bodies until light."

"It's light now. They may have found them. I haven't heard any sirens, but the airport is twenty sil from here."

Jad went to the window and peeked out at the street below. "Crap. The operative is here. He must have seen you come in."

"Where?" Leos jerked his head up. His heart pounded even faster, his forehead grew sweaty, and his chest tightened. He limped over to the window and carefully glanced out between the curtains. *Oh, God, if they've seen me—*

"That silver and blue vehicle. Across the street. That's the operative. Was that vehicle there when you came in?"

"Uh, no, I don't think so—no, I'm sure it wasn't." Leos relaxed, his heartbeat dropped. "I crossed the street right there. There wasn't any vehicle there. I'm sure of it." He exhaled a sigh of relief.

Jad turned from the window and began to pace around the apartment. "Crap. I can't let you stay here. That'll ruin everything. They'll . . ."

"It may take them a while to figure out how they got killed. Or who did it."

"What do you mean?"

"One of them is shot in the face, the other with a knife wound. I thought about this. They don't know about the knife. It may take them a while . . ."

"Shit, Leos, they don't have to know." Jad stopped pacing and approached Leos, still standing at the window. He'd grown agitated as he talked, but agitated for the taciturn Jad rarely meant little more than pacing, randomly, sometimes in a circle. "They know they assigned those two guards to escort you to your old ship, and they'll go to your place first."

"I figured. That's why I came here. I need to get away. God, this has been a nightmare. I killed someone. Do you know what that means? I killed two men. Esmerelda will be pissed . . ."

"Esmer . . . who? Oh, shit, I'll get caught up in this, and that'll . . . shit, no, you can't leave now, not with the operative out there. By now he already knows about it. He's waiting to see if you appear around here." A movement outside caught Jad's eye and he pulled the curtain back. "Wait—holy crap, he's leaving. Where's he going? Why's he driving off?"

"Maybe he's just finding out about this. I mean, I thought about this walking here. The two guards were drunk, at least one was. The other one, the senior one, you know, the one with the little . . . pip things on his collar, wasn't too drunk, but maybe they're just finding out who did it, and the other one was dead drunk, I mean, shit, I've been drunk, but even I've never been that drunk . . ."

"Shut up, Leos, you're rambling. We gotta get you to a safe place. You can't stay here. After they go to your place, they'll come here. You can stay with Tsee and Tsoder for a few days."

"Who's Tsee and . . . who?"

"You remember them. From the party? Live across the park. Just a short way from here. The operative's gone. He'll be back. Hurry."

"Hurry? I can't hurry. My foot's sore and I'm exhausted. I'm hungry, have you got any food? My clothes—shit, this is so . . ."

Jad opened the door to his apartment but Leos made no effort to walk down the stairs. "Leos, just shut up and get your ass going. You really are somethin', ya know, I gotta hand it to you. In the space of about twenty days, you've gone from being an honored guest on this fuckin' planet to being a fugitive, wanted for killing two guards. 'Bout the worst fuckin' thing you could do. You've got your mother's knack for getting into trouble. I sure hope you have her staying power."

They walked across the street and through the park and climbed three floors to Tsee and Tsoder's apartment. Jad knocked.

CHAPTER 40

FUGITIVE

"Jad! What are you doing here?" Tsee stepped out into the hallway in front of her apartment and closed the door. Her face was flushed and her eyes were red, swollen and bloodshot. Jhontu eyes were so conspicuous and prominent anyway, and hers were now even more so. Before Jad could say anything, she broke into a cry. "Jad. Tsoder hasn't come back. He's gone and I don't know what to do. He's been gone all night and I don't know where he went or if he'll come back."

Jad looked around at the empty hallway, apparently suspicious of being overheard. "Let's go inside."

They entered the apartment and stood in the living area. A simple one-bedroom apartment, bare and sparse, it reminded Leos of his and Jad's apartments—a dirty brown couch in the far corner bordering a small table with two chairs where Tsee and Tsoder ate. A separate cooking area in an alcove off the main room—it seemed a stretch to call it a kitchen—held a two-burner gas stove and noisy refrigerator. A brand new, glossy black video screen hung from the wall across from the couch, always on, always playing music the state preferred, or the movies they allowed, or the government programs that told you what great things the state did for its citizens. At the front of the apartment, a window overlooked the city park below. Jad turned to Tsee.

"What happened? When did he leave?"

"Last night. He said he had an errand to run, but he didn't come back."

"Did he say where he was going? Or what he was doing?"

"No, he said nothing, and I'm worried. It's not like him to stay away this long."

Jad didn't speak for a few seconds. His face didn't betray any emotion, but he seemed to be thinking. "I don't know."

To Leos, Jad's response was an obvious lie. Jad knew where Tsoder was—of course, he knew. Jad knew a lot more than he let on and it concerned—and even fascinated—Leos. Leos shook his head.

"I'll try and look into it. But even I can't do much. Leos needs to stay here for a few days."

"What? Jad—no! He can't stay here! Tsoder may be back anytime."

"He's got to. He can't stay at my place, and he can't go to his own a-partment. The Talatan will be back to talk to me as soon as they find he's not there."

Tsee hesitated. She studied Jad, who looked away. "Jad? What's going on? What did he do?"

"He killed two Talatan Guards."

"What! Oh, my God, Jad, no!" She shook her head violently. She looked at Leos, her eyes radiating fear, the fear of discovery, the fear of Leos, the fear of what he might do to her. She took a few steps away from Jad, backing into a corner near a floor lamp with a torn, brown faded shade. Her eyes shifted rapidly from Jad to Leos and back. "He can't stay here. Jad, this is—no, no, *no*. What they'll do to us if they find out."

Jad put his hands on his hips and stared at Tsee. He remained quiet for a second or two, then spoke in a subdued voice. "Tsee, I think I know what happened. Tsoder may be gone for a few days."

"Jad? What do you think Tsoder did? Do you know something? Jad—tell me. Tell me!"

"I can't tell you. I don't know for sure, but I think he may have been caught up in a curfew sweep."

Tsee raised her hands to her face and stared at Jad. "Oh, no," she cried. "Not that. He'll be—no, no Jad, he can't stay here. Take him to Thembo's place. Or Kazeh's. Jad—"

"They live too far away. You're closest. I don't have a vehicle. My eyes—Leos can't walk. They're looking for him now. We—"

"Kazeh has a vehicle. He could pick you up."

"It's too late for that. I can't contact him. We don't dare go out again. He'll be seen."

"Jad—he can't stay here. Tsoder will be angry."

"They won't find out. It'll just be for a few days. I'll contact someone and we'll get him out of here. We'll get him to the farm. They won't suspect anything there."

Tsee grew quiet, apparently mollified by Jad's explanations, though fear still held her face. She continued to stare at Leos, perhaps wondering . . . would he? . . . but Leos breathed a little easier. She seemed to be weakening in her protestations, and may agree to let him stay here after all. But his foot still hurt and he still breathed heavily. He'd never been a fugitive before, outside of a few times when he was five years old in his home on Anthanos when he swiped a few cookies from the cookie jar and hid in his bedroom. It had become a game with him and his mom. She'd rummage through the house, wondering in a mock angry voice, "Who stole the cookies?" and he'd giggle in his little hiding place in the closet, always a closet, and always loud enough, of course, for her to hear. She never spanked him, though she'd take back the cookies he hadn't eaten and tell him he was naughty. She'd let him have one after dinner, if he ate his fruits and vegetables, most of which he hated. Except for yanto. What he wouldn't give for a good yanto right now. But he was a fugitive, wanted for murder, though he would call it self-defense. That would be a distinction lost on the Talatan government.

"He can sleep there, on the couch. I'll make arrangements."

"Jad, no. He can't stay here. I . . . Tsoder will be angry." She put a hand over her mouth as several tears trickled down her cheek.

"It's just for a few days. I'll make arrangements. I told you."

Tsee said nothing more. She simply stared at Jad, her face wet with the tears of bewilderment and confusion.

"I'll bring some food over. He won't have to eat from your ration."

Tsee stayed quiet, but her face had turned from fear to anger, and she glared at Jad. "Jad, if they find out . . ."

"I promise, they won't. I'll get him out of here in four days, five, most."

"You get him out of here in four days, or else."

*　　*　　*

Leos stayed with Tsee four days. He slept on the couch, and Tsee supplied a blanket to warm him during the cool nights. Jad brought a small amount of food over on the second day, though Tsee took pity on him and shared some of her food, a few starchy vegetables and an alcoholic drink so foul in its taste it made the kaadz seem positively refined. But most of the time she stayed in the bedroom with the door closed and paid little attention to him, leaving him alone on the couch to watch the video or to nap. She regarded him with a mixture of pain and suspicion. He knew, because Jad had impressed on him with a compelling certainty that if they found him in her apartment, she would be sentenced to the Callus, and that was a loss Jad wasn't about to accept. She was willing to cook some of the food Jad brought over for him, but after the second day that was as far as she went.

Leos's stay with Tsee had given him a chance to calm down and try and think about what was to come. Jad had mentioned a 'farm,' and though most of his experience with farms came from his stay on Nytandra, he knew that farms were where food was grown. He and Esmerelda had visited a small farm, one of the few single-family farms that hadn't been assimilated into the larger corporations that dominated the farming industry on Nytandra. He tried to imagine life on a farm, the open fields of crops stretching for several anthans in all directions, the various grains and fruits and vegetables flourishing in the soil moistened with water pumped from the underground reservoirs, luxuriating in the warm, dry breezes that swept in from the surrounding desert. It couldn't be all that bad, he thought, and began to look forward to it.

By the fourth day, Leos was ready to leave. His apprehension about his fate only multiplied with each passing day. His confinement reminded him of the 500 T-sectors he spent on Grok's ship, wondering what was to become of him. At least then he could imagine a satisfactory conclusion to the trip, even if his mind was filled with ominous and frightful endings. Now he couldn't bring his mind to think of someone as lovely as Esmerelda to welcome him when he left this dreary apartment. What, he wondered, would the farm be like? Will there be a beautiful farmer's daughter, or a wonderful family that will take him in and shield him from the Talatan? That wasn't likely, but he couldn't stop thinking about it. At least it kept him from going stir-crazy waiting for Jad. And it gave his foot a chance to rest.

Late in the evening on the fourth day, Jad and Kazeh arrived with a vehicle. The vehicle was Kazeh's. As a physician, he was allowed personal transportation — they called it a 'car' — to make his rounds of the various hospitals, though it shook and rattled and clunked about so badly it seemed it would break down before they got very far out of town.

"I think it took them a day to put together what happened," Jad said as the car jounced along the road. "They didn't ask me if you'd visited me after the guards were killed until the next day. I told them no, and I said I didn't know where you were. They haven't been back since. But they're putting the details together now. I think you made a mistake coming to my apartment. If you had gone directly to your apartment, they may have assumed the two guards were killed after they dropped you off."

"Maybe," Leos said, his voice and mind barely registering Jad's comments. "It's too late now."

"No, no," Kazeh said. "They would have arrested him immediately.

What he did was right, and Jad was right to hold him with Tsee. Now we must find a way to get you off this planet."

"Off the planet? Where can I go? I can't go back to Nytandra, I'd be arrested. I can't go to the green planet, there's a war going on there."

Jad and Kazeh turned quiet. The car jolted on, clunking about the road, ready, it seemed, to come apart with each jolt.

"We can't keep him here much longer," Jad said quietly to Kazeh. "He'll fuck up the good thing we've got going." Kazeh nodded.

But when Leos asked what this "good thing" was, Jad remained quiet and said nothing.

CHAPTER 41

THE FARM

Oh, boy, the farm. About 350 sil from Marktu-Ahdenu (to Leos, about 100 anthans) near the town of *Tes-tset*, a small farming community of about 300, it certainly wasn't the farm Leos expected. No large fields of grain waving gently in the breeze, no farmer's daughter to share a laugh with. The only female he met was Zhinta, wife of the proprietor of the farm.

Tall like Mlada, but with a face that could fry vegetables, she had a disposition that made Mlada look positively radiant. She reminded Leos of the zolopil: thin, severe, flitting around the farm, always on the move, cawing her orders to the farmhands, snapping at them, almost taking their heads off. Her husband, Deack, on the other hand, became the zil in Leos's mind, an overweight, lumbering oaf, bellowing at the help as though he had nothing better to do. He owned the farm and did most of the administration, though Zhinta saw to it his orders were carried out. Like a foreman, but without the sparkle on her cloak. Or in her personality.

Zhinta didn't seem surprised to see Jad and Kazeh when the vehicle drove up the long, muddy driveway from the road; she'd apparently been told Leos was coming. As soon as he stepped out of the vehicle, she threw him a shovel and told him to start shoveling the manure from a pile near the barn to a waiting wagon. Jad said a few words to Zhinta before they left, then explained to Leos that she was just as upset as Tsee with Leos staying at the farm. She, too, knew that if he was caught at her farm, she would be sentenced to the Callus. And he would share her fate.

As the light in the sky faded toward night, Zhinta showed Leos to his room on the third floor of the main house. A small room, only about eight links by eight, with a single bed and one small window that overlooked the barn. Fortunately, the window seemed to have been painted shut so the putrid odor from the manure pile didn't penetrate. He was the only one on the third floor. The three other men who worked at the farm had rooms on the second floor, and Zhinta and Deack kept to themselves on the first.

Zhinta gave Leos a dark hooded cloak, like the cloaks everyone else wore, and told him to keep the hood up when outside. And to take his boots off before entering the house.

As the darkness of evening rolled over the house at the end of his first day on the farm, Leos lay on the bed in his room and began to appraise his chances for the future. He tried to remain as dispassionate as possible to keep the depression that was slowly seeping into his brain from coloring his thoughts. But no matter what he came up with, it always came down to the fact that he was a wanted man and would always be hunted for the deaths of two Talatan Guards. Even Jad had no further plans for him after his stay at this farm, other than the nebulous "get your fuckin' ass off this planet."

Yeah, right. There are no spaceflights off this planet. How's he going to do that?

This planet had been his escape from the warfare of the green planet, and meeting Jad those first few days after arriving had raised his spirits immensely. Knowing someone who spoke his own language and could introduce him around in Jhontu society had made him feel welcome so much sooner than he could ever have anticipated. He naïvely expected to stay here for a while, then get a ship out to . . . somewhere. But things had gone so terribly wrong, and now he was hunted by the planet-wide Talatan Guards, hiding in a hot, stifling cloak, shoveling manure. He wished he'd been more forceful with Esmerelda and stayed with her after the war broke out. He'd had plenty of time to think about it during the long solo voyage from *Jon-Set-Tom* to *Non-Dre-Ahdenu*, and he'd first come to the reluctant conclusion that Esmerelda had panicked when she told him to leave the welcoming green planet where he'd planned to spend the rest of his life. Now he was beginning to change his mind. She certainly knew of the dissension in some of the tribes. Had she *really* panicked? Or did she want Leos to leave so he wouldn't be killed by her own people? Was that her motive? It made little difference. He would have been killed had he stayed, either by Coreaje's men, or by Esmerelda's people. One way or another, he had to leave. He could never have avoided it.

How much lower could he go? Ever since his kidnapping from Anthanos, his life had degenerated into one episode after another of staying one step ahead of disaster, and now he had sunk so low he shoveled manure for his food, and faced the frightening potential of being captured and sentenced to death.

If Jad and the others do manage to get me off this planet, where could I go?

Nytandra? No — I can't go there. The green planet? Not with the war still going on — but wait, is there still a war? It's been a long time since I left. What's happened in the meantime? His spirits rose — maybe, just maybe, if I can just get my fuckin' ass off this planet . . .

The only other alternative would be Anthanos. Could Jad wrangle a way to get him back to his home planet? Maybe Jad would come with him.

Unlikely, for several reasons. Unlikely that this planet even has a spaceship capable of traveling to Anthanos. After all, that's a hundred light years away. Unlikely because Jad is too old for spaceflight any more, and he's settled here and wouldn't give that up for a long, tedious trip to an uncertain return on Anthanos. Unlikely, too, that the government, so repressive and secret, would allow him to leave. So, barring a sudden change in his fortune, he came to the somber and discouraging conclusion that he was stuck here for a long time, perhaps permanently, never to see Tama, never to see Esmerelda again. At least, he consoled himself, he was reasonably secure in his own room and safe from the Talatan. For a while, anyway. He drifted off to sleep, but didn't stay asleep long. He woke before morning, tired and depressed.

*   *   *

Zhinta kept Leos hidden in the house when the Guards came to make their routine inspections. Farms were inspected by the food service teams, and Leos was impressed that the government, for all its repressive and overpowering tactics against the population, would take the time to inspect farms to make sure the meat and milk that went on the market was at least edible. But his gullibility sank like a stone in still water when he found out that all the inspectors did was shake down Zhinta and threaten her if she said anything. She'd discovered long ago that the key to getting a good rating was to pay off the inspectors. Once, he overheard her admitting to Deack that she came close to revealing the presence of Leos in the house. Had she done so, though, she'd have been arrested for harboring a fugitive. As far as he knew they never looked at her records or they would have found out she had one more person working for her than was on her government allocation work sheet. One more than she was allowed. One person more that . . . he didn't let himself consider what would happen beyond that.

So Leos tread carefully around Zhinta, keeping out of her way and going about his business as quietly as possible. He fed and watered the animals and shoveled manure, and though he never liked it — the smell could make a zil puke—he got good at it, and he hoped she understood she could rely on him to do his job. That was his best defense. Don't antagonize the head lady.

"I have received a message from Jad," Zhinta told Leos ten days after he arrived. She found him at the manure pile near the barn. Leos stopped shoveling and looked deeply into her eyes, but all she did was motion to him. "Come over here," she whispered, and led him to a secluded corner of the barn, away from the house. Shaded by several large trees and isolated almost completely from the rest of the farm, they talked in secretive tones. "About Tsoder."

"Yes? What happened to him?" Zhinta turned away, scanning the area around the barn, especially the dirt road that led down the hill to the paved road in front of the farm. She spoke quietly, unusual for her, so often bellowing orders to the hands.

"I have known Tsoder for many years. He worked on this farm for a short time when he was young. But he was a radical. He could not keep still. He talked constantly for change, for a way to release himself and Tsee and his people from the oppression of this government. He longed for action, like many young men. I cannot say I disagree with him. But he was caught, as were many of his kind, and sentenced to the Callus. I do not work for change. I work this farm and produce food for the regime. And for the people of this regime. That is all I do." She turned back to him. "Do not be fooled, Leos of Nytandra, the Talatan are sophisticated. They infiltrated Tsoder's unit and many were arrested. The leaders of the group were executed, certainly. Tsoder was lucky, he was young, merely a low-level worker, and was sent to the Callus where he will live for the rest of his life. Which will be short."

Gulp.

"You will be sent there, too, if they find you here." Now Zhinta's voice rose slightly. "You will stay here as long as it takes to get a spaceship to remove you to another place."

"But I talked to Jad about this. There's no place I can go."

Zhinta became quiet for a nanosector and a scowl came over her face. That was not what she wanted to hear. "This I understand. I will see Jad at the market in Marktu in a few days. I will ask him about this. You cannot stay here. It is too risky."

She left Leos and turned toward the house.

CHAPTER 42

THE HELICOPTER

Not far from Zhinta's farm, about ten anthans east down the paved road, and on several square anthans of prime farmland, the Talatan had built a military base, including a small airport, for operations in this province. They kept helicopters and small planes at the airport, and low-level flights over the town and surrounding countryside were fairly common. Helicopters weren't new to Leos, they'd been used on Anthanos for years, though they weren't used much. They raised too much dust, and in the squeaky clean atmosphere of his planet—a point of pride with the Anthanians—that was sufficient reason for keeping them grounded.

The helicopter the Guards used was a small two-seater, open frame, with an engine that produced a loud metallic *pop-pop-pop* sound in addition to the characteristic whir of the blades. It could be heard several nanosectors before it arrived. Most of the time the copter held only the pilot, most days the same pilot. He seemed to possess a sadistic streak—he loved to buzz the farm, coming in at only a few links above ground, forcing the farmhands to fall to the ground as he roared by. Sometimes he'd swoosh through the narrow opening between the house and the barn, and the heavy downdraft from the blades would stir up krills and krills of dirt and dust, soiling Zhinta's wash hanging on the line, and she'd run from the house shaking her fist at him, but that never stopped him, he'd do it again and again until Zhinta took the clothes off the line and ran into the house with them and ignored him and he'd give up and fly away. Other times, he'd buzz the pasture, frightening the animals, scaring them so badly they'd scatter, and Leos and the others would have to spend several subsectors rounding them up, not arriving back at the barn until well after nightfall.

Night didn't fall as abruptly on *Non* as it did on Nytandra. The heavy cloud layer diffused and scattered the light from the sun, and the day died down quietly and gracefully, until everything was engulfed in total darkness. The complete and profound darkness of the nightime unnerved Leos. He hated it, so unused as he was to the total lack of light. It magnified his sense of isolation. He longed for the constant light of Anthanos, or the city lights of Nytandra, or at the very least, the orange glow of the tree that was his home on the green planet. Yet every time he looked out the window in his room toward the forest that bordered the rear of the house, he was met with total and absolute blackness. He longed for any light at all—a glimmer, a glint, a shimmer, even a mere flicker or a twinkle—something to take away the absolute profoundness of the night. Anything to destroy the deep shadow that had settled into his soul and threatened to quash any hope he had of ever getting off this planet.

Against the helicopter, though, Leos did have one defense. Dressed in his dark cloak and heavy black gloves, he looked like any other worker on the farm, and as long as he didn't look up at the helicopter as it zipped over the farm, he was safe. His umber skin would have given him away immediately.

*　　*　　*

About a hundred days after he arrived, Leos had gone to the lake, about a half-anthan from the farm. A large finger-like lake, about a hundred anthans long but a few thousand links wide, it served as reservoir for the cities and towns situated along its banks. Wild, virgin forest lined the lakeshore through most of its length, green and inviting during the warm season, barren and gray when the cold arrived. A small stream fed the lake at its southern end where Leos visited.

Leos was good at mechanical things so Zhinta assigned him the job of maintaining the pump that sent water from the lake to the farm. The little pump house, a sturdy concrete block structure, had been built on a narrow, gravelly beach near where the stream emptied into the lake. It sat at the bottom of an eroded scarp about five links high, and access was down a set of eight concrete steps. Mostly Leos performed routine maintenance—kept the motor and pump bearings lubricated, checked the pump for water or oil leaks—things that could be done without stopping the pump. Once every fifty days he had to stop the motor and disassemble the pump for inspection and heavy lubrication, and today was one of those days. He'd finished his work, restarted the pump, closed the door to the pump house, and had taken only two steps toward the stairs when the helicopter came spitting over. In the rumbling vibration of the pump and motor, he didn't hear it approach. It skimmed the top of the pump house and sent him sprawling to the ground. He jumped up screaming.

"What the hell! Whadda you think you're doing?" He watched as the pilot swung around to make a second pass. Leos stood there, shaking a fist at him, the hood of his cloak collapsed around his shoulders.

"Oh, shit," he yelled, and pulled the hood over his head and bolted for the steps. At the top of the steps the terrain was open field all the way to the farm. But even a half-anthan was a long run. He stared at the field, frightfully aware of what a helicopter could do to him in the open, but he started running as fast as he could. The pilot came in low again, directly over Leos as he ran. Caught in the open, he could do nothing but drop to the ground. The pilot made pass after pass, forcing Leos to turn and run back toward the shelter of the pump house. But as he reached the steps, the copter came over so low that one of the landing skids whacked him on the side of his head and sent him tumbling down the steps to the gravelly beach below. Dazed, his head throbbing, he lay still for a few nanosectors, but just as he tried to rise to his feet, another pass by the copter sent him flat on his face again.

Now the pilot began hovering, the copter swinging back and forth a few links above Leos, forcing him to remain on the ground. The heavy wash from the copter's blades had blown the hood of the cloak off his head, and he and the pilot stared blankly at each other, a few links apart through the plastic bubble that enclosed the cockpit. Then the pilot took off again and made a wide sweeping curve around for another pass. Leos remained still, stunned and disoriented from the noise and heavy wash. He'd wrenched his ankle in the fall, and, wouldn't you know, it was the same one he'd injured in the landing of the spaceship, and it ached and throbbed as he lay on the ground. He sat up, figuring to try and stand and limp back to the pump house. That was when he realized he sat on top of a rope coiled up on the ground.

About a hundred links long, the rope had a small loop a few deci-links in diameter at the free end. The rope was used to tie up small boats because there was no dock, and the other end was tied to the bottom of the handrail at the stairs. His head still throbbed where the helicopter landing skid had bumped it, and as the pilot made another pass, Leos, out of abso-lute frustration and anger, hurled the end of the rope at the helicopter as it zipped past.

"Go away!" he yelled. "Leave me alone!"

That didn't do anything other than relieve some of his frustration, but the end of the rope knocked against one of the copter's landing skids and dropped to the ground. The two landing skids, tubular metal bars about four decilinks in diameter, projected forward from beneath the copter a few links. That gave Leos an idea.

The pilot made another pass, coming in low from the land, swinging out over the water. Leos held the loop behind him, and as the copter came over, exactly head high, he squatted and tried to flip the loop up over the right-hand skid.

He missed — *no, that tiny loop will never slip over the skid. I'll have to make a larger loop. But how? The only way is to thread the other end through the loop, and it's tied up at the steps. There isn't time to untie it and . . . but hold on a microsector . . .*

As the copter buzzed out over the lake, Leos made a bend in the standing end of the rope and forced it through the small loop to form a running loop, like a lariat. When the copter came around for the next pass, he tried again, dropping to his knees, holding the loop behind him and flipping the loop up toward the oncoming skid.

It caught — right through the loop — almost too easy. The pilot probably didn't realize the rope was there as he swung out low over the lake. Leos stumbled out of the way as the rope payed out behind the copter, and when it reached full length, it tightened with a vibrant ringing *thwang*, and the copter flipped upside down and plunged into the lake.

The blades churned up a spray of water, but they stopped after a couple of loud flaps, and the hot engine of the copter exploded with a deafening *swoosh*, throwing a geyser of water, steam, and metal twenty or thirty links into the air. Leos pulled the rope back and threw it where it'd been near the stairs, then hobbled up the steps. He glanced back at the remnants of the helicopter, but didn't see the pilot.

But the damage had been done. The pilot had certainly identified Leos and communicated it to the Talatan. Leos was the only dark-skinned person on the planet, and the Talatan couldn't fail to realize who he was. Making pass after pass was the pilot's way of keeping him pinned down until the Guards could arrive, and they were certainly on their way by now. Leos headed for the farm, but stopped after he'd taken only a few steps. His foot and ankle throbbed, his head ached where the copter had struck it. Where should he go? The farm lay in the distance, the smell drifting faintly toward him. If he went to the farm, he'd walk right into the Guards as they arrived, and that would compromise Zhinta and her husband, and even the plot. He wished mightily for the forest of the green planet, or the protective hallways of the Nytandran Palace and Esmerelda's smiling face and comforting voice. He heard something in the distance. It was what he thought it was. The typical wailing of a Talatan vehicle. Several of them.

Back down the steps he ran, limping toward the trees on the other side of the stream that fed the lake—crap, that water was cold on his sore foot. Here come the Guards. Sirens—men—tracking animals making a squealing sound as they latched onto Leos's scent.

Go, man, go. Run—run—run.

Leos reached the relative safety of the forest when the Guards spotted him, yelling and screaming behind him. The tracking animals screeched and shrieked in pursuit, but the trees of this forest didn't have branches that reached all the way to the ground like those on the green planet, and he couldn't just hide and climb up to escape his pursuers. He ran on through the trees. As he got deeper into the forest, the trees got tighter together, dimming the light, shielding him from the oppressive clouds, but he wasn't relieved. He continued to run. The animals were behind him, the whistles of the Guards screeching in his ears. He stopped, looked around. He had few options. From under his cloak he withdrew his knife, prepared to fight if necessary.

But hold on—fight? No way. *There must be fifty, maybe a hundred men after me now. Maybe more. I can't fight that many—I'm just one man with a knife. Doesn't matter how good I am. Nobody could fight all of them. I might kill a few of them, but there's too many. They'd just blow me away.* He stashed the knife, still in its sheath, in a decay-filled hole in the crotch of a dead tree, and ran on.

I'll come back and get it.

When they caught him, they tackled him and beat him and tied him up and bound him hand and foot and held their weapons on him until the leader of the contingent of Guards came by. Then they took him back to Marktu-Ahdenu in a rickety old van with one Guard sitting on top of him the whole way so he could barely breathe, and they threw him in the deepest, darkest dungeon they could find. At least it seemed so.

CHAPTER 43

PRISON

What is this place? Where are we going? This looks like a dungeon of some sort. It's dark in here. I can't see where we're going. We're walking a long way, it seems downhill all the way. We've stopped—now what? That looks like a prison cell, is that my cell?

"Take your boots off!"

"Take my boots off? What for?"

"Get in there!" A voice boomed behind him. *Where's that voice coming from?*

"Hey—don't push—there's water all over the floor. What the hell! The water's cold."

Crap, did you have to push me into the water? Now all my clothes are wet. How the hell am I supposed to live in this godforsaken place? There's only a small bench here—it's hard and my clothes are soaking wet—I'll have to take off my clothes, they're so wet—but it's freezing in here—hey, don't turn off the light. Shit. Might as well try and get some sleep . . . but how can I sleep when it's freezing in here? It's like trying to sleep on the cold side at home. At least there we had warm clothing. And dry.

"Hey, leave me alone, let me get some sleep."

That's easy for you, you've got boots on, they look waterproof. You can walk in the water, I can't. God, that water is cold. Where are we going? Another room. At least it's a little warmer here than in my cell.

"Sit in the chair."

At least I know the word for 'chair.' "Hey! Turn out that light!"

"Tell us about Jad."

"Who are you? Don't yell. I can hear you."

"Where did he come from? Was he in the resistance? What was his position? Was he a leader? How much did he know? Who else is in the resistance?"

"Sorry, I don't speak your language that well. I don't know what you're asking. I've told you everything I know. I don't know anything about the resistance. If Jad was in it, he never told me. That makes sense, doesn't it? Why would he tell me? I know nothing, I tell you."

"Was Jad in the resistance? Was Zhinta in the resistance? Tell us! The sooner you tell us, the sooner you can go."

"I don't know! I don't know! How can I tell you something I don't know?"

"We know Tsoder was in the resistance. What about his wife, Tsee? Was she in the resistance? Tell us—now!"

"I don't know. I only met them at a party. I don't know much about them."

"Was she a runner for the resistance? Did she transmit messages to Jad?"

"I don't know. I told you, I met them at a party. That's all I know about them."

"How did you kill those two guards? With a knife? Where did you get the knife?"

"What? I don't understand. Oh, knife. It was just a pocket knife. I've had it for a long time. I threw it away. I don't know where it is. Probably in the lake somewhere. It was just self-defense. They attacked me. I had to defend myself."

"That's ridiculous. You couldn't kill two people with a puny pocket knife. Where's the knife?"

"I told you, in the lake."

"Where in the lake?"

"I told you. I threw it in the lake."

"Where in the lake?"

"I told you — how long is this going to go on?"

"Until you tell us what we want to know."

How long have we been here? I only got about a subsector of sleep. Cold sleep. All these questions. "I've told you all I know. I don't understand your language that well."

"You will return to your cell."

How long have I been here? All these questions. How much more. I can't take much more. God, that water is cold.

I hear screaming. It keeps waking me up. Who is it? I don't get much sleep in this cold anyway. Must be other prisoners. Or is it me? Do I wake myself up screaming?

"Make it easy on yourself. Tell us what we want to know and we will let you go. The more you resist, the longer you will be here."

More likely, the sooner I tell you everything I know, the sooner you'll dispose of me. God, that water is cold, do I have to walk through the water on the floor of my cell every time we come back here? It's cold and I'm cold, and I think I've caught a cold.

"Achoo!"

Are you playing with germ warfare? Did you deliberately give me germs?

"That sergeant you killed was a friend of mine! He and the private with him were given a medal for their service. But now they are dead and you will pay!"

"Friend of yours, sorry, I didn't know."

Oh, God, who are these guys? They're new. I've never seen them before. They look like sergeants, just like the one who tried to kill me. If I'd known, I wouldn't have killed him. Like I told those other guys—they must have been officers—it was self-defense.

"They were drunk. It was self-defense."

"How could it be self-defense? No friend of mine in the Talatan Guards would try to kill you. We uphold the law. We do not kill. You must be mistaken."

"They were drunk. They threw my knife at me, but it didn't work. I grabbed the knife and threw it back at them. Self-defense."

What is that? Hey! Why are you taking my pants off? Yow! Not there! I have to pee through that. That's my private part. Ahhhh! No more! No more! No more electric shocks, please—it's bleeding—can't you see the blood? Stop it! Stop it! God that hurts.

Oh, God that water is cold. Leave me alone—it hurts so much to pee.

No! No! Not there! My arms are stretched so much it hurts. My legs too. Ouch! Not there! No! No! Not more electric shocks—not there—it hurts too much. How will I ever be able to go to the bathroom again? It must be bleeding—I can't see—it hurts too much, I just want to go back to my cell. Oh, no! Not the cold water. I can't pee, I can't crap—what the hell did they do to me? All these electric shocks—front and back—what do they want—I can't tell them, it hurts too much. I can't sleep. They won't let me sleep anyway. So many questions.

"Tell us about Jad. Tell us how you killed the Talatan Guards. Tell us about your knife. Are there any others in the resistance? The sooner you tell us, the sooner you can go. All we want is a few answers. Then we'll let you go. It's that simple."

Oh, God, not upside down again. I hate being hung upside down. My head hurts, it's so full of blood. My feet are numb, I can't feel them anymore. Oh, God, just let me pass out—just become unconscious again. No, no not the cold water again! Do they have to let me wake up in the cold water on the floor of my cell? That hurts so much, the freezing water. So cold. So cold.

"Tell us about Jad. About the resistance. About the others. Who are they? Tell us! Tell us!"

"I don't—Ahhhh! Stop it! Stop it!"

My feet hurt so much—I can't walk—oh, God, the cold water hurts so much, even on my numb feet. I don't know how it can happen, I can't feel the cold water, but my legs ache so much from all the cold.

"Who are the others in the resistance?"

"I told you I don't know. Ahhhh! Stop! Stop!"

"Turn up the voltage! Higher! Higher!"

"No, don't! Okay, okay, I'll tell you. Zhinta! Zhinta at the farm—she's part of the resistance—I swear—I don't know who else—I swear—I swear . . . yes, it's true, she was! Stop! Stop! I don't know if Jad was in the resistance. He didn't tell me—why would he tell me? It doesn't make sense . . . oh, God, stop, stop, stop."

Shit, that water is cold. Let me sleep, just let me sleep. Now what? Who are these people? Mlada? Is that you? No, just someone who looks like Mlada. Except uglier. And in a Talatan uniform. Why are you taking my pants off? What is this? No! No! I can't make an erection—are you kidding? What the hell—no, no—not with you—I'm engaged to be married—Tama, where are you? I need you now. This woman is ugly. Who wants to fuck an ugly bitch? Get off me! Get off me! No, I don't know about the resistance. Jad was a friend of mine, that's all I know.

"Once you said Jad was in the resistance. Now you say you don't know. What is the right answer? What is the answer?"

"I never said Jad was in the resistance—I don't know if he was or not. Honest, I never knew. He didn't tell me."

No! No! Not upside down again! Unconscious—please, God, unconscious.

"Ahhhh!" *What the hell—what's going on—where am I—oh, I'm still in my cell—I woke up screaming—that's okay, other guys wake up screaming—at least I'm not losing my mind . . .*

"You said Jad was in the resistance. Now tell us again. We want to hear it from you. Again."

"I never said Jad was in the resistance. I said I didn't know."

My feet are so numb. And they still hurt so much.

"I'll get you, you miserable bastards! If it's the last thing I do, I'll get back at you! No! No! Not my feet again! Ahhhh! Stop it! Stop it!"

"Turn up the voltage!"

"Stop it! Stop it!"

Shit, that water's cold. Did they have to flood my cell here with water? I think they must put more water down every day.

How long have I been here? Must be days. A hundred or more. I can't tell. I can't sleep. I just want to sleep. God, let me sleep.

Where are they taking me now? I don't recognize this part of the dungeon.

Who is this guy? He looks like a judge. I wonder if I can . . .

"Your honor, I protest my treatment . . ."

"Silence, Mr. Leos. You will speak only when asked a direct question. It has been determined that your sentence will be that you will spend the rest of your days on the Callus. We would like to execute you for the capital crimes of murder and treason, but because of your friendship with the traitor Jad of Nytandra, and other places, and your involvement in the resistance, and your killing, execution style, of two of our Talatan Guards, we have determined that death would be too good for you, and therefore you will be taken to the Callus immediately where you will live out your days under the strictest, harshest conditions possible. Remove the prisoner."

The Callus? I've heard of it, Kazeh told me about it, about some people prisoners there, but nobody told me where it is. Is that where we're going? It's so dark out, I can't see where we're going. What T-sector is it? What time is it? God, my feet and penis and butt are so fuckin' sore.

In the darkness in the city of Marktu-Ahdenu that was so profound the streetlamps could barely project their light all the way to street level, and the headlights of the vehicle could illuminate the street only about twenty links ahead, they drove Leos to the airport.

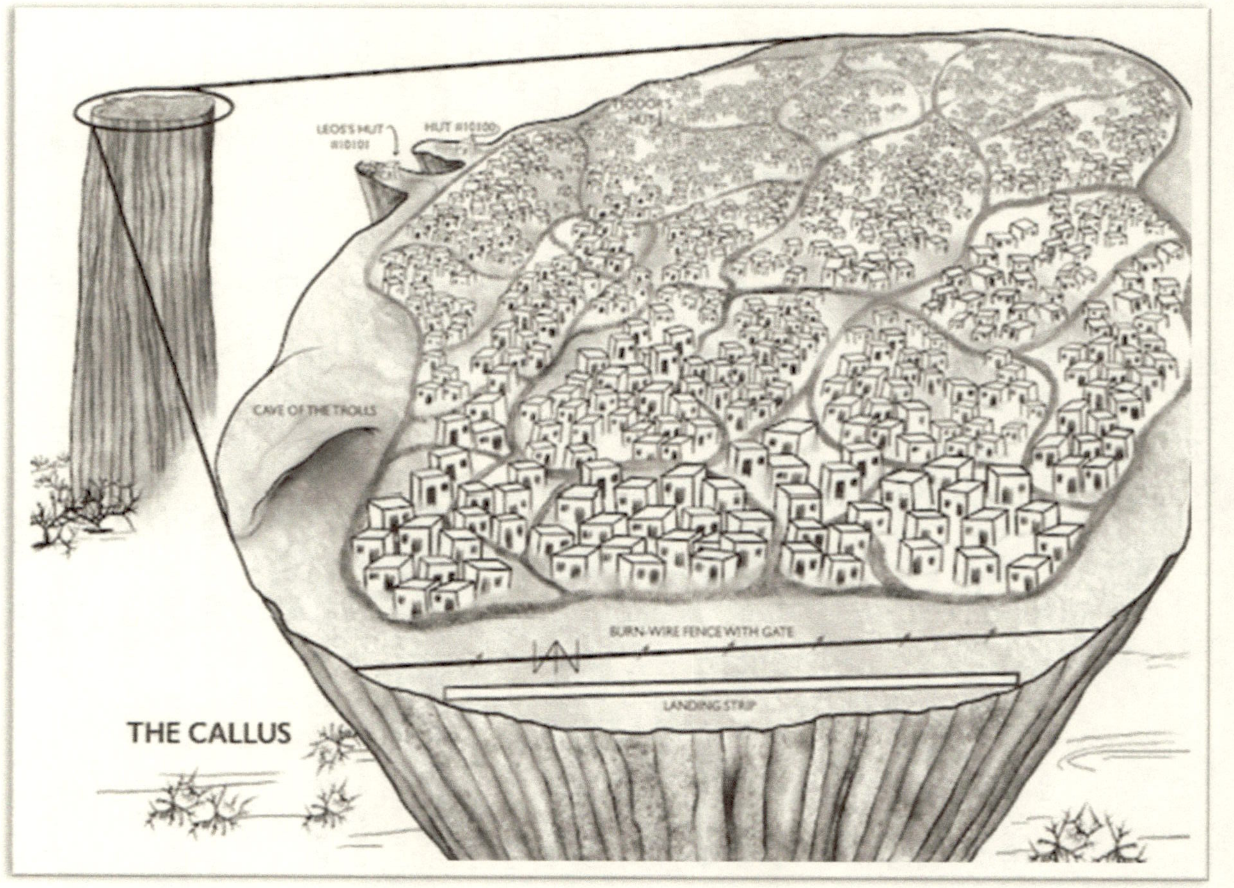

LEOS'S HUT #10101
HUT #10100
TEODOR'S HUT
CAVE OF THE TROLLS
BURN-WIRE FENCE WITH GATE
LANDING STRIP
THE CALLUS

CHAPTER 44

THE CALLUS

Leos had never seen a propeller-driven airplane. Not one as large as this.

They removed his leg bindings so he could board the plane, but he could walk only slowly and gingerly across the tarmac in spite of being urged on by the front ends of two rather vicious-looking weapons held by a couple of Talatan guards.

"Stop poking me. I'm walking as fast as I can."

A twin-engine plane with the engines mounted on the wings, and an unusual twin-rudder tail, the plane had sixteen seats, eight on each side of a center aisle. He dropped into one seat and his guard clamped his bindings to the armrest.

The only propeller airplanes Leos had seen were models of antiques in a museum on Anthanos, so with the tiny amount of curiosity that he was able to muster—occupied as much as he was with the pain and anger that still racked his body and consumed his mind—he watched with little more than mild curiosity when the engine out his window started. A flash of blue-white smoke erupted from the exhaust, and the propeller swirled into an invisible disk to produce the force that pulled the plane down the runway and into the wet dawning sky. He understood almost none of it, but he didn't care either.

Near midday, the plane landed near a small town at the edge of a desert. Here, he and one of his guards transferred to a six-seat single-engine plane that took him to the Callus. Another prisoner and his guard accompanied him. Two subsectors later they landed.

The Callus sat in the middle of the barren Khontodu desert, a desert so large it encircled the planet at the equator. A maze of dense canyons and open plateaus, desiccated valleys and rocky prominences, the desert lay like an tannish-gray scar fully around the planet, five hundred anthans north and south of the equator. From this impenetrable wilderness rose the Callus, a single erection thrust five thousand links into the sky, the same pale dusty color as the desert but so conspicuous and unmistakable as to appear preposterously out of place in the surrounding wasteland. The granite plug of a long-extinct volcano, the top lay much closer to the clouds than did the lowlands, and the oppressive mood that plagued the rest of the planet was here so much more pronounced.

At its top, an irregular circle over three anthans in circumference, the Callus was wide open and nearly flat, as though trimmed by a gigantic razor. Along the western edge rose one prominent hill, perhaps a hundred links tall, several hundred links from the airstrip where the plane landed.

The airstrip had been smoothed out of the rocks and gullies along the south edge of the Callus. Nothing else existed nearby, no buildings, no other airplanes, just a fence that demarcated the strip from the rest of the Callus. The opposite side of the strip was the edge of the Callus, a sheer cliff that went straight down into the wasteland below.

It was here on the Callus that Leos first met the trolls.

Ugly, misshapen, with a blunt, flattened nose, short stubby arms and legs, only three-and-a-half to four links tall, and rotund, like a ball, their eyes seemed miniature versions of the bright open eyes of the Jhontu, glassy and reflective in the light of day. Their uniforms were the same red and brown as those of the Talatan Guards, but cut differently to fit their short, stocky frame. Clearly these were the Talatan of the Callus, and they undoubtedly took their orders from Talatan headquarters. Most carried shoulder weapons, though a few had hand weapons in holsters, each a smaller version of the ones the regular Guards carried. Smaller to fit their smaller hand, but presumably as deadly. One of the trolls had two pips on his collar, like a corporal. He seemed to be in charge.

"Out of the plane!" the corporal bellowed. He had a high-pitched voice, so different from the much lower-pitched voices of the other Jhontu, and his enunciation was slightly garbled. Vowels were glossed over and a couple of consonants were run together.

A chilly wind whipped around the landing strip on the Callus, and blew dust into Leos's eyes as he and the other prisoner left the plane. Immediately, he was aware of the smell that permeated the Callus, but it wasn't just the dry, dusty flavor of the air. A squalid odor, grimy with a touch of sordidness, it faintly resembled the odor of the bar on Nytandra. But this wasn't the smell of the working man, this had a tinge of morbidity and mortality to it, a melancholy flavor that hinted at death and dying.

The trolls escorted them to a six-seat, three-wheeled cart-like vehicle, which took them through a gate in the fencing. The fence had been constructed of horizontal strands of heavy wire set every few decilinks with a triad of sharp, vicious-looking spines that would certainly shred your skin into painful strips were you foolish enough to try to wiggle through. The cart sped out over the open plain, spewing noxious fumes from the exhaust of the little engine that reminded Leos, both in smell and noise, of the helicopter. They came shortly to the mouth of a cave hollowed out of the one prominent hill on the otherwise flat Callus.

"Everyone out!" the corporal yelled. "Out! Out!"

During the trip to the Callus, Leos hadn't felt too much apprehension about his fate. He was still alive—*thanks to the Great God Arteamos*—and glad to be out of the torture chamber where he'd been held for so long. The "judge" he saw just before leaving Marktu had made it clear the Callus was for his permanent incarceration, not execution, though that was about all he knew. Curiously, though, he wondered, *why would they take the time and energy to send me to this out-of-the-way place? If they'd wanted to, they could have executed me by now. They could have done it so easily in Marktu.*

But when he saw the cave, his musings ended abruptly, his heart jerked into high gear, and his chest tightened. A dark hole in the side of the hill, a yawning, gaping mouth with several trolls holding weapons standing in its maw, and a guardhouse to one side with another troll holding what looked like an automatic weapon. And it was trained on him. The rough outline of the opening gave the cave an ugly, ominous look, with huge teeth hanging from the top, ready to devour anyone who entered.

Holy shit. What is this? Maybe I was wrong. This can't be good.

The other prisoner gasped and began yelling.

"No! No! Help me! Save me! Save me from this place!"

He turned and tried to run, but he couldn't move very fast in leg irons, and two of the troll guards grabbed him and knocked him to the ground. Five or six more trolls poured from the cave and pounced on him, overwhelming him in a burst of roly-poly fisticuffs. They shocked him with a pistol-shaped device that didn't knock him out, but when he stood, he trembled and shook, and seemed disoriented. The trolls pushed him toward the cave and he went—meekly, staggering and whimpering, and with leg tremors that made it hard to walk.

The troll guarding Leos prodded him with the front end of his weapon to follow. Leos didn't want to enter that dreadful-looking opening any more than the other prisoner, and in his own insolent way, he admired the guts of the other one, but defiance had been beaten out of him in Marktu, and he too obediently entered the cave.

They walked in darkness down a narrow passageway hollowed out of solid rock. About twenty links from the entrance, they turned into a lighted hallway that led toward a set of double doors. Machinery hummed in the background. More trolls lined the walls, all with weapons, all staring at Leos, and many of the trolls fell in behind him as they walked. The double doors opened into a large room, lit by bare bulbs hanging from the ceiling. Perhaps forty or fifty more trolls milled about in the room. Near the center of the room sat an older man, same chunky build and same snout face as the trolls, behind a large, solid-looking wood table. He wore the mostly red uniform of a high-ranking Talatan officer, but it seemed too small to cover his corpulence. One separate ceiling light illuminated him and his table in a brilliant cone of light, and several papers lay scattered across the table. The comparison with the Grand Hall of the Imperial Palace didn't come immediately to Leos, but he wasn't immune to its effects either. But this wasn't the Grand Hall, this was a dreary dungeon-like cave, crawling with creatures of sin and hell, and Leos's knees trembled as he stood waiting his turn.

The old man stared at Leos as the group approached, but switched his attention to the other prisoner when the trolls pushed him forward into the light in front of the table. The corporal handed the old man a sheaf of papers. He glanced at them and spoke briefly to the other prisoner. The guards removed his hand and leg bindings, and led him from the chamber.

Now it was Leos's turn. Two trolls nudged him toward the light.

"The Judge wants to talk to you," one troll said, but Leos hesitated. Other trolls congregated around, staring at Leos, perhaps incredulous at the presence of such a dark-skinned prisoner. His skin could have been bright purple, and he wouldn't have stood out more. A screechy murmuring of hushed whispers and subdued rumblings began among the trolls, not silenced until the Judge spoke.

"You, there, the one with skin dark through and through. Step forward and let me get a good look at you."

The troll guards pushed Leos harder, and he reluctantly stepped into the light.

"Mr. Leos, I say, several people you killed. Several Talatan Guards, how shall you be billed? Speak up for yourself, what have you to say? Speak up, O you dark man, we don't have all day."

"I-I killed no one." Leos consciously tried to suppress the tremor in his voice. "E-Except in self-defense." He thought he was being honorable, even principled in his attitude, but the trolls took his comments very differently. They burst into laughter. Even the Judge roared.

"It certainly was, self-defense, he did say. I'll wager the Talatan don't see it that way! Several women and children. I bet it's all true. What have you to say? Are you deaf and blind, too?" He roared even louder.

What? Women and children. What the hell is he talking about. "That's a lie. I never—"

"There was also the old man, your best friend, as they say. Chopped his poor head off—out the window one day."

The room roared.

An old man? What old man? What's he talking about—oh, my God.

Too stunned to respond, Leos's knees weakened, his eyes watered, and he looked down at the floor. His feet seemed to pain him more than usual. He couldn't think, his mind swirled, and all sorts of thoughts penetrated his brain. He grew dizzy and nauseated. For the first time, he began to comprehend what the Talatan had done to him. They'd accused him of many more crimes than he'd actually committed, even, apparently, of killing Jad—if Jad were really dead. They hadn't told him any of this. He'd been held for all those days in the prison in Marktu then brought directly here, stopping only to change planes at the little airport on the edge of the desert. He'd seen no one, not a judge or jury, not even an attorney.

"I d-don't know what you're t-talking about," he muttered as well as he could through his tears.

"Speak up, O you dark man, your words are too weak. We can't hear you at all. It's your voice that we seek."

"Speak up," one of the trolls said, and whacked Leos across the knee with his weapon. Leos didn't even blink. "The Judge wishes to hear your voice."

The Judge roared much more, and the laughter continued. Not a deep laughter like Leos had heard as he sat in the Kazo Dela Tan with his neck trapped between those cold, hard metal plates, but high pitched, shrill and penetrating, like a nasal squeal. It came from all the trolls around the cave, laughing and screeching, shrieking and yowling, and it hurt his ears much more than the laughter of the Nytandrans. He almost wished for the Kazo Dela Tan—at least he got out of that. His chances of getting out of this didn't look as good.

"Nytandran beauties through here never come, and this one that did, oh, he's pretty dumb."

"Boil him in brine," one of the trolls yelled. "That'll bleach him white." The Judge chuckled.

"Cut off his fingers," another said, giggling and snickering, and the laughter increased.

"Tear out his fingernails," a third said. That was an interesting remark because the trolls didn't appear to have fingernails. Several trolls grabbed Leos's hands and ran their grubby, stubby fingers over his nails and began a repetitive chant, "One by one, out they come."

"Let's pin a tail on him," a fourth one said, and with that the laughter — vibrantly high-pitched already — became so loud it reverberated and rebounded throughout the room, echoing off the walls, one wall to another and back, concentrating itself in the center of the room where Leos stood. A pitcher of water on the Judge's table vibrated and shook. The lamp above the table swung and gyrated in a circular orbit.

"He's ugly!" screeched another troll who looked female, with longer hair and a marginally higher voice. The sound grew louder, and the papers on the table undulated across the surface.

"Gouge his eyes out!"

"Cut off his ears!"

"Cut off his balls!"

"Does he even have balls?"

More laughter, louder. Lights around the room flickered.

"Scratch his left eye," another one said. Larger than the others with three pips on his collar, a sergeant. But with that suggestion, the laughing stopped so abruptly it could have been turned off at a switch. Many of the trolls gasped, and a death-like pall settled over the room. Most of the trolls backed timidly away from the light of the table, and the sergeant took over holding Leos's bindings — the only troll who didn't retreat. The Judge, too, stopped laughing and his face morphed into a black scowl that scared Leos more than the laughter. Leos's heart pounded into high gear, his knees resumed their weak and wobbly ways, and he started breathing heavily.

"Yes," the Judge said, quietly, though it seemed a stretch to say thoughtfully. "Yes."

"Wha— What are you saying? Scratch—my eye?"

The Judge leaned forward and stared intently at Leos. "If we must, dear Leos, the way's open still. But not right now, let's wait until . . ."

"Un . . . until?"

". . . until it's required, then our promise fulfill. Behave yourself Leos, or I warn you we will."

"Er, o-o-okay."

"Can you guess in your mind just what it will do? What route it will take? What will happen to you?"

Leos shook his head, dreading to hear what was coming. He swallowed hard and tried consciously to suppress the knocking of his knees.

"Your sight will be skewed, your eye a bit tight. But all that you see, you'll think is just right."

"You've g-g-got to be kidding."

The scowl on the Judge's face deepened and he stood up at his table and thrust a stubby digit at Leos. "I do not kid you, Leos, my friend. Your eye I will nick, and it will not mend. Here is the knife—I'll do, it I'm sure. The way is too clear, be warned there's no cure."

From the side of the table, the Judge picked up what at first looked like a rock, perhaps three decilinks long and a half-decilink wide. He held it directly in front of Leos's face and his eyes opened wide at the sight. One end of the rock tapered to a highly polished knife-like edge, and a single ray of light twinkled from the edge. Just a slight flickering, a momentary spectrum effect, but enough to let Leos know it was sharp—seriously sharp. Looking at it made him tremble. He swallowed hard.

"Many a prisoner we've had to do here. It changes them, yes, for the better, it's clear. Look around you, tell me, what do you see? Prisoners all—their eyes just like me!"

"What . . . ?" Leos looked around at the trolls. While the ceiling lights sparkled brilliantly in the right eye of each troll, the left eye was faintly dimmer and slightly hazy, as though a film covered it, or it had a roughness about it, like a piece of sandpaper.

"We don't do all, Leos my friend. That man here before you—compliant—he'll bend. But you, Leos, anger's filled up your mind. If you cross us, well, we've handled your kind. You'll regret it, I'm sure, Leos I say, regret it you will to your dying day. I know you, Leos, I know well your type. A day's work to you is just so much tripe. I put it to you, will you work to survive? Many men do—if they work, they thrive. But those who don't—the cold's on its way. Make up your mind, Leos. What do you say? Starvation may simmer at your front door. The route is too clear. Need I say more?"

The Judge paused and sat back down on his throne. He stared directly at Leos, but his face seemed to relax somewhat. "Now, where shall we send you? Which hut is for you? I'm thinking perhaps of—" He broke off his talk and stared at the ceiling. The room turned quiet and a murmuring spread through the trolls. Soon, one troll yelled, "To the North Fork!" and several more joined him yelling, "Yes! To the North Fork!"

"To hut 10101!" several others yelled.

"Yes. Yes!" the Judge said, and a big grin spread over his face. "To the North Fork. Hut one-oh-one-oh-one. I've given my order, now let it be done!"

At this, the Judge started laughing, and everyone else joined him. The hall was again filled with the screechy laughter of the trolls, but this time and even more so than before, a terrible feeling of the macabre saturated that laughter, and it filled Leos with the trepidation of his eventual demise. The Judge stood again and pointed directly at Leos. "But I warn you, friend Leos, of fences we've none. Escape is impossible. Where would you run? We have no ladders, no elevators, no stairs. Don't try to climb down—don't give yourself airs! Many have tried and many have died. Not one is alive, not one who tried. The bottom is deep—quite a distance down there. Four thousand siltos of nothing but air."

A silto was a Jhontu unit of linear measurement, somewhat more than a link, but as Leos tried to form a mental picture of the Callus and how high above the desert he stood, the Judge continued his diatribe.

"The soul of a man who stays careful and clean will last for ten years, unmarked and serene. Be quiescent, I tell you, within yourself stay. Life is hard here, day after day. Your new home awaits you, all shuttered and shut. The guards will take you—your new home, your hut!"

The troll sergeant stepped forward and nudged Leos toward the doors.

CHAPTER 45

THE NORTH FORK

When Leos and the trolls guarding him neared the opening to the cave, the sergeant unlatched Leos's arm and leg bindings. Leos rubbed his wrists where the shackles had bitten into his skin. He was glad to be rid of them, but that wasn't his most pressing worry. *Where is the hut the Judge mentioned?* He'd been expecting a cell, something like the jail cells he knew about on Anthanos or Nytandra, or the dungeon in Marktu.

"Follow me." The sergeant motioned toward the cave entrance and Leos followed. Another troll with a weapon trudged behind and slapped him in the butt or poked him in the ribs if he straggled, even just slightly. They boarded one of the three-wheeled vehicles and drove off toward the northern part of the Callus. "You are free to roam the Callus," the sergeant said as he drove, and swept his right arm out over the land. "But remember, there is no way down." He chuckled to himself.

For the first time, Leos turned his attention toward the main section of the Callus, to his right as they drove. The terrain on the Callus was depressingly monotonous. Largely flat, but with low, rocky hills in places and covered with a fine-grained sandy-brown soil. Everywhere, knife-edged rocks poked up from the soil. But the most prominent features of the Callus were the huts. Small, one room, gray cement-block huts about ten links square and maybe eight links high, with a dried, decaying number board above the wooden door. Only a small number of the huts were visible, but they seemed to be everywhere. There might have been thousands of them. Beside some of the huts stood a person, presumably another prisoner, each dressed in an ill-fitting dark brown outfit, all the same, all very uniform. Some watched as Leos passed, some worked in a small garden beside the hut, a few urinated into the garden. What vegetation existed on the Callus grew only in the little gardens beside the huts.

"These are your neighbors," the sergeant said. Then he laughed again in that high-pitched cackling laugh all the trolls had. "We are going to your hut. The cold season is coming. You will be warm in your hut."

This time he laughed so hard he nearly drove off the road.

The numbers on the number boards grew increasingly greater the farther they got from the cave, as though the numbering system started near the cave and proceeded outward. "We are taking you to hut 10101," the troll said after he calmed down enough to drive. "That is the last hut. Way out on the North Fork. The worst hut on the Callus. A perfect place for a visitor from Nytandra. You will like it there. Dead and dreary. Desolate and deserted."

Then he started laughing and almost drove off the road again.

If I'm going to hut 10101, does that mean there are over ten thousand huts on this place? That's a lot . . . a lot of people.

A projection of two roughly parallel fingers of land, the North Fork pushed northward from the main section of the Callus, like the tines of a two-pronged fork. Leos's hut had been built on the westernmost of the two fingers, placed precariously near the tip on the only area of flat land around. Behind the hut, a large pile of rocks and boulders rose ten to twelve links above ground level, and to the right side of the hut lay the remnants of a garden. Little grew in the rocky soil, and it was that fact alone that gave Leos the most dread.

Do I have to grow my own food? Deserts he'd seen, but this total lack of vegetation dismayed him.

The hut was dark and deserted.

The sergeant pulled up to the door. He jumped out and opened a hatch on the back of the cart that covered a small trunk-like carrier. He pulled out a quilted brown one-piece oversuit, thickly padded for insulation during the cold season; two blankets; and six packets of seeds.

"These are for you," he said. "Do not plant the seeds now. Nothing will grow in the cold weather that is coming. You will stay in this hut. It will be your home forever. In the cold weather, the food truck comes around twice a day, and once every ten days we fill the water jugs."

Then he laughed as he jumped back on the little cart and yelled, "Good luck!" as he turned the cart around and putt-putted off, leaving Leos standing at the door of the hut wondering what the hell was going on.

Leos turned and gazed at the hut. The same cement bricks as all the others, a flat, wooden roof covered the top. He'd hoped that the fact that the hut had the highest number meant that it'd been one of the last ones built, but as soon as he got a good look at it . . . *Yes, the troll was right, it probably is the worst hut on the Callus.*

The decayed and rotten door, warped almost beyond repair, hung loose on rusty, disintegrating hinges. There was no latch to lock the door. A small window beside the door was covered by decrepit shutters on rusty hinges. Instead of entering immediately, Leos circled the hut. Around back, he found another window, wide open, the shutters pushed aside. He looked in the window, but saw little in the dim interior. Around a third corner, a rusted hoe and small spade lay on the ground beside the garden, nestled against a blank side of the hut.

When he returned to the front, he pushed the door open and walked inside. The only piece of furniture, a long, hard, wooden bed, sat against the wall to the left. He dumped his stuff on the bed and tried to close the shutters of the rear window, but the wood, like that of the door, had become so thoroughly dried out and warped the shutters wouldn't close completely. *How well will they be able to keep out the bitter temperatures of the coming cold season?*

An empty plastic jug that could hold several trilinks of water stood on a metal shelf attached to the wall near the door. Beside it hung a rusty cup for drinking and a similar bowl for eating. He considered cleaning out the place, but other than kicking a few rocks on the dirt floor out the door, there was little he could do. He ventured outside to investigate the garden more closely. Remnants of dead plants poked gnarly brown shoots above ground, and he yanked a few out and tossed them aside. In the certainty that nothing would ever grow in the hard-packed, arid soil of that garden, he went back inside and sat down on the bench and placed his head in his hands. He sat motionless, his mind saturated with hatred and revulsion and disbelief. His was a life turned upside down.

*   *   *

For the first time since his captivity and torture at the hands of the Talatan, Leos had time to contemplate his fate. No more will a guard in a hideous brown-and-red uniform come to the door of his cell and take him to that room in the Marktu dungeon where unanswerable questions were asked and indefensible assaults were perpetrated. But that was not his most pressing problem. His situation had changed, radically and drastically, and the speed of that change had sent his mind spinning. No longer confined to a six-by-six link cell with ice-cold water all over the floor, here on this immense granite rock he was free — *that's almost unbelievable* — to stroll about the Callus and make as much of his life as he could.

I'm on my own here. I have to grow my own food. That'll be difficult given the almost nonexistent resources. The trolls obviously have everything controlled.

There's no way down, no place to go, no access to weapons, no access to the airstrip, no airplanes to leave in. What do you do on this God-forsaken rock? What do you do to keep from going out of your mind? A little gardening in the warm season, but that seems to be all. What about the cold season? Now I see why they send people here instead of executing them. This could be a fate worse than death. Fighting the boredom will be the hardest part. There are other people here, maybe I can get to know them. I remember, Tsoder's here. I wonder where he is. But I don't remember much about him, and I'm not sure I'd recognize him if I saw him. I'll try to find him. Later.

He leaned back against the cold, rough, cement block wall and turned his mind to reflect on other things.

What did he do to deserve this punishment? He scanned his life and found nothing but questions. He killed a couple of Guards, of course, but that was self-defense, regardless of what the trolls—or the Talatan—thought. And, yes, he shouldn't have pilfered that oroban, but Gasz left it behind, and he didn't know what it was, so did that justify terrorizing him by almost cutting his head off, and kicking him off Nytandra? And he didn't have anything to do with the death of Gasz, that was Jaiete's decision, so why did he have to leave the green planet? He seems to have been in so many of the wrong places at all the wrong times.

What confused him most was the actions of the two Guards he killed. Why hadn't they just arrested him when his knife slipped out of his roll of clothing? They were drunk, yes, of course, and perhaps they weren't thinking straight, but why go through all that knife throwing? What were they trying to accomplish, other than to kill him? Their actions seemed so baffling and idiotic. They could have just turned him in and he might have served a few days in jail for possessing a knife, but that would have been all.

But had that happened, the Talatan would have confiscated his knife and he'd never see it again. In retrospect, he'd had to put up with a lot—torture, imprisonment, cold, indifference—but now, *I still have my knife.* His heart rate doubled at the thought. *It's probably still stuck in that tree. If I ever get out of here . . .* He rose from the bench and began to pace about the hut.

Idiotic bastards. He snickered at the mental image of the two guards lying on the ground. *Perhaps they deserved to die.*

As he'd done so many times in that dungeon, he turned his mind to Anthanos, to Tama and Kalarias, to his dream of joining Spaceflight Command and becoming a pilot or navigator. He fantasized about flying off into the deepest darkest reaches of outer space, of swaggering around the galaxy in his own special, souped-up spaceship, of visiting new planets and meeting new civilizations, and—most especially—of finding a new planet that would be the perfect home for his people. It would be his discovery, of course, and his fantastical thoughts always drew to a magnificent conclusion when they pinned medals all over his chest, and his exploits would be deep-blue news on the Information Services for all the right reasons instead of simply being the son of the world-famous explorer Lilea Kalatarian. He hated that. He wanted to be known for something *he* did, not his—yuck—*mom*. Then he would marry Tama and live happily . . .

But his dream ended when he remembered where he was, and not likely to leave this place alive. His dream of research and exploration, of commanding men and supervising explorers, of piloting spaceships to planets of great and memorable beauty, was totally and unmitigatedly dead, pulverized by the consummate ruthlessness of fate, sabotaged by indifferent kidnappers, erased by shortsighted supreme rulers, wrecked by manic-depressive guards, and trashed by trolls whose sole reason for existence seemed to be to make fun of him.

He returned to the bed and remained there for an uncounted number of subsectors, and finally donned the body suit and lay down in the absolute darkness and pulled the blankets over himself. No light penetrated his hut—he couldn't see his finger were he to touch his nose. The darkness enveloped him in a great hand of wretchedness, the gloom so exhaustive it seemed to suck the desire to live right out of him. The clouds were much closer to the surface here than in the city of Marktu, and that gave the night a much more oppressive feel.

Why should I continue to exist? I could so easily jump off this great rock. They'd probably never find my body down there.

His future, indeed his present, appeared as dark as the blackness that encompassed him. *What have I got to live for? What's left for the rest of my life? To die on this gigantic rock?*

He slept fitfully, catching a wink here and there, perhaps a subsector total, until the faint light of morning crept between the boards of the shutters, and he woke. He looked at the door, still in the position he'd left it the evening before. With no lock, someone could come in easily by simply pushing the door open. He didn't like that at all.

During the day, his second on the Callus, the trolls repaired the shutters and the door. Two of them did the work while a third held Leos away from the hut with his weapon. After that, the shutters worked much better and kept most of the cold out. But the door still had no lock.

*   *   *

Behind the hut lay the rocks. A long, slender extension of land about a hundred links wide at the base, the North Fork projected several hundred links northward into the desert that surrounded the Callus. The other finger, fifty or sixty links across the abyss that separated them, was narrower, and no huts had been built on it.

Leos's hut stood about twenty links south of the rocks that made up the tip. His impression was that the rocks had been piled there when the hut was built since the area around the hut was reasonably smooth and level. Even his little garden seemed to be mostly free of rocks. When he climbed the rock pile on his second day, he found he could gaze out over the Callus and see most of its northern region. Hundreds, maybe even thousands of other huts lay scattered throughout the area, all made of the same cement blocks and all depressingly similar. From this vantage point, he could see the top of the hill the cave was in, though he couldn't make out the cave entrance or the fence around the air strip. Antennas bristled from the top of the hill. *The cave must be a half-anthan away, maybe three-quarters.* If he turned around, he had what, under more benign circumstances, might be considered a picturesque view of the surrounding desert.

Below and in all directions from where he sat lay an arid and barren wasteland. Even more rugged than the deserts of Nytandra, here were sharp, craggy escarpments, jutting peaks, torturous gullies, and vast, sweeping sand dunes. They filled his view from the base of the Callus to the horizon, everything in uninspiring shades of brown, tan, and gray, totally devoid of vegetation. No green or purple alleviated the parched dustiness of the desert.

No wonder they picked this place for incarceration. The smooth, steep, vertically-grooved sides of the Callus precluded climbing down, unless, of course, you had ropes and climbing equipment and knew how to use them. Even if you somehow managed to get to the bottom, you'd die in the bone-dry desert. The nearest outpost of civilization lay hundreds of anthans away. He found later, though, that the pile of rocks at the end of the finger did provide meager protection against the cold north winds that swept across the Callus during the cold season.

From his second day on the Callus, Leos spent several subsectors every day sitting on that rock pile, staring at the landscape, sometimes north toward the desert, sometimes south toward the main section of the Callus. Later—about twenty days after he arrived, when the weather cooled and cold north winds began to sweep off the desert and over the Callus—he stayed in his hut, venturing out only for gruel or to answer nature's call. He thought of Tama, of Esmerelda, and of his knife still lodged in that tree. He thought of his mom, of Jad, and many of the others he'd known in his thus-far short life. So many emotions swept through his mind—of good times and bad, of laughter and tears, of confidence and embarrassment—that he couldn't concentrate on only one. But he was so cut off from everyone he knew and loved, he might as well have been a billion light-years away in a distant galaxy, unable to get back, unable to communicate, destined to spend the rest of his life on this godforsaken erection in the middle of a vast derelict desert.

CHAPTER 46

THE FIRST YEAR

The food truck came around twice a day. Similar to the three-wheeled carts, the two rear seats had been removed and replaced with two steaming cauldrons of gruel. Almost tasteless and more watery than it should have been, the swill was at least hot. The trolls said it had all the nutrients a prisoner needed to survive on the Callus, though Leos doubted that—it tasted too weak and thin to hold much nutrition. To receive his portion, Leos had to take his bowl to the intersection where the road turned toward the other huts on the Callus since the food cart driver refused to drive down the road to Leos's hut. Too rough, he said. Might upset the cauldrons.

Near midday on Leos's third day on the Callus, after he'd finished his morning dole and was rinsing the bowl with a small amount of water, the Judge of the trolls drove up. The little corn-popper engine of the three-wheeled carts was difficult to miss. As Leos flipped the dirty water into his garden, three trolls, including the one with three pips on his collar, jumped out and held their weapons on him, forcing him back against the hut. The Judge dismounted and took a few awkward steps forward, but stayed close to his cart. He didn't venture near Leos. He surveyed the area, planted his fists firmly on his hips, and glared at Leos, his face stern, his eyes intense.

"Leos of Nytandra," he bellowed. "Three types of men inhabit this world, the good, the bad, and the evil. But only two types inhabit this place, the bad, and those of the devil. The bad have made a single mistake, their penalty will be severe. Yet of all of those that around you see, only a few of the bad stay here.

"The truly evil are depraved and vile, of insurrection they've been known to foment. Filled with the anger that kills and rapes, your life they will take in a moment.

"There are many of these men here. Be careful in your wanderings. Stay in your hut, keep to yourself, stay private in your ponderings. Into our cave you may not go, nor through the gate where the airplanes land.

But the Callus is yours and explore it you will. I'm sure; I've seen your hand."

Leos said nothing, he stayed where he was, pinned to the front of his hut by the guards. He'd taken an instant dislike to the Judge, whom he called the "old man" in his mind, dating from his first contact with him in the Cave of the Trolls—a wild, blustering old fool, he thought—though if you were to press Leos, he would admit—grudgingly, to be sure—that much of what the old man said was probably true. The Judge continued his tirade, shaking his finger at him.

"We'll be watching you, Leos, that much is clear. Be warned, be careful, we watch all men here. We know what you're doing, in darkness or in light, you're always in our reach, always in our sight."

The Judge turned abruptly and entered his cart. The three trolls followed; one drove while the other two threw rocks at Leos out of the back of the cart as it rumbled down the road that led off the finger. Leos watched the cart crest a slight rise near the middle of the Callus, then it disappeared from eye and ear-shot. He returned to his hut.

*   *   *

Of all the emotions that flowed through Leos as he began his stay on the Callus, the most common, and by far the most intense, was anger. It swelled through him every day—the anger that began with the unholy treatment of him by his captors in the prison, the anger that rose in his chest during the long, cold nights on that hard bench in his hut on the Callus with only the padded brown suit and two blankets for warmth, the anger that magnified the sharp pains that throbbed through his pelvis every time he urinated through a penis damaged by repeated assaults.

During his stay in the prison, his anger was unfocused, and he lashed out at everything and everyone that came within sight. But that only brought on more beatings, which engendered more anger. By the time he'd been transferred to the Callus, he'd learned to hold it in, to suppress it to avoid the beatings. But now, free of the physical torture, the anger grew deeper and more malevolent. It smoldered and festered like a cancer within his chest. He fumed and ranted, at first to himself, later out loud. He shouted and bellowed to the four walls of his hut, asking always, "Why? Why?" and the reverberation kicked back, a maddening echo of exasperation and frustration. He shouted himself silly. And hoarse. He cared not a whit if anyone could hear him—surely others must have gone through the same rage at being sentenced to this abominable Callus. Undoubtedly, they'd been treated badly by the Talatan, too.

He searched his life, looking for a single ray of hope, something on which to pin his memories—a valuable object, or lesson to be learned. Mom? Tama? Esmerelda? All, yes, of course, but too far away. His knife— hold on, yes.

It's still here on this planet. I can get to it. And it will help me get away from here. But how to get to it? To do anything, I'll have to get off the Callus. But that's so unlikely. I'll have to think about that.

The knife stayed alive in his mind as though it called to him from the notch in that tree, so far away. He bled for that knife—his feet bled, this hands, his genitals. He'd sacrificed so much for it, and he wanted it back as much as anyone can want anything. The knife had become more to him than just an instrument for cutting—or killing. It had become a symbol of release, a talisman to his freedom, a marker on his way back to civilization. *I've got to get that knife.*

Finally, after around forty-five days of raving, of blustering, of massive self-doubt and self-loathing, Leos's anger began to ease. Explored and finalized, he let it drain of its own accord. His voice hoarse, he bellowed less, he paced the hut more, and he focused on an outlet.

Anger for its own sake is destructive. But anger taken in the right direction can be constructive. I can use it to get away from here. I'm going to leave this place. One way or another, I'm getting my ass off this gigantic butt plug. I'm going to find my knife and I'm going to make sure a few people pay for what they did. I'll find Jad, and see if he's really dead.

On about the fiftieth day after he arrived, he stepped outside his hut for a reason other than to get food or answer nature's call, or climb the rocks behind the hut. He set out to explore the Callus and find Tsoder.

*   *   *

Leos walked down the dusty road that led off the finger and onto the major portion of the Callus. Many more of the huts lay scattered across the landscape. At the base of the finger, the road forked—this was the intersection where he received his ration of gruel. Straight ahead would take him to the cave of the trolls and the airstrip—he remembered that from the drive over. Left, though, led into the unknown. It seemed to point toward the densest concentration of huts in the center of the Callus, and he reasoned someone there might know Tsoder. He turned left and started out, coming shortly to the hut nearest the intersection. As he approached, he couldn't see anyone, but a gentle scraping sound came from nearby. The number of the hut, 10100, was barely readable in faded black letters on the usual wooden board tacked above the door. At the side of the hut, an old man scratched with a hoe in the soil of a small garden. Nothing grew in the man's garden, he seemed to be pulling out old shoots and roots, perhaps preparing the garden for the next growing season. What was left of the man's white hair was soiled and squalid, and his scraggly beard flopped about him as he poked at the hard soil. "Do you know Tsoder?" Leos asked, but the man kept pounding at the soil. Leos asked again. Still no response.

Maybe he's deaf. Leos walked on.

The next hut he came to was 9756. He inquired of the inhabitant, a middle-aged man urinating on his garden in the side yard. "Do you know Tsoder?"

"No," the man replied and Leos walked on.

He stopped at hut after hut, seemingly in random order, receiving at the least a curt, "No" when he asked about Tsoder. Many times he was ignored, occasionally threatened, and once the occupant of the hut threw his spade at him.

"Go away! Leave me alone!" the man yelled.

Leos continued on as the amount of light in the sky faded. Surprisingly, almost every hut was occupied and he wondered about the population of the Callus. *There must be ten thousand people or more in this place. I wonder how many of them could be recruited to attempt an escape? That many people could overwhelm the guards easily.*

He turned right onto another road and worked his way into an area heavily concentrated with huts. He inquired again and again, working his way down the road, from one hut to another. Finally, after what seemed his hundredth try, he got a positive reply when he asked, "Do you know Tsoder?"

"Over there." The man pointed in the general direction of several huts. "Twenty-five."

Leos looked around and scanned the huts, finally coming to rest on 3125, set diagonally across the intersection of two dirt roads near where he stood. He walked over and spoke to a youngish-looking man standing outside the hut. "Tsoder?" he inquired.

"Who are you?" the man said. Much younger than the elderly men he'd encountered on his walk, this man had a full head of dark brownish-black hair and large wire-rimmed glasses that did nothing to hide the openness of his Jhontu eyes. Leos looked carefully—both eyes seemed normal. A thickness in the hands and a short, stocky neck suggested the strong physique that Leos remembered from the party. This man may have worked out with weights in the past, though it was unlikely he did around here.

"I'm Leos. We met at Jad's place."

Strangely, that didn't elicit the response Leos'd expected. He'd hoped Tsoder would remember him, but Tsoder glanced warily at him. "What do you know of Jad?" He turned away.

"Well, I—"

Tsoder abruptly turned back and glared at Leos, a subtle anger in his eyes.

"You know, Leos, you should mind your own business. You should get back to your hut. Darkness approaches. You should not be caught out here after dark. Someone may steal your blankets." Tsoder went inside his hut and closed the door.

Leos started to go after him and considered knocking at the door, but he hesitated. He stared briefly at the door, and remembered the door to his own hut—it had been repaired, yes, but still no latch—then turned and scanned the area around the hut. Several other prisoners stood in front of their huts, watching him. All held a gardening tool. Like a weapon.

"Stay away from Tsoder's door," was their silent but unmistakable message. With the Callus so wide open and so little solitude in each man's life, a hut must remain private, even sacrosanct. A man's life was exposed here, not even allowed the privacy of a bathroom to carry out the most basic needs. He reluctantly decided not to knock and turned around and began the long return to his hut, back-tracking his route as the sky darkened.

When he entered, he found that someone indeed had stolen his blankets. He went outside and looked around. The sky had turned almost completely dark. Only a faint band of somber ochre-gray clouds in the west provided any light at all for his endeavors. He saw no one, but his suspicion was aroused. He walked back down the road to the nearest hut—the hut of the supposedly deaf man—and tiptoed over to the front window and pushed the shutters aside. In the darkness, he could tell only that the old man was asleep, a thin emaciated form lying on the bench, blankets draped over him. Leos went to the door but hesitated. He scanned the area around him but in the deepening darkness he saw no one watching him. He pushed the door open.

Privacy be damned, I need my blankets.

The hinges creaked and spit as the door swung open, but the old man didn't seem to hear. His breathing was heavy. Not really snoring, but strained and asthmatic, as though he had difficulty drawing air in and letting it out. He shivered in the cold, the only teeth he had left chattering against empty gums. Leos approached the bed and felt at the blankets, counting: one, two, three, four. One blanket had a small tear in the edge, near a corner. He recognized it—it was one of his. He lifted the two blankets from the top as quietly as he could and left.

The next morning Leos awoke to the sound of the bell on the meal truck. The morning chill penetrated his padded suit more than usual, and he wrapped his blankets around his shoulders before he left the hut. The clouds hung lower than he'd ever seen them, a mere ten, or perhaps fifteen links above his head. He watched them closely as he walked, concerned they might drop without warning and engulf him.

After the trolls filled his bowl, they moved on to the next hut. As usual, Leos began to drink the watery gruel as he walked back to his hut, but the trolls rang the bell on the cart much longer than usual. Leos stopped and turned around. No one left the hut. One of the servers cautiously entered the hut, a weapon in his hand, but he returned a few seconds later and said something to the driver who appeared to call on the truck's radio. The meal truck went on, and soon another of the three-wheeled carts arrived and two trolls carried the old man out on a stretcher, covered with his blankets.

Oh, shit. Did he freeze to death because I took back my blankets? Would he still be alive if I hadn't taken my blankets back? Well, shit, it doesn't matter. He would have been dead in a few days anyway. They were my blankets. I deserved to have them back.

*   *   *

After his meal, Leos set out to talk to Tsoder again. As the temperature rose during the day, the clouds migrated higher than the day before, but he kept an eye on them as he walked. He'd never been on a planet with clouds as thick as these. Anthanos had none at all, and Nytandran clouds were little more than high, thin, streaks in the sky. Even clouds on the green planet stayed well above the tops of the tallest trees. From the first day he was on this planet, he regarded the clouds with a mixture of suspicion and dread, never really trusting them to maintain their place above him. He just wanted them to leave him alone.

Today he slung his blankets over his shoulder and crammed the packets of seed in one of the pockets of the oversuit. After turning down one or two wrong roads, he found Tsoder's hut—he remembered the '25' of the number—and, trying to observe some touch of privacy, called his name quietly.

"Yes, I remember," Tsoder said as he came to the door. "At Jad's place. The party to welcome you to our planet. But what are you doing here? Wait, do not talk here. The huts are monitored. Let us go away from the hut."

Tsoder and Leos walked down a rough gravel path toward the intersection of the two roads that ran through this part of the Callus. As they walked, Tsoder looked up at the clouds and frowned.

"The cold season has arrived," he said. "We may be immersed in fog in a few days. But, enough about the weather. Tell me—"

"The fog? What is the fog?"

"When the clouds come to the level of the Callus. Even below. It is very white. You can see very little."

"Oh. It's not dangerous, is it?"

"No, not dangerous. But the trolls cannot see well to drive. There will be no ration of food until the fog lifts. Then only one. But tell me, what act did you perform to end up here?"

"Uh . . . I killed two Talatan Guards." Tsoder's big brown eyes blinked twice, a typical reaction of Jhontu when confronted with surprising news. Leos went into a short description of the killing and how he had to stay with Tsee, and later at the farm with Zhinta. "She told me you'd been sent here."

At the mention of his wife's name, Tsoder's eyes blinked twice again and he stared at Leos. His face turned even more pale than usual.

"Do you know how she is? How is she doing?" He grabbed Leos's arm and shook him. "How is she doing?" he repeated.

"I stayed with her only a few days after the killings, before they took me to the farm. She is well, but she worries about you."

"She will worry forever." Tsoder turned from Leos and closed his eyes, wiping them with the dusty sleeve of his suit.

"I'm sure Jad told her what happened to you."

"Yes, I'm sure he has. He knows a lot, that guy. Has he told you of our plans?"

Leos shook his head. "Zhinta gave me a few details, but she didn't tell me much. Even when I asked. Jad wouldn't tell me anything, either. It's like there's a conspiracy . . ."

"You are right, Leos, there was a conspiracy to prevent you from learning too much. That was for the sake of the plan. No one knows everything, except a few at the top. Jad, and some others. Even Kazeh knew only what he was supposed to know."

"Jad said something was about to happen, but he didn't give me any details."

"This is true. He wished you to remain outside. For your own protection. And ours. Much is to take place, and if you knew much and you were caught, you could be forced to tell."

Leos's penis ached. "Well, I was caught. And tortured. I told them what I could, and made some other stuff up." Leos stopped, hesitant as to whether he should reveal this last information. Tsoder might become angry if he admitted divulging even some small aspect of the plot. It might even affect his friendship with him for the rest of his stay on the Callus. He wanted a friend, someone to talk to. He might even need to recruit Tsoder into an escape attempt. He looked at the ground and shuffled his feet. "I told them about Zhinta. And the farm."

Tsoder didn't seem surprised. He didn't react at all, his eyes didn't blink, neither did he fly into a rage. His voice remained low and calm. "Do not blame yourself. We all divulge some. They are very good at making us talk, but mostly we make stuff up and they do not know the difference. I know little of the farm. I worked for Zhinta for a short time. I was very young. I remember very little. I remember going to the market. That is all."

Leos felt better at Tsoder's acceptance of his performance under torture, and that meant his friendship with him could continue at least for a while, though that didn't seem to make his revelations about Zhinta any easier to live with. "Okay, I'm here, now. What's going on?"

The plan, as Tsoder laid it out, was for a rebellion to begin on a specific day, a day known only to the select few who made up the ruling council of the underground. Because of his youth, Tsoder was not in that group, and he, too, had been given limited information. Jad, though, knew most of the details of the rebellion and the others involved. Tsoder's face became flushed as he spoke, and anger erupted. He pounded a fist into his hand. "I worked for the underground for only two years," he said. "But now I am isolated here, out of the way."

Leos paused a nanosector to let Tsoder's anger recede. "Maybe there's a way we can get out of here," he said.

"There is little we can do. The security is tight, and we cannot get down." Tsoder looked around at the other huts on the Callus, the flush on his face draining, his anger turning to resignation.

"I could probably fly one of the airplanes that lands here."

"Leos—" Tsoder, his eyes wide open, turned and looked directly at Leos. "How would you get to them? There is very high security at the air strip. The planes come in only to drop a new prisoner or supplies, and they leave. Security is very heavy around the planes. No planes are based at this airport. The fence is burn wire and the trolls have weapons."

"Burn wire?"

"It has sharp points on it which have a poison. If you even slightly touch it, you will receive a terrible burn. Even the trolls are not immune. Do not think about it."

"Maybe if a lot of us got together and stormed the gate—"

"Leos, do not be foolish. Look around. Do you see any prisoners here who could do that?" Leos scanned the area of Tsoder's hut, but the only prisoners he saw were older men, weak, lanky, bent over, even decrepit. Some could barely hold the hoe they tended their garden with. "You and I are in good condition," Tsoder continued, "but only because we have been here a short time. These men have been here many years, and it takes its toll. The food they give us will keep us alive, but that is all. Men do not thrive here. We have come here to die, and many of those you see around us will be dead by the next warm season. Do not fool yourself." The anger returned to Tsoder's face and he glared at Leos. "We are trapped here. We must wait."

"Wait for what—?"

Tsoder's eyes opened even wider than normal and he stared past Leos down the road. A small dust cloud hung in the air. "Tsit!" he yelled. "The trolls come now on their morning rounds. They will throw stones at us. You must leave. Go to your hut. Run!"

*   *   *

As the weather drew colder, the clouds did descend to the level of the Callus and below, enveloping it in a fog so thick you could barely see your feet from your face. Later, during the day, as the air warmed, the fog ascended and formed the customary morose blanket that hovered over the Callus. Sometimes the fog would last for several days and food would be rationed to one bowl of hot gruel per person because the trolls had to drive so slowly over the rough roads of the Callus. Not until it lifted would the ration return to twice a day.

Leos spent most of the time during the cold season in his hut, sitting on the crude bed, wrapped in his blankets. The blankets were old and torn, one in particular, and he asked once when the meal cart came around if he could have another blanket, but they laughed at him and went on without speaking. But the next day, when they came through on the morning meal run, they tossed another blanket on the ground.

He slept during the day because he didn't get much sleep at night. The blankets and the heavy outfit he wore were reasonably effective in keeping out the chill of the night, and he usually got a few subsectors of sleep. But he was forced to try to make up for it by sleeping during the day when the air temperature was marginally warmer.

When he did sleep, he had wild dreams. Funny shaped animals invaded his dreams—some had seven heads, others had thirteen tails. They attacked him and he couldn't defend himself, he stood naked and motionless and he would wake up just before he was to be devoured. In other dreams, a fire would sweep the Callus and engulf him in his hut, and he couldn't move, as though he was being burned alive, and behind it all came the sound of laughing, a high-pitched laughter, squealing and taunting. In all his dreams a soft woman's voice kept calling his name, beckoning to him—

"Come, Leos, come" the voice said. He wanted to run, but he couldn't.

But the greatest reason Leos didn't sleep well at night, even during the warm season, was the anger—still the anger. As he lay in the profound darkness of his hut, he thought more and more about getting away from the Callus, and many nights that excluded anything else. He worked on a plan, he imagined rejoining Jad and Tsoder and Tsee and getting a spaceship away from this planet. Back to the green planet he would go, to see Esmerelda once again and enter her warm, beautiful body. How he would get off this planet and into outer space he didn't consider. He focused largely on the first step, getting off the Callus.

CHAPTER 47

THE WARM SEASON

The warm season finally came again to the Callus, and Leos planted his garden, exactly according to the instructions on the packets of seeds. He fertilized it with his own excrement, the same way he'd been pissing and pooping in the garden during the cold. That was a suggestion from Tsoder, though Leos had seen others doing it. Tsoder'd warned him, "Don't use your drinking water for the garden. Use only your urine. Use the drinking water for drinking only, and let the fluid pass through your body. Then, pee in your garden. Drink from the water in your jug every day. Keep yourself hydrated. Pour only the dregs from your jug on the garden. Let them fill the jug with fresh water."

Leos nodded. "I can do that."

As his garden grew, as well as it could in the hard, rocky soil of the Callus, Leos continued to explore, especially to visit Tsoder. Tsoder pressed him about Tsee each time, as though Leos should have fresh news, but Leos calmly reminded him that he could offer nothing new, and Tsoder would turn away for a few seconds. Then Tsoder would turn back and talk to Leos in a calm and matter-of-fact voice.

On one particularly mild day during the warm season, Leos and Tsoder stood near the intersection of several roads outside Tsoder's hut, and Leos again brought up the subject of escape. "We have to do something. We can't just sit here and take this."

"Leos, we must wait. The revolution will start soon, and they will liberate us. This is most important. We must be patient and wait."

"Wait? I can't wait. I've got to get off here. You said yourself that most men do not live here very long. If we wait, we will not be here to rescue."

"And just what do you propose that we do?" Tsoder snapped. His face frequently had an angry expression, and now he turned even more sullen and crabby than usual.

"Maybe we could form a demonstration, like throw rocks back at the trolls when they come around."

"No, Leos, I do not throw rocks at the trolls. I saw one man who threw rocks back at them, and they took him away. It was many days before he came back. He was in worse shape than before. I do not know where he went, but others say they put him in solitary confinement, and they nicked his left eye. He degenerated into a troll, and now he travels with the other trolls and throws stones at us. I do not wish to become a troll. Now you should travel back to your hut and stay there. It is not good for us to be seen standing here talking too much. They will think we are plotting against them."

"We are."

Tsoder said nothing further, and returned to his hut. Leos went back to his.

*　　*　　*

"Tsoder, where do they get the rocks they throw at us? They've got an unlimited supply."

"I have not seen." Tsoder and Leos stood outside Tsoder's hut. "But I have heard that as they are enlarging their cave, they make rocks all the time. Sometimes they come around at night and collect the rocks they threw on previous days. Do not venture outside your hut after darkness is complete. They do not like to be interrupted in their collections. You may not come back."

"Oh."

*　　*　　*

"Maybe we could slip past the fence when they open the gate to bring supplies in," Leos said another day, standing near Tsoder's hut. Tsoder shook his head, and seemed exasperated.

"Leos, they have weapons. And there are many of them. They would kill you. Or at the least, injure you and nick your eye. Do you want that? I do not want to be a troll when the revolution starts. That is when they will liberate us from this prison. It is the only chance we have of getting out of here. We must wait—"

"But we can't just wait around for something to happen. We have to make it happen."

"Leos, we must be patient. I myself have gone through all this. Every man here has gone through this." He swept his arm around, as if to point out to Leos the entire population of the Callus. "We all wish to escape, but there is nothing we can do. The trolls have security well in hand, and there is no way out of here. We must wait for the revolution. Wait, Leos." Tsoder turned and walked back into his hut just as the troll rock-throwing contingent turned the corner at the crossing of the nearby dirt roads.

*   *   *

"Tsoder, could we grab some of the trolls and hold them hostage and force them to give us an airplane?"

"Leos, your mind is degenerating. You have been on this place for too long. How long has it been?"

"A hundred days or more, I lost count a long time ago."

"I do not think it would work. The trolls mean nothing. I saw once when a troll died. They threw his body in the trash heap. They can make trolls any time. Do not delude yourself, Leos. If you capture a troll, they will take you and put you away, like they did that other man. And they will turn you into a troll."

*   *   *

"Tsoder, where do they get the fuel for the airplanes?"

"I do not know. I believe the airplanes are not fueled here. I believe they have enough fuel to land and take off again. Why do you ask?"

"An exploding fuel tank might create enough of a diversion so that a few of us could a grab a plane and fly out of here."

Tsoder looked surprised. "And what of the ones who are left here? What of them? Will you leave them behind to be punished for your reckless attempt to escape? No, Leos, I will have nothing to do with that. Tsit! The trolls are coming. You must leave."

"Well, if you won't help me, I'll do it myself or die trying." Leos walked away from Tsoder's hut as Tsoder's last words assailed his ears. A rock hit him in the back as he walked.

"You are a fool, Leos," Tsoder yelled. "An admirable one, but nevertheless a fool."

*   *   *

Tsoder's anger and combativeness dwindled as his stay on the Callus progressed, and he and Leos became good friends. They talked every few days, and Tsoder explained many details of Jhontu society. Leos, in turn, told him of Tama and Anthanos, and of Esmerelda, Nytandra and the green planet.

Tsoder laughed out loud when Leos described his relationships with his two girlfriends. "Leos, you are a rascal," he said. "You are mated to one and engaged to the other!"

Leos shrugged.

"Could your friends on Anthanos not rescue you? You say they have spaceships and—"

"No," Leos replied. "I've thought a lot about that. I've come to the conclusion they don't know where I am. They're probably still searching for me on Anthanos. Even if they did start looking for me off-world, they wouldn't know where to go. The universe is a big place and we are a hundred light-years away. Getting off this place will be up to me. I can't rely on them."

Leos was pleased that Tsoder's mood had improved and that he seemed genuinely interested to learn about other worlds and civilizations. Tsoder's admonitions to "cool it" had helped him survive the day-to-day hardships of life on the Callus. It prevented him from running off and doing something stupid that would have gotten him thrown in solitary confinement, and perhaps even his eye nicked and turned into a troll.

Many days, though, Tsoder would become angry, and these occasional outbursts, commonly directed at his comrades in the underground for not starting the revolution that would liberate the Callus, belied his usually unflappable demeanor.

"When will they come?" he'd cry and blink his eyes rapidly.

But Tsoder largely took everything in stride, and that impressed Leos. He tried to imitate Tsoder's cool. But Leos's anger stayed with him, simmering just below the surface. He had to force himself to keep in it when the trolls threw rocks at them, as they did most every day. Like Tsoder, he didn't want to be turned into a troll.

"Tsit! The trolls come!"

CHAPTER 48

THE PLAN

By the time Leos had spent a year on the Callus, he'd devised an escape plan. Or at least the outlines of one. It would be his plan—he couldn't rely on the other prisoners to help him. In his conversations with those few of the other prisoners who agreed to talk with him—frequently grudgingly—he'd come to the dismaying conclusion that they'd been so frightened and intimidated by the trolls into acquiescence and submission they would never agree to join him in his plan, no matter how likely the chances of escape. Even Tsoder had been beaten into resignation by the constant harassment. He wanted nothing to do with any of Leos's plans.

They won't push me down. I'll get out of here if it's the last thing I do. I may die trying, but at least I'll try.

To make his plan work, Leos would take advantage of the fog. He recognized early that the key to getting off the Callus was the airstrip, and that realization had led to his aborted earlier ideas to storm the gate or set off a container of airplane fuel as a diversion. Tsoder's insistent admonitions scuttled those notions, and he was probably right to do so. Any escape would have to be done furtively, with no loud demonstrations. *Sneak past them and get away quietly. Before they can stop you.* The trolls certainly knew the importance of the airstrip, hence the burn wire. He would have to get inside that fence and grab one of the planes himself. That's right—hijack one of them. That would be the way. Quietly and sur- reptitiously.

But how to do that . . .?

He'd thought about it during the long, cold season, and formulated a plan by the time warm weather arrived. Difficulties constantly arose with his plan, and dealing with them required even more deliberation, but he came up with a concept he considered workable. It required, first, that he do a lot of walking. Day after day throughout the warm season, he walked from his hut to the airstrip, memorizing every detail along the way, step by step. Sometimes the trolls followed him in a cart, but at a distance, and he tried to make it look as though he was simply out for exercise.

In the beginning, the trolls questioned him about his wanderings.

"What are you doing, Leos of Nytandra?" they'd yell at him.

At first he ignored them, then, after several days, when they confronted him, pushing their weapons into his belly, he told them he liked to walk, that he was only out for a stroll, for exercise. Later he smiled and waved to them when he passed, and the look on their faces was exquisite. Frowns and sneers and dirty looks they'd seen a million times. But a smile? That puzzled them.

One day around the middle of the warm season, he changed his route to the airstrip. He walked past Tsoder's hut, but that was a much longer walk, almost two anthans, and he did it largely to confuse the trolls, to take the emphasis off the main route. But he invariably returned to his hut by his usual way.

On rare occasions, he'd get lucky in his travels, and a plane would land at the strip at the same time he was nearby. It would disgorge one or two prisoners and he'd watch as everything unfolded. Never more than two because the plane had only six seats. He took a special interest in the plane: where the pilot sat, if he got out of the plane and how long he stayed out, and when he got back in, and the northerly route he used after he took off.

He also noticed that on the other side of the dirt airstrip were several piles of large rocks, as though when they constructed the airstrip, they'd pushed the rocks to the side. Behind those rocks lay — *aha* — natural hiding places. This plan is definitely coming together!

His scheme was simple: slip inside the fence when the fog obscured everything so the trolls wouldn't see him, and then hide behind the rocks. Once safely inside, he'd grab the plane when the pilot left. He knew he could figure out how to fly it once he got in. It was the same plane every time, too — he recognized the markings on the side. It landed at around the same time on the days it came, but it never came on a regular schedule — only when prisoners were to be delivered. That was the weak point in his plan, and he decided he needed a scenario not dependent on chance for success, so he turned his attention to a different airplane.

Once every ten days a two-engine plane landed. The same type of plane in which he was brought to the little airport on the edge of the desert, before transferring to the six-seater. It delivered only supplies: water, food for the trolls, and the powder from which that god-awful gruel was made. It spent more time on the ground than did the single-engine plane as the supplies were unloaded. Two pilots flew this plane, but they both got out during off-loading. Because that plane came on a regular schedule, it removed the element of chance, and Leos decided to hijack that plane instead of the single-engine one. That took care of that problem, but others remained.

One day, early after he began his regular walk to the strip, he stopped just outside the gate and watched as the single-engine plane landed. This time, he concentrated on the trolls as they opened the gate and drove in with their little three-wheeled cart to pick up the new prisoner.

The latch on the gate was a simple sliding bolt, locked with a large, ancient-looking black padlock. The heavy bolt was as thick as Leos's forearm and twice as long, and it took two trolls to slide it open. Occasionally, in trying too hard to pull the bolt back, one of the trolls would nick himself on a prong of the burn wire and fall to the ground screaming and yelling. After a microsector or so, he would get up and run to the cave as fast as his stubby legs would carry him. The trolls always looked so comical when they tried to run. They couldn't bend their knees very far, and they ran straight-legged, clomping along in a zil-like trot. The other troll usually ignored him and would continue pulling on the bolt until the gate opened.

On another day, during his walk near the landing strip, and after the trolls closed and locked the gate, several of them ran Leos off by throwing rocks at him, and he retreated to his hut. But he couldn't stop thinking about that padlock and bolt. They had a formidable look, and he would suffer through many more days of deliberation to get past them.

*　*　*

Now that he had a plan in mind, a plan that had a real chance of working, Leos's heart pattered a little faster and the excitement rose in his chest. He could already feel the airplane under his control as he left the Callus headed — ah, that's the real problem, isn't it? Where would he go?

He had no idea where the Callus was on this planet, other than that it lay near the equator. He'd tried to follow the flight path as the twin-engine plane took him from Marktu to the airport where he changed to the smaller plane, but they closed the window beside his seat shortly after take-off. It had been a four subsector flight, but that told him little. The flight of the single-engine plane took almost two subsectors, and he could see the ground, but that was over the rugged terrain of the equatorial regions, so desolate and deserted that he couldn't recognize landmarks along the route. He knew nothing of the cities or towns nearest the Callus, and couldn't find them even if he did. Were he to get lucky enough to steal an airplane and get off the Callus and land near a town, he'd certainly be captured by the Talatan and brought back here and his left eye nicked and . . . well, that would be the end of Leos.

Even if he was lucky and managed to find the resistance, he couldn't go back to Marktu. They'd have to hide him, and the Talatan would be looking for him. But most importantly, would he be able to get off the planet at all? There *are* no ships that leave *Non-Dre-Ahdenu.*

So why leave the Callus?

To get out of here — to get away from this place — this despicable godforsaken place — to be free — just to be free. Free like Esmerelda's people. Free to go where I want. Free to make my own decisions. Free to go back and get my knife. Yes, I'll do it because I can do it. If I have to die on this planet, let it be as a free man. A wanted man, a hunted man, yes, but nevertheless free. I'd rather die free than live in this wretched hut and eat the tasteless gruel and the disgusting vegetables from the garden.

Just the thought of getting off the Callus—regardless of where he went or who he ran into—and of fondling his knife again sent him into waves of ecstasy. *The knife — the knife!*

More immediately, he turned his attention to his biggest problem: the padlock on the gate to the airstrip. He'd have to find a way to open it. He also had to wait until the cold season came. During the warm season, the fog didn't descend far enough to hide access to the strip.

That means I will have been on this humongous desert erection over a year. He lay on his bunk one evening in the middle of the warm season. He looked forward to the trolls starting the twice-daily ration of gruel. After a summer of growing and tending to his vegetables, he decided he preferred the gruel even though it was more insipid than the vegetables. The vegetables produced such severe gas that his bowels were constantly flatulent and diarrhetic, and they acidified his urine so strongly it burned even more than usual when he urinated.

At least I have a plan. But how do I get past that damn padlock?

*   *   *

The padlock stuck in Leos's mind for days. He even dreamed about it. Nothing occurred to him until one day, working in his garden, he hit a rock with the tip end of his hand trowel. The trowel was old and rusty, especially around the edges. It had been the hand tool of an unknown number of prisoners who'd been housed at this hut. The tip bent easily in its contact with the rock, and he found that by working the rusty areas back and forth with his fingers he could pinch off small areas of the edge. That tapered the trowel tip and made it look narrow and irregular, like an old saw blade, damaged and rusty after years of use.

No, not a saw blade . . . it looks more like . . . a key.

A key? Yes, a key. I can use this. A key to open the padlock. It just might work. Worth a fuckin' try.

* * *

During this, his first full summer on the Callus, Leos kept walking. The trolls stopped him almost every day. They were confused by his activity. Very few other prisoners walked around the Callus, and from what Leos could gather from the ramblings of the trolls, their excursions were short and random, rarely venturing far from their hut. No one else, Tsoder included, got out and exercised as much, though Tsoder did do stretching and calisthenics regularly, keeping himself in as good condition as the poor diet would permit. Leos continued to visit him, memorizing the route, step by step, turn by turn, dirt clod by dirt clod, rutted road by rutted road.

Soon, the trolls got angry and told Leos to stay near his hut. They threw rocks at him if he ventured too far, and he curtailed his walking for five days. He didn't stop completely, though, and the trolls got tired of harassing him and allowed him to walk wherever he wanted, toward the airstrip or not.

* * *

As the chilly winds of Leos's second cool season swept over the Callus, an ache developed in his bones much more than the previous winter. Walking was harder now, and he moved more slowly and stiffly. The abominable nutrition of the gruel and vegetables was so much less that what was necessary for even minimal sustenance that he couldn't help but lose weight. He figured he'd lost at least a quarter of what he weighed when he arrived. His muscles were down, the strength he'd developed in his arms and shoulders from tree-climbing on the green planet had disappeared long ago. His legs were like toothpicks. Sores appeared all over his body and in his mouth, and they took many days to heal. His teeth hurt and felt loose in his jaw, but he resisted the temptation, as others had succumbed, to pull them out, one by one. It had now become essential that he get through the gate and hijack an airplane soon, before he grew too weak to make the trip. This cold season would be the time. He had no choice. The clouds were descending again, enveloping the Callus in the dense, chilly miasma that was so familiar from last winter. But his mind stayed clear, and he remained focused on his plan.

Most every day, after his walk, Leos climbed the rocks behind his hut. He sat on the tallest rock, his favorite seat, where he could look out over the Callus. If the clouds were lower than usual he could reach up and swirl the clouds with his hand the way a spoon swirls liquid in a glass. He could swear the clouds were so close his hand looked fuzzy, out of focus, extended like that.

It won't be long. It won't be long.

*   *   *

A day came once, early during this, his second winter on the Callus, when the air was warmer than usual and the clouds had not descended. Almost warm-season-like, with barely a nip in the air. As he returned from his walk, he climbed the rock pile behind his hut and sat on his rock. He stared north, toward, as he'd been told, several major population centers in the northern hemisphere of this planet. The Callus projected so high that the horizon was several hundred anthans away, but the permanent cloud cover, regardless of how high it went, always covered the horizon and kept him from seeing the verdant landscape of the cities and farms. Today, though, something unusual caught his eye, a faint, dark haziness on the horizon. Just a smear of blackness, only slightly darker than the surrounding air at the point where the clouds met the land. You'd miss it if you weren't looking for it. But Leos had spent so much time staring off in that direction that any irregularity, no matter how small, stood out to his discerning eye. He shaded his eyes and scanned right and left, and at least two more hazy-smoky-like areas appeared, and there was even perhaps a fourth one much farther to the west. Without binoculars or a vision aid, he could make out little detail.

I wonder what that's all about. I'll talk to Tsoder about it.

As he turned around and left his seat, he heard the faint sputtering of the twin-engine plane approaching the airstrip far across the Callus.

Okay, only ten more days. The days are getting colder and the clouds may descend far enough to cover me by then. My chance is coming. I will get out of here!

* * *

Four days later, the single-engine airplane arrived at the Callus, disgorging two more prisoners. After that the oddest thing happened—the plane arrived every day. One day it came twice, bringing four prisoners. Never had so many prisoners come at one time. From the fifth until the eighth day, twelve prisoners arrived, all shuttled into the cave of the trolls then hurried out to huts across the Callus.

During these days, descent of the clouds was sporadic. Some mornings Leos would wake up in a thick fog which lasted until midday, and that would slow the trolls in their round to dole out the morning ration of gruel. Other mornings, the day would dawn with clouds still hundreds of links above his hut and the trolls would arrive bright and early, ringing their bell and he would have to run out to the intersection to get a meal. On the ninth day, a heavy, thick fog greeted him as he left his hut to pee. In the chilly air, he wrapped his blankets around his shoulders to venture outside.

The air is getting colder, so there's better than a fifty-fifty chance the clouds will be this thick tomorrow. Tomorrow is the day for the twin-engine plane to arrive. He returned to his hut to wait for the trolls to come by.

They came by about the fifth hour. "Will you walk today?" they asked him as they doled out his portion.

"I will, or I will be a troll."

They didn't like that and they threw rocks at him as he scampered back to his hut. Running was difficult now, and even walking took more energy than usual. Some of the gruel spilled as he ran, but he didn't care.

I'm getting out of here soon. Tomorrow. I hope it's damn foggy tomorrow.

He finished his meal, rinsed the bowl with a little water, and poured it on the garden. He returned to his hut, grabbed his blankets and started his walk. He turned east, onto the road to Tsoder's hut. He shuffled along the dusty road, his legs weak and crampy. As on most of his walks, he thought of Anthanos and Tama, of Esmerelda and the green planet. He wondered if she survived the war Jaiete started when he ordered the execution of Gasz. She might have been killed in that war. And what of Coreaje? And Jad. Is he dead, or not? So many thoughts went through his mind he had difficulty focusing on only one. He forced himself to watch the road, passing each landmark he'd set for himself, the particular clod of dirt, a rock here and there, the ruts the troll's carts made as they roamed the Callus doling out the meals and throwing rocks. Sometimes he looked for markers he'd made himself, pushing rocks with his foot into definite formations or making scratches in the dirt to identify a particular point because he knew in the heavy fog he'd be able to see only down at his feet, and he'd have to know the route by heart.

After about three millisectors on the road, he looked up, scanning the clouds above. They'd ascended high now, almost back to their summer position. He turned onto the road that led to Tsoder's hut. Two other prisoners were out, tending their gardens, but he was the only one on the road, and the area was quiet. The Callus could be amazingly peaceful, especially in the early morning. His mind was filled with the uncertainty of whether he'd be able to make his try at escaping tomorrow, when he was startled by the piercing sound of two dark blue jet aircraft thundering by directly overhead, splitting the still air with a roar that blasted eardrums and destroyed concentration. They came in from the east, skimming the bottoms of the clouds, perhaps three hundred links above the Callus. Instinctively, he ducked. "What the hell?" he yelled, cupping his hands over his ears. Other prisoners bolted from their huts, their eyes blinking rapidly at the shock, a mixture of fear and wonder on their faces.

Both aircraft had two jet engines molded into a single slender fuselage, short trapezoidal wings, and twin tail fins canted outward at, perhaps, twenty degrees from vertical. They reminded Leos of a series of fighter jet aircraft developed on Anthanos many years before he was born, during a time of perceived threats from outer space, threats that were eventually found to be bogus.

He looked for some sort of markings or insignia on the underside of the craft, or on the tail, and was able to make out an odd symbol on the right wing of one of them. He had only a fraction of a nanosector to look at it, they sped by so fast, yet in that brief time the symbol seemed almost recognizable, familiar. He'd seen it before, but where?

They're undoubtedly high-performance aircraft, capable of supersonic speeds. But what are they doing here? Perhaps the Talatan sent them to demonstrate the advanced technology they have in producing weapons of war. Maybe we've misjudged them.

Both aircraft circled back, and one split off and made a second approach from the east, but it slowed, the pilot throttling back, perhaps to get a good look at the mountain below. *He's flying over the airstrip. I can't see the cave from here . . . but the trolls must be panicking by now. They wouldn't know what to make of that thing. Stupid trolls. Wait—was that gunshots? Yes, it was. Ha! They're shooting at it*

The other jet made a slow pass over the Callus, but from the north, passing again directly over Leos's head, and this time he got a clear look at the markings on the underside. What he saw confused him. Tsoder scurried up to him as well as he could in that doddering gait residents of the Callus developed over years of eating abysmal food, bellowing as he ran.

"I told you, Leos, the revolution has begun! The revolution has begun!" For only the second or third time since Leos had known Tsoder, he smiled, his face animated with delight. "It is now time, Leos!" Tsoder thrust a fist in Leos's face. "It is now *time*! We will be away from here within days!"

As Leos watched the aircraft, he realized he might be wrong in thinking they were Talatan planes, unless, by some strange and unlikely coincidence, they were using a familiar insignia. On the underside of the right wing of each aircraft was a gold seven-pointed star.

CHAPTER 49

ACTION

Leos stayed near his hut the rest of the day. The jet aircraft left after their third pass, and solitude returned to the Callus. But it was a troubled solitude. A murmuring Leos couldn't identify undercut the usual detachment of the prisoners from one another. They talked among themselves very little normally, and today seemed no different. No one ever came to visit Leos. Even Tsoder never came to Leos's hut. Yet the appearance of the two aircraft—so bold, so loud, so markedly unusual in the skies of *Non-Dre-Ahdenu*—certainly had to have changed the interpersonal dynamics of the Callus. There must be a buzz among the other prisoners, perhaps inaudible, though probably not. And Leos himself began to wonder— was Tsoder right? Was the revolution beginning? Had it already begun? *Will* we be liberated? Holy dinfrizzle, should I postpone my plan now?

Yet within the day-to-day operation of the Callus, nothing had changed. The single-engine plane brought two more prisoners, and the trolls came around on their evening run and filled the bowls again, but they said nothing and Leos didn't ask them about the unusual aircraft. He'd decided to focus on his plan. Tomorrow, if the clouds cooperated, he would go. The plan was ready. He was ready. The twin-engine plane was due, and the time was right.

He slept little that night, his mind full of the plan, going over it again and again, imagining every step along the way. He decided to take the direct route that ran from his hut to the airstrip. That would be the shorter route so he'd get there in the least time. At this time of year the fog might be short lived—that occasionally happened—and he might not have much time. It was the more dangerous route, though, because it took him directly past the cave and the one troll guard in the guardhouse at the entrance.

As he lay on his bed, wrapped in the blankets against the chill, the difficulties of the plan swirled through his mind and he almost talked himself out of it several times.

I can wait until next time—that was the most common excuse he gave himself. *By the next arrival of the plane, the temperature may be lower and the*

310

fog will be heavier and last longer.

No, I can't wait. I'm losing weight and I'm not as strong as I was. I need whatever strength I've got to carry out the plan. It's now or never. I've got to get out of here.

But if I fail — I could be executed, or turned into a troll. That would be worse than death.

No, I've got to go. I've got to risk it. Think, you stupid idiot, about the chance of success, not failure.

But Tsoder may be right about the revolution. I could wait for them to liberate us. That may not be long.

No — no — no — that may take too much time. I must go. I will go. Tomorrow.

He drifted off to an intermittent sleep, and finally woke to a cold, foggy day as the light of morning gave him barely sufficient illumination to see. *Good, a heavy fog. A cold fog. This will last. Just what I need.* He stepped outside, his blankets around his shoulders. He hesitated a few microsectors, waiting for the light to intensify so he could visualize the road. He picked his trowel from the ground near the door where he'd set it the night before and started walking, watching the road as he shuffled along, carefully noting the various landmarks as he passed. He could see only a few links in front of his feet and those landmarks were so important. The road curved slightly left at this marker, slightly right at that one. Other markers designated the position of huts, and he took special care to be quiet lest the residents get suspicious. The shoes the trolls issued him were worn and threadbare now, the soles reduced to little more than thin fabric. They didn't cushion the irregularities in the road as well as they did when he first wore them, but they had the advantage that they were quiet.

Soon he reached the marker that designated the cave — three stones in a triangle formation. Turn slightly left at the next set of stones, watch for the marker that indicates a turn to the right. Look out for the guardhouse near the mouth of the cave — four stones in a square. Be very quiet here, the troll guard's probably asleep, but can't be too careful. Stay on the trail to the airstrip. Almost a quarter-anthan to the strip where things will be quiet. Look for the little pile of pebbles that indicates the approach to the gate. Yes, there it is — the gate is just beyond.

*   *   *

Leos paused to consider his position. "I'm here," he murmured, but quietly so the trolls wouldn't hear. "I'm really here. Probably no one has

311

ever gotten this far in trying to escape. I'm the first." His heart throbbed and he smiled at his good fortune. He glanced around. The fog swirled heavily about him. Its drifts and eddies curled aimlessly in and out, back and forth, but showed no sign of letting up. *That's good, I've got work to do.* He turned to the padlock and latch bar.

He tried his trowel on the padlock but the spade end was too large to fit the keyhole.

No problem. I can break off a few rusted areas – there, let's try it now.

Again it didn't fit, and he ticked more metal off both sides until he'd worked it down to a piece of metal vaguely resembling a key just small enough to fit the keyhole. He wiggled it around, left and right, jiggling and fidgeting, bending, turning, twisting and rotating until he thought, *God, it's never going to work. I may have to go back to my hut . . .* He stopped for a couple of nanosectors to let his arm rest, then tried again, pressing it farther in, this time feeling a solid resistance, and with one firm right-hand turn, the padlock clicked opened. *It worked. It actually worked.* He exhaled and chuckled to himself.

Wow, the latch bar is heavy. Now I know why it takes several trolls to maneuver it.

This was the first time he'd seen the bar up close, and it appeared intimidating. He yanked hard, but it was lodged tight. He draped both blankets over the bar to stifle the sound if it squeaked, and lapped one corner of a blanket over the nearby burnwire to protect his arm. He yanked again, putting his back into it. It moved a fraction of a decilink and a muffled squeal came from under the blanket. He pulled again and again, but the bar slid by only microscopic degrees. Another screech from under the blanket, louder this time, but they wouldn't hear it at the guardhouse. *It's too far away and the fog dampens the sound.* He jerked hard again and it moved a fraction more, but his muscles grew tired and began to cramp. He rested for a microsector, and tried again. Two or three more hard pulls and it was out. He opened the gate and slipped inside, carefully avoiding the burnwire. From the inside he replaced the bolt, but it didn't slide any more easily back into place than it did coming out. The padlock was last.

He scurried across the dirt runway and found the rocks on the far side. This was the South Ridge of the Callus, heavily bouldered. Sharp-edged rocks stabbed painfully through the worn soles of his foot covers, but he didn't mind. He was on his way. The rocks had been pushed right up to the edge of the Callus when the runway was graded, and in many places beyond them was nothing but a five-thousand silto drop. He crept toward the west end of the strip, skulking behind large boulders, and found a safe niche near the far west end of the runway where he could wait hidden from view. He wrapped himself in his blankets and settled down to wait for the fog to lift.

The plane will be here soon. I'll just get a few minutes of sleep.

*   *   *

Leos woke an unknown number of subsectors later. The fog had risen and visibility was clear. He hurriedly checked his situation. *Can they see me?* He peeked through a cleft between two of the boulders toward the gate—no activity, no one has entered. The plane should be here soon. He settled back on the ground and pulled his blankets around him. The air temperature was rising, though still chilly.

He was awakened by the sound of a twin-engine plane. It came from the east as it always did, touched down at the far end of the runway and taxied up to the vicinity of the gate. Usually it stopped there and turned around, but this time it didn't. It continued slowly past the gate, headed for the west end of the runway near where Leos lay.

Leos had a good view of the pilot through the front windshield. What's he doing? I've never seen him come past the gate like that. He usually stops right beside the gate. Why? Have they seen me?

About fifty or sixty links from where Leos crouched behind the rock, the plane turned completely around, coming to rest facing back down the runway. The engines stopped, but in the silence he became aware of the sound of another plane approaching. It's another of the same kind of aircraft, twin engines and twin tail.

What's going on? Have they discovered my hiding place? They most certainly know I'm gone because the trolls would have tried to deliver some gruel this morning and I'm not at my hut.

Most of the time the trolls don't do much when they find an empty hut. They just notify the sergeant of the guard and go on about delivering to the rest of the Callus. Someone comes out later in the day and pokes around. Missing prisoners are not treated seriously. Most are assumed to have fallen or jumped off the Callus. They don't even send a detail down to look for the body.

The second plane taxied up behind the first, right next to the gate. It too turned around, facing down the runway. The trolls opened the gate, and doors opened on both planes. From the first plane only the two pilots exited. The trolls brought up three of the three-wheeled carts and began unloading. Nothing unusual there.

They must have so many supplies they had to send two planes. I'll have to wait until the second plane is unloaded.

From the second plane, three people emerged on the far side. Dressed in dark blue uniforms, each carried a weapon that looked familiar, though Leos couldn't immediately place where he'd seen it before. It definitely wasn't Nytandran or Jhontu. One of them walked around the rear of the plane and surveyed the area, but Leos remained hidden. After the armed guard returned to the other side of the plane, five more people stepped out.

What in the name of the Great God Arteamos . . . what's going on here?

All were dressed in the same dark blue uniforms and black boots— wait, one wore a white uniform and black oxford-type shoes. Two Jhontu also came out, probably the pilots. Several three-wheeled carts driven by trolls picked them up and they headed toward the gate. Leos turned back to the first plane. The unloading of supplies was almost complete. A few microsectors later both planes were empty and unguarded.

Several millisectors will elapse after the supplies are unloaded before the pilots return and the plane takes off again. But the second plane—the one with the passengers—blocked the supply plane, and Leos will have to take it. It stood facing down the runway, ready for take-off, just waiting for him. No one else was around. The trolls and visitors were all at the cave. They'd gone inside. He made his move.

He pulled his blankets around his shoulders and bolted down the runway and across to the plane's door and cautiously peeked in. Empty. He scrambled inside and pulled the door closed and threw the locking lever. Finally, inside. Safe. Now all that remained was to get off the ground.

This plane was outfitted for passengers, two rows of seats on each side of a narrow center aisle. He ran up the aisle into the cockpit and dropped into the pilot's seat and pumped a fist in the air. His heart continued to throb with an excitement that caused his hands to shake and his knees to quiver.

"I'm here! I'm finally fuckin' here! I'm going to get off this revolting rock. What do I do now?"

Over the years Leos had been on *Non-Dre-Ahdenu*, he'd picked up enough of the Jhontu language to be able to interpret some of the various tags and labels on the instruments, and he took a minute to study the control panel. He found two buttons that, in his limited knowledge he thought said "Engine Start." He pressed the left one and pushed the throttle lever forward. The left engine coughed and sputtered and the propeller began to rotate, and he pushed the throttle farther and a big plume of blue-white smoke exploded from the exhaust as the engine started. He did the same with the right engine. Both engines were running, but they were grinding and grumbling, vibrating in their mountings much more than he remembered. He pushed the throttles farther forward, but the vibration became stronger. The plane rumbled and shook, straining against the brakes. Smoke continued to pour from the engines.

I don't remember all that smoke from before. How did they — Uh-oh.

"Oh, crap."

Now the one big problem that Leos hadn't thought much about suddenly became clear—he didn't know how to fly a propeller-driven airplane. He didn't understand the engines and how they work. To him, all that was required was merely to advance the throttles and the plane would fly, and while he was basically correct, he didn't know the appropriate number of revolutions for takeoff. There was no listing of that setting anywhere in the cockpit. He hadn't thought anything about flying propeller-driven airplanes during all the time he was concentrating on getting off this immense plug. He'd pushed that part of his escape plan into the back of his mind, intending to get around to it, but he never did. He scanned the controls in front of him, all the levers and buttons, and translated the labels and indicators. Two throttle-like levers were set off to the side of the main throttles and marked with two words. The first word was 'Air'—he knew that word right away. But the second word he wasn't as familiar with. It could be 'combination' or 'mixture' or even 'blend.' Jad had used the word to mean 'brew.'

Brew? Mixture? Air? Air mixture? Okay, that makes sense. The mixture of air with the fuel. He cautiously pushed both levers forward, and the roughness of the engines smoothed out and they stopped belching smoke. But while he was watching the left engine, through the smoke still hanging in the air he was able to make out two trolls driving one of the three-wheeled carts speeding toward the gate in the fence. Two of the blue-uniformed guards sat in two other seats. The trolls weren't armed, but they were yelling and waving their arms. "Stop! Stop!" they yelled. Then one of the trolls recognized the plane's pilot.

"Leos!" the troll yelled as he pointed toward the front of the plane. "Leos! Leos!"

"Leos?" one of the blue-uniformed guards yelled in a strangely familiar language. "Is that Leos? Leos! Wait! We're here—holy shit!"

One of the blue-uniformed guards fired into the air. The trolls ran up to the plane and banged on the door.

"Open the door! Open the door!" A couple of shots ricocheted off the left wing near the engine, but didn't do any serious damage. "Leos! Stop the plane! Stop the plane!" the guards yelled, still in that familiar language. One shot hit the window at the side of the cockpit and sent fragments of glass and metal careening through the window into Leos's face. He screamed as the debris peppered his left forehead, cheek, and chin. Blood spilled into his eye and dripped onto his clothes. But he retained enough presence of mind to throw a fist out the window toward them, and his heart pounded even faster with the excitement of release from the Callus. *Finally—escape!*

"I'm getting off this place!" he yelled out the window of the plane, and released the brakes and pushed the throttles forward. "Goodbye, you ignorant piles of glokshit!"

The plane began to move down the runway, faster and faster as Leos pushed the throttles even farther.

"Off we go!" He pulled back on the control column and the plane lifted into the air and cleared the end of the runway.

CHAPTER 50

RUNNING

Leos banked left and set a course of 000, due north toward the edge of the great rift around the middle of the planet. He leveled the plane just below the clouds. He dared not enter the clouds or he wouldn't be able to see the horizon, even though the horizon on this planet was little more than a hazy, indistinct line between the clouds above and the rugged desert below. The altimeter read 5,500 siltos. But the real altitude didn't matter, he stayed just below the clouds and began to relax in his seat.

Yes, but would *relax* be the proper word for what he was doing? For what he was feeling? Did he really *relax*? This had been a tremendously exciting and momentous day, no doubt about it, and he had a right to sit back and enjoy the flight. He'd gone through so much just to get to this point. Two years on the Callus—all that vapid, insipid gruel—all those repulsive vegetables—the unending cold nights—the rocks thrown at him by the trolls—all that walking he'd done—all that work in his garden just to get his vegetables to grow. He had every goddamn *right* to loosen up and take it easy. Yet, *relaxation* seemed not quite the right word at this moment. It was more than that. *I'm off the damn Callus! Yes!* He'd pushed himself so hard to get to the airstrip and grab an airplane and take off that the strain on his weakened body, the exertion just to get here, and even the excitement of giving the trolls an unapologetic goodbye pushed his heart to beat faster than it ever had since his first day on the Callus. Now all he wanted was to be able to settle back in his seat and enjoy the flight. That was important—he had a long way to go to be really free, and he should conserve his strength. *No telling what's going to happen when I get to the inhabited area.* But the overwhelming emotion that engulfed him in the first few microsectors as the plane left the vicinity of the Callus was not simple relaxation, not even excitement at being away from the imprisonment, but laughter. He broke into a deep, broad belly laugh. It came upon him suddenly, like a slap in the face and he bellowed out loud. Maybe they even heard him back on the Callus. It felt so good to be able to laugh for the first time in two years, two of the elongated years on this planet, so much longer than a year on Nytranda, or even Anthanos. Measured in Anthanian years, he'd probably been imprisoned on the Callus for as much as three years, and to be able to laugh out loud, to do something that would have gotten him weird stares if not downright physical assaults from the trolls or the other prisoners was so important. Perhaps that's why so many prisoners on the Callus lived only a few years after they arrived. Life was hard there—nothing to laugh about. No way to relieve the frustration of life there, nothing to take a prisoner's mind off the necessity to pee and poop in the garden to make the vegetables grow, or suffer through the cold, endless nights in a hut with no heat and only two blankets with which to try and keep warm. None of the prisoners on the Callus ever made a wisecrack or a gag about their situation, neither did anyone tell a witticism or a joke. That was just not done.

But it was important to laugh now. It had to be. To release the frustration of the Callus, to let it out and evacuate the bowels of pent-up anger and outrage. He laughed so hard he strained his abdominal muscles, or rather, what was left of them. Still, in his seriously weakened state, he couldn't keep up the level of excitement that he needed for all the convulsions and howls he wanted, and after a couple of microsectors the laughter left him and he calmed down. As soon as that happened, he looked at the magnetic compass and set in his mind the course he wanted, then fell asleep.

It wasn't a deep sleep, he'd had little of that over the past several years. He jerked himself awake every now and then, and would hurriedly and in a state of near panic glance at the horizon and scan the instruments—*am I still on course, still 5500 siltos altitude, still pointed at the horizon, airspeed still at whatever that number indicates?*—but the vague, fuzzy horizon looked the same from every direction. *How do you know if you're headed toward the same spot all the time?* But he wasn't worried; he was free of the Callus and anywhere he landed on this planet would suit him just fine.

After about the fifth time in this cycle of sleeping and awakening, the forested area that marked the habitable portion of the planet came vaguely into sight. At first, it was just a thin gray line on the horizon, as if splitting the clouds from the desert below. But it grew thicker as he approached, and eventually he could make out individual trees. Not green as in the warm season, on this planet, trees turned a mottled gray in the cold season. He glanced at the gauges on the plane's control panel marked "Fuel."

Low on fuel. Gonna have to find a place to land pretty soon.

He flew on past the dividing line between the trees and the desert, and entered airspace over the forest. After a few microsectors, he spotted a small town nestled within the forest, with a narrow dirt road that split the trees and entered the town from the east. He circled the town, reducing his altitude to about 1000 siltos. At first he saw very little. No signs of life. Some of the buildings seemed to be damaged or burned. Many had collapsed in on themselves. But as he circled, several townspeople ran from some of the more intact buildings and from the forest that surrounded the hamlet. A few had weapons, and they fired at Leos in his plane. Most of the shots missed the plane, but a few struck it, though at first he wasn't aware the plane had been hit. One or two shots hit the plane in the wings and in the fuselage. One shot came through the cockpit floor and exited through the roof.

"What the hell—what are you doing?" he yelled out the window. Why—?" But when another shot went through the left wing from below, he decided to get the hell out of there. He swung the plane back north and left the village.

Why would they shoot at me? I'm not the Talatan—wait, hold on a microsector, this is a Talatan plane. That could mean the village down there must be . . . Resistance. That means Tsoder was right—the revolution has begun. The Talatan did that damage to the buildings down there. But they think I'm part of the Talatan forces. If I could land there and contact them, maybe I could persuade them that I'm not . . . but if I go back, they'll just shoot at me again. Might even shoot me down. How much fuel do I have?

He glanced at the fuel gauges and noticed with a start that the left-hand gauge read 'empty.' And the other had very little fuel remaining. *Holy shit—one of those shots must've hit the fuel tank.* As if to confirm his theory, the left engine sputtered and quit. He could maintain the plane in the air on one engine, but with limited fuel he couldn't go very far. The plane's airspeed had dropped to what he read on the airspeed indicator as '25', way too slow to get much farther, and he had trouble keeping the nose of the plane up.

Start looking for a place to land. A road, or an opening in the forest.

Then the right engine died.

Well, that eliminated the problem of keeping the nose up. It now pointed toward the forest below, and he searched desperately for an opening. Anything—a road—a clearing—a meadow like the one his mother showed him on some of the images from the Blue Planet—anything at all. But the plane dropped lower and lower and skimmed the tops of some of the trees. He maneuvered between two large trees, but the wings began clipping the tops of the taller trees, and that slowed the plane just enough that it sank into the forest and struck the ground in a narrow ditch-like depression. It skidded along for several hundred links until it came to rest at the base of a large gray-and-white-barked tree. Both wings had been sheared off where they were attached to the fuselage. And what remained of the plane rolled slightly to the left.

Leos wasn't seriously hurt, though as the plane plunged toward the ground below it was knocked side-to-side against the trees, and he banged his head several times against the window frame. That just made the wounds on his face and forehead throb all the more intensely. And—wouldn't you know—he'd wrenched his left foot again, the same one that had been injured when he landed on this planet in the first place. He gathered his blankets around his shoulders and carefully made his way toward the rear of the plane. The door of the plane opened outward, and he had to force the door to scrape along the ground that blocked its opening in order to get it wide enough that he could squeeze through.

The ground was hard, the soil cold and black. The cold penetrated the thin soles of his foot coverings in icy slivers. The tree trunks were streaked in black and gray, and everything around him took on leaden shades of smoky white. During the cold season, the leaves of the trees rolled themselves into tight, slender cylinders six to eight decilinks long. They lost their green color and turned a ghastly dusky gray. When seen against the milky clouds, they looked like vicious black spikes. Hundreds of them on each tree, as if the tree was ready to defend itself from some unknown or obscure outside force. Leos worked his way to the rear of the downed plane and continued on, hoping this route would take him toward the village. But . . . yet . . .

If they shot at me, it's probably because they thought I was Talatan 'cause that's a Talatan plane. So, I need to find that village and show them I'm not. Maybe they can hide me. But would they accept me? They wouldn't know who I am. But what else is there? I'm off the Callus . . . so what do I do now? Where can I go?

Above, an airplane flew over at about one thousand links and began to circle the wreckage. Familiar Talatan insignia marked the wings. *That's another Talatan plane. They're looking for me. I've got to get away.* He kept walking, but his sore foot held him back. After he'd gone a few hundred links from the plane, he came to a small creek, only a couple of links wide. He didn't see it until his sore left foot stepped into the cold water. *Ahh! Damn, that's cold.* He followed the creek downstream to where it dribbled

into a small lake, maybe five hundred links across. It looked vaguely familiar. He waded out into the water and splashed some on his face to cleanse
it of the blood that caked his left temple and jaw. The water numbed his
left foot and dulled the pain. But the water was so cold, so achingly cold,
that he left the lake and dried his feet with a corner of one of his blankets.

*Where's the pump house? I can hide in the pump house. Or the farm. Zhin-
ta will hide me if I can get to the farm.*

He looked around for the pump house and the steps that led to the
open field between Zhinta's farm and the lake. But he saw neither, and he
left the lake and continued on through the forest.

Maybe I'm at the wrong end of the lake.

He came across a tree with a split trunk and a notch at the split. *My
knife. Is that where I stashed my knife?* He ran over to the tree, but his knife
wasn't there. *I don't understand. I stashed it right here. It should be here. Someone stole it. No, there was more decay in the tree where I stashed it. That's right, I
remember now. There must be other trees. I'll look around. It's around here somewhere. It wasn't that far from the lake.*

The numbing effect of the cold lake water had worn off and his left
foot had begun throbbing again. He staggered on through the forest, lurch-
ing from tree to tree, expecting at any moment to discover the one tree
which held his knife. The knife was important—he'd spent so much time
making it—so many Anthanian subsectors, so many Nytandran hours—
that it had become an extension of his arm. More than that, it became an
extension of his will. It went where he threw it, where he willed it. It did
his bidding. With it he could handle any emergency. He could defend himself against any animal that might attack, or any Talatan he might come a-
cross.

*I showed them. I got that one Guard. It took only one flick of my knife and
that guy was dead. I'll do it again if they come my way. But where is it?
Goddammit, where is it?*

The sky had begun to darken overhead and light in the forest was
dwindling. The air temperature had dropped and he tugged his blankets
all around him. Several hours of light were left in the sky, but in the forest,
the light, filtered through the grim, forbidding trees, faded so much more
rapidly than on the Callus. *It's getting late. I've got to find that knife.*

He staggered on, scanning each tree for that characteristic notch
where his knife would be hidden. *It's around here somewhere. It's got to be. It
wasn't far from the lake.*

Farther he walked, into the slowly fading twilight. The light seemed to diminish with every painful step he took, but he wanted that tree and his knife. One tree he came across had a crotch formed by three branches only a few links off the ground, and with darkness almost complete, he climbed in and made himself as comfortable as he could. "I'll get my knife tomorrow," he mumbled. He was so tired he fell immediately asleep.

*   *   *

Leos slept sporadically in the crotch of that tree. His blankets kept falling open and exposing him to the cold night air, and he woke several times. A knob on one of the limbs poked him in the back or side depending on how he turned, and his feet were numbingly cold. He had nightmares; he saw the trolls coming after him, driving their three-wheeled carts, coming through the forest, surrounding him, throwing rocks at him, grabbing him and taking him into their cave and nicking his left eye and he became a troll. Twice he woke screaming, "No! No! You'll never get me!" Or, the Talatan Guards came for him in that dungeon, and they tortured him and beat him and made him sleep in that cold room with the frigid water all over the floor, and it was all so horrible . . .

When light started filling the clouds of the sky, slowly increasing the illumination that filtered into the forest, he slipped from his perch and curled up on the ground at the base of the tree, if for no other reason than to try and regain the sleep he never got.

In frustration, he stood. The forest was quiet, a quiet he'd never heard in a forest. Not just quiet, but still. Nothing moved. Not a whisper of breeze. The forests of *Jon-Set-Tom* were always alive with sounds, even on the few occasions when he woke in the middle of the darkness—a breeze rustling the leaves of the trees, or a gentle rain that dribbled down the leaves, or the small animals that scampered up and down the leaves outside the tree, or the cawing of the zolopil high in the sky—something always to let him know where he was and he was not alone and Esmerelda was right beside him nestled into his groin, silently urging him to return to sleep. Even on the Callus, especially in the cold season, the wind whipped around his hut in the early morning, stirring up those tiny dust grains that got inside the hut through the cracks in the door or the shutters on the window. But here, in this forest there was no breeze, and all was bizarrely quiet.

Which way did I come? From which way did I approach this tree? Every direction looked the same, the same trees all around. In the eerie silence he started walking. But which direction? *Any direction. I'll go this way.* His ankle felt better now, though still sore. Taking his weight off it last night had given it a chance to partially recover. Where was that lake? *I'm so thirsty. And hungry. I haven't had anything to eat or drink since . . . let's see, two nights ago. I didn't get any of their crappy gruel yesterday.*

He'd walked maybe an anthan when he stopped and looked around. In the silence of those isolated woods, something seemed not right. A feeling of disquiet came over him, and he trembled. He looked in all directions and finally isolated the source of his unease. From behind and slightly to his left came a sound that at first was just a faint high-pitched wail, a wavering sound from very far away, a tremolo he didn't recognize. It might have been one of the sounds one might normally hear in the forest, nothing consequential, a typical sound from forest animals. But since he'd left his nest in that tree, the forest had been alarmingly quiet, as though no animals were around, and the mere fact of the presence of an unusual sound forced him to listen closely. The sound grew louder and its familiarity began to bother him. *Holy crap, that's the wail of tracking animals. The Talatan are on their way. I've gotta get outta here. They're comin' to get me!*

He started running as best he could on his sore ankle, and he could make surprising speed through the forest. But he tired easily and after about a thousand links he slowed and stopped to catch a breath. *They're comin' to get me! I gotta get outta here. They'll torture me and cut off my penis. I can't let them find me. Where's my knife? I'll fight them to the death if I have to.*

He started running again, but his foot had begun to hurt more and it held him back and he couldn't run like he did before. He stumbled more, tripping over rocks and exposed tree roots, and his blankets became soiled and he stopped every now and then to brush them off. *I need those blankets. Gotta keep them clean. They keep me warm.*

The wailing behind him had become louder now. He looked back but couldn't see anything or anybody coming through the forest. He kept trying to run, but his weak body and sore foot kept him from going as fast as he wanted. He tripped over more roots and soiled his blankets again and again. Once he banged his head against a tree limb and that hurt, and the wounds on his face began to bleed again. But the sound behind him kept getting louder and louder and he began to yell, "Stop it! Stop it! Get away from me!" He stumbled over another root and fell on his face. From behind he heard a voice.

"Leos! Leos!" He knew that voice. It was one of trolls, the sergeant of trolls. He knew that troll well. *Oh, no! They've tracked me down and they're going to take me back to my hut and I'll have to eat that worthless gruel and pee and poop in my garden just to get those god-awful vegetables to grow. They'll take me into their cave and nick my left eye and turn me into a troll. Oh, no! Not that — not that!*

He turned and looked back. Two of the trolls waddled through the forest yelling his name. Behind them were two of the blue-uniformed guards, the ones who'd fired on his plane. He ran on, but the blue-uniformed guards passed the trolls and also began yelling his name. They caught up with him, but stayed a few links behind.

"Leos! Stop! Wait!"

Leos didn't listen; violent anger overwhelmed him. In a spasm of rage and frustration that mushroomed from his inability to get away from his pursuers, and intensified by the pain of his foot and the wounds on his face, he turned and lowered his head and threw up his left arm over his face and charged the guards. "You fuckin' bastards can't keep me from getting away from here!" The trolls ducked behind two trees but the guards held their position.

"Leos, wait, we're here — holy shit!"

The lead guard raised his weapon and fired at the onrushing Leos. It was only a stun blast, but it burned the right side of Leos's face and scorched his hair and beard. It paralyzed him temporarily and he tumbled unconscious to the ground.

CHAPTER 51

RELEASE

Leos woke lying on some sort of hard surface, possibly a bench. At first his thoughts and feelings were fuzzy and unfocused, and he felt dizzy. His head hurt in so many places he couldn't count them all, or understand why. Slowly his mind cleared and he could feel the bandages that covered the left side of his face, but the uncovered skin on the right side burned as though he had a terrible sunburn. *Where's my beard? They shaved my beard. Why'd they do that?*

But beyond other sensations, what he felt most was the soothing warmth from a cloth that'd been placed over the bare-skin side of his face. He hadn't felt anything like that for so long it startled him. Warmth is not a feeling one experiences on the Callus. He opened his eyes, but the left eye was held shut by the bandages and the right eye was partially obscured. His blankets still covered him from the chest down.

He appeared to be in a metal hut or room. Corrugated metal formed the roof, and the only light came from a bare bulb hanging from the ceiling. He whipped the cloth from his face and turned his head to peer around. A few links away, bathed in the light from the bulb, stood a man dressed in all white, talking to another man, obviously Nytandran by the look of his face. A young woman wearing the same dark blue uniform as the others knelt beside him. Several more people in dark uniforms and holding weapons stood nearby. The higher-pitched busy grumblings of trolls whispered in the background, though he couldn't see them.

"He's awake." The woman's voice had a soft pastel timbre to it. "Leos, how do you feel?"

"What?" The man in white turned around and looked down at him.

Leos said nothing. His mind swirled—all he could think of was getting away from this place. *Where is this place? Where am I?* The woman's voice was familiar, but he didn't stop to place it. The anger still lay within him, as powerful as ever, and he was confused. The memories of his escape from the Callus were fresh in his mind and he tried to understand where he was and why he was here and he needed to get out of here and get back to the Resistance. They'll protect him from the Talatan and maybe find a way to get him off this planet and get back to *Jon-Set-Tom* and Esmerelda. She would keep him safe—oh no, he can't go back there, there's open warfare—he'll have to go back to Nytandra and—oh no, he can't go back there either, they kicked him off and he stole something and they almost chopped his head off—that's right, he can't go anywhere—he'll have to stay here and stay in his hut and eat the worthless gruel and the vegetables . . . but he'd get into trouble if he stayed around here much longer. The trolls might nick his eye and turn him into a troll, so he had to get out, get back to the airplane and find the Resistance. He sat up but the woman pressed gently on his chest.

"Leos. Lie down. You need to rest." She spoke a different language than he was used to, and though he understood it, he didn't immediately comprehend why she was speaking it. It wasn't Jhontu or from *Jon-Set-Tom*, and it wasn't Nytandran.

"Please, old friend, lie down." Another voice—a male voice—familiar—but in still a different language.

"I'm gettin' my fuckin' ass off this place," Leos blurted, the words exploding from his mouth. He spoke Jhontu and tried to stand.

"Leos, you mustn't—" came the male voice again. Now he recognized the language—Nytandran.

"Leos. Please lie down," the female said, and she pressed even more forcefully on his chest, but Leos wasn't ready to take anyone's advice. All these different languages were confusing and he didn't want to have anything to do with any of them. He pushed them aside in his mind and focused on only one thing: getting out of this place—wherever it was—and back into the forest.

"I've got to get out of here!"

Against the woman's insistence, he stood and pushed past her, almost knocking her to the floor. He tried to run but his legs were weak and he took three or four steps and fell forward, almost collapsing on top of one of the blue uniformed guards. As they helped him to his feet, he became vaguely aware of a flurry of activity behind him accompanied by voices in several languages. As the woman screamed, "No-no! You don't need to—" a slight prickling sensation tickled the right side of his neck and turned into a burning.

Then his lights went out.

*   *   *

"Leos, don't try to get up," the woman's voice told him. So soothing, that voice, and so familiar. The language was Anthanian, yes, but that meant little to him—he wanted only to get away from this place . . . wherever it was.

He opened his right eye. Bandages still covered the left side of his face, and a dim gray light came through a window of the room in which he lay. His head still ached and the skin on his face burned. His lips were swollen to twice their normal size. A salve or ointment had been applied to the bare part of his face and lips. Another light, faint and white, on the other side of the room illuminated several people, but he couldn't identify them or the source of the light. He felt soft bedclothes, and briefly thought he might be back in his room in the Nytandran Palace. So many recognizable things assaulted him as he struggled to get his bearings—the languages, the people, the voices, the feelings—it was all so overwhelming he couldn't make sense of most of it. He forced himself to suppress the confusion, to concentrate on leaving. He tried to get up again.

"I have to get out of here," he said through swollen and inflamed lips.

"Leos, no!" The woman's voice came again. "Stay in bed. You need to rest." She pressed him firmly back into the bed.

"Leos," a man's voice came again, but a different man's voice. He spoke in Jhontu. "Do you recognize me? I am Kazeh. We met at Jad's place. You are injured. You must rest. I will give you some medicine to help you rest, and we have dressed your injuries."

Kazeh—yes, I remember you. You and Jad took me to the farm. Leos nodded and hesitantly lay back on the bed as the woman pulled the covers over him. Kazeh was a good friend, and he was a friend of Jad's, and with Kazeh's soothing voice he was reassured, and knew he was in good hands. *But what's she doing here? Who is she? Why is she here? Where am I, anyway?*

"Please, Leos. Stay still. You need to rest." The woman again. *Such a nice woman. Her face looks familiar.*

Maybe I'll be transferred back to my hut on the Callus as soon as I recover. Yes, the hut. I'll go back to my hut. That was important, and Leos put the airplane and his crash landing in the forest out of his mind and hoped he could go back to his hut. *Yes, the hut, I need to go back to my hut.* That hut was supposed to be his home for the rest of his life. He was tired and he just wanted to go back to the Callus and eat the obnoxious vegetables and the worthless gruel, and pee and poop in his garden like he always did. No more escape attempts, he promised himself. He listened as Kazeh explained more.

"You must have been injured when your airplane crashed in the forest," he said. "You are lucky your astrosoldier put his weapon on stun, and you were burned only slightly. It was good you lowered your head before the blast, your corneas were not scarred. You are no longer on the Callus. You are in a hospital in a small town about a hundred sil from MarktuAhdenu. Your friends are here with you. We will transfer you later."

"Leos," the woman said again. "Do you remember me?"

He stared at the woman. She didn't have the big, wide eyes of the Jhontu, like Kazeh or Mlada, but she didn't have the puffy eye slits of the Nytandrans either. A slender woman, very light skin—no, no, not green skin, she's not from the green planet—reddish-blond hair cut way short— those light green eyes, that fair skin, that hair, that figure—even dressed in an unflattering dark blue jumpsuit, he'd recognize that figure anywhere. That could only be . . .

Oh, but no, he told himself, it couldn't be. *She couldn't be here.* Kazeh's presence he could understand—he was injured and needed medical attention. But, her? *They're playing with my mind. They have to be. Did they nick my eye? I can't tell. It doesn't feel like it. I would know if they had. Maybe you don't feel it. But there are bandages over my left eye. I can't open my left eye. Is this the first stage of turning into a troll? Do old memories come flooding back into your mind? I remember her, but she could never be here— there's no way. She's a hundred light-years away. Why would I be thinking of her? Good God, what's happening to me?* He closed his right eye, trying to put *her* out of his mind.

The woman spoke again. "Leos, do you remember me? We came a long way to find you. We want to take you back to Anthanos with us."

Anthanos? Don't give me that, young lady—it'll never happen. I just want to go back to my hut on the Callus and eat the disgusting vegetables and worthless gruel and . . .

He stared at the woman, intently, longingly, her face so familiar, her features so soft, as soft as those of Esmerelda. There's only one other person in the universe who looks like that. *Maybe she could be here. Oh, it would be so nice if she was . . . no, it'll never happen . . . but what if it did . . . it couldn't be . . . maybe it is . . .*

"Tama?" Leos muttered, but his lips didn't work well, all swollen and sore. It came out more like "Tmmaa?"

Tama smiled. "He remembers."

CHAPTER 52

GOODBYE

As soon as Leos's mind cleared sufficiently for him to talk coherently with Tama and Kazeh and the others, and with Kazeh's good ministrations and Tama's sensitive nursing skills (she had to take nursing courses to qualify for a position on *Star Voyager*), Leos recovered well enough to be transferred back to the same hospital he was in when he first arrived on *Non-Dre-Ahdenu*. The next day after the transfer, as the swelling in his lips had subsided enough to make himself understood, he began to translate for the various visitors. He had so many questions, he almost couldn't wait to ask. Now, around the beginning of the fourth hour of the day, so many people had crowded into his room they almost spilled out into the hallway. Tama sat cross-legged on the bed beside Leos, and most of the others stood around the walls of the room: Kazeh; Tsoder and Tsee; several other of Jad's friends from the revolution; some former prisoners whom Leos befriended on the Callus; as well as Tam and two medical and four security personnel from *Star Voyager*; and Dr. Gadomer from Grok's ship.

"We had to bring someone along who spoke Anthanian and Nytan-dran to speak to Esmerelda," Tam explained.

"Before we begin, what time is it?" Leos asked when everyone had finally squeezed into Leos's room. "I mean, Anthanian time. How long have I been gone?"

"It's 488.672," Tam said. It's been almost five years since you left."

"Wow." Leos had to struggle to put the time in perspective. "I didn't realize I'd been gone that long." He stayed quiet for a few nanosectors, mulling the import of that time factor.

I'm twenty-six and a half years old, but I feel almost a hundred. I'm sure I'll get over that.

He reached over and captured Tama's hand in his.

"Tell me about how you came here. How'd you know where to come?"

Tam launched into a brief description of the evidence that led them to *Non*, going into detail about each planet they approached. "We stopped

329

at Nytandra first when we entered this solar system. When we mentioned your name, everyone pointed to the sky, but we didn't understand what they were trying to tell us. We tried to speak to Coreaje, but he refused to hear us. Apparently, he's still angry with you. He did assign Dr. Gadomer to translate for us, though. He told us about you and Esmerelda and said you'd been sent to the green planet but he didn't know anything more. He assumed you were still there so we went there and met Esmerelda."

"Esmerelda? You met her? How's she doing?"

Tam nodded. "She's doing well. She's their queen. She runs the place."

"Queen?" Leos's eyes opened wide. He searched his memory. "Holy dinfrizzle. I remember they were talking about something they didn't want us to know about. We were always so puzzled. But that explains the legend."

"The legend?"

"The legend of the young woman. Senalar told me. Her mate was killed by a zil—"

"Zil?"

"The big animals. Maybe you saw one or two of them."

"Oh, yes, we had to kill a couple of them. They charged at us. The indigenous people actually appreciated it."

"I can imagine. But tell me about Esmerelda. Didn't they attack you when you landed?"

"No, at first they began yelling at us, and a bunch of guys with big knives surrounded us and looked real threatening, but when we mentioned your name, the guy who seemed to be in charge, this older guy with white hair—"

"That must have been Jaiete," Leos said.

"—he recognized your name, and he sent a runner down the trail, and after about a subsector, Esmerelda appeared. She recognized Dr. Gadomer, and he could talk to her, and she smiled when he told her we were here to pick you up. She told us about the war and said you'd escaped. Most of Coreaje's troops were killed and fed to those animals—what did you call them, the 'zil'?—except for a small number that were allowed to take Coreaje back to Nytandra. She thought you'd gone back to Nytandra, too. When we told her you weren't there, she got really worried, and she said you may have come to this planet. That scared her most of all. So we came here. But finish that legend."

"After her mate was killed, in her grief she climbed the tallest tree in the forest and never came down. Senalar said she was taken by *Moreno*, the spirit of darkness and death, but she returned twenty years later and they made her queen. Just like Esmerelda. But, go on, tell me, what happened when you landed here?"

"Our arrival here seemed to jump start the revolution, and when we landed, we were attacked by the Talatan, and, from what Kazeh tells us, that gave them the encouragement they needed. They recognized the confusion of the Talatan forces—they thought we were part of the resistance—and the rebels took advantage of their disorganization. We retreated to *Star Voyager* and waited a few planetary rotations until the fighting diminished, then came back down."

"The revolution is almost over," Kazeh said. "The Talatan have been routed in many places, and *Marktu-Ahdenu* has been returned to control by the revolutionaries."

"But how did you find me?"

"We couldn't speak the language, but—and this was really odd—we found several people who spoke some Anthanian, and they recognized your name and they got out a map and pointed to the Callus. When I questioned how they could speak Anthanian, they said Jad taught them, and I was surprised to hear that name, but I discounted it at first. Of course, I recognized the name immediately, how could I not? But I couldn't understand how Jad could be here. When I thought about it—about him being missing for more than twenty years—I realized, yes, it could have been." Tam's voice dropped, and he looked at the floor. "I asked about him, you know, like where he was and was he still alive and so on, and they told us they hadn't seen him in more than a year, and they put their hands over their hearts—"

"That means they think he's dead."

"Jad even wrote in a book a list of words and phrases in Jhontu and their equivalent in Anthanian." Tam produced a small, loose-leaf notebook, written in Jad's hand, and showed it to Leos. "It was originally for Jad's own use to help him learn the language, but he also used it to teach others. Kazeh showed it to me." Tam paused and swallowed, his eyes glistening even in the dim light of the room. "I was sorry to hear he was dead. I'd hoped to see him once again. It'd been so long . . ."

"Has anyone found his body?"

"No," Kazeh said. "He may be buried in an unmarked grave. We have many of those on our planet."

Leos nodded as if to say, "I understand." The room turned quiet for about a nanosector when Tam cautiously continued his story.

"We sent a couple of interceptors over to the Callus to take a look. Kazeh arranged for a twin-engine plane the next day, and we followed the regular cargo plane." Tam broke into a broad smile that illuminated his expressive, freckled face. "But we didn't know you were planning on hijacking one of the planes."

"So, those jet fighters were yours?"

Tam nodded. "We didn't know what we'd run into when we entered this solar system. Kept the Talatan off our back until we could return to our ship."

Leos listened intently, fascinated about how the events had played out. Then he related his story, from his kidnapping by Grok and Krok to the Kazo Dela Tan.

"Oh, my God, Leos," Tama exclaimed. "I didn't realize how close you'd come to . . ."

Dr. Gadomer left during the final part of the story. "Excuse me," he said. "I have always had difficulty accepting that instrument. As have many of my colleagues." Leos continued about living on the green planet with Esmerelda, the death of Gasz, and coming to *Non*.

"Because of Jad's disappearance, we thought to postpone the rebellion," Kazeh said. "We lost an important figure in our plans, and it caused us much pain. But the rebellion had to go on schedule, Jad or no, and we knew Jad would want us to continue without him. It was so unfortunate.

"But now I must remind you it is almost the eighth hour. We have been here four hours, and I perceive many are growing tired of this meeting. Leos needs his rest. Let us break up, and we can meet again in a few days. If Leos will agree."

Leos nodded, and everyone filed out of the room, many expressing their good wishes to Leos and Tama, and soon the room was empty, except for Tama who closed the door after the last person left. In the quiet of the small hospital room, punctuated only by occasional random shots from outside of gunfire of Jhontu still celebrating the overthrow of the hated Talatan, she turned back to Leos. She had a funny expression on her face that Leos had never seen before. It seemed part anger, part frustration. She took one or two quiet steps toward him, still in bed. He reached out to her. Then she exploded.

"Oh, my God, Leos! How could you?"

*　　*　　*

"Tama, what are you talking about? I don't understand. What . . ."

"I thought you and I were going to get married. Now I find out you married this green-skinned woman from another planet. How could you?"

"Oh, I see. Tama, sweetheart, you have to understand that when I was taken to Nytandra, I thought I'd be there for the rest of my life. That's what they told me. That's where I met Esmerelda. Then, when I went to the green planet, I thought I'd be *there* for the rest of my life. I couldn't see escaping. Then I went to *Non-Dre-Ahdenu* and I thought I'd be *there* . . . er here, for the rest of my life. Especially when I was sentenced to the Callus. The Callus is where you go to die. Everybody does. No one is rescued. I had no idea. You can understand that, can't you?"

"I guess so." She folded her arms across her chest.

"I thought when I went to Nytandra that was the end of our relationship. They wanted me to marry Esmerelda. Maybe you'll meet her sometime. I held out as long as I could, but other things got in the way and they kicked me off. I already explained how Esmerelda came with me and I had to accept the fact that I was going to have to spend the rest of my life on *Jon-Set-Tom*. We lived there over a year when Coreaje came. I never expected him to try and bring Esmerelda back. But the people there hated Gasz so much, they killed him and started a war, and, well, I had to leave."

To her credit, Tama listened quietly as Leos spoke. Not interrupting, not commenting.

"Everything was set. It always had been. I couldn't believe we'd ever see each other again. It didn't look good. I never believed you'd find out where I was. It never entered my mind. I thought no one would ever figure out where I was taken."

"The two guys who kidnapped you talked too much. Tam and SpaceComm figured out where you'd gone. They put it all together."

"I understand, but are you okay with what's happened? I'm sorry it's difficult to accept. I didn't mean to hurt you. I didn't mean it that way."

"I don't know. I was hoping . . . maybe I shouldn't have . . . maybe that was too naïve . . . did you fall in love with her? Are you still in love with her? Can we get married now? Or are you mated to Esmerelda permanently?"

There were two questions there, and Leos, somewhat blindsided by Tama's simple and sincere honesty, couldn't come up with a straight answer to either immediately. "I don't know," he said, opting to reply to the second. "That's never come up. But, hold on a microsector, there may be someone who can tell us."

"Who?"

"Do you have your PersComm? Mine was confiscated when they kidnapped me."

Tama handed Leos her Personal Communicator. The small communicator didn't have enough power to reach *Star Voyager* in synchronous orbit above *Marktu-Ahdenu,* so Leos contacted Tam and explained his predictament. Tam returned his call a few millisectors later. Leos handed the PersComm back to Tama.

"Tama," Leos said. "This is Tandor, the legal affairs officer on *Star Voyager.* You must have met him by now."

"Yes, we've met. Hello."

"Tama," Tandor explained, "a mating on an unsophisticated planet such as the Green Planet won't be recognized on Anthanos, especially without a ceremony and some sort of permanent record. You and Leos will be free to get married when you get back."

"Now do you see? It's time to think about our marriage. Are you ready?"

"I'm still not sure. I wasn't expecting anything like this when we arrived here. Especially not you mated to someone else. And having consummated the marriage. I was hoping I'd be your first."

"I wasn't expecting to be the mate for Esmerelda either. I didn't find out until I got to Nytandra. Quite a surprise. They didn't tell me anything during the trip out there. And *Jon-Set-Tom.* And *Non-Dre-Ahdenu.* I don't know what more I can say. I've traveled to three of the four planets in this system, always involuntarily. Always without you. You were in my mind, yes, constantly, but there was never any possibility of seeing you again. I'm sorry, I wish things had been different, but they weren't. Are we okay?"

"Maybe. But you still haven't answered my question. Are you still in love with Esmerelda?"

There it was again. The consequential question Leos had never thought about, but which he knew he'd have to answer sooner or later, and which he'd better answer correctly, or . . . he didn't want to think about the possible consequences if he gave the wrong reply. Disaster lurked.

"I don't think I ever was. It was a mating of convenience. I was brought to Nytandra just to marry Esmerelda. I was expected to, regardless of how I felt. I never meant to hurt you. Are you okay with it?"

"I guess so. I don't really have anything to say about it, do I?" She lay down on the little cot that had been placed in Leos's room and turned her back to Leos, in his bed. Leos said nothing more.

*   *   *

The surface-orbit shuttle that brought Leos and Tama from *Star Voyager* to *Jon-Set-Tom* touched down on the dirt landing strip and rolled to a stop at the eastern end. Several of the old landing ships that had brought Coreaje and Gasz to the surface still littered the area, corroding and disintegrating in the warm, humid atmosphere. Leos and Tama went first down the short ramp onto the dark soil of the runway, and Tam and a couple of security guards descended a few steps behind. Tama gasped and went into a fit of giggling.

"Oh my gosh, Leos, they're naked."

"Didn't you see them before? When you stopped here before?"

"No, I didn't go down in the shuttle. Just Tam and a few others."

A small group of Leos's old friends stood just inside the edge of the forest, and he went over to them. Senalar stepped forward to greet him.

"Welcome, my old friend. We rejoice in the return of a member of our tribe." He gave Leos a great big Anthanian-type hug, then asked him, "Will you stay with us for a few days? Esmerelda waits to see you."

"I'm sorry, old friend, I can't stay for more than a short time. As you guessed, I came to see Esmerelda. Then I must be on my way."

One by one, Leos greeted the others who stood with Senalar. Even Jaiete had come to see him, though no one else from Jaiete's tribe came with him. Leos introduced them to Tama, and they frowned slightly, but greeted her warmly. Then Leos turned to Esmerelda.

Esmerelda stood near the edge of the forest in front of the tree they'd climbed their first day on the green planet. She didn't participate in the celebration, she still maintained the regal bearing Leos had known since he first met her.

"Oh, my gosh, Leos. She's beautiful," Tama whispered. "Now I understand why you were so attracted to her. But why is everyone so quiet? They seem to be glad to see you."

"Too much noise might attract a zil. Maybe more than one."

"A zil? Oh, the big animals. When you lived here, did you take your clothes off, too?"

"No, I kept mine on. Well, most of the time."

Esmerelda was Queen all right, with a much different ribbon around her neck now, wider and bright red, with two lines of lettering in different colors—green, gold, blue, and silver—that proclaimed her royal office. The

335

ends of the ribbon hung farther down her right side, almost to her elbow. She had a different knife too, with fancy engravings and carvings on the handle. She still wore her hair in a ponytail, still held by a piece of zil leather, but it fell farther down her back, almost to her waist. Her deep green skin still glimmered in the sunlight that illuminated the opening in the forest. Two women, apparently attendants to Her Majesty, stood beside her. One carried a familiar looking object.

"Leos, I worried so much about you," Esmerelda said. She touched the scars on the left side of his face as they embraced. "I was so scared when they told me you'd gone to the white planet. I knew of things there. Mlada told me."

"Things turned out okay." Leos cast his eyes nervously at the ground. "I got out of there. There was a revolution. Things are different now. They're getting better. Even Mlada would approve, I'm sure. But I'm not going back."

"Is this Tama? Your fiancé whom you spoke of? Many times you spoke of her."

"Yes it is. I hope my bringing her here doesn't . . . I mean . . . I hope it's all right with you. But I wanted you to meet her, and her to meet you."

Esmerelda smiled. "Yes, Leos, it is fine. I will release you from your obligation to me. As Queen, I have the authority to annul a mating. Even my own."

That made Tama smile.

"Please also accept my blessing on your marriage. That is another of the privileges of being Queen. I can bless a mating, too." She turned to one of her attendants who held the familiar-looking object. "Leos, I would like for you to have this. A zil blanket. Freshly made only ten days ago. Please accept it with my blessing."

"Oh, my gosh, thank you, Esmerelda. I wasn't expecting . . ."

"Keep it to remember our friendship. Remember our time together on this planet. Remember the trees and the people who live in those trees and who loved you in spite of everything."

Esmerelda gave Leos a big parting hug, but tears washed down her cheeks when she gave Tama a brief goodbye embrace and wished her well. "You will have a long and happy life. I know it. Good-bye. Now I must leave." She turned and ran into the forest. Her two attendants followed.

Leos and Tama waved "Good-bye," and returned to the shuttle. By the time the shuttle took off for *Star Voyager* to prepare for the long voyage home, one or two inconspicuous tears dribbled down Leos's cheeks, too.

CHAPTER 53

ADDRESS

Assembly Hall was crowded—congested—overloaded. People wanting to enter the visitor's gallery jammed the hallways in lines three and four across, almost preventing the Assembly members from getting to the doors to the Chamber. The Hall Security Service finally gave up on trying to admit anyone else, so they drove everyone out, closed the doors leading to the Chamber and all the hallways around it, and posted "No Admittance" signs outside. Inside, the packed Legislative Chamber of the Anthanian General Assembly buzzed and whispered, murmured and reverberated in the excitement as the time approached for the post-election acceptance speech by the newly-elected President.

Finally, all 224 members had taken their seats in the Chamber. They'd come to witness a new tradition in Anthanian politics, a President who would take an active role in the administration of the government and the running of the planet. By tradition, Presidents had been elderly men or women who'd finished their career in politics, usually as Vice President, and were elected to the largely ceremonial office of President. They did little other than sign the documents the Vice President put before them, and make a once-yearly trip to SpaceComm to show their support for the agency. (There was a standing joke around SpaceComm as to how much of what these old guys were shown they really understood.) Their infirmity invariably prevented them from doing much else, and the important administrative duties were carried out by the Vice President.

But times had changed. In the twenty-two years since Leos returned, not one candidate planet suitable for colonization had turned up, and the population was restless. Astronomers published chart after chart predicting in excruciating detail the effects the planet would experience in the not-too-distant future—the warming, the increase in the force of the breeze from the cold side, the approach of the sun's surface toward Anthanos, the eventual spiraling of the planet into the sun. The concern and anxiety that all this had on the population had infiltrated Anthanian politics and the population demanded change—a change to calm the rage, a change in the structure of the government to assure the nation-planet that help was on its way, a change that would force the government to take a more active role in finding a new home planet and end the nightmare of not knowing.

Often the exploration of the Blue Planet was brought up in the media. Articles, essays, op-eds, and scientific papers were written, distributed, and vocalized, demanding that the disaster of the Blue Planet not be repeated. "We need a new home," they implored, "but a safe one, not one where so many of the settlers are wiped out." We need assurance, they said. Protection. Safeness. Refuge.

Into this cry came a new name.

The youth and vigor of this new President had captured the imagination of the Anthanian people in a way that no politician ever had. He was one of the first to suggest the change in the structure of the Presidency, and he campaigned on a platform to make its holder a forward-thinking leader, rather than the reactionary old man usually the last to be consulted on matters of state. By the time of his election, measures had been introduced into the Assembly to make those changes. Now it came time for the new President—brought into office by one of the largest electoral margins in Anthanian politics—to make his introductory remarks, and the whole world quieted down to listen.

A visitor's gallery of seven rows of seats ran almost all the way around the upper level of the circular hall. Seated in the second seat off the aisle of the middle row within the VIP section, directly behind the speaker's platform as the speaker faced the Assembly, sat Tama, her two children, both boys, to her left. Beside the boys sat Lilea Kalatarian, now in her seventies, her hair a delicate blondish-white. Next to Lilea sat a tall thin gentleman, dark hair and immaculate white clothes but contrasting shiny black boots. But the first seat in that row, and by Anthanian custom, remained empty.

From the highest vault of the ceiling hung a chandelier, a superb creation of the expert glass blowers and silicoartisans of Anthanos. Flowers, bells, trees, icicles, animals of all description, existing and extinct, real and fantastic, monsters with horns and talons, aerial and ground-dwelling, (including one that looked suspiciously like a zil), spaceships and shuttle craft, real and imaginary, hung from the graceful boughs of the chandelier, each lit from within by a small, colored LED.

At precisely 510.999.9.9.0, the outgoing President entered the Chamber through a door to the left of the speaker's platform and the Chamber quieted. He strode to the exact center of the circular room within the midst of the assembled, directly beneath the chandelier. By tradition, he held directly upward a small remote control which increased the illumination of the chandelier, signifying the beginning of the session. The low murmuring and quiet whispers between members of the Assembly ceased, and everyone took their seats. Then he began to speak.

"Ladies and gentlemen. It is my duty and very great honor—and, I might add, a very great pleasure—to introduce to you the fifty-second President of the Anthanian General Assembly, the honorable—" But before he could utter the incoming President's name, he was drowned out by the spontaneous uproar that filled the Hall. Cheers reverberated through the chamber, and the chandelier jingled and tinkled in the noise and vibrations as the new President entered through the same door. A faint smile crossed his face and he looked around at the assembled delegates as if to acknowledge the applause. He marched to a small table to one side of the speaker's platform. The table was covered with a deep blue cloth, and on the cloth was coiled the Emperor's chain, the symbol of the office of President of the Anthanian Assembly. The outgoing President likewise approached the table from the other side and picked up the chain. Made originally of a silvery alloy of lead, the chain had been covered with a gold and platinum sheath in recent years, and it seemed to weigh an entire kilokrill. Then, in a re-creation of the occasion when the first President was presented the chain by the Emperor Samaros IV—himself quite elderly and frail at the time—at the beginning of the year 001, the old President intoned the Charge to the President:

> **"With this chain, I, acting as successor of and on behalf of Samaros IV, Emperor of all Anthanos, do charge you, as the next President of the Anthanian Assembly, and by receipt of this chain, forged in the fires of the discord between our city-nations and resulting in our determination to tie together the original twenty cities of Anthanos in perpetual peace and prosperity, to retain the primary symbolism of this chain, to hold together the cities of this nation-planet against all forces, internal and external, and to judge, arbitrate, and consider all matters that may arise on this planet or its possessions, with equanimity, patience, and justice. Do you accept this chain and this charge?"**

"I do," said the new President, and as the old President held the chain out to him, he took it and held it in both hands, being careful to not let any link touch the table. He held it for a couple of nanosectors until the timer above the President's seat behind the speaker's lectern turned to "511.000.0.0.0," exactly the beginning of the New Year, marking the end of the former President's term and the beginning of the new. Whoever held the chain at this precise time of the new year was President, carrying on the tradition of all new Presidents since the office was established at the beginning of the year 001. The applause began again.

The new President set the chain carefully on the table and stepped over to the lectern on the speaker's platform several steps above the level of the Assembly floor. He acknowledged the applause, then held up one hand asking for quiet. He unsnapped his chronometer from his wrist and set it carefully on the lectern beside the com screen that scrolled his speech. Again, he held up his hand, but the adulation continued.

"My fellow Anthanians," he began in the midst of the clamor. He paused again and the Assembly quieted. "These last few years have been difficult for us on this planet. We have watched the temperature on our planet rise slowly and relentlessly for many thousands of years, and our scientists and astronomers tell us our sun is still on course to wipe out all life on our planet by its extreme heat. Our lives have been kidnapped, as it were, by the progressing heat. The erection of domes over some of the smaller cities has brought many of us to feel as though we are being held captive within these glass and metal enclosures. I quite understand.

"Over the past forty years, we have sent expeditions to many planets, beginning with the expedition to the Blue Planet, but none of those have met our conditions for colonization. The three planets around the major star in the constellation Diinn, despite their inviting outward appearance, especially Nytandra, were likewise not acceptable, and we kept looking. We've sent our spaceships to planets a hundred and even two hundred light-years away, difficult trips that exhausted our travelers and resulted in finding nothing we could colonize. Many of these worlds looked good on the surface, but did not meet the needs of our people.

"The improvements and refinements in the control mechanisms of our starships — the addition of the fourth and even fifth propulsion coil and second control coil — promise to cut travel times to only a few tens of T-sectors, and make travel among the stars agreeable, if not downright pleasant.

"We have met new civilizations, and we have acquired many new friends in our small section of the galaxy, and their friendship has been invaluable, but they have not been able to show us the way to a suitable home."

The President continued, summarizing the historical record as it was known to the people. He frightened them with facts—"the planet may be too hot for our continued existence in only a hundred years, give or take twenty." Many in the Hall shifted uncomfortably in their seats. "Many children born this year will live to see that time. The temperature will continue to rise, and there is little we can do. And the rise is accelerating. The higher the temperature, the faster it rises." He paused to let the reality sink into their minds, then he plied them with platitudes:

"We are in a difficult situation through no fault of our own."

"We will put the greatest minds of our planet to work on this."

"Some things we cannot understand, but we will come to understand them in time."

"We will undoubtedly try a lot of things that won't work before we find the one thing that does."

"We will have to take what we've got and turn it to our advantage."

"Many things may sound crazy at first, but new ideas always sound crazy. The best new idea in the long run may be the one that sounded craziest at the time."

"Hesitation may be deadly. We may have to try something without delay. We must take the initiative."

"Once we start on a course of action, we will have to continue. We can't stop midway even though the outlook may be bleak at the time."

The President spoke for nearly a subsector, though he expressed very little the citizens of his planet hadn't heard before. The inexorable swelling of the sun, the rising temperature, the engulfment of Anthanos by the sun, the looming nova blast, the results from the various missions to other planets—these were already well-known around the world. But coming from the mouth of a respected and popular President, a President who'd promised to find a new home or die trying, they meant so much more than the dry pronouncements of the scientists who said the same things. The open expression of all the facts told them that the government was at least sensitive to their concerns.

A mystique had developed about this man. His exploits in space as navigator and pilot on missions to other solar systems, his knowledge of languages of other civilizations, and his ability to communicate with alien cultures, his calm demeanor and analytical nature, especially in perilous situations, all contributed vitally to an almost magical aura that surrounded and enveloped him. The facts he laid before his people were the same, the problems old and timeworn, the difficulties exasperatingly familiar. The electorate was renewed and excited. Pre-election polls had confirmed repeatedly that the populace wanted a scientist as head of government, someone who appreciated the difficulties the people faced, yet was familiar with the scientific method that would get them out. They responded by electing him in the largest majority in recent memory.

The population always had an expectation, an unwritten hope, an optimistic dream that a new planet would be found within plenty of time to move, leaving their expanding sun in their wake. Previous Presidents subtly, and perhaps a little absentmindedly, contributed to this assumption. They threw the challenge to Spaceflight Command.

"You take care of it," they said.

SpaceComm responded with astronomical surveys that demonstrated planets circling almost every star out there. Yet virtually none of those planets were worth considering. Many were gas giants with toxic atmospheres, or rocky bodies devoid of atmosphere and searingly hot or abysmally cold, or their orbit was a long, looping ellipse, or they were far too big with crushing gravity or so miniscule as to be laughable. Many of the planets circled red dwarf stars, with orbital periods of only a few hundred T-sectors, and the fear of never finding anything soared within the populace

"And so, my fellow Anthanians," the President continued. "If my experiences in traveling between worlds in outer space have taught me anything, it is this—that this is not the time for pinning medals on the chests of explorers. This is a time for reflection. It is a time for all of us to work together to solve the problem of our collective future. I ask you to take a look at your own lives and decide what *you* can do to aid in the great exploration we are to undertake to find our new home. It will not be cheap, it will not be simple, it will not be easy, but it must be done, and I ask you to join me in this quest. I bring my comments to a close with this counsel: don't ask what your planet can do for you, ask what you can do for your planet. Thank you to one and all."

The new President took one step back and, as was the custom for Presidents in ending their speeches, nodded briefly to the assembled. A roar exploded through the Hall as everyone rose to their feet. Even the visitors in the gallery stood—Lilea and Tama applauded vigorously. The President, taken by surprise by the sudden acclaim, lurched back another step or two, and a wide smile covered his face. But he recovered sufficient grace to walk down the few steps to the level of the Assembly floor where many members of the Assembly surged forward to meet him. They shook his hand and patted him on the back and congratulated him on the speech, surrounding him in a gaggle of admirers and well-wishers.

"Wonderful!" one of them exclaimed. "Exactly what we needed." They threw their arms around him and called him buddy and friend and comrade and partner. They called him by his first name and last, but mostly they called him "Mr. President." He spoke a few words to each, shaking their hands and smiling at the adulation, enjoying the camaraderie, remaining on the Assembly floor for several millisectors, paying little attention to the passage of time. Abruptly, one of the President's assistants, who'd edged his way into the group, placed a light hand on his shoulder.

"Excuse me, Mr. President," the assistant whispered, interrupting him as he was about to speak to an elderly colleague. "You left your chronometer on the lectern."

"Holy dinfrizzle," the President said, scratching an old scar on the left side of his face. "I must be of the forgetting type."

END

ACKNOWLEDGEMENTS

My sincerest and most grateful thanks go to Kathy Schuit for being a beta reader of the manuscript, and for producing the cover art and the illustrations within the text. My thanks also go to Cornelia Gamlen for taking on the task of being a beta reader even though she'd never read science fiction before.

But my most especial thanks go to my editor Cara Lockwood for a thorough and critical reading of the manuscript, and for her numerous suggestions, recommendations, and exhortations that made the book so much better than anything I could have produced myself.

And a final thanks to all who take the time to read this book. I hope it meets all your expectations. Or at least comes close.

ABOUT THE AUTHOR

Roger Floyd is a retired PhD researcher in the field of virology, the study of viruses. He spent most of a 40+-year career working in hospitals and medical schools around the United States, examining various viruses to see how they work and how they interact with one another and how to kill them and how to isolate them from infected patients. He received his Bachelor of Arts degree from Trinity University in San Antonio, Texas, in 1963, and his PhD degree from Baylor College of Medicine in Houston, Texas, in 1971. He's been a life-long reader of books, both fiction and non-fiction, especially including science fiction. In 1998, after so many years of reading and writing scientific papers, he decided the time had come to write his own novel. What the hell—that can't be too difficult, can it? Little did he know. . . That first book, **EXPLORER**, as well as this book, and the third volume, **WARRIOR**, which together comprise *The Anthanian Imperative* Trilogy, were the eventual result of that decision. And he doesn't regret it one bit.

He maintains a website and blog at *rogerfloyd(dot)com*, where copies of this book and the others of the trilogy can be purchased.

Albuquerque, New Mexico, July, 2025